GREATEST HITS

Also edited by
Robert J. Randisi

The Eyes Have It (1984)
Mean Streets (1986)
An Eye for Justice (1988)
Justice for Hire (1990)
Deadly Allies [co-edited w/ Marilyn Wallace] (1992)
Deadly Allies 2 [co-edited w/ Susan Dunlop] (1994)
Lethal Ladies [co-edited w/ Barbara Collins] (1994)
Lethal Ladies II [co-edited w/ Christine Matthews] (1995)
First Cases (1996)
First Cases II (1997)
First Cases III (2000)
Tin Star (2000)
The Shamus Game (2000)
Mystery Street (2001)
First Cases IV (2002)
Most Wanted (2002)
White Hats (2002)
Boot Hill (2002)
Black Hats (2003)
High Stakes (2003)
Lonestar Law (2005)
Greatest Hits (2005)

GREATEST HITS

ORIGINAL STORIES OF ASSASSINS, HITMEN, AND HIRED GUNS

Edited by

ROBERT J. RANDISI

CARROLL & GRAF PUBLISHERS

NEW YORK

GREATEST HITS
Original Stories of Assassins, Hit Men, and Hired Guns

Carroll & Graf Publishers
An Imprint of Avalon Publishing Group Inc.
245 West 17th Street
11th Floor
New York, NY 10011

AVALON
publishing group incorporated

Copyright © 2005 by Robert J. Randisi
First Carroll & Graf edition 2005

Library of Congress Cataloging-in-Publication Data is available.

ISBN: 0-7867-1581-2
ISBN-13: 978-0-78671-581-7

9 8 7 6 5 4 3 2 1

Interior design by Maria E. Torres

Printed in the United States of America
Distributed by Publishers Group West

CONTENTS

Introduction

Hit Man.
Hitter.
Button Man.
Mechanic.
Torpedo.
Assassin.
Killer.

A HIT MAN BY ANY OTHER NAME is still a Hit Man. In this book, you will read about hit men—and women—of all shapes and sizes. Lawrence Block's "Keller" and Max Collins's "Quarry"—who have been appearing in series over the years—are here. But the hit man is not like the police detective, or private eye, or thief, or amateur detective. There have not been as many series characters who kill for a living. My guess would be they are not perceived as being very sympathetic. Interesting, yes, but not sympathetic. And haven't we all been told that series characters need to be sympathetic to appeal to the reader?

Well, it's my contention that you will find the characters in these stories not only interesting, but odd, quirky, unusual and, in some cases, even downright likeable. Given the quality of the authors I invited—best sellers like Jeffery Deaver, Lee Child, and James Hall; experts at their craft like Ed Gorman, John Harvey, and Jeff Abbott; dangerous and talented ladies like Barbara Seranella, Jenny Siler, and Christine Matthews; and relative but no less talented new-comers such as Kevin Wignall, Marcus Pelegrimas, and Paul Guyot, as well as the aforementioned Block and Collins—into this book, there was no question that the stories would be good. For me, that was a given (although I know some critics will disagree—but that's their job). But the characters they've come up with, and the situations, are, I think, standouts.

I submit, dear reader, for your approval and enjoyment—as I try to do with each anthology I present—these tales of murder for profit. And I hope the one who profits the most will be you.

Keller's Karma

BY LAWRENCE BLOCK

This is the only reprint in this book, but we couldn't very well do a hit-man anthology without Larry Block and Keller. This may be the only legitimate "hit man" series around. The two Keller books, *Hit Man* and *Hit Men*, are both collections of short stories. Mr. Block is so busy with his Bernie Rhodenbarr series and his Matt Scudder series that he has not had the time—or the inclination?—to do an entire novel featuring Keller. He did have time recently, though, to appear on the *Late, Late Show* with Craig Fergussen, and acquitted himself quite well as a talk show guest.

The newest Block novel is *All the Flowers Are Dying*, featuring Matt Scudder.

IN WHITE PLAINS, Keller sat in the kitchen with Dot for twenty minutes. The TV was on, tuned to one of the home shopping channels. "I watch all the time," Dot said. "I never buy anything. What do I want with cubic zirconium?"

"Why do you watch?"

"That's what I ask myself, Keller. I haven't come up with the answer yet, but I think I know one of the things I like most about it. It's continuous."

"Continuous?"

"Uninterrupted. They never break the flow and go to a commercial."

"But the whole thing's a commercial," Keller said.

"That's different," she said.

A buzzer sounded. Dot picked up the intercom, listened a moment, then nodded significantly at Keller.

He went upstairs, and he was with the old man for ten or fifteen minutes. On his way out, he stopped in the kitchen and got himself a glass of water. He stood at the sink and took his time drinking it. Dot was shaking her head at the television set. "It's all jewelry," she said. "Who buys all this jewelry? What do they want with it?"

"I don't know," he said. "Can I ask you something?"

"Ask away."

"Is he all right?"

"Why?"

"I just wondered."

"Did you hear something?"

"No, nothing like that. He seems tired, that's all."

"Everybody's tired," she said. "Life's a lot of work and it tires people out. But he's fine."

Keller took a train to Grand Central, a cab to his apartment. Nelson met him at the door with the leash in his mouth. Keller laughed, fastened the leash to the dog's collar. He had calls to make, a trip to schedule, but that could wait. Right now he was going to take his dog for a walk.

He headed over to the river. Nelson liked it there, but then Nelson seemed to like it everywhere. He certainly had a boundless enthusiasm for long walks. He never ran out of gas. You could exhaust yourself walking him, and he'd be ready to go again ten minutes later.

Of course you had to keep in mind that he had twice as many legs as a human being. Keller figured that had to make a difference.

"I'm going to have to take a trip," he told Nelson. "Not too long,
I don't think, but that's the thing, you never really know. Sometimes
I'll fly out in the morning and be back the same night, and other
times it'll stretch to a week. But you don't have to worry. As soon as
we get back to the house I'll call Andria."

The dog's ears pricked up at the girl's name. Nelson was an Australian cattle dog, and Keller wasn't sure where the breed ranked in
comparative intelligence, but he figured it had to be pretty close to
the top. The dog didn't miss much.

"She's due to walk you tomorrow anyway," Keller said. "I
could probably just stick a letter of instructions next to your
leash, but why leave anything to chance? As soon as we get home
I'll beep her."

Andria, who earned a living walking people's dogs and watering
their plants, had a standing appointment to take Nelson for a walk
on Tuesday mornings and Friday afternoons. For this service Keller
paid her fifty dollars a week, which Andria had assured him was
higher than her customary rates. When Keller had to leave town, the
price went to fifty dollars a day and Andria saw to such additional
aspects of dog maintenance as feeding Nelson and freshening the
water in his dish.

Because Andria's living situation was as tenuous as her career, the
only number Keller had for her was that of the beeper she carried on
her rounds. He called it as soon as he got home and punched in his
number, and the girl called him back fifteen minutes later. "Hi," she
said. "How's my favorite Australian cattle dog?"

"He's fine," Keller said, "but he's going to need company. I have
to go out of town tomorrow morning."

"For how long, do you happen to know?"

"Hard to say. It might be a day, it might be a week. Is that a
problem?"

She was quick to assure him that it wasn't. "In fact," she said, "the
timing's perfect. I've been staying with these friends of mine, and it's
not working out. I told them I'd be out of there tomorrow and I was

wondering where I'd go next. Isn't it amazing the way we're always given guidance as to what to do next?"

"Amazing," he agreed.

"But that's assuming it's all right with you if I stay there while you're gone. I've done it before, but maybe you'd rather I don't this time."

"No, that's fine," Keller said. "It's more company for Nelson, so why should I object? You're not messy, you keep the place neat."

"I'm housebroken, all right. Same as Nelson." She laughed, then broke it off and said, "I really appreciate this, Mr. Keller. These friends I've been staying with, they're not getting along too well, and I'm kind of stuck in the middle. She's turned into this jealous monster, and he figures maybe he ought to give her something to be jealous about, and last night I just about walked the legs off a long-haired dachshund because I didn't want to be in their space. So it'll be a pleasure to get out of there tomorrow morning."

"Listen," he said, impulsively. "Why wait? Come over here tonight."

"But you're not leaving until tomorrow."

"So what? I've got a late evening tonight and I'll be out first thing in the morning, so we won't get in each other's way. And you'll be out of your friends' place that much sooner."

"Gee," she said, "that would be great."

When he got off the phone, Keller went into the kitchen and made himself a cup of coffee. Why, he wondered, had he made the offer? It was certainly uncharacteristic behavior on his part. What did he care if she had to spend one more night suffering the dirty looks of the wife and the wandering hands of the husband?

And he'd even improvised to justify her acceptance of the offer, inventing a late evening and claiming an early flight. He hadn't booked the flight yet, and he had no plans for the evening.

Time to book the flight. Time to make plans for the evening.

The flight was booked with a single phone call, the evening

planned almost as easily. Keller was dressing for it when Andria arrived, wearing striped bib overalls and bearing a forest-green backpack. Nelson made a fuss over her, and she shucked the backpack and knelt down to reciprocate.

"Well," Keller said. "You'll probably be asleep when I get home, and I'll probably leave before you wake up, so I'll say goodbye now. You know Nelson's routine, of course, and you know where everything is."

"I really appreciate this," Andria said.

Keller took a cab to the restaurant where he'd arranged to meet a woman named Yvonne, whom he'd dated three or four times since making her acquaintance at a Learning Annex class, "Deciphering the Mysteries of Baltic Cuisine." The true mystery, they'd both decided, was how anyone had the temerity to call it a cuisine. He'd since taken her to several restaurants, none of them Baltic. Tonight's choice was Italian, and they spent a good deal of time telling each other how happy they were to be eating in an Italian restaurant rather than, say, a Latvian one.

Afterward they went to a movie, and after that they took a cab to Yvonne's apartment, some eighteen blocks north of Keller's. As she fitted her key in the lock, she turned toward him. They had already reached the goodnight-kiss stage, and Keller saw that Yvonne was ready to be kissed, but at the same time he sensed that she didn't really want to be kissed, nor did he really want to kiss her. They'd both had garlic, so it wasn't a reluctance to offend or be offended. He wasn't sure what it was, but he decided to honor it.

"Well," he said. "Goodnight, Yvonne."

She seemed for a moment to be surprised at being left unkissed, but she got over it quickly. "Yes, goodnight," she said, reaching for his hand, giving it a comradely squeeze. "Goodnight, John."

Goodnight forever, he thought, walking downtown on Second Avenue. He wouldn't call her again, nor would she expect his call. All they had in common was a disdain for Northern European cooking, and that wasn't much of a foundation for a relationship.

The chemistry just wasn't there. She was attractive, but there was no connection between them, no spark.

That happened a lot, actually.

Halfway home, he stopped in a First Avenue bar. He'd had a little wine with dinner, and he wanted a clear head in the morning, so he didn't stay long, just nursed a beer and listened to the juke box and looked at himself in the back-bar mirror.

What a lonesome son of a bitch you are, he told his reflection.

Time to go home, when you started having thoughts like that. But he didn't want to get home until Andria had turned in for the night, and who knew what kind of hours she kept? He stayed where he was and sipped his beer, and he made another stop along the way for a cup of coffee.

When he did get home the apartment was dark. Andria was on the sofa, either asleep or faking it. Nelson, curled into a ball at her feet, got up, shook himself, and trotted silently to Keller's side. Keller went on into the bedroom, Nelson following. When Keller closed the bedroom door, the dog made an uncharacteristic sound deep in his throat. Keller didn't know what the sound meant, but he figured it had something to do with the door being closed, and Andria being on the other side of it.

He got into bed. The dog stood in front of the closed door, as if waiting for it to open. "Here, boy," Keller said. The dog turned to look at him. "Here, Nelson," he said, and the dog jumped onto the bed, turned around in a circle the ritualistic three times, and lay down in his usual spot. It seemed to Keller as though he didn't have his heart in it, but he was asleep in no time. So, eventually, was Keller.

When he woke up, the dog was missing. So was Andria, and so was the leash. Keller was shaved and dressed and out the door before they returned. He got a cab to LaGuardia and was there in plenty of time for his flight to St. Louis.

He rented a Ford Tempo from Hertz and let the girl trace the route to the Sheraton on the map. "It's the turn right after the mall," she said helpfully. He took the exit for the mall and found a parking place, taking careful note of where it was so he could find it again. Once, a couple of years ago, he had parked a rental car at a mall in suburban Detroit without paying attention to where he'd parked it or what it looked like. For all he knew it was still there.

He walked through the mall, looking for a sporting goods store with a selection of hunting knives. There was probably one to be found; they had everything else, including several jewelry stores to catch anyone who hadn't gotten her fill of cubic zirconium on television. But he came to a Hoffritz store first and the kitchen knives caught his eye. He picked out a boning knife with a five-inch blade.

He could have brought his own knife, but that would have meant checking a bag, and he never did that if he could help it. Easy enough to buy what you needed at the scene. The hardest part was convincing the clerk he didn't want the rest of the set, and ignoring the sales pitch assuring him the knife wouldn't need sharpening for years. He was only going to use it once, for God's sake.

He found the Ford, found the Sheraton, found a parking place and left his overnight bag in the trunk. It would have been nice if the knife had come with a sheath, but kitchen knives rarely do, so he'd been moved to improvise, lifting a cardboard mailing envelope from a Federal Express drop-box at the mall entrance. He walked into the hotel lobby with the mailer under his arm and the knife snug inside it.

That gave him an idea.

He checked the slip of paper in his wallet. *St. Louis, Sheraton, Rm 314.*

"Man's a union official," the old man in White Plains had told him. "Some people are afraid he might tell what he knows."

Just recently some people at a funded drug rehabilitation project in the Bronx had been afraid their accountant might tell what she knew, so they paid a pair of teenagers $150 to kill her. The two of them picked her up leaving the office, walked down the street behind her, and after a two-block stroll the sixteen-year-old shot her in the head. Within twenty-four hours they were in custody, and two days later so was the genius who hired them.

Keller figured you got what you paid for.

He went over to the house phone and dialed 314. It rang almost long enough to convince him the room was empty. Then a man picked up and said, "Yeah?"

"FedEx," Keller said.

"Huh?"

"Federal Express. Got a delivery for you."

"That's crazy," the man said.

"Room 314, right? I'll be right up."

The man protested that he wasn't expecting anything, but Keller hung up on him in mid-sentence and got the elevator to the third floor. The halls were empty. He found Room 314 and knocked briskly on the door. "FedEx," he sang out. "Delivery."

Some muffled sounds came through the door. Then silence, and he was about to knock again when the man said, "What the hell is this?"

"Parcel for you," he said. "Federal Express."

"Can't be," the man said. "You got the wrong room."

"Room 314. That's what it says, on the package and on the door."

"Well, there's a mistake. Nobody knows I'm here." That's what you think, thought Keller. "Who's it addressed to?"

Who indeed? "Can't make it out."

"Who's it from, then?"

"Can't make that out, either," Keller said. "That whole line's screwed up, sender's name and recipient's name, but it says Room 314 at the Sheraton, so that's got to be you, right?"

"Ridiculous," the man said. "It's not for me and that's all there is to it."

"Well, suppose you sign for it," Keller suggested, "and you take a look what's in it, and if it's really not for you you can drop it at the desk later, or call us and we'll pick it up."

"Just leave it outside the door, will you?"

"Can't," Keller said. "It needs a signature."

"Then take it back, because I don't want it."

"You want to refuse it?"

"Very good," the man said. "You're a quick study, aren't you? Yes, by God, I want to refuse it."

"Fine with me," Keller said. "But I still need a signature. You just check where it says 'Refused' and sign by the X."

"For Christ's *sake*," the man said, "is that the only way I'm going to get rid of you?"

He unfastened the chain, turned the knob, and opened the door a crack. "Let me show you where to sign," Keller said, displaying the envelope, and the door opened a little more to show a tall balding man, heavyset, and unclothed but for a hotel towel wrapped around his middle. He reached out for the envelope, and Keller pushed into the room, boning knife in hand, and drove the blade in beneath the lower ribs, angling upward toward the heart.

The man fell backward and lay sprawled out on the carpet at the foot of the unmade king-size bed. The room was a mess, Keller noted, with an open bottle of Scotch on the dresser and an unfinished drink on each of the bedside tables. There were clothes tossed here and there, his clothes, her clothes—

Her clothes?

Keller's eyes went to the closed bathroom door. Jesus, he thought. Time to get the hell out. Take the knife, pick up the FedEx envelope, and—

The bathroom door opened. "Harry?" she said. "What on earth is—"

And she saw Keller. Looked right at him, saw his face.

Any second now she'd scream.

"It's his heart," Keller cried. "Come here, you've got to help me."

She didn't get it, but there was Harry on the floor, and here was this nice-looking fellow in a suit, moving toward her, saying things about CPR and ambulance services, speaking reassuringly in a low and level voice. She didn't quite get it, but she didn't scream, either, and in no time at all Keller was close enough to get a hand on her.

She wasn't part of the deal, but she was there, and she couldn't have stayed in the bathroom where she belonged, oh no, not her, the silly bitch, she had to go and open the door, and she'd seen his face, and that was that.

The boning knife, washed clean of blood, wiped clean of prints, went into a storm drain a mile or two from the hotel. The FedEx mailer, torn in half and in half again, went into a trash can at the airport. The Tempo went back to Hertz, and Keller, paying cash, went on American to Chicago. He had a long late lunch at a surprisingly good restaurant in O'Hare Airport, then bought a ticket on a United flight that would put him down at LaGuardia well after rush-hour traffic had subsided. He killed time in a cocktail lounge with a window from which you could watch takeoffs and landings. Keller did that for a while, sipping an Australian lager, and then he shifted his attention to the television set, where Oprah Winfrey was talking with six dwarfs. The volume was set inaudibly low, which was probably just as well. Now and then the camera panned the audience, which seemed to contain a disproportionate number of small people. Keller watched, fascinated, and refused to make any Snow White jokes, not even to himself.

He wondered if it was a mistake to go back to New York the same day. What would Andria think?

Well, he'd told her his business might not take him long. Besides, what difference did it make what she thought?

He had another Australian lager and watched some more planes take off. On the plane, he drank coffee and ate the two little packets of peanuts. Back at LaGuardia, he stopped at the first phone and called White Plains.

"That was fast," Dot said.

"Piece of cake," he told her.

He caught a cab, told the driver to take the 59th Street Bridge, and coached him on how to find it. At his apartment, he rang the bell a couple of times before using his key. Nelson and Andria were out. Perhaps they'd been out all day, he thought. Perhaps he'd gone to St. Louis and killed two people while the girl and his dog had been engaged in a single endless walk.

He made himself a sandwich and turned on the television set. Channel-hopping, he wound up transfixed by an offering of sports collectibles on one of the home shopping channels. Balls, bats, helmets, caps, shirts, all of them autographed by athletes and accompanied by certificates of authenticity, the certificates themselves suitable for framing. Cubic zirconium for guys, he thought.

"When you hear the words 'blue chip,'" the host was saying, "what are you thinking? I'll tell you what I'm thinking. I'm thinking Mickey Mantle."

Keller wasn't sure what he thought of when he heard the words 'blue chip,' but he was pretty sure it wasn't Mickey Mantle. He was working on that one when Nelson came bounding into the room, with Andria behind him.

"When I heard the TV," she said, "my first thought was I must have left it on, but I never even turned it on in the first place, so how could that be? And then I thought maybe there was a break-in, but why would a burglar turn on the television set? They don't watch them, they steal them."

"I should have called from the airport," Keller said. "I didn't think of it."

"What happened? Was your flight canceled?"

"No, I made the trip," he said. "But the business hardly took me any time at all."

"Wow," she said. "Well, Nelson and I had our usual outstanding time. He's such a pleasure to walk."

"He's well-behaved," Keller agreed.

"It's not just that. He's enthusiastic."

"I know what you mean."

"He feels so good about everything," she said, "that you feel good being with him. And he really takes an interest. I took him along when I went to water the plants and feed the fish at this apartment on Park Avenue. The people are in Sardinia. Have you ever been there?"

"No."

"Neither have I, but I'd like to go sometime. Wouldn't you?"

"I never thought about it."

"Anyway, you should have seen Nelson staring at the aquarium, watching the fish swim back and forth. If you ever want to get one, I'd help you set it up. But I would recommend that you stick with freshwater. Those saltwater tanks are a real headache to maintain."

"I'll remember that."

She bent over to pet the dog, then straightened up. She said, "Can I ask you something? Is it all right if I stay here tonight?"

"Of course. I more or less figured you would."

"Well, I wasn't sure, and it's a little late to make other arrangements. But I thought you might want to be alone after your trip, and—"

"I wasn't gone that long."

"You're sure it's all right?"

"Absolutely."

They watched television together, drinking cups of hot chocolate that Andria made. When the program ended, Keller took Nelson for a late walk. "Do you really want a fish tank?" he asked the dog. "If I can have a television set, I suppose you ought to be able to have a fish tank. But would you watch it after the first week or so? Or would you get bored with it?"

That was the thing about dogs, he thought. They didn't get bored the way people did.

After a couple of blocks he found himself talking to Nelson about what had happened in St. Louis. "They didn't say anything about a woman," he said. "I bet she wasn't registered. I don't think she was his wife, so I guess she wasn't officially there. That's why he sent her to the bathroom before he opened the door, and why he didn't want to open the door in the first place. If she'd stayed in the bathroom another minute—"

But suppose she had? She'd have been screaming her head off before Keller was out of the hotel, and she'd have been able to give a certain amount of information to the police. How the killer had gained access to the room, for a starter.

Just as well things had gone the way they did, he decided. But it still rankled. They hadn't said anything at all about a woman.

There was only one bathroom. Andria used it first. Keller heard the shower running, then nothing until she emerged wearing a generally shapeless garment of pink flannel that covered her from her neck to her ankles. Her toenails were painted, Keller noticed, each a different color.

Keller showered and put on a robe. Andria was on the sofa, reading a magazine. They said goodnight and he clucked to Nelson, and the dog followed him into the bedroom. When he closed the door the dog made that sound again.

He shucked the robe, got into bed, patted the bed at his side. Nelson stayed where he was, right in front of the door, and he repeated that sound in his throat, making it the least bit more insistent this time.

"You want to go out?"

Nelson wagged his tail, which Keller had to figure for a yes. He opened the door and the dog went into the other room. He closed the door and got back into bed, trying to decide if he was jealous. It struck him that he might not only be jealous of the girl, because Nelson wanted to be with her instead of with him, but he might as easily be jealous of the dog, because he got to sleep with Andria and Keller didn't.

Little pink toes, each with the nail painted a different color. . . .

He was still sorting it out when the door opened and the dog trotted in. "He wants to be with you," Andria said, and she drew the door shut before Keller could frame a response.

But did he? The animal didn't seem to know what he wanted. He sprang onto Keller's bed, turned around once, twice, and then leaped onto the floor and went over to the door. He made that noise again, but this time it sounded plaintive.

Keller got up and opened the door. Nelson moved into the doorway, half in and half out of the room. Keller leaned into the doorway himself and said, "I think the closed door bothers him. Suppose I leave it open?"

"Sure."

He left the door ajar and went back to bed. Nelson seized the opportunity and went on into the living room. Moments later he was back in the bedroom. Moments after that he was on his way to the living room. Why, Keller wondered, was the dog behaving like an expectant father in a maternity-ward waiting room? What was all this back-and-forth business about?

Keller closed his eyes, feeling as far from sleep as he was from Sardinia. Why, he wondered, did Andria want to go there? For the sardines? Then she could stop at Corsica for a corset, and head on to Elba for the macaroni. And Malta for the falcons, and Crete for the cretins, and—

He was just getting drifty when the dog came back.

"Nelson," he said, "what the hell's the matter with you? Huh?" He reached down and scratched the dog behind the ear. "You're a good boy," he said. "Oh yes, you're a good boy, but you're nuts."

There was a knock on the door.

He sat up in bed. It was Andria, of course, and the door was open; she had knocked to get his attention. "He just can't decide who he wants to be with," she said. "Maybe I should just pack my things and go."

"No," he said. He didn't want her to go. "No, don't go," he said.

"Then maybe I should stay."

She came on into the room. She had turned on a lamp in the living room before she came in, but the back lighting was not revealing. The pink flannel thing was opaque, and Keller couldn't tell anything about her body. Then in a single motion she drew the garment over her head and cast it aside, and now he could tell everything about her body.

"I have a feeling this is a big mistake," she said, "but I don't care. I just don't care. Do you know what I mean?"

"I know exactly what you mean," Keller said.

Afterward he said, "Now I suppose you'll think I put the dog up to it. I wish I could take the credit, but I swear it was all his idea. He was like that donkey in the logic problem, unable to decide between the two bales of hay. Where did he go, I wonder?"

She didn't say anything, and he looked closely and saw that she was crying. Jesus, had he said something to upset her?

He said, "Andria? Is something wrong?"

She sat up and crossed her arms beneath her breasts. "I'm just scared," she said.

"Of what?"

"Of you."

"Of me?"

"Just tell me you're not going to hurt me," she said. "Could you do that?"

"Why would I hurt you?"

"I don't know."

"Well, why would you say something like that?"

"Oh, God," she said. She put a hand to her mouth and chewed on a knuckle. Her fingernails weren't polished, just her toenails. Interesting. She said, "When I'm in a relationship, I have to be completely honest."

"Huh?"

"Not that this is a relationship, I mean we just went to bed together once, but I felt we really related, don't you think?"

Keller wondered what she was getting at.

"So I have to be honest. See, I know what you do."

"You know what I do?"

"On those trips."

That was ridiculous. How could she know anything?

"Tell me," he said.

"I'm afraid to say it."

God, maybe she did know.

"Go ahead," he said. "There's nothing to be afraid of."

"You—"

"Go ahead."

"You're an assassin."

Ooops.

He said, "What makes you think that?"

"I don't think it," she said. "I sort of know it. And I don't know how I know it. I guess I knew it the day I met you. Something about your energy, I guess. It's kind of intangible, but it's there."

"Oh."

"I sense things about people. Please don't hurt me."

"I'll never hurt you, Andria."

"I know you mean that," she said. "I hope it turns out to be true."

He thought for a moment. "If you think that about me," he said, "or know it, whatever you want to call it, and if you were afraid I might . . . hurt you—"

"Then why did I come into the bedroom?"

"Right. Why did you?"

She looked right into his eyes. "I couldn't help myself," she said.

He felt this sensation in the middle of his chest, as if there were a steel band around his heart and it had just cracked and fallen away. He reached for her and drew her down.

On the floor at the side of the bed, Nelson slept like a lamb.

In the morning they walked Nelson together. Keller bought the paper and picked up a quart of milk. Back at the apartment, he made a pot of coffee while she put breakfast on the table.

He said, "Look, I'm not good at this, but there are some things I ought to say. The first is that you have nothing to fear from me. My work is one thing and my life is something else. I have no reason to hurt you, and even if I had a reason I wouldn't do it."

"I know that."

"Oh?"

"I was afraid last night. I'm not afraid now."

"Oh," he said. "Well, the other thing I want to say is that I know you don't have a place to stay right now, and as far as I'm concerned you can stay here as long as you want. In fact, I'd like it if you stayed here. You can even sleep on the couch if you want, assuming that Nelson will allow it. I'm not sure he will, though."

She considered her reply, and the phone rang. He made a face and answered it.

It was Dot. "Young man," she said, in an old lady's quavering voice, "I think you had better pay a call on your kindly old Aunt Dorothy."

"I just did," he reminded her. "Just because it was quick and easy doesn't mean I don't need a little time off between engagements."

"Keller," she said, in her own voice, "get on the next train, will you? It's urgent."

"Urgent?"

"There's a problem."

"What do you mean?"

"Do you remember saying something about a piece of cake?"

"So?"

"So your cake fell," Dot said. "Get it?"

There was no one to meet him at the White Plains station, so he took a cab to the big Victorian house on Taunton Place. Dot was waiting on the porch. "All right," she said. "Report."

"To you?"

"And then I report to him. That's how he wants it."

Keller shrugged and reported. Where he'd gone, what he'd done. It only took a few sentences. When he was done he paused for a moment, and then he said, "The woman wasn't supposed to be there."

"Neither was the man."

"How's that?"

"You killed the wrong people," she said. "Wait here, Keller, okay? I have to relay this to His Eminence. You want coffee, there's a fresh pot in the kitchen. Well, a reasonably fresh pot."

Keller stayed on the porch. There was an old-fashioned glider and he sat on that, gliding back and forth, but it seemed too frivolous for the circumstances. He switched to a chair but was too restless to stay in it. He was on his feet when Dot returned.

She said, "You said Room 314."

"And that's the room I went to," he said. "That was the room I called from downstairs, and those were the numbers on the door. Room 314 at the Sheraton."

"Wrong room."

"I wrote it down," he said. "He gave me the number and I wrote it down."

"You didn't happen to save the note, did you?"

"Oh, sure," he said. "I keep everything. I have it on my coffee table, along with the boning knife and the vic's watch and wallet. No, of course I didn't keep the note."

"Of course you didn't, but it would have been nice if you'd made an exception on this particular occasion. The, uh, designated victim was in Room 502."

He frowned. "That's not even close. What did he do, change his room? If I'd been given a name or a photo, you know—"

"I know. He didn't change his room."

"Dot, I can't believe I wrote it down wrong."

"Neither can I, Keller."

"If I got one digit wrong or reversed the order, well, I could almost believe that, but to turn 502 into 314—"

"You know what 314 is, Keller?" He didn't. "It's the area code for St. Louis."

"The area code? As in telephone?"

"As in telephone."

"I don't understand."

She sighed. "He's had a lot on his mind lately," she said. "He's been under a strain. So, just between you and me—" For God's sake, who was he going to tell? "—he must have looked at the wrong slip of paper and wound up giving you the area code instead of the room number."

"I thought he seemed tired. I even said something."

"And I told you life tires people out, if I remember correctly. We were both right. Meanwhile, you have to go to Tulsa."

"Tulsa?"

"That's where the target lives, and it seems he's canceling the rest of his meetings and going home this afternoon. I don't know if it's a coincidence or if the business two floors down spooked him. The client didn't want to hit him in Tulsa, but now there's no choice."

"I just did the job," Keller said, "and now I have to do it again. When she popped out of the bathroom it turned into two for the price of one, and now it's three for the price of one."

"Not exactly. He has to save face on this, Keller, so the idea is you stepped on your whatchamacallit and now you're going to correct your mistake. But when all this is history there will be a little extra in your Christmas stocking."

"Christmas?"

"A figure of speech. There'll be a bonus, and you won't have to wait for Christmas for it."

"The client's going to pay a bonus?"

"I said you'd get a bonus," she said. "I didn't say the client would be paying it. Tulsa, and you'll be met at the airport and somebody will show you around and point the finger. Have you ever been to Tulsa?"

"I don't think so."

"You'll love it. You'll want to move there."

He didn't even want to go there. Halfway down the porch stairs he turned, retraced his steps, and said, "The man and woman in 314. Who were they?"

"Who knows? They weren't Gunnar Ruthven, I can tell you that much."

"That's who I'm going to see in Tulsa?"

"Let's hope so. As far as the pair in 314, I don't know any names. He was a local businessman, owned a dry-cleaning plant or something like that. I don't know anything about her. They were married, but not to each other. What I hear, you interrupted a matinee."

"That's what it looked like."

"Rang down the curtain," Dot said. "What a world, huh?"

"His name was Harry."

"See, I told you it wasn't Gunnar Ruthven. What's it matter, Keller? You're not going to send flowers, are you?"

"I'll be gone longer this time," he told Andria. "I have to . . . go someplace and . . . take care of some business."

"I'll take care of Nelson," she said. "And we'll both be here when you get back."

His plane was leaving from Newark. He packed a bag and called a livery service for a car to the airport.

He said, "Does it bother you?"

"What you do? It would bother me if I did it, but I couldn't do it, so that's beside the point. But does it bother me that you do it? I don't think so. I mean, it's what you do."

"But don't you think it's wrong?"

She thought it over. "I don't think it's wrong for *you*," she said. "I think it's your karma."

"You mean like destiny or something?"

"Sort of. It's what you have to do in order to learn the lesson you're supposed to learn in this lifetime. We're not just here once, you know. We live many lives."

"You believe that, huh?"

"It's more a matter of knowledge than belief."

"Oh." Karma, he thought. "What about the people I go and see? It's just their karma?"

"Doesn't that make sense to you?"

"I don't know," he said. "I'll have to think about it."

He had plenty of time to think about karma. He was in Tulsa for five days before he had a chance to close the file on Gunnar Ruthven. A sad-eyed young man named Joel met his flight and gave him a tour of the city that included Ruthven's suburban home and downtown office building. Ruthven lived in a two-story mock-Tudor house on about half an acre of land and had an office in the Great Southwestern Bank building within a block of the courthouse. Joel drove next to the All-American Inn, one of a couple dozen motels clustered together on a strip a mile from the airport. "The reason for the name," Joel said, "is so you would know the place wasn't owned by Indians. I don't mean your Native Americans, I mean Indians from India. They own most of the motels. So this here place, the owners changed the name to the All-American, and they even had a huge signboard announcing the place was owned and operated by hundred-percent Americans."

"Did somebody make them take the sign down?"

Joel shook his head. "After about a year," he said, "they sold out, and the new owners took the sign down."

"They didn't like the implications?"

"Not hardly. See, they're Indians. Place is decent, though, and you don't have to go through the lobby. In fact you're already registered and paid in advance for a week. I figured you'd like that. Here's your room key, and here's a set of car keys. They belong to that Toyota over there, third from the end. Paper for it's in the glove box, along with a little .22 automatic. If you prefer something heavier, just say so."

Keller assured him it would be fine. "Why don't you get settled," Joel said, "and get yourself something to eat if you're hungry. The Sizzler across the street on the left isn't bad. I'll pick you up in say two hours and we'll sneak a peek at the fellow you came out here to see."

Joel picked him up on schedule and they rode downtown and parked in a metered lot. They sat in the lobby of Ruthven's office building. After twenty minutes Joel said, "Getting off the elevator. Glen plaid suit, horn-rimmed glasses, carrying the aluminum briefcase. Looks space age, I guess, but I'd go for genuine leather every time, myself."

Keller took a good look. Ruthven was tall and slender, with a sharp nose and a pointed chin. Keller said, "Are you positive that's him?"

"Shit, yes, I'm positive. Why?"

"Just making sure."

Joel ran him back to the All-American and gave him a map of Tulsa with different locations marked on it—the All-American Inn, Ruthven's house, Ruthven's office, and a southside restaurant Joel said was outstanding. He also gave Keller a slip of paper with a phone number on it. "Anything you want," he said. "You want a girl, you want to get in a card game, you want to see a cockfight, just call that number and I'll take care of it. You ever been to a cockfight?"

"Never."

"You want to?"

Keller thought about it. "I don't think so," he said.

"Well, if you change your mind, just let me know. Or anything else you want." Joel hesitated. "I got to say I've got a lot of respect for you," he said, averting his eyes from Keller's as he said it. "I don't guess I could do what you do. I haven't got the sand for it."

Keller went to his room and stretched out on the bed. Sand, he thought. What the hell did sand have to do with anything?

He thought about Ruthven, coming off the elevator, long and lean, and realized why he'd been bothered by the man's appearance. He wasn't what Keller had expected. He didn't look anything like Harry in 314.

Did Ruthven know he was a target? Driving around in the Toyota, keeping an eye on the man, Keller decided that he did. There was a certain wariness about him. The way to handle that, Keller decided, was to let him get over it. A few days of peace and quiet and Ruthven could revert to his usual way of thinking. He'd decide that Harry and his girlfriend had been killed by a jealous husband, and he'd drop his guard and stick his neck out, and Keller could get the job done and go home.

The gun seemed all right. The third afternoon he drove out into the country, popped a full clip into the gun, and emptied the clip at a Cattle Crossing sign. None of his shots hit the mark, but he didn't figure that was the gun's fault. He was fifteen yards away, for God's sake, and the sign was no more than ten inches across. Keller wasn't a particularly good shot, but arranged his life so he didn't have to be. If you walked up behind a guy and put the gun muzzle to the back of his neck, all you had to do was pull the trigger. You didn't have to be a marksman. All you needed was—

What? Karma? Sand?

He reloaded and made a real effort this time, and two shots actually hit the sign. Remarkable what a man could do when he put his mind to it.

The hard part was finding a way to pass the time. He went to a movie, walked through a mall, and watched a lot of television. He had Joel's number but never called it. He didn't want female companionship, nor did he feel like playing cards or watching a cockfight.

He kept fighting off the urge to call New York.

On one of the home shopping channels, one woman said earnestly to another, "Now there's one thing we both know, and that's that you just can't have too many earrings." Keller couldn't get the line out of his head. Was it literally true? Suppose you had a thousand pairs, or ten thousand. Suppose you had a million pairs. Wouldn't that constitute a surplus?

The woman in 314 hadn't been wearing earrings, but there had been a pair on the bedside table. How many other pairs had she had at home?

Finally one morning he got up at daybreak and showered and shaved. He packed his bag and wiped the motel room free of prints.

He had done this routinely every time he left the place, so that it
would never be necessary for him to return to it, but this morning
he sensed that it was time to wind things up. He drove to Ruthven's
house and parked around the corner at the curb. He went through
the driveway and yard of a house on the side street, scaled a four-
foot Cyclone fence, and jimmied a window in order to get into
Ruthven's garage. The car inside the garage was unlocked, and he got
into the back seat and waited patiently.

Eventually the garage door opened, and when that happened
Keller scrunched down so that he couldn't be seen. Ruthven opened
the car door and got behind the wheel.

Keller sat up slowly. Ruthven was fumbling with the key, having a
hard time getting it into the ignition. But was it really Ruthven?

Jesus, get a grip. Who else could it be?

Keller stuck the gun in his ear and emptied the clip.

"These are beautiful," Andria said. "You didn't have to bring me
anything."

"I know that."

"But I'm glad you did. I love them."

"I didn't know what to get you," Keller said, "because I don't
know what you already have. But I figured you can never have too
many earrings."

"That is absolutely true," Andria said, "and not many men
realize it."

Keller tried not to smirk.

"Ever since you left," she said, "I've been thinking about what you
said. That you would like it if I stayed here. But what I have to know
is if you still feel that way, or if it was just, you know, how you felt
that morning."

"I'd like you to stay."

"Well, I'd like it, too. I like being around your energy. I like your
dog and I like your apartment and I like you."

"I missed you," Keller said.

"I missed you, too. But I liked being here while you were gone, living in your space and taking care of your dog. I have a confession to make. I slept in your bed."

"Well, for heaven's sake. Where else would you sleep?"

"On the couch."

Keller gave her a look. She colored, and he said, "While I was away I thought about your toes."

"My toes?"

"All different colors."

"Oh," she said. "Well, I had trouble deciding which color to go with, and it came to me that when God couldn't decide on a color, he created the rainbow."

"Rainbow toes," Keller said. "I think I'll take them one by one into my mouth, those pink little rainbow toes. What do you think about that?"

"Oh," she said.

Later he said, "Suppose someone got killed by mistake."

"How could that happen?"

"Say an area code turns into a room number. Human error, computer error, anything at all. Mistakes happen."

"No, they don't."

"They don't?"

"People make mistakes," she said, "but there's no such thing as a mistake."

"How's that?"

"You could make a mistake," she said. "You could be swinging a dumbbell and it could sail out of the window. That would be a case of you making a mistake."

"I'll say."

"And somebody looking for an address in the next block could get out of a cab here instead, and here comes a dumbbell. The person made a mistake."

"His last one, too."

"In this lifetime," she agreed. "So you've both made a mistake, but if you look at the big picture, there was no mistake. The person got hit by a dumbbell and died."

"No mistake?"

"No mistake, because it was meant to happen."

"But if it wasn't meant to happen—"

"Then it wouldn't."

"And if it happened, it was meant to."

"Right."

"Karma?"

"Karma."

"Little pink toes," Keller said. "I'm glad you're here."

The Catch

BY JAMES W. HALL

James Hall's long-running "Thorn" series was recognized in 2003 by the Private Eye Writers of America when they awarded the Shamus award for Best Novel to his book *Blackwater Sound*. His most recent novel is the best-selling stand-alone *Forests of the Night*.

Hall sets his stories—as he has done the majority of his books—in Florida, but his character is very unlike his series hero. As you'll see, he's a bit of a throwback to the torpedoes of old. . . .

"TWO HUNDRED BUCKS? You're kidding, right?"

"A hundred now, the rest when it's done."

"You can't be serious."

"You're asking me to charge more?"

"I always heard it was like five thousand or something."

"Yeah? Where'd you hear that?"

"The movies, I guess. Somewhere."

Mason took a second to appraise the guy—shoulders pulled back, trim waist, the look of command. Wearing a dark blue corporate suit, oxblood cordovans polished to a deep gleam. Gray hair clipped in a military style. Ice-blue eyes clicking here and there, but a little pouchy underneath them like he wasn't getting his full eight hours. Fifty-nine, sixty years old. Stock broker, he said. Probably pulled down half a million a year. Manicured and massaged with a leased Porsche and slinky girlfriends a third his age. An apartment with a ten-mile ocean view, decorated with furniture too chrome and weird-angled to sit in. To this guy, two hundred bucks was tip money for a valet parker.

"Some get five thousand, some get more," Mason said. "The rip-off artists. The hotshots. How hard it is to pull a trigger? Two hundred dollars. I been getting that for forty years. It's my rate."

"But the chances you take. Prison, the death penalty. I don't know, it just sounds cut-rate."

"Think of me as the generic alternative. Same drug, lower price."

"Weird," the guy said. "Very weird."

"You want to pay more, I got some phone numbers, guys'll be glad to take your cash."

On his prehistoric Motorola, *Jeopardy* was playing. Some red-haired twerp was getting everything right, been winning for a solid month, like they were feeding him the answers. Trying to draw in a larger audience. Mason wouldn't put it past the TV assholes. That's how it worked. Couldn't trust anything that came out of that box. Which didn't keep him from having it on twenty-four hours a day. Playing in the background like Muzak with pictures. Kept him company, kept him from drifting off into memories, bad dreams, regrets or worse.

Mason sat in his green corduroy chair. One lamp on. Lighting up the oversized oil painting of Jesus with his hands upraised like he was calling a heavenly touchdown.

The painting belonged to his wife, long dead. He kept it as a reminder of her and her ridiculous faith.

"Do they know what you do, your relations?" The guy motioned toward the front house where his son lived with his anorexic wife and three brats.

Mason shrugged, and the guy took a deep breath and blew it out.

"So how'm I doing so far?" Mason said.

"I'm sorry, what?"

"You're interviewing me, how'm I doing?"

"Hey, I'm just trying to get a feel for this thing. Who you are, what I'm getting into. How much danger I'm putting myself in. You're so nonchalant, 'cause yeah, you do this all the time. But this is a big deal for me."

"I just told you," said Mason. "I never been in jail. Never arrested, or seen the inside of a courtroom. Nothing like that. If that isn't good enough, take a hike."

"But I found you. A normal guy like me. What's to keep the cops from doing the same thing? Sniffing you out."

Mason just smiled. The people Mason got rid of, shit almighty, the cops should give him the keys to the city.

"All I'm saying, the kind of reputation you've got, if I were you, I'd charge more." The executive dug his hands in the pockets of his nicely tailored trousers. "I'd raise it to two, three thousand at least."

"So buy a gun," Mason said. "Hang out a shingle."

The guy turned away from Mason, glanced at Jesus, at the TV, at the empty bird cage. The cage was another leftover from his wife. Mason hated birds. How could anybody love a bird? Like loving a radish with feathers. But his wife had adored the thing. Broke her heart when the chirping, shitting, pecking creature died. Wept for weeks, stayed in bed. Mason kept the cage for the same reason he held on to the Jesus picture. Something from that other time, that life when she fussed over that bird, fussed over Mason, fussed over their boy. The boy who now lived in the ten-thousand-square-foot mansion and let Mason stay rent-free in the poolhouse.

"Just so you know," the executive said. "I got your name from a shoeshine guy in the lobby of my building downtown."

"I'm supposed to be surprised? That's how it works."

"It's amazing," the guy said. "I sort of hinted around I wanted a person removed, made it sound like a joke. Just said it to this one guy, kind of a shady character. Made it sound like I was fooling around. Then yesterday he gives me your name and address. Whispers it while he's putting a shine on."

"Word of mouth," Mason said. "A killer's best friend."

"So I guess you want to know who I want dead."

"Either that, or I go shoot somebody at random."

The guy tried a smile but after a nervous second it curdled and slipped off his lips. He lowered his butt to the arm of a chair and watched *Jeopardy* for a minute. The executive had a name, Arnold Chalmers, an old-fashioned moniker like the name of some loser from a black-and-white Bogart movie.

In the back yard, one of the brats, his grandson, was playing with a neighbor kid. They were passing a football back and forth, getting pissed off over something. Squawking at each other. Always with the squawking. His son and the anorexic, not the greatest parents.

Truth be told, Mason hadn't been either. A downright shitty father. Moody and irritable. Feeling low a good percentage of the time. Nothing much to celebrate, a professional hitter with a busy schedule. Leaving the child-rearing to his wife, giving her something to do while Mason flew in and out of Miami all the time. Two hundred bucks plus expenses. Which had been a decent wage in the early sixties when he started out.

But Chalmers was right. Mason should ask a thousand at least, more likely five or ten. But he stuck with the two hundred out of stubborn habit. Funny thing was, these days since it was such a ridiculous amount, and since Mason was such a withered-up old fart, an oddity in this age of bleached blond punks from Odessa and Gdansk, covered in tattoos and flashing their chrome nine millimeters, Mason had acquired a certain status. A retro celebrity. His name getting around in circles he'd never cracked before. Becoming a minor legend. Funny. A thing like he did, requiring no skills whatsoever, all of a sudden people treating him like he's Babe Ruth.

Not that he was ever a second-rater. Back in the old days when Miami Beach was the mob's winter playground, Mason had more business than he could handle. Things getting so routine at one point, he even had a regular commute. Up and back to New York. Some goombah wanted his son-in-law whacked, guy had been cheating on the goombah's daughter or maybe it was a bookie skimming receipts. Next week, a Miami dog track boss calls up and gives Mason the address of somebody to clip in Long Island—retaliation and more retaliation. Back and forth, back and forth, Miami International to Newark or LaGuardia. Mason working both sides. Though he had to admit, he got more of a zing from doing the New York assholes. Their loud-mouth arrogance annoyed him. The way they treated Miami like a bumpkin patch. Their bus-station urinal. Miami was Mason's town. Had been since birth. As bad as it was turning out with the Cubans and the Nicaraguans and the Haitians and the Russians crowding the roads and stinking up the evening news, he'd take Miami over New York any day of the week. A paradise. As good a place as there was to get old and wait to die.

Chalmers dug out his wallet. He fingered through the bills and extracted two fifties. Held them out to Mason.

"On top of the TV," Mason said.

He aimed the remote and flicked through the channels, looking for what he watched after *Jeopardy*. Lately he'd been on a *Seinfeld* binge. Reruns. Those four kooks hanging out in Jerry's apartment or the diner downstairs. The goofball with the big hair always sliding into Jerry's apartment like it was an ice rink. The goony faces he made. And the fat little schmuck who reminded Mason of his own son. Such a loser, he was actually funny.

"So there it is," Chalmers said. "Aren't you going to count it?"

The guy smirked at him. Proud of his stupid joke.

When Mason didn't smile back, Chalmers walked over to the bird cage and peered inside the bars. Everything was still exactly like the day the bird died. Same newspaper on the floor. Hulls, bird shit, little plastic swing.

"Okay," the guy said. "There's the money. Now what's the catch?"

"The catch," Mason said.

"There is one, isn't there?"

Mason watched Jerry spooning cereal into his smug New Yorker mouth while Elaine yakked about some new boyfriend. George on the couch clipping his toenails. Gross and annoying as usual. Annoying and oblivious. He could picture shooting them, one by one, make the remaining ones watch what was coming. They made him laugh, though. Funny but irritating.

Mason said, "Well, I wouldn't call it a catch exactly."

"Christ, I knew it," Chalmers said. "Two hundred dollars, there had to be a catch."

"I'm not a sociopath," Mason said. "That's the catch."

"Yeah, okay? What's that supposed to mean?"

"I got a sense of shame. I'm not some robot, wind him up, he goes and shoots a guy, then comes home makes a plate of spaghetti and sleeps his eight hours. I used to be that guy, but I'm not any more."

"I still don't get it."

Seinfeld's latest girlfriend comes strutting out of the back bedroom, making a grand entrance. She's tall and wearing a super-tight low-cut blouse which naturally shows off her mammoth boobs. Jerry introduces her to Elaine and Elaine looks at her and slips up and says something about knockers. She can't help herself. For the next minute everything out of her mouth is about tits. All tasteful enough for TV, but still a little on the raunchy side. Seinfeld was a TV show his wife would never sit still for. The morals of America were in steep decline, that was her view. From the time she was born in some redneck coal town in West Virginia, American morals had been sliding downhill. For seventy-two years, everywhere the woman looked, everything she saw confirmed it. America was going to hell. Their entire married life, the woman thought Mason sold medical supplies.

"Okay, so you got a conscience. How's that change things?"

"It means you gotta convince me."

"Convince you to murder this person?"

"Something like that. I gotta hear what he did. I got to see this from your point of view, be converted."

"Jesus Christ."

"You don't like the rules, take your money and go."

"You want me to plead with you, grovel, is that it? Get on my knees."

"What I'm saying is, I got scruples. Only way I can do what I do, I gotta be convinced it's necessary."

The executive stared at Mason for half a minute then sighed and walked to the door. He opened it, gave Mason a parting look, and headed out into the dusky light and shut the door behind him.

Todd, the bratty grandson, screamed at his little brat friend and the two of them came whooping over to the poolhouse. A few seconds later, Todd threw open the door, stuck his fat sweaty head inside and screeched for a full five seconds, then slammed the door and ran back into the yard. His little game. Scream at the boogeyman. That's what he called his grandfather. Not Granddad. Not some cute goo-goo name left over from when he couldn't pronounce. No, Mason was boogeyman.

A minute later, Mason was back with *Seinfeld*. The show was almost over and he'd only caught the basic outline. The bosomy girlfriend, Elaine's breast jokes. George and Kramer in awe of the woman, falling all over themselves as she approached. Not the funniest one Mason had seen.

As the final commercial came on, the door opened again and Chalmers walked back in. He was shaking his head like he couldn't believe he'd returned to this nuthouse.

"It's my son," the guy said. "I want you to kill my son."

"Okay, that's a start."

The man's neat haircut look rumpled now. Like he'd been grinding his head in his hands. Giving him a wretched look.

"You're not shocked. A man wanting his own son dead."

"Wouldn't be my first," Mason said. "Wouldn't be my second or third."

The brats were practicing their banshee yells outside Mason's bathroom window. Cranking up the volume, trying to outdo each other. Hateful little turds.

"Here's a picture," Chalmers said.

He dug a snapshot out of his jacket pocket and held it out. Mason told him to put it on the arm of his chair. Not like he was obsessive-compulsive about fingerprints or any of that DNA bullshit. He just didn't want to touch things if he didn't have to.

Chalmers set the photo on the chair arm, nudged it around so Mason had a good view, then stepped back.

Chalmers was wearing bathing trunks and had his arm around the shoulder of the boy. There was a lake behind them, other swimmers. The boy was maybe thirty, thirty-three. Wearing shorts and a Bud-weiser T-shirt that fit tight enough to show the hump of his belly. Wide simple face, bad haircut, blunt features, too much forehead.

"Retarded?" Mason said.

"Learning-disabled." Chalmers turned his back on Mason and watched the commercials jabbering on and on.

"So 'cause he's dumb, he's got to die?"

Chalmers came around slowly. A look forming on his face, going from the gloomy dread he'd been wearing to something with more edge. His business face. Take it or leave it, that's my best offer. A bully-boy look.

"You trying to piss me off?"

Mason reached into the crack of the cushion and extracted a Ruger .22 auto with the long silencer cylinder.

He lay the pistol on his lap and watched Chalmers's face drain of hardass. The same effect the Ruger usually had—making the lungs tighter, the eyes more focused.

"He's retarded," Mason said. "For thirty years you put up with it, now enough's enough. Is that it? He's cramping your style. Your bachelor ambitions. The girls find out about him, it turns them off?"

"Fuck this," Chalmers said and headed for the door again. Then remembered the photo and about-faced and came over and plucked it off the chair.

"So, help me," Mason said. "What changed? What made it sud-denly intolerable to live with this pitiful creature? Your son."

"He raped a girl."

Mason gave it a few seconds' thought, then nodded.

"Okay. That would change things."

"Raped her and then threw her off a bridge."

"Here in Miami?"

"In Lauderdale."

"I didn't see it on the news," Mason said. "I watch the news and there wasn't anything about a rape and a girl off a bridge."

"I got there in time," Chalmers said.

"And you covered it up," said Mason. "You buried the girl."

Chalmers took a deep breath and looked at the photo, at himself and his son. Same blood bumping through their veins. But Mason knew that didn't count for shit. Look at his own flesh-and-blood son. Look at his grandson. They might as well be from Gdansk themselves, for all he knew them, understood them, cared about them. Or vice versa.

"His name is Julius," Chalmers said. "I call him Jules."

"And you buried the girl. The two of you."

"I did it," Chalmers said. "I dug a hole and put her in it and Jules stood there the whole time complaining about his pecker. How it itched. He raped this girl, killed her, and he's grumbling about how she gave him some disease. Crabs or something. While I was digging out in the dark, he's going on about feeling prickly between his legs."

"You wanted to hit him with the shovel. Smack him in the face."

Chalmers raised his eyes and gave Mason a level look.

"Is this some kind of game you play?"

Mason said, "Yeah, it's a game. That's right. You enjoying it?"

He picked up the Ruger, unscrewed the suppressor a couple of turns, then tightened it back down.

"Okay, so we're at the bridge. You're digging and Jules is whining about crabs."

"That's all," Chalmers said.

Mason shook his head.

"I said that's all. That's all there is. He killed a girl. And, I don't know, maybe he knew what he was doing, maybe he didn't. Maybe he has a guilty conscience. But I don't think so. I'm afraid he found out he liked it, raping girls and killing them, and he's going to do it again and then again after that, and one of those times I won't be able to cover it up."

"So?" Mason lay the Ruger across his lap. "So the kid gets caught, goes to jail, problem solved. You save two hundred bucks, don't have to live with the guilt you killed your own boy."

Out in the yard the brats were splashing in the pool. School night, but they might be going at it till ten, eleven o'clock before the anorexic or Mason's fat, sloppy son called them in to bed.

Already dark out there, but the floodlights from the rear patio were on. Sometimes his son and the anorexic forgot and left the floodlights on all night, blasting into Mason's bedroom. Penetrating the slats in his worthless mini-blinds. Mason would lie there and stare at the slits of light and he'd think of what his wife would say. She wouldn't complain about there being too much light to sleep. No, that old woman would be blathering about the wasted money. Ten dollars at least, all those lights running through the night. You know how hard people in her generation had to work for ten dollars, the things she had to do. Take in sewing, baby-sit, all the pennies she put away, and look at that waste, those big fancy lights burning for no good reason.

Mason didn't miss his wife. He didn't miss her bird and if something happened to his own son and the grandchildren, hell, he wouldn't miss them either. All three of them were brats. Screaming in the pool, going out of their way to raise the volume. And did his fat, lazy son put down his cocktail for a second to go out and see what they were screaming about? Never. Not once. They could be drowning, or being molested by a passing pervert.

"I don't want my son going to jail."

"You don't mind killing him," Mason said, "but what is it, you don't want some big black guy bulldozing your baby's butt. That it?"

"You're a crude man."

"I don't get paid for my refinement and urbanity."

Chalmers watched a few seconds of the TV show, another sitcom set in New York City. *Friends.* A bunch of do-nothing twenty-year-olds who could spend half an hour whining about an ingrown toenail or a soufflé that collapsed. Mason usually switched over to CNN after *Seinfeld*, spent the evening catching up on all the ways the world was going to hell. Something the dead wife would appreciate. See there. See there. See there. Gloom, gloom, and more gloom.

Chalmers sat down in the chair beneath the Jesus picture. He raised both hands and finger-combed his hair, raking it back into place.

"I don't want my boy going to jail."

"Yeah, we established that. We just haven't figured out why that's worse than him being dead."

"Don't you have what you wanted? Isn't it enough he killed this girl?"

"That's a start, yeah. I'm getting into your head a little, seeing your misery. Yeah. Digging a hole, rolling a dead girl into it, son scratching his nuts the whole time. I'm warming up to it, I'm just not quite there yet."

"I'll give you five hundred dollars. Shit, I'll give you ten thousand. I don't care. Just no more questions, okay?"

"That's a good sign, resisting like that. Means we're getting closer, a layer or two more, we might have a deal."

"Look, maybe you should just shoot me. Just shoot me now. Right here, right now. Do it. Take all my money, get rid of my corpse. Nobody knows I'm here. You could get away with it."

"That what you want?"

"I don't know. Maybe it is."

"Do me a favor, Chalmers. Before we go any farther with this, get up, take down that picture."

Chalmers looked at Mason for a few seconds then turned his head and looked up at Jesus.

"That?"

"That."

Chalmers rose and lifted the painting off its hook. Grunted a little. The thing was heavier than it looked.

He set it down, propped it against the TV.

"So?"

"The wall," Mason said.

Chalmers looked back at the wall. Chunks missing in the drywall, fist-sized holes, dried blood, some fragments of bone and hair.

"Fuck."

Chalmers swung back, giving Mason a wild stare.

Expecting the Ruger to be aimed his way. But it lay on Mason's lap.

"What is this?"

Chalmers's mouth was open, a ribbon of drool showing at the corner.

"You execute people in here? This is a murder chamber?"

"That makes it sound creepy."

"You shoot people. Clients coming in to hire you. You kill them instead."

"Right where you're standing. Ten, twelve. I don't keep a total."

"Why?"

"They ask me to. Sometimes they beg."

"Jesus, this is fucking crazy. You're a crazy man."

"Some guys, they come in, tell their story, I bully till it's all out, last bit of puke from their guts, then bingo, they ask me to do it. They plead. Well, sometimes they plead, not always. Different people, it works different ways."

"And how's it working with me?"

"Don't know yet. We're not there. Not at the end. We're sort of stuck on why you'd rather your son be dead than go to jail."

"I'm out of here," Chalmers said.

"No one's stopping you."

Chalmers stared at the wall again as if counting the holes. That wasn't a reliable way to figure out how many had died because sometimes it took two shots, sometimes, Mason hated to admit, he missed with the first one, sometimes the second one too. So there had to be a few more holes than victims.

"What were you wearing?"

"Wearing?"

"We're back at the hole, the grave for this girl. What'd you have on?"

"Hell, I don't know. Why's that matter?"

"I'm trying to get a picture. I'm trying to put myself there, inside your skin. Get the feel."

"A suit," Chalmers said. "A black suit."

"Armani, that's what you wear?"

Chalmers swallowed.

"How'd you know that?"

"I got an eye for tailoring. I'm not a clotheshorse myself, but some of the guys I associated with in my younger days, they dressed nice. I made it a hobby. So you're in your black Armani, five-, six-thousand-dollar coat and pants. You're sweating like a pig. Your son is all cranky about his itchy dick. I bet there were mosquitoes out there too."

"A few, but I wasn't feeling much."

"Too focused on the inner turmoil. Cleaning up after your son's murder. A guy wouldn't feel a few mosquito bites."

"I got blisters on my hands from the shovel. I remember that."

"Bleed a little, did you?"

"Where's this going?"

"Hey, you were there, not me," Mason said. "I don't know where it's going."

On the TV, the good-looking blonde girl who is also the resident airhead is trying to cook something for Thanksgiving dinner. But she'd read the recipe wrong. That was supposed to be funny? Maybe his wife had a point. The world was going to hell. Men wanted to hire other men to kill their retarded sons while there were all those people in an audience laughing at a girl who couldn't cook.

"I buried the girl, then Jules and I drove back to my apartment and we took showers and changed clothes and I ordered a pizza."

"A pizza."

"Jules has a very limited range of foods he'll eat."

"Picky boy."

"It's part of his disability. He gets stuck in ruts."

"Happens to the best of us," Mason said.

Chalmers glanced back at the wall behind him.

"What do you do with the bodies?" Chalmers said it, then he swung around to face Mason and said, "Never mind, that's none of my business."

"I use a wheelbarrow," Mason said. "Roll 'em out to my car, put them in the trunk. I got a canal I like out in the 'Glades. Shovels, no way, I'm too old for shovels. This canal, though, it has gators."

"No one's ever been found?"

"Not that I heard."

Chalmers sat down in the chair again. His body seemed heavier than it had a few minutes earlier.

"So you and Jules are eating pizza. How's his itch doing?"

"Still there," Chalmers said.

One of the girl brats, fourteen, fifteen, Mason could never remember, she turns on the music in her bedroom. Window open, this ghetto rap, hip-hop bullshit starts booming. The boys in the pool yell for her to turn it down. It turns into a war out there. Girl screeches and little boy screeches, and the volume of the music gets higher. And where's Daddy and anorexic Mommy? No fucking where to be found.

"I told Jules he had to go see a psychiatrist. He had to get this new lustfulness under control."

"Lustfulness? That's what you think?"

"Whatever the right word is. I'm no shrink."

"So this just started? Came out of the blue, did it? He's thirty, all of a sudden he's horny?"

"As far as I know."

"Nothing set it off?"

"What're you saying?"

"I'm asking questions. I'm not saying anything."

"You're suggesting something I did might've set it off. That I'm responsible for what my son does. My adult son. My dating habits influenced him to go out and rape a girl."

Mason looked across at the holes in his wall. Seeing a little fragment of a blouse wedged into one of the ragged craters. Mason remembered that one. She was one of the pleaders. Yeah, down on her knees. Begging with her hands pressed together like Mason was the Pope. Pretty woman. Mason made her stand up. Made her look him in the eye. Made her stop crying. Made her stand up straight. Then that was that.

"If Jules went to jail, it would all go public. It would be a major story. The people I represent, they're the movers and shakers in this community. Names you'd know. Owners of the sports franchise, the cruise-ship company. You know who I mean. I'd be ruined. My business is built on trust and confidence. How's anybody going to give me their life savings to manage if they know what's in my family's bloodstream?"

"So, your boy's got to die to protect your net worth."

"He could rape and kill again. Another innocent girl. That's my number-one concern. But, yeah, to be completely honest, the money's an issue too. I've got obligations."

"Mortgage, things like that."

"Alimony payment, mortgage, I've got obligations like everybody else."

"So Jules gets two in the brain."

"Oh, fuck it. Forget this. I'm out of here. Go ahead, try to shoot me. I'm gone."

But Chalmers didn't get up from the chair. They usually didn't.

"Pizza is over, you had some ice cream, whatever, and what then?"

"I don't remember."

"Sure you do. That's a night you're not going to forget."

"I had an appointment. I went out."

"Left your boy in your condo, blood on his hands, while you went out on a date."

"Where'd you get 'date'? I went out."

"With a woman."

"Okay, okay. I had a date. It was important to me. I was in love with this woman."

"Not any more, though."

Chalmers shook his head. Watched a little of the end of *Friends.* Everyone laughing their heads off about the fucked-up recipe. Poor air-headed blonde.

"Jules," Chalmers spoke softly, watching the TV show. "He followed me that night. He waited till I was gone from Sheila's condo, and he broke in and raped her."

"Yeah, okay. But there's a topper. Something worse."

"How do you know that?"

"There's a topper. What is it?"

"Sheila had a security video. She runs it to make sure her nanny isn't abusing her kid while she's off at work."

"Okay," Mason said. "So she's got the whole rape thing on tape. Now she's blackmailing you. Or she goes to the police and there goes your career."

Chalmers stared at Mason.

"Jesus, where do you get this stuff?"

"I'm an old man. There's only so many ways people can treat each other badly."

"I been sending her ten thousand a month."

Mason nodded. "Ten thousand's a bargain."

"It's pinching me. That and everything else. The alimony. All of it, the market dipping, it's making life difficult."

"So killing Jules, how does that fix anything?"

He rocked forward, settled his elbows on his knees, giving Mason an earnest look. Salesman's eyes, man to man.

"I thought if Jules turns up dead, clearly a murder, it would scare her off. Show her what I'm capable of."

Mason shrugged, picked up the remote and cut to CNN. People starving somewhere in Africa. Their bellies swollen, flies all around their eyes. Little kids who looked two hundred years old. Bones showing through.

"Yeah, I guess, a certain woman, that could work."

"It's to scare her away, but it's also because I'm worried what that boy'll do next. I don't see any other choice."

"So two hundred bucks, that's a bargain. Saves you a fortune."

"It's not the money."

"It's never the money."

The little brat, his grandson, came screeching one more time at Mason's door, swung it open, stuck his blocky head through, closed his beady eyes and wailed for five seconds, then slammed the door and ran off to the big house where the anorexic and Mason's sad, unhappy son were burying themselves alive.

Chalmers looked over his shoulder at the wall.

"I don't want to die."

Mason said, "I'm not trying to convince you of anything."

"I got things I want to do, places I want to see. I've got appetites. I'm not suicidal."

"That's good. Everyone needs something to live for."

The starving kids in Africa were living in camps behind barbed wire. Their mothers pressed them to their breasts. Dying faster themselves so their kids could live a few more days. No men anywhere. All of them had been macheted or machine-gunned by another tribe. One tribe versus another tribe. Women nursing kids. People starving. Babies dying. Flies everywhere.

"You can put Jesus back on the wall."

Chalmers's frown relaxed and his eyes lingered on Mason.

Chalmers rose and hung the Jesus picture on the wall. Covering up the gashes and bloody streaks.

He adjusted the angle of the painting, stepping back to make sure he'd gotten it lined up.

"You're a religious man?" Chalmers said.

"Water to wine. People coming back to life? Yeah, right."

Chalmers looked away from Christ and stared at the empty birdcage.

"Your bird died."

"I hated that bird. It was a fucking nuisance. The old woman liked it. I was glad to see it fall off its perch."

Mason watched Chalmers draw a hard breath. A quick glance at the painting to see if he had it straight.

"If you hate a bird," Chalmers said, "it's simple to break its neck, be done with it."

"I look like a guy who murders parakeets?"

Chalmers turned and eyed Mason. He drew a long breath.

Then he clenched his face into a tight scrunch like he'd stepped on a tack. When his features relaxed, he looked different. Not any smarter, not any richer or happier, but his suit fit better. His eyes were a quieter shade of blue.

One more slow look around Mason's pathetic poolhouse apartment, then Chalmers dug out his wallet and fingered through the bills and came out with two more fifties and set them on the television.

Mason was quiet. Some did it this way. You never knew how it would play out. It was what kept him interested, these conversations, these surprises at the end.

"Keep it," Chalmers said. "You earned it."

"I didn't kill anybody."

"That's what I mean."

"Two hundred for an hour of talk," Mason said. "They'll bust me for practicing without a license."

The commercial was on. That dark-haired woman with the pouty lips, lounging in a doorway making eyes at her husband who has finally taken the right drug and gotten his pecker working again. Modern science. Too bad they couldn't find a pill for those starving babies with the flies all over them.

"Hey, listen," Chalmers said. "How would it be if I brought Jules over sometime? Just for some talk, nothing more than that."

Chalmers heard his own words, then shook his head. A preposterous idea. Sorry he'd mentioned it.

He headed for the door.

Was halfway out when Mason said, "Sure, why not? Bring the kid over. Let's hear his side."

Quarry's Luck

BY MAX ALLAN COLLINS

Max Allan Collins wears many hats—filmmaker, historian, publisher of classic calendars, author of comic books, illustrated novels, historical mysteries, contemporary thrillers. His illustrated novel *The Road to Perdition* was filmed by Stephen Spielberg with Tom Hanks and Paul Newman. 2005 saw the publication of the prose sequel *Road to Purgatory*. Mr. Collins has twice been presented the Shamus for Best Novel. His character Quarry is a legitimate hit man who appeared in a series of novels in the 80's. While this story did appear in a small-press publication, this is its first appearance in a mass-market format.

ONCE UPON A TIME, I killed people for a living.

Now, as I sit in my living quarters looking out at Sylvan Lake, its gently rippling gray-blue surface alive with sunlight, the scent and sight of pines soothing me, I seldom think of those years. With the exception of the occasional memoirs I've penned, I have never been very reflective. What's done is done. What's over is over.

But occasionally someone or something I see stirs a memory. In the summer, when Sylvan Lodge (of which I've been manager for several years now) is hopping with guests, I now and then see a cute blue-eyed blonde college girl, and I think of Linda, my late wife. I'd retired from the contract murder profession, lounging on a cottage on a lake not unlike this one, when my past had come looking for me and Linda became a casualty.

What I'd learned from that was two things: the past is not something disconnected from the present—you can't write off old debts or old enemies (whereas, oddly, friends you can completely forget); and not to enter into long-term relationships.

Linda hadn't been a very smart human being, but she was pleasant company and she loved me, and I wouldn't want to cause somebody like her to die again. You know—an innocent.

After all, when I was taking contracts through the man I knew as the Broker, I was dispatching the guilty. I had no idea what these people were guilty of, but it stood to reason that they were guilty of something, or somebody wouldn't have decided they should be dead.

A paid assassin isn't a killer, really. He's a weapon. Someone has already decided someone else is going to die, before the paid assassin is even in the picture, let alone on the scene. A paid assassin is no more a killer than a nine-millimeter automatic or a bludgeon. Somebody has to pick up a weapon, to use it.

Anyway, that was my rationalization back in the seventies, when I was a human weapon for hire. I never took pleasure from the job— just money. And when the time came, I got out of it.

So, a few years ago, after Linda's death, and after I killed the fuckers responsible, I did not allow myself to get pulled back into that profession. I was too old, too tired, my reflexes were not all that good. A friend I ran into, by chance, needed my only other expertise—I had operated a small resort in Wisconsin with Linda— and I now manage Sylvan Lodge.

Something I saw recently—something quite outrageous really, even considering that I have in my time witnessed human behavior of the vilest sort—stirred a distant memory.

The indoor swimming pool with hot tub is a short jog across the road from my two-room apartment in the central lodge building (don't feel sorry for me: it's a bedroom and spacious living room with kitchenette, plus two baths, with a deck looking out on my storybook view of the lake). We close the pool room at ten P.M., and sometimes I take the keys over and open the place up for a solitary midnight swim.

I was doing that—actually, I'd finished my swim and was letting the hot tub's jet streams have at my chronically sore lower back—when somebody came knocking at the glass doors.

It was a male figure—portly—and a female figure—slender, shapely, both wrapped in towels. That was all I could see of them through the glass; the lights were off outside.

Sighing, I climbed out of the hot tub, wrapped a towel around myself, and unlocked the glass door and slid it open just enough to deal with these two.

"We want a swim!" the man said. He was probably fifty-five, with a booze-mottled face and a brown toupee that squatted on his round head like a slumbering gopher.

Next to him, the blonde of twenty-something, with huge blue eyes and huge big boobs (her towel, thankfully, was tied around her waist), stood almost behind the man. She looked meek. Even embarrassed.

"Mr. Davis," I said, cordial enough, "it's after hours."

"Fuck that! *You're* in here, aren't you?"

"I'm the manager. I sneak a little time in for myself, after closing, after the guests have had their fun."

He put his hand on my bare chest. "Well, *we're* guests, and *we* want to have some fun, too!"

His breath was ninety proof.

I removed his hand. Bending the fingers back a little in the process.

He winced, and started to say something, but I said, "I'm sorry. It's the lodge policy. My apologies to you and your wife."

Bloodshot eyes widened in the face, and he began to say something, but stopped short. He tucked his tail between his legs (and his towel), and took the girl by the arm, roughly, saying, "Come on, baby. We don't need this horseshit."

The blonde looked back at me and gave me a crinkly little cha-grined grin, and I smiled back at her, locked the glass door, and climbed back in the hot tub to cool off.

"Asshole," I said. It echoed in the high-ceilinged steamy room. "Fucking asshole!" I said louder, just because I could, and the echo was enjoyable.

He hadn't tucked the towel 'tween his legs because I'd bent his fingers back: he'd done it because I mentioned his wife, who we both knew the little blonde bimbo wasn't.

That was because (and here's the outrageous part) he'd been here last month—to this very same resort—with another very attractive blonde, but one about forty, maybe forty-five, who was indeed, and in fact, his lawful wedded wife.

We had guys who came to Sylvan Lodge with their families; we had guys who came with just their wives; and we had guys who came with what used to be called in olden times their mistresses. But we seldom had a son of a bitch so fucking bold as to bring his wife one week, and his mistress the next, to the same goddamn motel, which is what Sylvan Lodge, after all, let's face it, is a glorified ver-sion of.

As I enjoyed the jet stream on my low back, I smiled and then frowned, as the memory stirred . . . Christ, I'd forgotten about that! You'd think that Sylvan Lodge itself would've jogged my memory. But it hadn't.

Even though the memory in question was of one of my earliest jobs, which took place at a resort not terribly unlike this one. . . .

We met off Interstate 80, at a truck stop outside of the Quad Cities. It was late—almost midnight—a hot, muggy June night; my black T-shirt was sticking to me. My blue jeans, too.

The Broker had taken a booth in back; the restaurant wasn't par-ticularly busy, except for an area designated for truckers. But it had the war-zone look of a rush hour just past; it was a blindingly white but not terribly clean-looking place, and the jukebox—wailing "I Shot the Sheriff" at the moment—combated the clatter of dishes being bused.

Sitting with the Broker was an oval-faced, bright-eyed kid of about twenty-three (which at the time was about my age, too) who wore a Doobie Brothers t-shirt and had shoulder-length brown hair. Mine was cut short—not soldier-cut, but businessman-short.

"Quarry," the Broker said, in his melodious baritone; he gestured with an open hand. "How good to see you. Sit down." His smile was faint under the wispy moustache, but there was a fatherly air to his manner.

He was trying to look casual in a yellow Ban-Lon shirt and golf slacks; he had white, styled hair and a long face that managed to look both fleshy and largely unlined. He was a solid-looking man, fairly tall—he looked like a captain of industry, which he was, in a way. I took him for fifty, but that was just a guess.

"This is Adam," the Broker said.

"How are you doin', man?" Adam said, and grinned, and half-rose; he seemed a little nervous, and in the process—before I'd even had a chance to decide whether to take the hand he offered or not—overturned a salt shaker, which sent him into a minor tizzy.

"Damn!" Adam said, forgetting about the handshake. "I hate fuckin' bad luck!" He tossed some salt over either shoulder, then grinned at me and said, "I'm afraid I'm one superstitious mother-fucker."

"Well, you know what Stevie Wonder says," I said.

He squinted. "No, what?"

Sucker.

"Nothing," I said, sliding in.

A twentyish waitress with a nice shape, a hair net, and two pounds of acne took my order, which was for a Coke; the Broker already had coffee and the kid a bottle of Mountain Dew and a glass.

When she went away, I said, "Well, Broker. Got some work for me? I drove hundreds of miles in a fucking gas shortage, so you sure as shit better have."

Adam seemed a little stunned to hear the Broker spoken to so disrespectfully, but the Broker was used to my attitude and merely smiled and patted the air with a benedictory palm.

"I wouldn't waste your time otherwise, Quarry. This will pay handsomely. Ten thousand for the two of you."

Five grand was good money; three was pretty standard. Money was worth more then. You could buy a Snickers bar for ten cents. Or was it fifteen? I forget.

But I was still a little irritated.

"The two of us?" I said. "Adam, here, isn't my better half on this one, is he?"

"Yes, he is," the Broker said. He had his hands folded now, prayerfully. His baritone was calming. Or was meant to be.

Adam was frowning, playing nervously with a silver skull ring on the little finger of his left hand. "I don't like your fuckin' attitude, man. . . ."

The way he tried to work menace into his voice would have been amusing if I'd given a shit.

"I don't like your fuckin' hippie hair," I said.

"What?" He leaned forward, furious, and knocked his water glass over; it spun on its side and fell off my edge of the booth and we heard it shatter. A few eyes looked our way.

Adam's tiny bright eyes were wide. "Fuck," he said.

"Seven years bad luck, dipshit," I said.

"That's just mirrors!"

"I think it's any kind of glass. Isn't that right, Broker?"

The Broker was frowning a little. "Quarry. . . ." He sounded so disappointed in me.

"Hair like that attracts attention," I said. "You go in for a hit, you got to be the invisible man."

"These days, everybody wears their hair like this," the kid said defensively.

"In Greenwich Village, maybe. But in America, if you want to disappear, you look like a businessman or a college student."

That made him laugh. "You ever see a college student lately, asshole?"

"I mean the kind who belongs to a fraternity. You want to go around killing people, you need to look clean-cut."

Adam's mouth had dropped open; he had crooked lower teeth. He pointed at me with a thumb and turned to look at Broker, indignant. "Is this guy for real?"

"Yes, indeed," the Broker said. "He's also the best active agent I have."

By "active," Broker meant (in his own personal jargon) that I was the half of a hit team that took out the target; the "passive" half was the lookout person, the backup.

"And he's right," the Broker said, "about your hair."

"Far as that's concerned," I said, "we look pretty goddamn conspicuous right here—me looking collegiate, you looking like the prez of a country club, and junior here like a roadshow Mick Jagger."

Adam looked half bewildered, half outraged.

"You may have a point," the Broker allowed me.

"On the other hand," I said, "people probably think we're fags waiting for a fourth."

"You're unbelievable," Adam said, shaking his greasy Beatle mop. "I don't want to work with this son of a bitch."

"Stay calm," the Broker said. "I'm not proposing a partnership, not unless this should happen to work out beyond all of our wildest expectations."

"I tend to agree with Adam, here," I said. "We're not made for each other."

"The question is," the Broker said, "are you made for ten thousand dollars?"

Adam and I thought about that.

"I have a job that needs to go down, very soon," he said, "and very quickly. You're the only two men available right now. And I know neither of you wants to disappoint me."

Half of ten grand did sound good to me. I had a lakefront lot in Wisconsin where I could put up this nifty little A-frame prefab, if I could put a few more thousand together. . . .

"I'm in," I said, "if he cuts his hair."

The Broker looked at Adam, who scowled and nodded.

"You're both going to like this," the Broker said, sitting forward, withdrawing a travel brochure from his back pocket.

"A resort?" I asked.

"Near Chicago. A wooded area. There's a man-made lake, two indoor swimming pools and one outdoor, an 'old town' gift shop area, several restaurants, bowling alley, tennis courts, horseback riding. . . ."

"If they have archery," I said, "maybe we could arrange a little accident."

That made the Broker chuckle. "You're not far off the mark. We need either an accident, or a robbery. It's an insurance situation."

Broker would tell us no more than that: part of his function was to shield the client from us, and us from the client, for that matter. He was sort of a combination agent and buffer; he could tell us only this much: the target was going down so that someone could collect insurance. The double-indemnity kind that comes from accidental death, and of course getting killed by thieves counts in that regard.

"This is him," Broker said, carefully showing us a photograph of a thin, handsome, tanned man of possibly sixty with black hair that was probably dyed; he wore dark sunglasses and tennis togs and had an arm around a dark-haired woman of about forty, a tanned slim busty woman also in dark glasses and tennis togs.

"Who's the babe?" Adam said.

"The wife," the Broker said.

The client.

"The client?" Adam asked.

"I didn't say that," Broker said edgily, "and you mustn't ask stupid questions. Your target is this man—Baxter Bennedict."

"I hope his wife isn't named Bunny," I said.

The Broker chuckled again, but Adam didn't see the joke.

"Close. Her name is Bernice, actually."

I groaned. "One more 'B' and I'll kill 'em *both*—for free."

The Broker took out a silver cigarette case. "Actually, that's going to be one of the . . . delicate aspects of this job."

"How so?" I asked.

He offered me a cigarette from the case and I waved it off; he offered one to Adam, and he took it.

The Broker said, "They'll be on vacation. Together, at the Wistful Wagon Lodge. She's not to be harmed. You must wait and watch until you can get him alone."

"And then make it look like an accident," I said.

"Or a robbery. Correct." The Broker struck a match, lit his cigarette. He tried to light Adam's, but Adam gestured no, frantically.

"Two on a match," he said. Then got a lighter out and lit himself up.

"Two on a match?" I asked.

"Haven't you ever heard that?" the kid asked, almost wild-eyed. "Two on a match. It's unlucky!"

"*Three* on a match is unlucky," I said.

Adam squinted at me. "Are you superstitious, too?"

I looked hard at Broker, who merely shrugged.

"I gotta pee," the kid said suddenly, and had the Broker let him slide out. Standing, he wasn't very big: probably five-seven. Skinny. His jeans were tattered.

When we were alone, I said, "What are you doing, hooking me up with that dumb-ass jerk?"

"Give him a chance. He was in Vietnam. Like you. He's not completely inexperienced."

"Most of the guys I knew in Vietnam were stoned twenty-four hours a day. That's not what I'm looking for in a partner."

"He's just a little green. You'll season him."

"I'll ice him if he fucks up. Understood?"

The Broker shrugged. "Understood."

When Adam came back, Broker let him in and said, "The hardest part is, you have a window of only four days."

"That's bad," I said, frowning. "I like to maintain a surveillance, get a pattern down. . . ."

The Broker shrugged again. "It's a different situation. They're on vacation. They won't have much of a pattern."

"Great."

Now the Broker frowned. "Why in hell do you think it pays so well? Think of it as hazardous-duty pay."

Adam sneered and said, "What's the matter, Quarry? Didn't you never take no fuckin' risks?"

"I think I'm about to," I said.

"It'll go well," the Broker said.

"Knock on wood," the kid said, and rapped on the table.

"That's formica," I said.

The Wistful Wagon Lodge sprawled out over numerous wooded acres, just off the outskirts of Wistful Vista, Illinois. According to the Broker's brochure, back in the late '40s, the hamlet had taken the name of Fibber McGee and Molly's fictional hometown, for purposes of attracting tourists; apparently one of the secondary stars of the radio show had been born nearby. This marketing ploy had been just in time for television making radio passé, and the little farm community's only remaining sign of having at all successfully tapped into the tourist trade was the Wistful Wagon Lodge itself.

A cobblestone drive wound through the scattering of log cabins, and several larger buildings—including the main lodge where the check-in and restaurants were—were similarly rustic structures, but of gray weathered wood. Trees clustered everywhere, turning warm sunlight into cool pools of shade; wood-burned signs showed the way to this building or that path, and decorative wagon wheels, often with flower beds in and around them, were scattered about as if some long-ago pioneer mishap had been beautified by nature and time. Of course that wasn't the case: this was the hokey hand of man.

We arrived separately, Adam and I, each having reserved rooms in advance, each paying cash up front upon registration; no credit cards. We each had log-cabin cottages, not terribly close to one another.

As the backup and surveillance man, Adam went in early. The target and his wife were taking a long weekend—arriving Thursday, leaving Monday. I didn't arrive until Saturday morning.

I went to Adam's cabin and knocked, but got no answer. Which just meant he was trailing Mr. and Mrs. Target around the grounds. After I dropped my stuff off at my own cabin, I wandered, trying to get the general layout of the place, checking out the lodge itself, where about half of the rooms were, as well as two restaurants. Everything had a pine smell, which was partially the many trees, and partially Pine-Sol. Wistful Wagon was Hollywood rustic—there was a dated quality about it, from the cowboy/cowgirl attire of the waiters and waitresses in the Wistful Chuckwagon Cafe to the wood-and-leather furnishings to the barnwood-framed Remington prints.

I got myself some lunch and traded smiles with a giggly tableful of college girls who were on a weekend scouting expedition of their own. *Good,* I thought. *If I can connect with one of them tonight, that'll provide nice cover.*

As I was finishing up, my cowgirl waitress, a curly-haired blonde pushing thirty who was pretty cute herself, said, "Looks like you might get lucky tonight."

She was re-filling my coffee cup.

"With them or with you?" I asked.

She had big washed-out blue eyes and heavy eye makeup, more '60s than '70s. She was wearing a 1950s style cowboy hat cinched under her chin. "I'm not supposed to fraternize with the guests."

"How did you know I was a fraternity man?"

She laughed a little; her chin crinkled. Her face was kind of round and she was a little pudgy, nicely so in the bosom. "Wild stab," she said. "Anyway, there's an open dance in the ballroom. Of the Wagontrain Dining Room? Country swing band. You'll like it."

"You inviting me?"

"No," she said; she narrowed her eyes and cocked her head, her expression one of mild scolding. "Those little girls'll be there, and plenty of others. You won't have any trouble finding what you want."

"I bet I will."

"Why's that?"

"I was hoping for a girl wearing cowboy boots like yours."

"Oh, there'll be girls in cowboys boots there tonight."

"I meant, *just* cowboy boots."

She laughed at that, shook her head; under her Dale Evans hat, her blond curls bounced off her shoulders.

She went away and let me finish my coffee, and I smiled at the college girls some more, but when I paid for my check, at the register, it was my plump little cowgirl again.

"I work late tonight," she said.

"How late?"

"I get off at midnight," she said.

"That's only the first time," I said.

"First time what?"

"That you'll get off tonight."

She liked that. Times were different, then. The only way you could die from fucking was if a husband or boyfriend caught you at it. She told me where to meet her, later.

I strolled back up a winding path to my cabin. A few groups of college girls and college guys, not paired off together yet, were buzzing around; some couples in their twenties and up into their sixties were walking, often hand-in-hand, around the sun-dappled, lushly shaded grounds. The sound of a gentle breeze in the trees made a faint shimmering music. Getting laid here was no trick.

I got my swim trunks on and grabbed a towel and headed for the nearest pool, which was the outdoor one. That's where I found Adam.

He did look like a college frat rat, with his shorter hair; his skinny pale body reddening, he was sitting in a deck chair, sipping a Coke, in sunglasses and racing trunks, chatting with a couple of bikinied college cuties, also in sunglasses.

"Bill?" I said.

"Jim?" he said, taking off his sunglasses to get a better look at me. He grinned, extended his hand. I took it, shook it, as he stood. "I haven't seen you since spring break!"

We'd agreed to be old high-school buddies from Peoria who had gone to separate colleges; I was attending the University of Iowa, he was at Michigan. We avoided using Illinois schools because Illinois kids were who we'd most likely run into here.

Adam introduced me to the girls—I don't remember their names, but one was a busty brunette Veronica, the other a flat-chested blonde Betty. The sound of splashing and running, screaming kids— though this was a couples hideaway, there was a share of families here, as well—kept the conversation to a blessed minimum. The girls were nursing majors. We were engineering majors. We all liked Creedence Clearwater. We all hoped Nixon would get the book thrown at him. We were all going to the dance tonight.

Across the way, Baxter Bennedict was sitting in a deck chair under an umbrella reading *Jaws*. Every page or so, he'd sip his martini; every ten pages or so, he'd wave a waitress in cowgirl vest and white plastic hot pants over for another one. His wife was swimming, her dark arms cutting the water like knives. It seemed methodical, an exercise workout in the midst of a pool filled with water babies of various ages.

When she pulled herself out of the water, her suit a stark, startling white against her almost burned black skin, she revealed a slender, rather tall figure; tight ass, high, full breasts. Her rather lined leathery face was the only tip-off to her age, and that had the blessing of a model's beauty to get it by.

She pulled off a white swim cap and unfurled a mane of dark, blond-tipped hair. Toweling herself off, she bent to kiss her husband on the cheek, but he only scowled at her. She stretched out on her colorful beach towel beside him, to further blacken herself.

"Oooo," said Veronica. "What's that ring?"

"That's my lucky ring," Adam said.

That fucking skull ring of his! Had he been dumb enough to wear that? Yes.

"Bought that at a Grateful Dead concert, didn't you, Bill?" I asked.

"Uh, yeah," he said.

"Ick," said Betty. "I don't like the Dead. Their hair is greasy. They're so . . . druggie."

"Drugs aren't so bad," Veronica said boldly, thrusting out her admirably thrustworthy bosom.

"Bill and I had our wild days back in high school," I said. "You shoulda seen our hair—down to our asses, right Bill?"

"Right."

"But we don't do that any more," I said. "Kinda put that behind us."

"Well, I, for one, don't approve of drugs," Betty said.

"Don't blame you," I said.

"Except for grass, of course," she said.

"Of course."

"And coke. Scientific studies prove coke isn't bad for you."

"Well, you're in nursing," I said. "You'd know."

We made informal dates with the girls for the dance, and I wandered off with "Bill" to his cabin.

"The skull ring was a nice touch," I said.

He frowned at me. "Fuck you—it's my lucky ring!"

A black gardener on a rider mower rumbled by us.

"Now we're really in trouble," I said.

He looked genuinely concerned. "What do you mean?"

"A black cat crossed our path."

In Adam's cabin, I sat on the brown, fake-leather sofa while he sat on the nubby yellow bedspread and spread his hands.

"They actually do have a sorta pattern," he said, "vacation or not."

Adam had arrived on Wednesday; the Bennedicts had arrived Thursday around two P.M., which was check-in time.

"They drink and swim all afternoon," Adam said, "and they go dining and dancing—and drinking—in the evening."

"What about mornings?"

"Tennis. He doesn't start drinking till lunch."

"Doesn't she drink?"

"Not as much. He's an asshole. We're doing the world a favor here."

"How do you mean?"

He shrugged; he looked very different in his short hair. "He's kind of abusive. He don't yell at her, but just looking at them, you can see him glaring at her all the time, real ugly. Saying things that hurt her."

"She doesn't stand up to him?"

He shook his head, no. "They're very one-sided arguments. He either sits there and ignores her or he's giving her foul looks and it looks like he's chewing her out or something."

"Sounds like a sweet guy."

"After the drinking and dining and dancing, they head to the bar. Both nights so far, she's gone off to bed around eleven and he's stayed and shut the joint down."

"Good. That means he's alone when he walks back to their cabin."

Adam nodded. "But this place is crawlin' with people."

"Not at two in the morning. Most of these people are sleeping or fucking by then."

"Maybe so. He's got a fancy watch, some heavy gold jewelry."

"Well, that's very good. Now we got ourselves a motive."

"But *she's* the one with jewels." He whistled. "You should see the rocks hanging off that dame."

"Well, we aren't interested in those."

"What about the stuff you steal off him? Just toss it somewhere?"

"Hell, no! Broker'll have it fenced for us. A little extra dough for our trouble."

He grinned. "Great. This is easy money. Vacation with pay."

"Don't ever think that . . . don't ever let your guard down."

"I know that," he said defensively.

"It's unlucky to think that way," I said, and knocked on wood. Real wood.

• • •

We met up with Betty and Veronica at the dance; I took Betty because Adam was into knockers and Veronica had them. Betty was pleasant company, but I wasn't listening to her babble. I was keeping an eye on the Bennedicts, who were seated at a corner table under a buffalo head.

He really was an asshole. You could tell, by the way he sneered at her and spit sentences out at her, that he'd spent a lifetime—or at least a marriage—making her miserable. His hatred for her was something you could see as well as sense, like steam over asphalt. She was taking it placidly. Cool as Cher while Sonny prattled on.

But I had a hunch she usually took it more personally. Right now she could be placid: she knew the son of a bitch was going to die this weekend.

"Did you ever do Lauderdale?" Betty was saying. "I got *so* drunk there. . . ."

The band was playing "Crazy" and a decent girl singer was doing a respectable Patsy Cline. What a great song.

I said, "I won a chug-a-lug contest at Boonie's in '72."

Betty was impressed. "Were you even in college then?"

"No. I had a hell of a fake I.D., though."

"Bitchen!"

Around eleven, the band took a break and we walked the girls to their cabins, hand in hand, like high school sweethearts. Gas lanterns on poles scorched the night orangely; a half-moon threw some silvery light on us, too. Adam disappeared around the side of the cabin with Veronica and I stood and watched Betty beam at me and rock girlishly on her heels. She smelled of perfume and beer, which mingled with the scent of pines; it was more pleasant than it sounds.

She was making with the dimples. "You're so nice."

"Well, thanks."

"And I'm a good judge of character."

"I bet you are."

Then she put her arms around me and pressed her slim frame to me and put her tongue half-way down my throat.

She pulled herself away and smiled coquetishly and said, "That's all you get tonight. See you tomorrow."

As if on cue, Veronica appeared with her lipstick mussed up and her sweater askew.

"Good night, boys," Veronica said, and they slipped inside, giggling like the school girls they were.

"Fuck," Adam said, scowling. "All I got was a little bare tit."

"Not so little."

"I thought I was gonna get laid."

I shrugged. "Instead you got screwed."

We walked. We passed a cabin that was getting some remodeling and repairs; I'd noticed it earlier. A ladder was leaned up against the side, for some re-roofing. Adam made a wide circle around the ladder. I walked under it just to watch him squirm.

When I fell back in step with him, he said, "You gonna do the hit tonight?"

"No."

"Bar closes at midnight on Sundays. Gonna do it then?"

"Yes."

He sighed. "Good."

We walked, and it was the place where one path went toward my cabin, and another toward his.

"Well," he said, "maybe I'll get lucky tomorrow night."

"No pickups the night of the hit. I need backup more than either of us needs an alibi, or an easy fuck, either."

"Oh. Of course. You're right. Sorry. 'Night."

"'Night, Bill."

Then I went back and picked up the waitress cowgirl and took her to my cabin; she had some dope in her purse, and I smoked a little with her, just to be nice, and apologized for not having a rubber, and she said, Don't sweat it, pardner, I'm on the pill, and she rode me in her cowboy boots until my dick said yahoo.

The next morning, I had breakfast in the cafe with Adam, and he seemed preoccupied as I ate my scrambled eggs and bacon, and he poked at his French toast.

"Bill," I said. "What's wrong?"

"I'm worried."

"What about?"

We were seated in a rough-wood booth and had plenty of privacy; we kept our voices down. Our conversation, after all, wasn't really proper breakfast conversation.

"I don't think you should hit him like that."

"Like what?"

He frowned. "On his way back to his cabin after the bar closes."

"Oh? Why?"

"He might not be drunk enough. Bar closes early Sunday night, remember? "

"Jesus," I said. "The fucker starts drinking at noon. What more do you want?"

"But there could be people around."

"At midnight?"

"It's a resort. People get romantic at resorts. Moonlight strolls. . . ."

"You got a better idea?"

He nodded. "Do it in his room. Take the wife's jewels and it's a robbery got out of hand. In and out. No fuss, no muss."

"Are you high? What about the wife?"

"She won't be there."

"What are you talking about?"

He started gesturing, earnestly. "She gets worried about him, see. It's midnight, and she goes looking for him. While she's gone, he gets back, flops on the bed, you come in, bing bang boom."

I just looked at him. "Are you psychic now? How do we know she'll do that?"

He swallowed; took a nibble at a forkful of syrup-dripping French toast. Smiled kind of nervously.

"She told me so," he said.

● ● ●

We were walking now. The sun was filtering through the trees and birds were chirping and the sounds of children laughing wafted through the air.

"Are you fucking nuts? Making contact with the client?"

"Quarry—she contacted me! I swear!"

"Then *she's* fucking nuts. Jesus!" I sat on a bench by a flower bed. "It's off. I'm calling the Broker. It's over."

"Listen to me! Listen. She was waiting for me at my cabin last night. After we struck out with the college girls? She was fuckin' waitin' for me! She told me she knew who I was."

"How did she know that?"

"She said she saw me watching them. She figured it out. She guessed."

"And, of course, you confirmed her suspicions."

He swallowed. "Yeah."

"You dumb-ass dickhead. Who said it first?"

"Who said what first?"

"Who mentioned 'killing.' Who mentioned 'murder.'"

His cheek twitched. "Well . . . me, I guess. She kept saying she knew why I was here. And then she said, I'm why you're here. I hired you."

"And you copped to it. God. I'm on the next bus."

"Quarry! Listen . . . this is better this way. This is much better."

"What did she do, fuck you?"

He blanched; looked at his feet.

"Oh God," I said. "You did get lucky last night. Fuck. You fucked the client. Did you tell her there were two of us?"

"No."

"She's seen us together."

"I told her you're just a guy I latched onto here to look less conspicuous."

"Did she buy it?"

"Why shouldn't she? I say we scrap Plan A and move to Plan B. It's better."

"Plan B being . . . ?"

"Quarry, she's going to leave the door unlocked. She'll wait for him to get back from the bar, and when he's asleep, she'll unlock the door, go out and pretend to be looking for him, and come back and find him dead, and her jewels gone. Help-police-I-been-robbed-my-husband's-been-shot. You know."

"She's being pretty fucking helpful, you ask me."

His face clenched like a fist. "The bastard has beat her for years. And he's got a girl friend a third his age. He's been threatening to divorce her, and since they signed a pre-marital agreement, she gets jack shit if they divorce. The bastard."

"Quite a sob story."

"I told you: we're doing the world a favor. And now she's doing us one. Why shoot him right out in the open, when we can walk in his room and do it? You got to stick this out, Quarry. Shit, man, it's five grand apiece, and change!"

I thought about it.

"Quarry?"

I'd been thinking a long time.

"Okay," I said. "Give her the high sign. We'll do it her way."

The Bar W Bar was a cozy rustic room decorated with framed photos of movie cowboys from Ken Maynard to John Wayne, from Audie Murphy to the Man with No Name. On a brown mock-leather stool up at the bar, Baxter Bennedict sat, a thin handsome drunk in a pale blue polyester sport coat and pale yellow Ban-Lon sport shirt, gulping martinis and telling anyone who'd listen his sad story.

I didn't sit near enough to be part of the conversation, but I could hear him.

"Milking me fucking dry," he was saying. "You'd think with six-teen goddamn locations, I'd be sitting pretty. I was the first guy in the Chicago area to offer a paint job under thirty dollars—$29.95! That's a good fucking deal—isn't it?"

The bartender—a young fellow in a buckskin vest, polishing a glass—nodded sympathetically.

"Now this competition. Killing me. What the fuck kind of paint job can you get for $19.99? Will you answer me that one? And now that bitch has the nerve. . . ."

Now he was muttering. The bartender began to move away, but Baxter started in again.

"She wants me to sell! My life's work. Started from nothing. And she wants me to sell! Pitiful fucking money they offered. Pitiful. . . ."

"Last call, Mr. Bennedict," the bartender said. Then he repeated it, louder, without the "Mr. Bennedict." The place was only moderately busy. A few couples. A solitary drinker or two. The Wistful Wagon Lodge had emptied out, largely, this afternoon—even Betty and Veronica were gone. Sunday. People had to go to work tomorrow. Except, of course, for those who owned their own businesses, like Baxter here.

Or had unusual professions, like mine.

I waited until the slender figure had stumbled half-way home before I approached him. No one was around. The nearest cabin was dark.

"Mr. Bennedict," I said.

"Yeah?" He turned, trying to focus his bleary eyes.

"I couldn't help but hear what you said. I think I have a solution for your problems."

"Yeah?" He grinned. "And what the hell would that be?"

He walked, on the unsteadiest of legs, up to me.

I showed him the nine-millimeter with its bulky sound suppresser. It probably looked like a ray gun to him.

"Fuck! What is this, a fucking holdup?"

"Yes. Keep your voice down or it'll turn into a fucking homicide. Got me?"

That turned him sober. "Got you. What do you want?"

"What do you think? Your watch and your rings."

He smirked disgustedly and removed them; handed them over.

"Now your sport coat."

"My what?"

"Your sport coat. I just can't get enough polyester."

He snorted a laugh. "You're out of your gourd, pal."

He slipped off the sportcoat and handed it out toward me with two fingers; he was weaving a little, smirking drunkenly.

I took the coat with my left hand, and the silenced nine-millimeter went *thup thup thup*; three small, brilliant blossoms of red appeared on his light yellow Ban-Lon. He was dead before he had time to think about it.

I dragged his body behind a clump of trees and left him there, his worries behind him.

I watched from behind a tree as Bernice Bennedict slipped out of their cabin; she was wearing a dark halter top and dark slacks that almost blended with her burnt-black skin, making a wraith of her. She had a big white handbag on a shoulder strap. She was so dark, the white bag seemed to float in space as she headed toward the lodge.

Only she stopped and found her own tree to duck behind.

I smiled to myself.

Then, wearing the pale blue polyester sportcoat, I entered their cabin, through the door she'd left open. The room was completely dark, but for some minor filtering in of light through curtained windows. Quickly I arranged some pillows under sheets and covers, to create the impression of a person in the bed.

And I called Adam's cabin.

"Hey, Bill," I said. "It's Jim."

His voice was breathless. "Is it done?"

"No. I got cornered coming out of the bar by that waitress I was out with last night. She latched onto me—she's in my john."

"What, are you in your room?"

"Yeah. I saw Bennedict leave the bar at midnight, and his wife passed us, heading for the lodge, just minutes ago. You've got a clear shot at him."

"What? Me? I'm the fucking lookout!"

"Tonight's the night, and we go to Plan C."

"I didn't know there *was* a Plan C."

"Listen, asshole—it was you who wanted to switch plans. You've got a piece, don't you?"

"Of course. . . ."

"Well you're elected. Go!"

And I hung up.

I stood in the doorway of the bathroom, which faced the bed. I sure as hell didn't turn any lights on, although my left hand hovered by the switch. The nine-millimeter with the silencer was heavy in my right hand. But I didn't mind.

Adam came in quickly and didn't do too bad a job of it: four silenced slugs. He should have checked the body—it never occurred to him he'd just slaughtered a bunch of pillows—but if somebody had been in that bed, they'd have been dead.

He went to the dresser where he knew the jewels would be, and was picking up the jewelry box when the door opened and she came in, the little revolver already in her hand.

Before she could fire, I turned on the bathroom light and said, "If I don't hear the gun hit the floor immediately, you're fucking dead."

She was just a black shape, except for the white handbag; but I saw the flash of silver as the gun bounced to the carpeted floor.

"What . . . ?" Adam was saying. It was too dark to see any expression, but he was obviously as confused as he was spooked.

"Shut the door, lady," I said, "and turn on the lights."

She did.

She really was a beautiful woman, or had been, dark eyes and scarlet-painted mouth in that finely carved model's face, but it was just a leathery mask to me.

"What . . ." Adam said. He looked shocked as hell, which made sense; the gun was in his waistband, the jewelry box in his hands.

"You didn't know there were two of us, did you, Mrs. Bennedict?"

She was sneering faintly; she shook her head, no.

"You see, kid," I told Adam, "she wanted her husband hit, but she wanted the hit man dead, too. Cleaner. Tidier. Right?"

"Fuck you," she said.

"I'm not much for sloppy seconds, thanks. Bet you got a nice legal license for that little purse pea-shooter of yours, don't you? Perfect protection for when you stumble in on an intruder who's just killed your loving husband. Who *is* dead, by the way. Somebody'll run across him in the morning, probably."

"You bitch!" Adam said. He raised his own gun, which was a .380 Browning with a home-made suppresser.

"Don't you know it's bad luck to kill a woman?" I said.

She was frozen, one eye twitching.

Adam was trembling. He swallowed; nodded. "Okay," he said, lowering the gun. "Okay."

"Go," I told him.

She stepped aside as he slipped out the door, shutting it behind him.

"Thank you," she said, and I shot her twice in the chest.

I slipped the bulky silenced automatic in my waistband; grabbed the jewel box off the dresser.

"I make my own luck," I told her, but she didn't hear me, as I stepped over her.

I never worked with Adam again. I think he was disturbed, when he read the papers and realized I'd iced the woman after all. Maybe he got out of the business. Or maybe he wound up dead in a ditch, his lucky skull ring still on his little finger. Broker never said, and I was never interested enough to ask.

Now, years later, lounging in the hot tub at Sylvan Lodge, I look back on my actions and wonder how I could have ever have been so young, and so rash.

Killing the woman was understandable. She'd double-crossed us; she would've killed us both without batting a false lash.

But sleeping with that cowgirl waitress, on the job. Smoking dope. Not using a rubber.

I was really pushing my luck that time.

A Trip Home

BY ED GORMAN

Ed Gorman has done it all in this business: published successful novels in the western, science fiction, horror, and mystery genres; co-founded and edited *Mystery Scene Magazine*; edited many successful anthologies; and he has a long-running regular column for *Cemetery Dance Magazine*. He has also been the recipient of the Western Writers of America Spur award for Best Short Story. There are other achievements, but they are too plentiful to mention here. When you have a Gorman short story in your hands, you are usually holding a gem. This one is no different.

SULLY DONLON WAS WORKING on deck when Kay came up from the cabin and said, "I was washing the windows down there and I noticed there's some guy up there on the cliff with a pair of binoculars watching you."

Donlon wore faded denim cut-offs, no shirt or shoes. She wore the same except for a red cotton halter.

McKenna's Cove was part of an island ninety miles north of Chicago. There were three summer houses on the island, one of them belonging to Donlon and his Woman of the Moment, as one of his more sardonic ex-roomies had described herself.

Kay was a nurse at a medical clinic. Donlon had met her six weeks ago at a disco on the Gold Coast. She'd been celebrating her divorce from a neurosurgeon she'd help put through med school, her repayment being a case of crabs he'd picked up from one of his numerous girl friends. She was spending one week of her vacation on Donlon's island.

She watched Donlon closely after bringing him the news. He didn't talk much about his life. All she knew for sure was that he was a wholesale salesman of power yachts. His own craft wasn't in that esteemed a class. It was a venerable old 19-footer that required a hardy seaman to keep it operating. Donlon's deep tan and muscular wiry body attested to the hours he put into keeping it in max condition.

Aware that she was watching him for a response to her news, he smiled and said, "Not me. The rig here. Everybody wants a look at it. Not many of these left."

He went back to polishing some of the custom-made stainless steel fittings.

"You're not even interested that somebody's up there watching us?"

"Nah. Why should I be? Free country, isn't it?"

"Well, it kind of spooks me."

Donlon grinned. "Flip him off. That'll get rid of him."

Later in the day, when they made love, she noticed how distracted he was. It was as if he'd sent a clone of himself to perform the sex.

Even in July, the wind off the lake cooled the harsh temperature. She slept, fanned by a breeze that gave her goosebumps until she covered her nakedness with a thin blanket. Then it was a perfect sleep.

Once he was sure she was out for a while, he slipped off the bed, went to his ancient army duffel bag, and took out the Glock.

The forest here ran to hardwood maples. The scent of loam and lake braced him for his search.

He spent half an hour searching the land around the cabin. Next he went down to the landing where the ferry for visitors docked.

He was ten feet from the landing when he heard the outhouse door upslope behind him squawk open.

A voice said: "You looking for me?"

Amazing what you could forget in ten years. Of course, the man hadn't been either fat or bald then.

They moved toward each other. No smiles, no arms open to manly embrace, no words of greeting.

Dave said, "I didn't want to come here. I mean, just in case you think I've changed my mind about what a sleazy bastard you are."

"You better have a damned good reason to be here."

The man was a stranger. Even the timbre of his voice was different. So damned strange. His own brother, with whom he'd shared a house for the first sixteen years of his life, utterly lost to him now.

"Well, it wouldn't be because of Mom. Because you wouldn't give a damn."

"I don't have anything against her."

"Well, that's damned nice of you."

"Nora?"

"No. Because you wouldn't give a damn about her, either."

Donlon said: "Sam."

"Yeah. Sam. The son you've haven't contacted since he was four years old."

Donlon didn't have to wait until his brother said the words. Donlon said them for him: "He died?"

"Yeah. He died."

"I'm sorry."

Dave smiled bitterly. "Don't get me wrong, brother. We're all very happy you kept your word and didn't contact him. But I wanted to tell you that he died. I wanted to see your face when I told you."

"How'd he die?"

"I should've known that's the part you'd be interested in. No tears for a young boy. Not good old Sully. I guess when you're a professional killer, that's the only thing that matters, huh? How he died?" Angry tears; his fat face jiggling with rage. "I helped raise him, Sully. I loved him. I took the wife you lied to and I made her my wife; and I took your son and we made him our son."

He was blubbering. Donlon was embarrassed for him. Wind soughing in the trees and perfect white clouds sailing the skies and the nearby water embracing the shore—a day to enjoy. Not a day to see a grown man blubber without any pride.

"I want to know how he died."

"What difference does it make, Sully? You didn't give a damn about him."

Donlon shook his handsome head. "Don't tell me what I think. I thought about him a lot. I paid a neighbor lady on the sly to take pictures of him for me. They're all over my condo. So don't tell me what I do or do not think because you don't know jack shit about it." He took two threatening steps closer. "What I want to know is how he died."

Dave had given up his dramatics. "He was murdered. There's no other way to say it. And the law isn't gonna do a damned thing about it."

"Why not?"

Wiping snot from his nose on the back of his shirt sleeve. Smiling and looking ugly doing it. The brains had gone to Dave, the looks to Sully. "Remember all those causes I used to get so caught up in back in high school? And you'd tell me only wimps gave a damn about stuff like that? Well, it was stuff like that, Sully, that got your son—*my* son—killed."

All Donlon could do was stand there and wonder what the hell his brother—his emotional, do-gooder brother—Dave was talking about.

"She wants you to fly back with me. The funeral's tomorrow morning. She says it's only right that you should be there."

"You don't sound real enthusiastic about that."

"Far as I'm concerned, Sully, I wish you would've died in the Gulf War. Because something snapped in you over there." Instead of emotional, he sounded cold, hard. "I wish you would've died over there. For everybody's sake. Including mine."

"You done with your little speech?"

"Fuck yourself, Sully."

"I need ten minutes to pack. You wait here."

The town looked the same except for a few more chain restaurants. An agricultural town of 32,200, a hub of supplies and entertainment pretty much since the first covered wagon stopped here in 1854 and a man set up a business that would later be called a general store.

Donlon rented a car at the airport and then drove to a motel eight blocks from where his brother and Jeannie lived. Dave had said that they'd see him at the funeral home.

On the way there, he passed the imposing and expanded area where the paint factory sat near the river. It had come here in the late fifties and had saved the town from virtually disappearing. But it'd brought some other things with it too, Donlon thought, his jaw bunching angrily.

Thomas Prescott, Sr. had passed away from pancreatic cancer three years ago, Donlon was told ten steps inside the bunker-like one-story building that stank of too-sweet flowers and too-sweet sentiments contained in plaques along the receiving area walls. The funeral home preferred by Catholics.

Thomas Prescott, Jr., half again as unctuous as his old man had been, said, "Dad put up a fight to his last breath. He just didn't want to go. Just didn't feel like his time had come quite yet."

Apparently Jr. saw no irony in this. His old man had died at age ninety-seven. Jr. was in his early seventies. His chin was raw with eczema.

He'd come early so he could slip out before he was forced to stand in the family line and get his hand shaken numb.

He eased himself down on the kneeler and looked into the casket. His son looked like somebody who hadn't survived a death camp. Not even makeup could disguise the gray pallor; not even the bulky black suit could hide the skeleton-like body.

The kid had gotten his mother's look, that slightly wan look—that quiet terror that something profoundly bad was waiting just around the next corner of existence—that would have been redeemed only by the almost alarming grace of the huge smile.

He remembered most of the words to the Our Father; half of them to the Hail Mary. When he stood up, his knees exploded like twigs being snapped.

Several people had quietly entered the room while he was looking at his boy. Three of his aunts, one of his uncles, two boys he'd played varsity baseball with. He'd had a damned serviceable right arm.

He could see that they were getting themselves ready for him. All they would know is that he'd deserted his wife and son after returning from the war, that he kept up the child support he'd been ordered *in absentia* to pay, and that as far they knew he'd never been back to town till now.

He started walking toward them then decided he just couldn't face them. He wasn't ashamed of himself in any way. He just detested awkward social moments, and this one would be about as awkward as you could get.

There was a side door and he took it.

The late dusk, the evening sky streaks and swaths of gold and purple and mauve, was cooler than he'd expected.

He had almost reached his rental when Dave pulled up in an elderly brown Volvo.

Dave got out first and came over to him. Other cars were turning into the small paved lot.

Dave said, "Janice wants to talk to you. Alone."

Donlon sighed. "I don't see what that would accomplish, Dave. Do you?"

"A part of her still loves you."

"I doubt it."

"I wish I could cut it out of her. It's like a cancer. It doesn't make any sense."

"She ever tell you that herself?"

"No. But I can tell."

"I forgot, brother. You know everything."

People leaving their cars watched the two brothers carefully. Best show in town. Dave had probably never hidden his hatred for his brother from them. Poor, poor Dave: the smart one; the good one; the one who spent half his time running the local Democratic party and handing out do-gooder bumper stickers and pamphlets. Poor, poor Dave. The sonofabitch reveled in the pity, Donlon knew.

Dave walked away quickly, going with a small group into the side door of the funeral parlor.

He recognized some of the people passing by. A few of them nodded reluctantly. Who wanted to be seen nodding to a wife-deserter like Donlon?

Janice finally got out of the car and walked over to him. She'd been crying, and understandably: her only son was dead. She wore a dark blue dress with a shawl that made her look older than necessary. She was still pretty, enough so that he could remember the exact feel, taste, and scent of her flesh in the high-school years when they'd made love everywhere possible. He had still never had a lover who could satisfy him the quiet way she could.

"I appreciate you coming back with Dave."

"He was my son, too."

"I wish you could have known him." She was going to cry and he was going to get uncomfortable and helpless. But she surprised him, caught her tears in her throat, dispersed them. Then: "You look good, Sully."

"So do you."

"Oh, that's nice of you to say. But you don't see my mirror in the morning light." She glanced away; cut a sob in half. Looked back at him. "That's all I do is cry."

"You loved him. That's only natural."

"It got worse, the paint factory, I mean. They'd always find some way to get out of cleaning up."

"That's what Dave said."

"They killed him, Sully. Our boy. They killed him."

She gave up fighting her tears. She clung to him, weeping. He held her. People walked by. They looked confused. Shouldn't it be Dave out here comforting her like this? But they went on inside. They'd talk about this later, of course. Poor, poor Dave. That was what a lot of them would say. He marries her and takes care of her. So what the hell's she doing in the parking lot of Prescott's funeral home in the arms of that no-good bastard Sully Donlon?

When Father Gilliam drove up in his black Ford—he'd driven black Fords since Sully was a boy; the parish folks chipped in every three years and put up half and he put up the other half—the old priest looked over at them, gave a little jerk of shock seeing them together the way they were, then gave them a wave and went on inside.

"I better go in, Sully," she said, her face a ruin of tears now.

"Yeah, I'll be at the mass tomorrow morning."

She put her hand on his arm as he started to turn away. "Dave's been very good to us, Sully. We couldn't have made it without him. After you left, he just took over."

"He always loved you. Ever since grade school."

"I know, Sully. But he could've done better than a woman with a child. He was popular at school."

He leaned over and kissed her on the cheek. Tasted breeze-cooled tears and makeup.

"I wish you could've known him, Sully," she said. "He was such a good kid. Just a good kid. Nothing special, I suppose. Just a good kid."

She went inside, muffling tears into her handkerchief.

• • •

After the burial, after the luncheon at the Knights of Columbus, after the goodbyes, Dave drove Donlon out to the graveyard. Their people were buried here, now including the youngster they both thought of as son.

Sometime during the luncheon, a giant wreath had been brought and set at the boy's grave. Now Dave, without warning, became more violent than Donlon had ever seen him. He tore the wreath apart with his hands and then picked up what remained and hurled it down the hill.

"The mayor's office," he said. "He's blocked every move we've made to clean up the toxic waste sites in town. He's on their payroll. But he always makes sure to send a wreath when one of us dies from all the poisons in the water and the ground." He choked on his tears. "I told you, that's what happened to Sam. Pancreatic cancer. Seven kids died of pancreatic cancer here in the last year. The statistics show that that's just about impossible unless pollution is a huge factor. The old doc, Cooney, he's the only one who'll stand up and tell the truth. The other two, the young ones, they're all buddy-buddy with the men who own the factory."

He then took Donlon around and showed him the gravestones of all those suspected of dying of pollution-caused cancer in the past ten years. The stones had small circles of green spray-painted on them.

Thirty-nine gravestones in all, the oldest victim being eighteen.

"And there'll be a lot more, you can bet on that."

They started down the hill to the car.

"It ever bother you?"

"Does what ever bother me?" Donlon knew what Dave was asking. He just wanted to make his younger brother say it out loud.

"Killing people."

"Not the people I kill. I'm doing society a favor."

"You ever sorry about the bargain you made?"

"Sometimes."

The bargain had been simple enough. Donlon's mother had found his suitcase open one morning. He kept newspaper clippings of every hit. Vanity. She asked him about them. Dave came in and when he heard what his mother was saying, he started asking Donlon, too. The whole family had been suspicious of how he'd supported himself since coming back from the war. Janice had over-heard a couple of strange phone calls. When Dave told her about the newspaper clippings, she realized how he was making his money. They gave him a choice—quit taking assignments, or leave town immediately, even though Janice was three months pregnant. He'd tried it for a month. But it didn't work for him. He took a job and did it fast, but they still suspected and called him on it. He left town.

Dave drove Donlon back to his car. "You stopping by the house?"

"Guess not."

"You're just leaving, huh?"

"Pretty much."

They sat in the front seat in back of the Knights of Columbus, where Donlon had left his rental.

"I'd appreciate it if you wouldn't come back."

"Nothing to worry about there."

"She told me last night that she still loved you."

"She loves you, too."

"Yeah, but not in the way I want."

"I'm sorry, Dave."

Dave put his head down and then raised it. "You would've liked him. He was a great kid."

"That's what Janice said."

"And nobody's going to pay for it, for him dying, I mean."

Donlon pushed his hand out. They shook.

"So long."

"Yeah, Sully. So long."

They were out on the water and had been all morning. The sun was hot and merry. Donlon wore his dopey fishing hat. Kay was stretched out on the hammock he'd strung. He didn't give a damn about news, but she did. She was giving her laptop a workout, reading all the papers online.

"Wow," she said, "listen to this."

Donlon was fishing off the side. "Do I have to?"

"You left your old home town too early."

"Yeah, how's that?"

"You were telling me about all the pollution there? Well, the guy who runs that paint plant? Somebody grabbed him when he was coming out of work two nights ago and stabbed him with a syringe. Gave him some kind of injection."

"The fish can hear you talking. That's why they're not biting."

"They did tests and they found that what he got injected with was some of the spill from one of his toxic waste dumps." She read a bit more of the story. "He's really sick but it could take him quite a while to actually die."

"Yeah," Donlon said, "too bad he has to suffer like that." A few minutes later, he got his first bite for the day and it was a damned good one.

Misdirection

BY BARBARA SERANELLA

Barbara Seranella is the author of the "Munch Mancini" crime novels, including 2003's *Unpaid Dues* and 2004's *Unwilling Accomplice*, both published by Scribner's. This tale of women in prison begins with a clever premise, and then throws in a twist.

THEY GAVE HER A CODE NAME, to keep her safe, they said. And then they stuck her in a 6 x 9 cell with the coldest-blooded murderer to ever do time in the Corona Institute for Women—keeping in mind that this was the same facility where the Manson family girls would grow old and toothless and eventually die.

"Double-oh-seven" they dubbed her. Her mission was to get her cellie to talk, to brag, to confide. The FBI agents sat with her in the warden's office and showed her photographs of murdered people. They had been killed in a variety of ways. Hit people, unlike serial killers, didn't have signature styles. That would be stupid and incriminating.

Double-oh-seven paused at one particularly gory shot of a murdered Latino man. His nose was jammed flat so that the two bloody nostrils were on the same plane as the lifeless eyes. The Feds explained that the cartilage had been forced into the brain, that even if the victim had survived, he would be unable to recount who had done this to him.

"And this is who you want me to buddy up to and then betray?" Double-oh-seven asked.

"We'll have your cell bugged," Agent Arness said. He was a nice enough seeming guy, Double-oh-seven thought. She would never have made him for a Fed. He seemed more like a minister in one of those churches where the ministers wore street clothes and got to get married if they wanted.

"Yeah," Double-oh-seven said, wiping her sweating hands on the legs of her jeans. "But what about if she attacks me somewhere else?"

"We'll be watching," Agent Bowler said. He was a thin guy, kinda geeky looking. He reminded her of a first-year public defender. Nervous like one of those young lawyers who the court appoints and right away you know he's in way over his head and that, with your courtroom experience and 10th-grade education, you could still do a better job of defending yourself than him.

She turned to Arness. "And what do I get out of all this?"

"The satisfaction of keeping a monster off the street."

"So she can be in here with the rest of us monsters?"

Arness acknowledged her sarcasm with a small smile. His younger partner hadn't developed a sense of humor yet, probably thought smiling at a criminal was a sign of weakness.

"You'll also get a favorable report at your next parole hearing," Arness said, correctly assessing what she wanted to hear.

"Is there a reward?" she asked. "You know, like money?"

"Don't push it," Bowler said. He took a sip of his Starbucks coffee and looked smug.

Double-oh-seven wanted to ask him who died and made him King Law. Though, in truth, she preferred young cops with egos. They were so much easier to manipulate.

"All right," she said, "how are we going to pull this off?"

The warden, who had been quiet until now, took over. Like the other inmates, Double-oh-seven was always polite to the guy, but only minimally. He had a thin moustache, a potbelly, and a combover. He looked like the kind of guy who took forever to come and never tipped.

"I'm issuing a facility-wide reassignment of cells and cellmates," he said now, twisting the ends of his moustache into small rattails. "That way, your reassignment won't stand out."

"Good thinking, sir," she said.

She was escorted back to her cellblock, what the CO's euphemistically termed "The Dorms." CIW was said to have a college-campus layout. There was a whole lot of learning going on, that was for sure, mostly cons trading tips.

Her escort was Officer Jesus, or so they called her behind her back. To her face, she was Officer Dwan, and at the prayer meetings she was always holding, inmates were encouraged to call her Sister Dwan. Her mission on earth, Dwan believed, was to save sinners from eternal damnation by getting them to accept Jesus.

What the hell, Double-oh-seven thought, at least her heart was in the right place.

The following day, Cass and Trinity were put together. Each did the appropriate grumbling at the interruption of their routine and living arrangement. But there really was no point in it. When you were inside, you gave up any sort of freedom of choice of where to be, when to be there, and what to do once you were there.

Cass was the older of the two. She kept her hair cropped close to her head, and might have been pretty in the right circumstances. A scar ran down the length of her face from the corner of her right eye to her jaw. It wasn't disfiguring and could be hidden by makeup. She didn't bother with flesh-toned paste and powder while on the inside. This sometimes led to questions about how she got the scar in the first place. She never answered those queries. In fact, she rarely answered anyone's questions. She barely said five words to Trinity the first day.

That was okay with Trinity. She wasn't in a particularly sharing mood either. Always best to start off slow with a new roomie. If nothing else, to at least give the illusion of each woman having her own space.

Trinity's people were from the Dominican Republic. She was a mocha-skinned Amazon with wavy black hair, high cheekbones, and a winning smile when she chose to use it. Both women were healthy after their prolonged, if unintentional, abstinence from their various poisons. Both were buff, their muscles well toned from the fire-crew training regimen. Firefighting was a good job, even when it meant clearing brush in the hot sun or picking up garbage. The detail got them out of the facility, away from the smell of cow piss from the neighboring dairy farms, and the usual harassments that went along with prison life. There were still guards, but the inmates were treated with respect by the people of the different communities. They could also count on some decent eats while they were out in the wilderness fighting brush fires.

On the second night of their new living arrangement, after lights out and lockdown, Trinity lay awake. The floodlights outside their opaque window lit the cell like dawn. There wasn't much to see—a stainless steel toilet with no lid, an equally austere sink, two upright storage lockers with no locks, a small writing table with a fixed seat. She missed movable parts, and colors. If the cell were tipped upside down, nothing would move except the thin mattresses on their bunk beds.

She listened to Cass breathe on the pallet beneath her. The other woman's respirations didn't follow the irregularity of sleep, the intake and exhales were too measured. After a half hour, she broke the silence.

"So what you in for?"

"A miscommunication," Cass said, not pretending that she had been asleep.

Trinity chuckled deep in her throat. "I've met the bitch myself a few times."

"What about you?" Cass asked.

"Zigging when I should have zagged."

Cass responded with a grunt that was her excuse for a laugh and went to sleep.

Agent Bowler removed his earphones and shook his head in disgust. "Man," he said to his partner, "at this rate, it's going to take forever."

Agent Arness took a sip of his coffee, but seemed unperturbed. "Double-oh-seven is playing it smart. Taking her time. She might just make it."

Agent Bowler didn't respond to that. He didn't like talking about past failures. After a moment he mumbled, "I don't trust her. That's all I'm saying."

Arness, halfway through another sip of his black coffee, had to spit what was in his mouth back in the white, styrofoam cup to make room for his laugh. "Trust her?" He chuckled, wagging his head in amusement. "Of course we don't trust her. She's a con, for Chrissakes."

Getting assigned to a fire crew was limited to inmates who met certain criteria. There could be no history of escapes, no arrests for or convictions of violent crimes, no history of trafficking or abusing drugs. Those rules were supposed to be cast in stone, but for the right reasons there was some wiggle room.

Participants also had to pass physical fitness, stamina, and agility tests. No extra points for resistance to pain, or the roommates would have scored higher. They took classes in firefighting and practiced handling the various pieces of equipment.

The last qualification for fire crew was that the inmate must have more than six months, and less than six years, to do in prison.

"So, how short are you?" Cass asked the second week. Her scar itched, but she didn't scratch it. She never touched the ridge of damaged skin in anyone's presence, even when they stared. She knew it was there. She kept to herself, not making friends, enemies, or alliances. Her disciplines gave her comfort, made her feel less like a caged animal and more in control of her destiny.

Trinity didn't act surprised by the question. Short-timers were often beseeched to look up family members on the outside, make phone calls, or pass a message. It was against the rules to ask or accept such favors, but CIW ran on its own currency.

"I've got a hearing in six months and they got no reason to turn me down," Trinity said. "What about yourself?"

"I meet with the parole board in seven months. They've turned me down twice before, but I think the third time is going to be the charm."

"I hate it when they play God," Trinity said.

"Yeah, but what are you going to do?" Cass said.

Neither woman answered the question out loud, but they both knew there were ways around anything.

Cass pressed her hand to the window beside her bunk. "I'm getting us a curtain," she said.

"That would be nice." Trinity said. "I was beginning to think nothing bothered you."

Cass laughed, pleased that her front was so believable.

"I sure would love it to get dark at night," Trinity said wistfully.

Putting something over the window was allowed. Trips to Home Depot were not. Most inmates made do with one of the institution-issued, notoriously thin and scratchy wool blankets spread across the window frames. The blankets beat doing nothing, but they were ugly and sometimes fell down in the middle of the night. Once, a blanket had fallen on Cass's face and added a new dimension of terror to her nightmares. So yeah, a few things still had the power to bother her.

"It's no big deal," she said, feeling slightly embarrassed. She should have just gone ahead and done it without saying anything.

"Still," Trinity said.

"Yeah, whatever." Cass wanted the conversation over with. She was turning into a regular Chatty Cathy, and that wasn't her way.

Trinity took the hint and returned to the book she was reading. She was probably wondering what other surprises her roomie held for her. They had plenty of time to find out.

"We do not have all the time in the world," Agent Bowler said.

"Not if you keep pulling me in here," Double-oh-seven said.

"Do you think this is some kind of a joke?" the Fed asked, his Adam's apple bobbing—something about it reminding her of a Thanksgiving turkey. "Are you playing me?"

"Playing you? Shit, man, you're the one sitting up here sipping coffee, listening to headphones. I'm the one with everything at stake. I'm taking it very seriously."

"What Agent Bowler means," Agent Arness said, "is that this operation is time-sensitive. Let me put it like this: The only way you get paroled is if she doesn't. And the only thing that will ensure that is if we can bring new charges against her. Also, our budget is limited and we might have to pull out of here before we get what we want. In that case, your only chance to help yourself will be gone, too."

Budget, huh? Maybe if they packed their own lunches, Double-oh-seven thought, eyeing the cartons of take-out. She also wondered what other traces of their presence they left lying around. Did they park their Fed car in the lot? Had they even bothered with a cover story to explain their presence? What had she gotten herself into this time? Bile built up in her throat; her stomach made a gurgling noise.

"You want an egg roll?" Arness asked.

"No, thanks. I seem to have lost my appetite." Arness was the one to watch, she thought. His eyes had that seen-it-all-and-haven't-for-gotten-a-bit-of-it look to them.

After she left, the two Feds smiled at each other. "Well, I guess we put the fear of God into her," Bowler said.

Arness smiled back, but he wasn't as sure. He'd been around a lot longer than his young partner. Rather than feeling like he knew it all,

Arness was more aware of the many variables in human nature and all that he didn't know. By the time he retired, he doubted if he'd be sure of his *own* thoughts and motives.

Cass came through with the curtain. It was double-layered and black, more than adequate to block out the tower search beams and give the roomies a break from the light.

They celebrated with a meal of tamales and chocolate cake. This was Trinity's contribution. She had hoarded the necessary ingredients, buying some from the commissary, stealing others, and getting creative with whatever was at hand.

"These tamales ain't half bad," Cass said.

Trinity smiled broadly. This was high praise coming from her taciturn roomie. "Wanna know my secret?"

Cass licked a finger, stained orange from the sauce. "Only if you wanna tell me."

"Crushed Doritos."

"I never would have guessed," Cass said, trying to sound interested.

"Shit, girl, don't try to bullshit a bullshitter. You wouldn't even try."

They exchanged small tentative smiles, a sign that the ground rules for their relationship were being established.

While they ate, they fantasized about the first meal they'd have when they were free, what they'd do and who with.

Cass bit into the chocolate cake, a concoction of crushed Oreo's, melted vanilla ice cream, Jello chocolate pudding and Hershey bars that had been "baked" in the dayroom's microwave oven. She made a rare personal admission. "Nobody ever gave me nothing for free, 'cept a hard time."

"Neither me," Trinity agreed, wondering if that scar had been one of the free gifts her roomie referred to. She leaned closer to Cass and confided, "I stabbed a pimp once, right through the heart. Thought he was gonna beat on me. I showed him."

"I hear you," Cass said. "A woman's got to do what she's got to do to make her mark." She sliced another piece of the decadent dessert.

"I've never met a pimp that didn't need killing. Some people are just begging to die. Sometimes they don't even know it."

Even though they were speaking hypothetically, Trinity felt a rush of adrenaline that was either fear or excitement.

The agents listening in the warden's office were beside themselves with frustration. After hearing the key word "secret" they had allowed their hopes to soar.

"Didn't anyone ever teach these broads to not talk with their mouths full?" Bowler said. "I'm only getting every other word." He threw his headphones down in disgust. "I can't even tell which one is talking."

"Maybe we can clean it up from the tape," Arness said. *Yeah,* he thought, *just like you see on TV. We'll just use all our high-tech equipment we're supposed to have in our batcave. Shit, they were lucky the listening devices worked at all.*

Bowler checked his notes. "Think we should check out the pimp story?"

"Probably a waste of time. We don't know when or where the alleged assault happened. For all we know, it's bullshit anyway. One con trying to impress the other."

Bowler rubbed his jaw thoughtfully. He felt this mannerism made him look like a deep thinker. "Or maybe she's testing the waters. Getting ready to open up."

"Ever the optimist, Rex." Arness chuckled to himself. *Testing the waters.* He hoped his young colleague was right. They needed some results soon. He'd like to coast into his upcoming retirement with a winner under his belt.

A week later, the first fire of the season broke out in Crest Line. The communities of Big Bear and Lake Arrowhead were threatened. The heavily wooded hillsides were filled with dry, resin-rich pines that all but exploded when the fire reached them.

Trinity and Cass joined the other women of the fire crew in the dirt parking lot on the west end of the prison. Officer Witten would be driving the transport, Officer Jesus rode shotgun. There was a festive atmosphere as the prisoners climbed aboard the equipment truck. The vehicle was fitted with locked toolboxes around the outside. Benches for the inmates lined the bed. A fireproofed canvas tarp, stretched over an arc-shaped framework, covered the women, and made the vehicle look like a motorized covered wagon.

Small triangular flaps allowed the fire crew peeks at the outside world. Once inside their transport, the women chucked their prison outfits of blue jeans and baseball jersey shirts. A few of the women wore boxer shorts under their pants, but no one raised an eyebrow.

During initial intake, these men/women would have been singled out for one of the Daddy Tanks. But once at CIW, they were mainstreamed into the population and easily absorbed by the prison community. Some were gay when they got there, others were gay for the stay. Trinity had a girl on the outside. They had met at CIW and vowed to be faithful to each other. Trinity needed that parole. Solange said she would wait, but she didn't say how long or what exactly she would be doing while she was waiting. Trinity had known better than to press the girl for details. Not knowing was killing her.

On the fire line, it didn't matter if they were black, white, purple, or wanted to dress like Little Bo Peep. As long as they could do the job, they were accepted. If they proved too weak, they sometimes didn't come back. And if they did come back, they resigned from the detail at the not-so-subtle urging of the other inmates.

Cass preferred to keep her sexual preferences to herself. She had a whole stack of Ben Franklins waiting for her when she got out, and he was all the man she needed. Those bundles of cash had better still be where she'd stashed them or there would be hell to pay. Each day inside, the worry about who might get to the money first grew. She was not doing this time for free. She didn't do anything for free.

Cass was new on the crew and felt the others' scrutiny. This would be the first fire she fought with the other inmates. She held their stares for a second and then all eyes shifted to the small makeshift windows in the tarpaulin as the gate swung open and the truck left the compound.

"You'll be all right," Trinity said. Her voice floated into Cass's ear as if by magic.

Cass recognized the accent, but never saw Trinity's mouth move or expression change.

The trustie in charge of the Nomex firesuit gear was a particularly nasty piece of work named Maxine, but more commonly referred to as Mad Max. Trinity had warned Cass that she was a sadistic bitch, with a following of like-minded psychos. The inmates who received the boots Max distributed kept their eyes averted as they accepted their footware.

"What size?" Max asked Cass, standing over the large wooden box full of sturdy black boots.

Cass made eye contact. "Nine."

Max handed her a pair of boots clearly labeled "7." Trinity clamped a hand on the trustee's arm. "She said nine."

"I didn't hear please," Max said.

Cass delivered a quick thrust with her right hand to the trustee's throat. It wasn't a punch so much as a finger stab. Blink your eyes and you would have missed the whole thing.

Mad Max started to say, "Bitch" but didn't get past "Bi—." Then she was on the floor of the truck, gasping for air and unable to speak. Cass reached over her writhing body and pulled a pair of size 9's from the box. *Why,* she wondered, *did people always have to fuck with you?*

Oblivious to the woman she had so easily and efficiently dispatched, Cass sat on the bench and pulled the boots on as if she were getting ready to go out square-dancing. "I fight my own battles," she told Trinity.

"Yeah, you're welcome," Trinity said, but couldn't keep from grinning. The finger stab to the throat was a sweet move. She'd have to get Cass to teach her that one before they parted ways. Maybe they could trade skills. Trinity had a few moves in her bag of tricks that Cass might find useful.

"You know her people are going to be looking for some payback," Trinity said.

"Yeah," Cass replied, settling down for a nap, "I'm terrified."

They drove for an hour, smelling the fire before they saw the smoke. The work crew was given pickaxes and shovels and instructed to widen the slash in the earth already started by a dozer with a single-bladed drag shovel. On the hilltop less than a hundred yards away, the flames ignited one pine tree after another, as if it were some ravenous beast on a binge. Trinity looked at Cass; flames had turned her cheeks and forehead red, and she was grinning. Trinity found her roomie's expression more terrifying than her glower. There was a strange intensity in Cass's eyes that Trinity couldn't quite get a handle on.

Sweat soaked their shirts as they labored over the fire line. The trench reminded Trinity of one long open grave stretching to hell. A place her step-daddy always predicted she'd end up. Her only crime then had been being an eight-year-old "temptress."

She had told him to save her a seat. He was her first.

Thinking of her step-daddy put more force behind her swing with the pickaxe. She imagined that the axe was a ball peen hammer, and that she was driving it into his body long after he was already dead.

Cass, meanwhile, was also in a world all her own. The repetitive action of digging left her mind free to roam. She loved fire and its cleansing flames. The smoke smelled like money. Easy money. She'd been paid up to a thousand dollars to torch an over-insured warehouse. That was a sweet gig until her partner got greedy and tried to cheat her out of her share. He was her first, and the last one she'd done for free. Cass thought of all the sins and, more importantly, the evidence of sins that fire consumed. Fire had always been her friend. Fire had no emotion, it took what was in its path to keep itself going, and never suffered a moment's regret. A person could learn a lot from nature.

That night, exhausted from the day's battle, Cass and Trinity filled their plates with food and then found a tree to lean against as they ate.

"So was that kung fu or something?" Trinity asked.

Cass finished chewing the food in her mouth, savoring the taste of fresh meat and vegetables. "Karate, I think. Some shit like that."

"Think you can teach me?"

"If you'll show me that trick you did with your voice."

Trinity drank from her steaming mug of coffee. She lifted her arm with her fingers curled, her thumb acting like a lower jaw. "You mean this?" her hand asked.

"Yeah. How do you make your voice come out somewhere else?"

"It doesn't. Not really. It's all about misdirection. My lips weren't moving, but my hand was. The brain puts the two together and thinks the thing moving is the thing making noise."

"Cool."

"Yeah, it can come in handy, but it takes lots of practice and a long time to do it smoothly."

"Time, I got," Cass said.

"I heard that." Trinity drew symbols in the dirt with a stick. "If we get this fire out in time, you going to the prayer meeting on Sunday?"

"I hadn't thought about it. Are you?"

"Yeah, you should come. Looks good for a parole report. Officer Jesus brings cookies and lemonade."

"I guess it couldn't hurt," Cass said.

"Speaking of hurt, I got time right now to learn some of that ka-ra-zy."

They stepped behind one of the tents, away from the prying eyes of the guards and the other girls, and Trinity got her lesson. How to hold her fingers so they were like one unit, where to put her thumb, and how to shift her weight for maximum thrust.

They took a break after half an hour, and went and got some pie that had been brought by grateful homeowners. Then Trinity gave Cass the basics of enunciating words without moving her jaw or lips.

"You got to practice in front of a mirror. Start with the vowels. Close your teeth, but keep your lips open a little."

"Like this?" Cass asked, the words coming out a bit slurred.

"Yeah, now say A, E, I, O, U."

Cass made the noises.

"Okay, now try some of the other letters."

"B," Cass said, growling in frustration when her lips moved.

"That's all right," Trinity said. "In fact, stay away from the words that begin with B, M, P, and W. They're damn near impossible to pronounce without moving your lips. Especially if you're a beginner."

The lesson continued until it was time for the final head count before bed.

"After you get good at that," Trinity said, "I'll teach you how to make the other voice different."

"Cool," Cass said through clenched teeth.

"Now you're getting it, girl." Trinity smiled her friendliest, knowing that her teeth would light up her face in the fading light. "Damn, you might even be a natural." Though, truthfully, she was unsure if her roomie had the patience to practice. Changing the sound of your voice to make it higher or lower involved stretching the vocal chords. At Cass's age, her vocal chords might not be stretchable enough. Time would tell.

Trinity had bigger things to worry about. Her girl, Solange, hadn't written or visited in three weeks. Trinity tried calling her apartment a few times, but all she ever got was the answering machine. She had to call collect. The prison payphone didn't take change. In fact, all calls to the outside had some operator saying the call was coming from the prison. Solange didn't leave instructions on the outgoing message of the machine that she would accept any collect calls from CIW, so Trinity couldn't even leave a message.

Solange should have known better. In her heart of hearts, Trinity suspected Solange did know exactly what she was doing. Trinity was being avoided. Her mama didn't raise no fools. Trinity had to get with that girl, in person, if she were going to salvage the relationship. Solange needed a reminder about why they were so right for each other, and why no one else would ever take her place.

Trinity needed that parole to make things right.

The inmates on fire duty returned to the prison midday on Sunday. Agents Bowler and Arness resumed their monitoring of the two women's conversation. The more time the prisoners spent together, the more they sounded alike. Sort of like some married couples who take on each other's mannerisms and expressions.

Arness took to transcribing their dialogue. He would ask Double-oh-seven to fill in the attributions at their next meeting. And then he'd ask the other one, Double-oh-eight, to cross-check. Putting the two suspected hit women together, each thinking they were there to gather incriminating information on the other, was his brainchild. He liked the irony of pitting the killers against each other while dangling out the hope of freedom.

Sunday afternoon, Cass and Trinity attended Officer Jesus's prayer group. Officer Jesus was a big black woman with a large gap between her front teeth. She sat with the inmates on plastic chairs which had been drawn into a circle. Each woman was issued a bible and a hymn book.

After an hour of standing, sitting, reading, and singing, the inmate to Cass's left confided, "This is the hardest time I've ever done."

Cass ignored her. She was doing her best to look interested, even enthralled. She had never played the religious card before, but she willing to look each member of the parole board in the eye and tell them she'd been saved. That the Father, Son, and Holy Ghost had all taken up permanent residence in her heart. Anything that it would take to get out of CIW and reunite her with her money was worth it.

The last song they sang was "Amazing Grace." Any other time, Cass would have scoffed outright, but now she was trying to appear moved by it. Her receptive posture and facial expression was back-firing. She really was touched by the lyrics and, for the first time in a very long time, wondered if it was too late to take her life into another direction.

After the meeting, Cass approached Officer Jesus. "Sister Dwan? Do you have a minute?"

Officer Jesus gave her a hard scrutiny, no doubt checking the inmate's sincerity on her own bullshit meter.

Cass remained humble-faced and didn't press it.

"What is it, Sugar?" Officer Dwan asked.

"What do I have to do to get, uh, like baptized?"

"Are you ready to accept Jesus into your heart?"

"Yes, ma'am, I believe I am." Cass heard the catch in her throat. Now she wasn't sure she was acting at all. She wiped away a tear that had crept out the corner of her eye.

Officer Dwan smiled broadly. "I'll talk to the sergeant in Receiving. He's a lay minister. I'm sure he would be overjoyed to lead you into the Kingdom of Light Everlasting."

"Thank you, ma'am," Cass said. "That would mean a lot to me."

Officer Dwan pressed a laminated bookmark into Cass's hand, along with one of the bibles. "You'll find everything you need in here. Love, comfort, peace, and hope. God bless you, child."

It had been a long time since anyone had called Cass a child. She felt the tears coming again and mumbled, "Thank you, Sister Dwan," then took her bible and fled to the solitude of her cell to sort out this unexpected spiritual windfall.

Maybe there was another way to go for her. According to Sister Dwan, it was never too late. Cass felt excitement at the prospect of starting over. She also didn't see the point of her extended incarceration. Surely God didn't want that for her either.

"What you reading?" Trinity asked.

"Officer Jesus gave me a bible. I'm checking out some of the stories."

Trinity laid the romance novel she had been reading face down on her chest. "You got any questions, go ahead and ask me. My mama had us reading the bible all the time."

"It's all new to me," Cass admitted.

"You're really getting into it, huh?"

"Well, I don't know. Maybe if I could get some quiet in here, I could concentrate."

"Pardon me for living," Trinity said. Then she smiled as she realized the opportunity that presented itself. She requested a meeting with her FBI friends the following day.

Agent Bowler studied his informant with undisguised suspicion. "I don't see, Ms. Fuqua, that you are in any position to bargain or dictate terms."

"I'm offering you an ironclad confession. Tell me about the hits you most want to close, including those details you guys never tell to the press, and I'll have her singing."

"And in return, we're supposed to grant you an immediate release?" Agent Arness said.

"And I want it in writing, with my lawyer here, or no deal." Cassandra Fuqua, aka Double-oh-seven, crossed her arms over her chest. "I don't know how long you've been after this broad, but you've got to want her pretty bad."

"Thank you, Ms. Fuqua," Arness said. "We will give your offer due consideration. And if we decide to accept, we'll need the deal signed off by the district attorney."

"You do what you have to," she said. "When you're ready, I can deliver."

An officer arrived to escort Cass back to her cell. "Please use the back stairs," Arness said.

After the inmate had left, Bowler turned to Arness. "What do you think?"

"She sounded pretty sure of herself," Arness said, wondering once more about the scar on the woman's cheek and why he found it so sexy. "Let's hear what Double-oh-eight has to say."

Bowler pushed the intercom button on the warden's desk. "Send in Ms. Canter."

Trinity strutted into the office, gracing the Feds with one of her bright smiles. "She's close to breaking."

"You've said as much before," Bowler said.

"I mean it this time, Poppy." She gave Bowler the full dose of her charm, treating him as if he were the only man in the room. She was long practiced at using her eyes and body to make promises that no red-blooded heterosexual man misunderstood. She knew she had succeeded when she saw the color rising in his cheeks. She suspected she had made other parts rise as well.

"And what do you base your newfound confidence on?" Arness asked.

"The girl is getting religion. She's gonna want to confess. You give me a wish list of the murders you want evidence on, and I'll make sure she tells us all about them."

"In exchange for?" Arness asked.

"My freedom. I can't hang around here after. It wouldn't be safe for me." She gave Bowler an almost apologetic look and said, "I'll need that in writing, sugar."

Arness buzzed the intercom again and the corrections officer appeared in the doorway. "We'll give you our decision as soon as we clear the legality of your deal."

"Don't make me wait long," she said to Bowler.

He tried to say something, but all that came out of his mouth was a dry cough. When Trinity turned her back on him to sashay out, he didn't see the satisfied smirk on her face.

Arness was also smiling. Maybe they could finesse a two-fer out of all this double-dealing. Neither woman had thought to ask for immunity. He had his loophole; the DA would love it.

Arness was able to get the documents guaranteeing immediate absolution on current convictions. Their individual lawyers both received copies and all was duly witnessed and notarized. The whole process had taken forty-eight hours. He caught himself singing

along to the radio as he drove out to Corona with the documents in
his briefcase. The song playing on the radio was, appropriately
enough, "I Fought the Law, but the Law Won." He beat time on the
steering wheel.

He couldn't wait to see the convicts' reactions when they realized
they'd screwed themselves as well as each other. The evidence each
woman would bring him to fulfill their end of the bargain would
result in new charges and warrants being issued before the ladies
were back in their street clothes.

Cass took extra care the morning of her scheduled baptism. She
invited Trinity to come along as a witness. The two had taken to traveling together as much as possible. The rumor was that Mad Maxine
had a shiv and planned to take them both out.

Cass was outwardly calm, but inside she felt keyed up. These were
her first steps to her new life. A sudden cloudburst caught the women
by surprise as they cut across the commons. They ran to the building
near Administration where the classrooms were.

"Looks like the Lord can't wait," Trinity said, shaking water from
her curls.

It was Sunday, so the classrooms, where some inmates were
training to be beauticians and others were learning basic computer
skills, were dark. Sunday was a big day for visitors, so most of the
population was in the large multipurpose room, anxiously awaiting
a glimpse of their loved ones.

Cass and Trinity walked down the dark hallway. The chapel where
Sister Jesus and Sergeant Chaplain waited was on the far side of the
schoolhouse.

Cass felt a cold wind on her back. Someone else was seeking
refuge in the deserted building. A figure emerged from the restroom
ahead of them. It was Maxine. So not refuge, Cass realized, but
revenge.

"Bring it on, bitch," she said.

Trinity spun around in time to block a blow from behind by one of Maxine's posse swinging a table leg. The woman was sloppy and undisciplined. Trinity kicked her in the knee, but she kept coming. Trinity squatted low and delivered a sweeping kick that knocked the woman off her feet.

Cass had her hands full, too. Maxine was holding her right arm to her side which could only mean she was armed with a knife and wanted to wait until the last possible moment before Cass saw it.

Cass pretended to fall for the trap, turning sideways at the last moment and letting Maxine's own momentum work against her. She sprawled across the wet linoleum, the shiv skittering away. She crawled after it, screaming in rage.

Trinity had managed to get her adversary in a head lock. She pressed on the woman's carotid arteries with her powerful forearm until the woman crumpled to the floor, unconscious and defeated.

"Go get help," Cass told Trinity.

Trinity ran for the chapel. Cass waited about ten seconds, then delivered a crushing blow to Maxine's throat. "If I were you," she told the gasping woman, "I'd work real hard on calming down. You'll need less oxygen that way. If we can get you to the infirmary in time, we still might be able to save your sorry life."

Maxine stared at Cass wild-eyed. Her face had already turned red. Her hands worked futilely to make her airway work.

Trinity returned with Officer Dwan and the sergeant. The sergeant went first to the contraband knife and secured it while he radioed for help. Officer Dwan, draped in a white choir robe, knelt beside Maxine.

"She asked for you, Sister," Cass said. "She wanted to get right with God. She said she didn't want to die with all her sins unconfessed."

"Speak to me, child," Officer Dwan said. "God loves you."

It took some minutes, with Trinity holding Maxine's other hand, for two of the stories of murders for hire to be told. Details were given known only to the killer and the Feds. Maxine acted like she wanted to say more, but her throat was rapidly swelling shut. She flopped like a fish out of water, gasping for air that never made it to her lungs.

Nobody thought to bring her writing paper and pen. They concentrated instead on giving the convict the last rites.

After five minutes, the color had drained from Maxine's face. Her lips, which had never stopped moving, turned blue. The medics arrived, but they were too late to save her.

"Rest in peace," Sister Dwan said.

"Amen," Cass said.

"Amen," Trinity echoed, taking care to remember to move her lips.

Trinity and Cass were granted their early release. Cass found her stash intact, and Trinity won her woman back. The death of Maxine was ruled justifiable self-defense, especially when only her fingerprints were found on the homemade shiv.

Arness was credited with closing two major murder cases. He had hoped for more, but you took what you could get.

What he didn't know was the difficulty the two roommates had had in finding two murders that Maxine had no alibi for. It would have looked awfully fishy if Mad Max claimed credit for a killing at a time when she was in custody.

As it was, the dying woman's confession couldn't have been more solid if it had been true. It was witnessed by two sworn officers of the state, and was ironclad in the eyes of the law. Arness was offered a promotion, which he accepted: it would mean a larger pension when he finally did retire.

Bowler also received a promotion to Special Agent in Charge of the western section of Riverside County, and was soon busting the balls of all the Special Agents who reported to him.

The results of the autopsy confirmed what Arness already knew in his heart. Maxine "Mad Max" Kelly had died from a severe contusion to her throat. Her windpipe had swollen shut, and she had asphyxiated. The coroner also noted that the same blow had crushed her larynx.

But since everyone had gotten what they wanted, nobody looked too closely at the implications of the postmortem examination, or how a person could confess without a working voice box.

Snow, Snow, Snow

BY JOHN HARVEY

John Harvey is the author of the popular "Charlie Resnick" novels, the first of which, *Lonely Hearts*, was named one of the 100 Best Crime Novels of the Century by the *London Times*. His recent standalone crime thriller *Flesh and Blood* (Carroll and Graf, 2004) was presented the Silver Dagger award from the Crime Writers Association as Best Crime Novel of the Year.

Here he creates not only an interesting hit man protagonist, but yet another appealing police detective. Fodder for another series of novels? One can only hope.

SNOW DRIFTED, soft, against his face.

Earlier, the wind had whipped each succeeding fall into a virtual blizzard, slicing into him as he stood, barely sheltered, on the edge of the fen.

Now it was this: the snow of fairy tales and dreams.

A pair of swans floated, uncaring, along the shuffled surface of the water, at home in the gathering white.

Malkin checked his watch and continued to stand.

Fifteen minutes later, Fraser's SUV appeared on the raised strip of road, headlights pale through the mist of falling snow.

Malkin waited until, indicator blinking, the vehicle slowed into the left-hand turn that would take it along a narrow, barely made-up lane to where the new house was in the process of construction, further along the fen.

The main structure was already in place: varying shades of yellow brick at each end and to the rear, the front partly clad in as-yet untreated wood. The frames for the large windows that would dominate the upper floor had recently been set. No glass as yet. Ladders leaned against scaffolding, secured with rope. A bucket half-filled and frozen fast. Tarpaulins that flapped in each catch of wind.

Fastidious, Fraser changed soft leather shoes for green Wellingtons and pulled on his sheepskin coat. Lifting back the mesh gates that guarded the site, he moved inside and, after a few moments, disappeared into the building's shell. Snow continued to fall. Malkin stood no more than forty meters away, all but invisible against the washed-out sky, the shrouded earth.

Cautious, Fraser climbed the ladder to the upper floor and stared out. He'd expected the architect to be already at the site, not limping in late with some excuse about the weather. A bit of snow. February. What else did he expect?

Treading with care across the boards, Fraser eased aside a length of tarpaulin and stepped inside what would be the main room, running almost the entire length of the floor. Views right out across open land, unimpeded as far as the horizon. But not today. He failed to hear Malkin's foot on the ladder's bottom rung.

Angry, Fraser pushed back his cuff and double-checked his watch. Damned architect!

Hearing Malkin's footsteps now, he turned. "What sort of time d'you call this?"

Malkin stepped through the space of the open doorway and out of the snow.

"Who the hell . . . ?" Fraser began, words fading from his lips.

Malkin smiled.

"Remember Sharon Peters?" he said.

For an instant, Fraser saw a tousled-haired girl of eight, playing catch ball up against the wall as she waited for her bus; her face, at the last moment, widening in a scream.

"You do remember," Malkin said, "don't you?"

The pistol was already in his hand.

"Don't you?"

Ashen, Fraser stumbled back, began to plead.

For jobs like this, Malkin favored a 9 mm Glock 17. Light, plastic, readily disposable. Two shots were usually enough.

Or sometimes one.

At the sound, a solitary crow rose, shaking snowflakes from its wings, and began to circle round.

Blood was beginning to leak, already, from the back of Fraser's head, staining the untreated wood a dull reddish-brown. Snow swirled into Malkin's face as he descended the ladder, and with a quick shake of his head he blinked it away.

The train was no more than a third full and he had a table to himself, plenty of room to spread the paper and read. Every once in a while, he looked out at the passing fields, speckled as they were with snow. Hedgerows and rooftops gleamed white in the fresh spring sun.

He read again the account, all too familiar, of a prison suicide: a nineteen-year-old who had hanged himself in his cell. According to his family, the youth had been systematically beaten and bullied during the weeks leading up to his death, and prison staff had turned a blind eye.

"My son," the mother was reported as saying, "made complaint after complaint to the governor and the prison officer in charge of his wing, and they did nothing. Nothing. And now they're as guilty of his death as if they'd knotted the sheet themselves and kicked away the chair."

Poetic, Malkin thought. A good turn of phrase. He tore the page from the newspaper, folded it neatly once and once again, and slipped it into his wallet. One for a rainy day.

When the train pulled into the station, he left the remainder of the newspaper on the seat, pulled on his coat, and walked the length of the platform to the exit, taking his time.

The first thing he saw, stepping into the broad concourse, was a police officer in helmet and body armor, sub-machine gun held at an angle across his chest, and he was glad that he'd disposed of the Glock before boarding the train. Not that any of this was for him.

Two other officers, similarly armed, stood just outside the station entrance, at the head of the pavement steps. Anti-terrorism, Malkin thought, it had to be. A suspect being brought in that day for trial. Some poor bastard Muslim who'd made the mistake of visiting Afghanistan, or maybe just sent money to the wrong cause. Most likely now he'd be slammed up for a couple of years in Belmarsh or some other top security hole, then released without charge.

But that wasn't why Malkin was here.

He crossed close to a bus holding as many as ten officers in reserve and descended a cobbled slip road leading to the canal. A short distance along, the high glass and polished stone of the new magistrates' court was guarded by yet more police.

All it needed, Malkin thought, was a helicopter circling overhead.

He showed his ID and explained his reasons for entry. The case he was interested in was due to conclude today.

Almost two years before, Alan Silver had been woken in the night by the sound of intruders; he had armed himself with the licensed shotgun that he kept close by the bed, gone to the head of the stairs, and emptied both barrels into the two youths he surprised below. One took superficial wounds to the arm and neck and was able to turn and run; the other was thrown backwards onto the tiles of the broad hallway, bleeding out, a hole torn in his chest.

Silver phoned emergency services, ambulance and police, but by the time the paramedics arrived, less than ten minutes later, it was too late. Darren Michaels, seventeen, was pronounced dead on arrival at the hospital.

Alan Silver—a sometime song-and-dance man and minor

celebrity—was both hero and villain. The more righteous of the media spoke of unnecessary force and questioned the right of any civilian to own firearms at all, while others championed him as a hero. Right-of-center politicians strutted in reflected glory, crowing about the right of every Englishman to protect house and home, his proverbial castle. When Silver, described in court as a popular entertainer, pleaded guilty to manslaughter and was sentenced to eighteen months' imprisonment, there was uproar. *Is this all a young man's life is worth?* demanded *The Independent; Jailed for doing what was right!* denounced the *Mail.*

Outside the court that day, Darren Michaels's father, sweaty, clinging to his dignity in an ill-fitting suit, was asked how he felt about the verdict. "My son is dead," he said. "Now let justice take its course."

More recently, Silver's lawyers had earned the right to appeal; the sentence, they said, was punitive and over-severe. Punitive, Malkin remembered thinking: isn't that supposed to be the point?

Riding on the back of a popular hysteria about the rising rate of crime they had helped to create, the tabloid press rejoiced in seeing their circulations soar, inviting their readers to text or E-mail in support of the campaign *Free Silver Now!*

"If this government," proclaimed a Tory peer in the Lords, "and this home secretary, have not totally lost touch with the people they are supposed to represent, they should act immediately and ensure that the sentence in this case be made to better reflect the nation's mood."

Malkin settled into the back of the public gallery in time for the verdict: after due deliberation, and having reconsidered both his previously untarnished reputation and his unstinting work for charity, Alan Silver's sentence was reduced to one year. Taking into account the time he had spent on remand awaiting trial, this meant Silver had less than one month still to serve.

Channel Five was rumored to have offered him a six-figure contract to host a weekly chat show; a long-forgotten recording of "Mama Liked the Roses," a sentimental country ballad initially made popular by Elvis Presley, had been reissued and was currently number seven in the charts.

No wonder, as he was led out to the waiting Securicor van, Alan Silver, gray hair trimmed short and wearing his sixty-three years well, was, none too surprisingly, smiling.

Malkin found Michaels's father staring into the water of the canal, smoking a cigarette.

"You still think justice should be allowed to take its course?" Malkin said.

"Do I fuck!"

Earlier that morning, Will Grayson and his four-year-old son, Jake, had been building a snowman at the back of the house: black stones for the eyes, a carrot for the nose, one of Will's old caps, the one he'd worn when he was on the police bowling team, snug on the snowman's head.

Inside, Will could see his wife, Lorraine, through the kitchen window, moving back and forth behind the glass. Pancakes, he wouldn't have minded betting. Lorraine liked to make pancakes for breakfast those mornings he didn't have to go in to work; Lorraine well into her eighth month and on maternity leave, the size of her belly showing their second kid almost ready to pop. Baby might come early, the midwife had said.

As Will crouched down and added a few finishing touches to their snowman, Jake sneaked round behind him and caught him with a snowball from close range. Will barely heard the phone through the boy's shrieks of laughter; didn't react until he saw Lorraine waving through the window, her knuckles banging on the pane.

Will touched her belly gently with the palm of his hand as he passed. Good luck.

"Hello?" he said, picking up the phone. "This is Grayson."

The change in his face told Lorraine all she needed to know, and quickly she set to making a flask of coffee; a morning like this, more snow forecast, he would need something to keep out the cold.

Will laced up his boots, pulled on a fleece, took a weatherproof coat from the cupboard beneath the stairs; the first pancake was ready and he ate it with a smudge of maple syrup, licking his fingers before lifting his son into the air and swinging him around, kissing him, then setting him down.

Lorraine leaned forward and hugged him at the door. "Be careful when you're driving home. In case it freezes over."

"Don't worry." He kissed her eyes and mouth. "And call me if anything, you know, happens."

She laughed. "Go get the bad guys, okay?"

When the car failed to start first time, Will cursed, fearing the worst, but then the engine caught and turned and he was on his way, snaking tire tracks through a film of fallen snow.

Some thirty minutes and two wrong turns later, he pulled over into a farm gateway and unfolded the map. Out there in the middle of the fens, a day like this, everything looked the damned same.

It was another ten minutes before he finally arrived, wheels cracking the ice, and he slid to a halt behind Helen Walker's blue VW, last in line behind the three police vehicles that were lined up alongside the fen. There was an ambulance parked further back, closer to the road.

Helen Walker: how had she got there before him?

"Afternoon, Will," she called sarcastically, leaning over the scaffolding on the upper level of the unfinished house. "Good of you to join us."

Will shot her a finger and began making his way up the ladder.

He and Helen had worked together the best part of three years now, Will, as Detective Inspector, enjoying the higher rank, but, most of the time, that wasn't how it worked. It was more as if they were partners: sometimes one would lead, sometimes the other.

"How's Lorraine?" Helen's first question when he stepped off onto the boards.

"She's fine."

"The baby?"

"Kicking for England."

She laughed at the grin on his face.

"What have we got?" Will asked.

Helen stepped aside.

The dead man lay on his back, one arm flung out, the other close to his side, legs splayed. Eyes opened wide. A dark hole at the center of his forehead. The blood that had pooled out from the exit wound seemed to have frozen fast.

"Someone found him like this?"

"Kids. Playing around."

Will crouched low, then stood up straight. "We know who he is?"

"Arthur Fraser."

"How do we know that?"

"Wallet. Inside pocket."

"Not robbery then?"

"Not robbery."

"Any idea what he was doing here?"

"Checking on his new house, apparently. The architect's name's on the board below. I gave him a call. He was with a client the other side of Cambridge." Helen took a quick look at her watch. "Should be here, another thirty minutes or so."

Will turned back toward the body. "He come from around here?"

"Not really. Address the other side of Coventry."

"What's he doing having a house built here?"

"I asked the architect that. Making a new start, that's what he said."

"Not any more."

Malkin and Wayne Michaels sat at one of a cluster of wooden tables out front of a canal-side pub. None of the other tables was occupied. The snow had held off, but there was a wind, driving in from the north-west, though neither man seemed bothered by the cold. Both were drinking blended Scotch, doubles; Malkin nursing his second, Michaels on his third or fourth.

"How much," Michaels asked, "always assuming I wanted to go ahead, how much is this going to cost?"

When Malkin told him, he had to ask a second time.

"That friggin' much?"

"That much."

"Then you can forget it."

"Okay." Downing the rest of his drink in one, Malkin got to his feet.

"No. Hey, hey. Wait a minute. Wait up."

"Look," Malkin said, "no way I want to push you where you don't want to go."

"Come on, it's not that. You know it's not that. Nobody wants that . . . nobody wants it more than me. That bastard. I'd like to get hold of that fucking shotgun of his and let him have it myself."

"And end up inside doing fifteen to life."

"I know, I know." Michaels shook his head. He was a heavy man and the weight sat ill upon him, his body lumpen, his face jowly and red.

Malkin sat back down.

"That sort of money," Michaels said. "I'd be lucky to earn that in a year. A good year, at that."

Malkin shrugged. "You want a job well done. . . ."

"Listen." Leaning in, Michaels took hold of Malkin's sleeve. "I could go down to some pub in the Meadows, ask around. Time it takes to have a good shit, there'd be someone willing to do it for a couple of hundred quid."

"Yes," Malkin said. "And ten days after that, the police would have him banged up inside and he'd give you up first chance he got. Listen to him, you'd been the one talked him into it, forced him more or less, did everything except pull the trigger."

Michaels knew he was right.

"You want another?" he said, eying his empty glass.

Malkin shook his head. "Let's get this sorted first."

"The money," Michaels said, "I don't see how. . . ."

"Borrow it," Malkin said. "Building society. The bank. Tell

them you want to extend. I don't know. Add on a conservatory. Put in a loft."

"You make it sound easy."

"It is if you want it to be."

For several minutes neither man spoke. Whoever had been the center of all the police attention at the court had been taken in under close guard and now, indeed, there was a helicopter making slow small circles above their heads.

"That bastard Silver," Michaels said. "He's going to make a fucking fortune out of this."

"Yes."

"Smelling of fucking roses won't be in it."

"That's true."

"All right, all right. But listen, I'm going to need a few days. The cash, you know?"

Malkin laid a hand on his arm. "That's okay. Within reason, take all the time you need. Silver's not going anywhere quite yet. Meantime, I'll ask around, make a few plans."

"We've got a deal, then?"

The skin around Malkin's gray eyes creased into a smile. "We've got a deal."

What was it they said about converts? They were always the strictest adherents to the faith? Since he'd turned away from a thirty-a-day habit two years ago, Will had been that way about smoking. Just about the only thing he found hard to take about Helen was the way her breath smelled when she'd come in from outside, sneaking a cigarette break at the rear of the building. Not so long back, he'd given her a tube of extra-strong mints and she'd handed them back, saying they were bad for her teeth.

It was the day after Fraser's body had been found.

Careful examination of the scene had found little in the way of forensic evidence; no stray hairs or fingerprints, no snatches of fabric snagged by chance on ladder or doorway. A series of footprints, fading in the slow-melting snow, had been traced across two broad fields; at the furthest point, close in against the hedge, there were tire tracks, faint but clear. A Ford Mondeo with similar-patterned tires, stolen in Peterborough the day previously, was discovered in the carpark at Ely station. Whoever had killed Fraser could have had another car waiting or have caught a train. South to Cambridge and London; east toward Norwich, west to Nottingham and beyond.

It was an open book.

"Fraser," Will said. "I've been doing some checking. Fifty-two years old. Company director. Divorced five years ago. Two kids, both grown up. Firm he was running went under. Picked himself up since then, financially at least, but it seems to have been pretty bad at the time."

"That was when the wife left him?"

"How d'you know she was the one who left?"

Helen touched her fingertips to her temple. "Female intuition."

"Bollocks!"

"Excuse me, is that a technical term?"

"Definitely. And you're right, she walked away. What with that and the business thing, Fraser seems to have fallen apart for a while, started drinking heavily. Two charges of driving with undue care, another for driving when over the limit. Just under three years ago he lost control behind the wheel, went up on to the curb and hit this eight-year-old. A girl."

Pain jolted across Helen's face. "She was. . . ."

Will nodded. "She was killed. Oh, not outright. She hung on in hospital for another five days."

"What happened to Fraser?"

"Fined six thousand pounds, banned from driving for eighteen months. . . ."

"Eighteen months?"

"Uh-huh."

"And that was it?"

"Two years inside."

"Of which he served half."

Will nodded. "Two-thirds of that in an open prison with passes most weekends."

"Fucking justice!"

"You said it."

Helen drew breath. "What time's the post-mortem?"

Will looked toward the clock on the office wall. "An hour from now."

"Okay. My car or yours?"

Malkin showed the appropriate credit card and booked a room at the Holiday Inn under an assumed name. It was a city he knew, though not well, and it was doubtful that anyone there knew him. Average height, average build, he was blessed with one of those faces that were instantly forgettable, save possibly for the eyes.

At the central library, he read through the coverage of Silver's appeal and then the reporting of the original shooting and trial. Aside from Silver's own faded celebrity, much was made of the delinquent life style of Darren Michaels and his companion that evening, Jermaine Royal. Both young men had been in trouble with the police since their early teens; both had been excluded, at various times, from school. An accident, one compassionate reporter said of Darren Michaels, just waiting to happen.

Malkin found a cut-and-paste biography on the shelves. *The Fall and Fall of Alan Silver*. He took it to one of the tables on the upper floor to read; just himself and a bunch of students beavering away at their laptops, listening to their iPods through headphones.

Silver's mother had been a chorus girl, his father a third-rate comedian in music hall and pantomime dame; Alan himself first appeared on stage at the age of six, learning to be his father's stooge. A photograph showed him in a sailor suit and hat. By the age of seventeen, he was doing a summer season at Scarborough, complete with straw hat and cane, Yorkshire's answer to Fred Astaire. There were spots on popular radio shows, *Variety Bandbox* and *Educating Archie*; even some early television, *Café Continental* with Hélène Cordet.

Three marriages, but none of them stuck; no children, apparently. A veiled suggestion that he might be gay. In the eighties, he had something of a comeback in the theater, playing a failed music-hall performer in a revival of *The Entertainer*. The part originally played by Laurence Olivier. Asked how he did it, Silver evidently replied, "I just close my eyes and think of my old man."

Soon after this, he was featured on *This Is Your Life* and had some brief success with *Mama Like the Roses*. Somehow he kept working into his sixties, mostly doing pantomime, trotting out his father's old routines at Mansfield and Hunstanton.

Oh, no it isn't!

Oh, yes it is!

He bought an old farmhouse between Newark and Nottingham. Retired, more or less.

Malkin phoned Michaels that evening, wanting to make sure he was still on board; asked a few questions about Darren's friends. Something Darren's pal, Jermaine, had claimed at the trial, that they'd been out to Silver's place before and he'd told them come back any time. Did Michaels think there was any truth it that?

Michaels had no bloody idea.

"Besides," Michaels said, "what difference if there was?"

None, Malkin told him. None at all.

"Too bloody right," Michaels said. "Dead is fucking dead."

The phone rang and before Will could reach it, Helen had snatched it up. Coat buttoned up against the cold, she had just come in from outside.

"Lorraine," she said, passing the receiver swiftly across.

Will's throat went dry and his stomach performed a double somersault, but all his wife wanted was to remind him to pick up an extra pint of milk on his way home if he could. Will assured her he'd do what he could.

"No news?" Helen asked, once he'd set down the phone.

"No news."

"Well, I've got something."

"You're not pregnant, too?"

"Chance would be a fine thing."

Will stood back and looked her over. "You want to get pregnant?"

"You're offering?"

He grinned. It was a good grin, took maybe ten years off his age and he knew it. "Not today."

"Damn!" Helen smiled back. She liked flirting with him; it was something they did. Somehow it helped them along; kept them, Helen sometimes thought, from ever getting close to the real thing.

"You want to tell me your news?" Will said.

"You know that expanse of water the other side of Ely. Close to the railway line. Locals call it the Wash."

"Yes, I think so."

"These kids were out there the day Fraser was killed. Late morning. They'd taken a makeshift toboggan, thinking the water might have frozen over, but it hadn't. Just a little at at the edges maybe, but that's all. Certainly not worth taking any risks; near the center it's pretty deep."

Will nodded, waiting, sitting perched on the edge of a desk. She'd get to it in her own time.

"While they were there, the Nottingham train went through. They didn't know it was that, but I've checked. One of the boys swears he saw someone throwing an object from the window between the carriages. Just for a moment, he thought it looked like a gun."

"How old? This kid, how old is he?"

"Nine? Ten?"

"You think he's any way reliable?"

"According to his mother, he's not the kind to make things up."

"Why's he only come forward now?"

"Mentioned it to his mum at the time. She didn't think anything of it till she saw something about the investigation on the local news."

"You know what the boss is going to say. Divers don't come cheap."

"Not even if they're our divers?"

"Not even then."

"Think you can persuade him?"

"What else have we got?"

"So far? Diddly-squit."

"Why don't I tell him that?"

Instant Tanning, the sign said, diagonally across the window. *Manicure, Pedicure* in similar lettering below. *Top Notch Beauty Salon* above the door. Lisa was sitting on the step outside, pink overall, sandals, tights, smoking a cigarette.

Malkin crossed toward her and as he came close, she glanced up and then away.

"Busy?" Malkin said.

She looked at him through an arc of smoke. "Takin' the piss, right?"

By appearance, she was a mixture of African-Caribbean and Chinese, but her accent was East Midlands through and through, Notts rather than Derby.

"Lisa?"

"Yeah?"

Malkin squatted low on his haunches, face close to hers. "You used to know Darren Michaels."

"So what if I did?"

"I'm sorry. About what happened."

"Yeah, well. Been and gone now, in't it?"

"You've moved on."

"Something like that."

"Good."

Something about his voice made her feel ill at ease. "Look, this place." She looked up at the sign. "It's what it says it is, you know. Not one of them massage parlors, if that's what you're thinking."

"Not at all. It's just, if you've got the time, I thought we could talk a bit about Darren? Maybe his mate, Jermaine? You were friendly with both of them, weren't you?"

Lisa narrowed her eyes. "You're not the police, are you?"

"Perish the thought."

"Not some reporter?"

Malkin shook his head. "I used to know Darren's father a little, that's what it is."

"Him told you 'bout me, I s'pose, were it?"

"That's right."

Lisa lit a new cigarette from the butt of the last. "Got a good twenty minutes till my next, why not?"

There were a pair of divers, borrowed for the occasion from the Lincolnshire Force, and they struck lucky within the first hour, Will grateful he could assure his boss there'd be no need for overtime. The weapon was a Glock 17, its bulky stock immediately recognizable. Any serial numbers had, of course, been removed. If they begged and pleaded with the technicians, another twenty-four hours should tell them if it was the gun responsible for Arthur Fraser's death.

Will and Helen were both parked up at the side of the road, a lay-by off the A10, the Ely to Cambridge road. They were sitting in Will's car, a faint mist beginning to steam up the insides of the windows.

"You thinking what I'm thinking?" Will said.

"Most probably." A hint of a smile on Helen's face.

"This shooting. Nothing to suggest any kind of fight or quarrel. Nothing personal. Every sign of careful planning: preparation. A single shot to the head with a weapon that's almost certainly clean. A professional job. It has to be."

"Someone hired to make a hit on Fraser?"

"It looks that way."

"Then you have to ask why."

"And there's only one answer," Will said. "Sharon Peters."

Helen nodded. "The family, the parents, we should go and talk to them?"

"Let's wait," Will said, "till tomorrow. Make sure the ballistics match up."

"Okay."

It was warm inside the car. Their arms close but not touching. An articulated lorry went past close enough to rock them in its slipstream. Still neither one of them made a move to go.

Finally, it was Helen who looked at her watch. "Shouldn't you be getting back?"

"If anything had happened, Lorraine would have called on my mobile."

"Even so."

He left her leaning against the roof of her VW, smoking a cigarette.

When Will arrived home, Lorraine was wandering from room to room, Cowboy Junkies on the stereo, singing quietly along. "A Common Disaster" playing over and over, the track programmed to repeat. To Will, it wasn't a good omen.

"Lol?"

"Huh?"

"Can we change this?"

"Change?"

"The music. Can we . . . ?"

"I like it."

Okay, Will thought, go with the flow.

A good few years back, when he and Lorraine had first started going together, she would fetch her little stash from where she kept it upstairs in the bedroom—her dowry, as she called it—and roll them both a joint. Now that he no longer smoked cigarettes and, Will supposed, with this latest promotion, if she ever suggested it, he passed.

Lorraine, he was sure, still partook from time to time, the sweet smell lingering in the corners of the house and in her hair. Maybe, looking at her slight, slow sway, she was stoned right now.

How would that be for baby, he wondered, if that were so?

Would it make him a cool kid or slightly crazy?

There were some cans of beer in the fridge, and he took one into the living room and switched on the TV. Lorraine had been vague about dinner, but he thought she was entitled, hormones all over the place like they were. Later he'd phone for a curry or, better still, a Chinese. It was ages since they'd eaten Chinese.

They were in bed before ten-thirty, Lorraine set to read a chapter or so of whatever book she had on the go, Will rolling away from her and onto his side, arm raised to shield his eyes from the light.

He must have fallen asleep straight away, because the next thing he knew it was pitch dark and the bed beside him was empty. Lorraine was sitting on the toilet with her night gown pulled high across her thighs.

"You all right?" Anxiety breaking in his voice.

"Yes. Yes, just woke with this pain." She indicated low in her abdomen.

"But you're okay? I mean, nothing's happened?"

"Nothing's happened."

When he bent to kiss her forehead, it was damp and seared with sweat. "Why don't you let me get you something? A drink of water? Tea? How about some peppermint tea?"

"Yes. Peppermint tea. That would be nice."

He kissed her chastely on the lips and went downstairs.

Back in bed, he found it near impossible to get back to sleep, dozed fitfully and got up finally at five.

Jake was fast asleep, thumb in his mouth, surrounded by his favorite toys.

Will made coffee and toast and sat at the kitchen table staring out, willing it to get light. At six-thirty he gave in and dialed Helen's number. She answered on the second ring.

"Not asleep then?"

"Hardly."

"Yesterday," Will said, "you think I was being over-cautious?"

"In the car?"

"What I said in the car, yes. About waiting to see if we had a match."

"You don't think there's any doubt?"

"Has to be some. But, shit, not really, no."

"You want to go over there now? Sharon Peters's parents?"

"What do you reckon? A couple of hours' drive? More?"

"Coventry? This time of the morning, maybe less."

"I'll meet you by the Travelodge on the A14. This side of the turn-off for Hemingford Grey."

"It's a deal." Will could hear the excitement rising in her voice.

Lorraine, at last, looked relaxed in sleep. Will left a note on her pillow decorated with a dozen kisses, looked in again on Jake, and closed the front door as softly as he could.

The traffic moving into and out of the city was heavy, and it was close to nine before they arrived at the house, a twenties semidetached in a quiet street with trees, leafless still, at frequent intervals. Cars parked either side.

There was a van immediately outside the house with decorating paraphernalia in the rear, partly covered by a paint-splodged sheet. The man who came to the door was wearing off-white dungarees, speckled red, blue, and green.

"Mr. Peters?"

He looked Will and Helen up and down, as if slowly making up his mind. Then he stepped back and held the door wide. "You'd best come in. Don't want everyone knowing our business up and down the street."

One wall of the room into which he led them was a virtual shrine to Sharon when she'd been alive, photographs almost floor to ceiling.

"The wife's out," Peters said. "Dropping off our other girl at school. Usually goes and does a bit of shopping after that."

Our other girl, Will was thinking. Of course, to them she's still alive.

"You know why we're here?" Helen asked.

"Something to do with that bastard getting shot, I imagine."

"You know about it, then?"

"Not at first, no. One of neighbors come around and told us. Saw it, like, on TV."

"And you didn't know anything about it till then?"

"'Course not, what d'you think?"

"To be frank, Mr. Peters," Will said, "we think someone paid to have Fraser killed."

"You reckon?" Peters laughed. "Well, I'll tell you what, if they'd come round here asking for a few quid toward it, I'd have shelled out double-quick. What he did to our Sharon, shooting's too good for him." Looking at Will, he narrowed his eyes. "Quick, was it?"

"I think so, yes."

"More's the sodding pity."

They talked to him for three quarters of an hour, pushing and prodding, back and forth over the same ground, but if he had anything to give away, it never showed.

Just as they were on the point of leaving, a key turned in the front door and Mrs. Peters stepped through into the hall, shopping bags in both hands. One look at her husband, another at Will and Helen, and the bags dropped to the floor. "Oh, Christ, they know, don't they? They bloody know."

Will contacted the local police station and arranged for an interview room to be placed at their disposal. Donald and Lydia Peters were questioned separately and together, always with a lawyer present. After her initial outburst, Lydia would say nothing; Donald, brazening it out, would not say a great deal more. Without an admission, without tangible evidence—letters, E-mails, recordings of phone calls—their involvement in Fraser's murder would be difficult to prove. All they had was the wife's slip of the tongue. *They know, don't they?* In a court of law, it could have meant anything.

Their one chance was a court order to examine the Peterses' bank records, turn their finances inside out. If they had, indeed, paid to have Fraser killed, the money would have had to come from somewhere. Unless they'd been especially careful. Unless it had come from other sources. Family. Friends.

Will knew full well that if he went to the CPS with what they had now, the prosecution service would laugh in his face.

It had taken a little time for Malkin to gain Lisa's confidence enough for her to take him to see Jermaine. Jermaine had served his time for attempted burglary and had been released into the care of his probation officer, one of the conditions that he move away from where he'd been living, steer clear of his former friends. Where Lisa took Malkin was no more than ten miles away, Sutton-in-Ashfield, Jermaine's gran's.

Jermaine and Malkin sat in the small front room, the parlor, his gran had called it, Lisa and the old lady in the other room, watching TV.

Jermaine was fidgeting constantly, never still.

"What you said in court," Malkin asked, "about having been to Silver's place before, was that true?"

"'Course it was true. No one fuckin' believed it, though, did they?"

"You'd both been there? You and Darren?"

"Yeah. What's this all about, anyway? What's it matter now?"

"Why were you there, Jermaine?"

"What d'you mean, why?"

"I mean Alan Silver's a has-been in his sixties and you're what? Seventeen. I wouldn't have thought you'd got a lot to talk about, a lot of common ground."

Jermaine's head swung from side to side. "He was all right, you know, not stuck up, not tight. Plenty to drink, yeah? Southern Comfort, that's what he liked."

"And money? He gave you money?"

Now Jermaine was staring at the floor, not wanting to look Malkin in the eye.

"He gave you money?" Malkin said again.

"He gave Darren money." Jermaine's voice was little more than a whisper.

"Why did he give Darren money? Jermaine? Why did he give—?"

"For sucking his cock," Jermaine suddenly shouted. "Why d'you think?"

Just for an instant, Malkin closed his eyes. "And that's why you went back?" he said.

"No. We went back to rip him off, didn't we? Fucking queer!"

Malkin leaned, almost imperceptibly, forward. "Silver's house," he said. "If I gave you some paper, paper and a pencil, d'you think you could draw me some kind of plan of the inside?"

"Look," Will called across the office. "Take a look at this."

Helen pushed aside what she was doing and made her way to where Will was sitting at the computer.

"There, you see. This has been nagging at me, and there it is. Two years ago. Lincoln. This man Royston Davies. Night club bouncer. Found dead in the back of a taxi. Single bullet through the head. Nine millimeter."

"All right," Helen said. "I see the connection."

"Just wait. There's more." Will scrolled down the page. "See. That was February. The August before, there was a fracas outside the club where Davies was working. Nineteen-year-old youth was struck with something hard enough to put him into hospital. Bottle, baseball bat. Went into a coma and never came out of it." Will closed the file. "I rang someone I know at Lincoln this morning. Seems Davies was brought in for questioning, quite a few witnesses pointing the finger, but they never got enough to make a case."

"Wait, wait. Wait a minute." Helen held both hands in front of her, palms out, as if to ward off the idea. "What you're suggesting, unless I've got this wrong, what you're saying, there's someone out there, some professional assassin, some hit man, specializing in taking out people who've killed and got away with it. Is that it?"

"That's it exactly."

"You're crazy."

"Why? Look at it, look at the evidence."

"Will, there is no evidence. Not of what you're saying."

"What is it, then?"

"Coincidence."

"And if I could show otherwise?"

"How?"

"If these weren't the only two instances, for instance, would you believe me then?"

"And are there?"

"I don't know yet. But I can find out."

Helen laughed and pushed a hand back through her hair. "Tell you what, Will, when you do, let me know."

He watched her walk, still laughing, back across the room.

Alan Silver's house was pitched between Colston Bassett and Harby, on the western edge of the Vale of Belvoir. Nice country. Hunting country, when the time was right.

Malkin had driven past it several times, learning the lay of the land. Earlier that evening, the light fading, he had parked close by the canal and made his way across the fields. Now he was there again, close to midnight, tracing a path back between the trees.

Cold, he thought, pausing at a field end to glance up at the sky. Cold enough for snow.

At just about the time Malkin had made his first visit to Alan Silver's house, Lorraine had been sitting with her feet up on the settee, watching television, one of those chat shows Will abhorred. Richard and Judy? Richard and Jane?

He was in the other room, leafing through the paper, when she called him.

"Look. That man who shot the boy trying to burgle him. The one there was all the fuss about, remember?"

Will remembered.

"He's on now."

As Will came into the room, a black and white image of a young Alan Silver was on the screen. White suit, straw hat and cane.

"My God!" said Silver in mock surprise. "Was that me? I'd never have known."

"But that was how you started?" said Richard. "A bit of a song-and-dance man."

"Absolutely."

"You don't suppose," said Jane or Judy, "you could still do a few steps for us now?"

Sprightly for a man of his years, Silver sprang to his feet and did a little tap dance there and then. Jane or Judy marveled, and the studio audience broke into spontaneous applause.

"Not bad for sixty-odd," Lorraine said.

Will said something noncommittal and walked back out of the room.

Alan Silver plumped up his pillows and reached for the glass of water he kept beside the bed. He was tired; his legs ached. The show had gone well, though, he thought. Sparkled, that's what he'd done. Sparkled. Still smiling, he switched out the bedside light. It wouldn't take him long to get to sleep tonight.

A short while later, he was wide awake.

Something had woken him. But what?

A dream? A noise on the stairs?

Imagination, surely?

But no, there it was again.

Silver felt his skin turn cold.

It couldn't be happening twice.

Carefully, he eased back the heavy covers and, rolling onto his stomach, reached beneath the bed.

It wasn't there. The bloody thing wasn't there.

The bedroom door swung open and Silver, turning clumsily, jabbed on the light.

"Looking for something?" Malkin said, leveling the shotgun toward the center of the bed.

Upon My Soul

BY ROBERT J. RANDISI

Mr. Randisi is the author of the "Joe Keough" novels, the most recent of which was *Arch Angels* (2004, SMP). His newest book is *Everybody Kills Somebody Some Time*, a tale of the Rat Pack in Vegas during the 1960 filming of *Ocean's 11*.

For temptation let me ply
be my wings, Lord, be my eyes
guard me when old Satan's nigh
upon my soul
　　　—Townes Van Zandt

1

The day Sangster woke and discovered he had a soul after all, everything changed.

Along with the soul came a conscience, something else he had never experienced in his thirty-seven years. He hadn't been awake five minutes when he began to weep. He wept not only for the people he'd killed over the years, but for their families, who had been deprived of their loved ones. He wept uncontrollably, and it was a day for firsts, for he had never cried before, not even as a child.

Sangster was a new man, but the question became . . . was he a better man?

He left his apartment that day and never returned. In fact, no one in California ever saw him again, and for many years he was presumed dead. Those who knew him figured that his line of work had finally caught up with him.

It seemed logical to assume that a man who was an assassin for hire would fall prey to an assassin, himself.

But that was not the case. . . .

2

Three years later . . .

Sangster looked up from the chessboard at the man who had appeared at the end of his front walk. In the almost three years he had been renting this house in Algiers, across Lake Pontchartrain from the French Quarter, the only person who had ever come up that walk was his neighbor, with whom he played chess at least three times a week.

"Know 'im?" Ken Burke asked.

Sangster looked across the table at the older man, who had not looked up from the board.

"Yeah," he said, "I know him."

The man advanced up the walk carefully, as if he expected somebody to take a shot at him at any moment. He probably would have felt better if he'd known Sangster hadn't touched a gun in three years.

When he reached the porch, he stopped and stared at Sangster before he spoke.

"Hello, Sangster."

"Primble."

Burke looked up at that, eyed Sangster, who could only shrug his shoulders.

"What do you want?"

"A lot of people think you're dead," Primble said.

"That was kind of the idea, Eddie."

"It worked pretty well," Eddie Primble said, "until now."

"Well, you didn't find me," Sangster said. "I know that much. Who was it?"

"Top secret," Primble said. "Is there someplace we can talk?"

"You don't want to talk in front of my friend?"

Primble looked at Ken Burke, who continued to eye the board intently.

"You have a friend?" he asked. "Things *have* changed quite a bit in three years."

Sangster looked at Primble.

"Yes," he said, "they have." He looked at Burke. The man had aged badly in three years. Sangster knew Primble must have been forty, but much of his hair had receded and he'd put on weight. He looked fifty—healthy enough, but fifty. The cut of his suit also bespoke of some progress, financially.

"I have to talk to this man," he said to his chess opponent.

"Go ahead and talk," Burke said. "I'm concentratin'."

Sangster looked at Primble.

"He won't listen, he's concentrating."

"I intend to talk very plainly," Primble warned.

"Talk as plainly as you want," Sangster said. "I have no secrets from Burke."

"Your friend," Primble reiterated.

"And neighbor," Sangster said. "He lives in the house next door."

"How much does the old-timer know?"

"Everything."

"Everything?" Burke asked. He ignored the "old-timer" remark. After all, he was seventy. If that didn't qualify as an old-timer, what did? "If I knew everything, this game would've been over a long time ago." Sangster knew—Primble did not—that Burke was not only talking about chess.

"Eddie," Sangster said, "you found me—or somebody found me for you. What do you want?"

"I need you," Primble said, "to . . . to do what you used to do."

"He wants you to kill somebody," Burke said, eyeing the board, chin in hand.

"That's what I used to do," Sangster said. He looked at Primble. "I don't do that any more."

"You don't—come on, Sangster," Primble said. "What else does a man like you do?"

"I'm retired."

"Retired?"

"I don't kill any more," he said. "I haven't killed anyone in three years. I don't even own a gun, and I haven't held one in all that time."

"You expect me to believe that?" Primble asked.

"I don't care what you believe, Eddie," Sangster told him. "It's the truth."

Primble thought a moment, put one foot up on the first step. It was warm, and he was sweating. He loosened his tie, undid the top button of his shirt.

"All right," he said. "For the moment let's assume that you haven't killed anyone in three years." He adopted a look of complete puzzlement. "Why not?"

"That's not important," the ex-assassin said. "All you need to know is that I don't do it any more. You need to find someone else."

"Do you know how long it took me to find you?" Primble demanded.

"Let me guess," Sangster said. "Three years?"

"I'm not just gonna take no for an answer, Sangster," Primble said. "That's not what I do, remember?"

"I remember very well."

"In fact," the man went on, "when you walked out, you left

behind an unfinished assignment. I had to have someone else do your job for you."

"Luckily," Sangster replied, "you hadn't paid me in advance."

"That's not the point."

"I know," Sangster said. "I've been trying to get you to see the point, Eddie."

"Sangster," Primble said, "you were the best I ever ran."

"I'm out of the business, Eddie."

"You can't get out of this business, Sangster," Primble said. "Why don't we just call the last three years a vacation?"

Sangster looked at the chessboard. The old man hadn't made a move yet. He had his chin in his left hand, and his right hand was down out of sight.

"Eddie—"

"You don't think I came alone, do you?" Primble asked.

"I don't really care if you came alone or not, Eddie," Sangster said. "You're leaving, either way."

"There are two guns trained on you right now. If I nod, you're dead, and your chess buddy, too."

It got quiet, and suddenly they all heard the sound of the hammer being cocked on a gun.

"I thought you said you didn't own a gun," Primble said.

"He don't," Ken Burke said. "I do."

Burke brought his right hand into sight. He was holding a big .45 Peacemaker, the kind they used to carry in the old West.

"You so much as twitch, let alone nod, and it'll be the last thing you ever do," Burke told Primble.

"Easy, old-timer," Primble said. "That thing's pretty old. It might explode in your hand."

"I guess you don't really know much about guns, do ya, mister?" Burke asked. "That probably comes from havin' other people do your killin' for ya. This here's a collector's item, and I keep it in pristine shape. It's the pride of my collection, and believe me when I tell you it's in fine workin' order."

That was the most Sangster thought he'd heard the older man say at one time in the three years he'd know him.

Primble was sweating even more, but it wasn't from the heat.

"Is he serious?" he asked.

"Dead serious," Sangster said. "Show him, Burke."

With his left hand, Burke took his wallet from his pocket and flipped it open to show Primble his badge.

"You're a cop?"

"Sheriff," Burke said, "retired, but I keep my hand in."

"Sangster," Primble said, "I just wanted to talk."

"Then you should have left the threats at home," Sangster said. "Come on." He stood up, as did Burke.

"Where we going?" Primble asked.

"You signal your boys to put up their guns," Sangster said. "We're going to walk you to the ferry, so nobody decides to take a shot at me."

"Look, I—"

"We're done talking, Eddie."

"I need you, Sangster!"

"You heard the man," Burke said. "Now give whatever signal you arranged so your men know to put up their guns."

Primble frowned, and for a moment looked like a man about to cry. Finally, he turned his body partially and waved his hand in disgust.

"They're leaving," he said.

"Good," Sangster said, "they'll be on the same ferry you're on. Let's go."

"I don't know why—" Burke prodded Primble in the back with the barrel of the Peacemaker and the man almost jumped out of his skin. They made the walk to the Algiers ferry in silence.

Sangster watched the ferry start across the lake back to New Orleans.

"You sure his men were on there, too?" Burke asked.

"I'm sure," Sangster said.

Sangster looked at the Peacemaker in his friend's hand.

"I'm glad you brought that over today to show me."

"Yeah," Burke said, with a grin. He took it off cock and lowered it to his side.

"Would it really have fired?"

"To tell you the truth," Burke said, "I don't know." He waited a beat, then added, "Maybe if it'd been loaded."

3

On the ferry, Silk Guiliano and Jimmy O'Malley walked over to where Eddie Primble was sitting.

"What the hell happened?" Silk asked.

"Yeah," Jimmy said. "He run us off?"

"He did," Primble said. "He's still as good as ever. Wants me to believe he hasn't pulled the trigger—hell, even held a gun—in three years, but. . . ." Primble shook his head in admiration. "He had that old man hold the gun. It was . . . brilliant."

Silk looked at Jimmy.

"He ran us off, and Eddie's impressed."

"I ain't so impressed," Jimmy replied. He looked at Primble. "Is the bet still on?"

"It's still on," Primble said. "I fingered him for you, didn't I? You both get a good look at him?"

"I did," Silk said. He was in his early thirties, dressed completely in black. His had christened himself "Silk" years ago, liking the name and all its connotations. "Smooth as silk," that's what he told women, and he also considered himself to be smooth as silk with a gun.

O'Malley, on the other hand, was just the opposite. Late twenties, he was rough, crude, but effective when it came to killing.

One of these men wanted to take the place of Sangster in Eddie Primble's operation, but Primble wouldn't pick one until he knew that Sangster was dead and was not coming back. So a wager was put in place between Silk and Jimmy. Whichever man managed to kill Sangster would get his spot. The other man would be relegated to second banana, and neither man wanted that.

"So," Primble said, "you both know him on sight, the rest is up to you."

Silk and Jimmy exchanged a look, then Silk asked, "Are you sure you didn't talk him into coming back?"

"Yeah," Jimmy said. "Maybe you told him about us?"

"He says he's done with it," Primble said. "If he's truly finished, I can't have him running around out here alive, not with what he knows. No, he didn't agree to come back. He's your target, boys, and there's a lot at stake."

"He didn't look so tough," O'Malley said.

"Don't underestimate him," Primble said. "That's the only advice I'm going to give you both."

"I'm not going to underestimate him," Silk said. "What's the point of killing him if he's not the best?"

"Oh, he was the best, all right," Primble said. "The best I ever saw. Probably still is."

"We'll see about that," Silk said, looking back at Algiers.

For want of something else to say, Jimmy O'Malley said, "Yeah."

4

It had taken Sangster a year to get to know Ken Burke well enough to tell him the truth. As a retired lawman, Burke didn't approve of the way Sangster had made his living, but as a man who had done his own share of killing—all in the line of duty, of course—he understood a man finding redemption. As a Christian, he forgave Sangster, and their friendship grew stronger after that.

They didn't finish their chess game after walking Primble to the ferry. Sangster told the old man he had some thinking to do.

"About leavin'?"

"Maybe."

"That'd be a shame."

"I know," Sangster said. "I love it here." He loved the house in Algiers, but he also loved the French Quarter and everything it had to offer, from its great bookstores to its countless musical venues, its food, and its women.

"Then don't let that feller ruin it."

"There's only one way I could be sure of that, Burke."

"By killin' him?"

Sangster nodded.

"And I'm not going to do that."

"Got to be another way, then."

"That's what I'm going to think about."

"Well, gimme a shout if you need me," Burke said. "I got guns that I know will shoot."

"I'll keep that in mind. Thanks, Ken."

After his neighbor left, Sangster walked to one of the front windows and stared out. He had known someone would find him sooner or later, but he'd hoped it wouldn't be his old boss, Primble. Now he was either going to have to deal with the man, take care of him, or move on and make a new life somewhere else. The only problem with the third one was, he knew Primble wouldn't stop looking. He had too much invested in Sangster just to let him go, and if he could find him—or have him found— once, he could do it again.

The problem with the second option was that he didn't kill, any more.

So the only option left to him was number one, deal with him.

From his vantage point he could see his mailbox, one of those big metal ones mounted on a pole and fitted with a red flag. When the flag was up, something was in the box. The flag had not been up in the three years he'd been living there, because nobody knew where he was to send him mail. He didn't even get junk mail because he'd instructed the post office never to deliver it.

Then why was the flag up now?

He went out the front door and down the walk to the mailbox. He saw that the door was slightly ajar. He hadn't thought about things like booby traps and tripwires for over two years. The first year, he'd kept expecting to find death around every corner, but eventually he was able to relax and start living a normal life—not "again," because he couldn't remember when he'd actually lived a normal life. Certainly not growing up. How normal could it have been to constantly be trying to avoid your parents in your own house? And certainly not since he killed his first man, at fifteen. So surely it had only been the past two years that he could call his life normal, by conventional means.

Now, as he stared at the mailbox, he had to summon back some of those old instincts. He examined the pole and the box on the outside, then used his fingers to search for wires of any kind. Finally, after pressing his ear to the box and listening intently, he eased the door open and looked inside. There was one single brown letter-sized envelope inside. He studied the interior of the box for several seconds before reaching in to remove it. Now that he was holding it, he had to be concerned that it might be a letter bomb. How could he have existed all those years having to deal with this kind of fear every moment?

He ran his finger over the envelope carefully before slipping his thumb under the flap and unsealing it. It came open rather easily, indicating it hadn't been sealed very long ago. Inside was a single piece of white paper with two handwritten lines on it:

I'M AT THE LAFITTE HOUSE
IF YOU WANT TO TALK.

It was signed: *E.P.*

He folded the note and put it back in the envelope. As he turned to go back to the house he swiped at the red flag to put it back down. As it came down it made a connection with a wire and a puff of smoke leaped into the air. Sangster took one step away from the box and watched the smoke rise and dissipate. Primble's sense of humor. He just wanted to show Sangster that he could be dead at that moment.

Instead of going back to his house, he walked across to Burke's.

"What are you going to do?" Burke asked.

"I'll have to handle it, somehow," Sangster said.

"You think he's here to kill you?"

"I think he was here to get me back," Sangster said. "Failing that, he'll have me killed."

"Not kill you himself?"

"No," Sangster said. "Primble doesn't kill. He has others do that for him."

"Like you?"

"Yes," Sangster said, "like me . . . at one time."

They were seated in Burke's kitchen, each with a Blackened Voodoo beer bottle in front of them. It was early, but they both thought the occasion called for it.

"He said he had guns with him," Burke said.

"I believe him."

"How many?"

"At least two."

"And you plan on takin' them out?"

"Not if I can help it."

Burke leaned back and regarded his friend across the table.

"You said you don't kill for a livin' any more."

"That's right."

"How about to survive?" Burke asked. "Could you kill then?"

Sangster stared at his beer bottle.

"I don't know, Burke," he said. "Are you a religious man?"

"No," Burke said, with no explanation.

"Do you believe men have souls?" Sangster asked. "Souls that tell them what's right and what's wrong? Souls that make them feel compassion?"

"You're confusing a soul with a conscience, son," Burke said. "I know you told me you woke up three years ago and discovered you had both, but maybe it was just one."

"Which one?"

"That's for you to figure out. If you decide it's a soul, then you might not want to put any black marks on it. But if you decide it's a conscience—well, you can kill and still have a conscience."

"Am I kidding myself, Burke?" Sangster asked. "A hit man is all I've ever been. Can I be a hit man who won't kill?"

"A hit man is what you used to be, son," Burke said. "Just like a cop is what I used to be."

"You're still a cop, you old coot," Sangster said. "You've told me that a hundred times."

"Have I?" Burke asked. "Then who is the one kiddin' themselves?"

5

It was an old house, and it creaked everywhere. After living there three years, Sangster had all of them memorized, so he knew right where the assassin was from the moment he stepped up onto the porch.

He sat in the dark in the living room, waiting. At one time he would have been holding a gun in his hand, but on this night instead of a Colt Woodsman or a Glock, he was holding a Louisville Slugger.

Whoever the mechanic was, he was at a window now, sliding it open as gently as he could. Unfortunately for him, the sound of the window was very familiar to Sangster who, even in the dark, was able to pinpoint it and position himself.

Entering from outside, the hitter had no night vision inside the room. That was a mistake. He should have taken steps to make sure he'd be able to see when he entered the room. Having been inside the entire time, not having to deal with moonlight, Sangster could see very well as first a leg came through the window, then a shoulder, and then a gun. Another mistake. The man

should have led with the gun, first. Where was Primble getting these guys?

Sangster's first swing knocked the gun from the hitter's hand. It flew across the room into the darkness and landed with a few clatters and a thud.

The man yelled, staggered as his other foot came in through the window. Sangster picked a knee and let fly with the bat. There was a satisfying popping sound accompanied by a nice tremor up through the bat and into his arms. It was like hitting a home run.

Primble's man screamed and went down, holding on to his knee with both hands. Sangster took a moment to turn on a nearby lamp, then moved it so that the light shone into the man's eyes, illuminating his face.

"Quiet down," Sangster said.

"Oh, man!" the guy shouted. "Aw, my knee!"

"If you don't shut up, I'll pop the other one."

"What the hell, man?" the guy moaned.

"Okay," Sangster said, and pulled the bat back for another swing.

"No, wait!" the man screamed.

"What?"

"I'll—I'll try to q-quiet down."

Sangster relaxed, letting the bat come back down. He pressed the barrel against the man's chest to get his attention again, prodded him a bit.

"Name?" he said.

"O-O'Malley," the man said, "Jimmy O'Malley."

"You work for Primble." That wasn't so much a question as it was a statement.

"Y-yes."

O'Malley's face was all screwed up in pain, but while one hand was clutching his knee the other one was moving down his leg.

"You pull that gun from your ankle holster and I'll split your head like a watermelon."

O'Malley's hand came away as if the gun was scalding. Sangste

retrieved the little twenty-two and sent it sailing in the same direction as the other gun.

"How many of you are here?"

"T-two."

"The other one outside?"

"No."

"What's the other one's name?"

"Guiliano," the injured man said, "Silk Guilianio."

"Silk?" Sangster asked. "Is that his real name?"

"Shit, man, I dunno," O'Malley whined.

Sangster put pressure on the bat, still pressing it into the man's chest, then patted him down. No third gun, no wallet. All he found was a King of Spades in the man's pocket.

"What's this?"

"W-we cut for you."

"What?"

"We cut the cards to see who would try you first," O'Malley said. "I—I won."

Sangster placed the barrel of the bat beneath the man's chin and said, "Now, Jimmy, I think you lost."

The next morning, Ed Primble met Silk Guiliani at Café Dumond for a breakfast of coffee and begnets. Primble was already present, working on his second cup of coffee. There was a fine mist of powder on the lapels of his dark suit. Normally fastidious about his appearance, he didn't seem to mind.

"He didn't come back," Silk said, sitting opposite Primble.

"He's probably dead."

"Then I win."

Primble licked three of his fingers, then waggled one of them at the younger man.

"Not until you've killed him," he said. "That was the wager."

"But . . . he can't win if he's dead."

"And neither can you," Primble said. "You'll have to take your

shot, Silk. That's the only way you'll win . . . or lose, clearly and fairly."

A waitress came over. Silk asked for coffee and then waved her off when she started to ask if he wanted a begnet. Primble, however, stopped her and asked her to bring him still another of the delicious powdered pastries.

"How can you come to New Orleans and not have a begnet from Café Dumond?" he asked.

"I'm not hungry."

"Could that be because you're a little nervous?"

"I'm a lot nervous, Primble," Silk said. "I'm not a fool. I know Sangster was your best, once."

"He was the very best I ever saw," Primble said.

"Well then, it's only natural that I'd be . . . concerned."

"Not . . . scared?"

"No, not scared. Jimmy was good, though. If Sangster took him out, then he's still got skills."

"Of course he's got skills," Primble said, "which is more than I could say for Jimmy O'Malley."

"You didn't think Jimmy was good?"

Primble made a face.

"Second-rate, at best."

"And me?"

"You?" Primble asked. He sat back then, fell silent as the waitress set his new treat in front of him.

"Sure you won't have a bite?" he asked Silk.

"Answer my question, Primble," Silk said. "Do you think I'm second-rate . . . or first?"

Primble took a bite of the begnet, sending a whole new curtain of powder down upon himself.

"That, dear boy," he said, "remains to be seen."

• • •

6

Sangster did not want to give Primble or his second man time to adjust to missing Jimmy O'Malley, so he caught the first ferry in the morning to Algiers. He refused Burke's offer of a gun, and also the old man's offer to go with him.

"If I don't come back, everything in the house is yours."

"Who you kiddin'? You ain't got nothin' in that house."

"There's good beer in the fridge."

"That I'll take."

The two men shook hands at the dock.

Once he was in the Quarter, he knew where Primble was staying, but not where Silk Guiliano was staying. That meant Primble had to tell him where Guiliano was, even if he didn't want to.

He arrived outside the Lafitte House early enough to catch Primble coming out. He followed the man to Café Dumond, watched him consume four begnets, two before a man joined him, and two after. Sangster assumed this was Silk Guiliani.

He watched while the two men spoke. Primble remained calm, Guiliani became agitated. Sangster knew this because the man did not eat a begnet. He had to be otherwise occupied to be able to resist eating just one.

When the two men left at the same time, Sangster followed Guiliani, since he already knew where Primble was staying.

Guiliani seemed to wander the Quarter aimlessly. Sangster remained half a block behind him and across the street, reasonably certain he had gone unnoticed. He trailed the man for a couple of hours. During that time, there were any number of locations that would have lent themselves to murder. One in particular was when the man ducked down Pirate's Alley which, at that time of the day, was not very busy. It would have been relatively easy to take the man right in front of The Faulkner House, drag him into the shadows of St. Louis Cathedral, and kill him—if he had been so inclined.

He was not.

After two and a half hours, Guiliani finally stopped somewhere—

a restaurant called Remalade's, on Bourbon Street. Sangster knew the place, had eaten there many times. He crossed the street and looked in the window. Since Guiliani worked for Primble, he halfway expected the man to be gone, perhaps out the back door. Instead, the other man had been seated at a table away from the few other diners in the place.

Sangster decided this was as good a place and time as any. . . .

"Silk Guiliani?"

The man looked up, frowned.

"Who's asking?"

"I think you know."

Silk's eyes widened.

"Sangster?"

"That's right. Mind if I sit?"

Before Silk could say a word, Sangster was seated across from him.

"I think we need to talk."

"About what?"

"Your friend O'Malley. He gave you up."

"He's not my friend."

"Colleague, then."

"Whatever."

Sangster looked around. The waitress who was approaching was unfamiliar to him. That was good.

"Have you ordered yet? I'd suggest a Po' Boy. They do them really well here."

"I . . . was just gonna have a drink."

"Good. I'll join you. A beer all right?"

"Fine."

As the waitress reached them, Sangster said, "Two Abitas, please."

"Yessir."

"You'll like it. It's a good beer."

"What do you want, Sangster?"

"I want to save your life."

"Save my life?"

"That's right."

"I thought you told Primble you don't kill any more."

Sangster smiled. The man had just admitted to working for Primble. That was on Primble's list of things not to do.

"That's right, I don't."

"Then what do I have to fear?"

"I don't know."

The waitress came with two sweating bottles of Abita.

"Ahh," Sangster said, after downing a good-sized swallow.

Guiliani lifted his bottle to his mouth, preparing to take a drink. Moving quickly, Sangster drove the heel of his hand into the bottom of the bottle, in turn driving that into the other man's mouth. Teeth broke, blood spurted, and Guiliani screamed. He dropped the bottle and pressed his hands against his mouth.

Sangster got to his feet, took Guiliani by the shoulders, and took him to the floor, chair and all.

"You're not good enough, Silk," he hissed into the bleeding man's ear before anyone could reach them. "Go home!"

He got to his feet and was out the door as the waitress and another person reached Guiliani and began to ask him what was wrong.

7

When Edward Primble entered his suite at the Lafitte House on Bourbon Street, he stopped short. His stomach muscles tensed as he noticed Sangster sitting in the large wicker chair at the far end of the room. He half expected a bullet to rip through his chest, but Sangster was sitting very calmly, his left ankle resting on his right thigh.

"How did you get in here?" Primble asked.

"Easy," Sangster said. "I just asked downstairs what the most expensive suite was. Then I asked if it was available. When they said no, I knew it was yours."

"Smart," Primble said. He'd been inching toward a small table near the door with one drawer in it. Sangster pretended not to notice. Finally, Primble lunged, opened the drawer and took out a handgun. It was small, a silver thirty-two that held five shots. He pointed it at Sangster and grinned.

"Now what?" he asked.

"It would work better with these." Sangster tossed all five bullets onto the floor between them. Primble paled as they struck the carpet, rolled, and lay still.

"What do you want to bet I can get to you before you can get one of those loaded?"

Sangster was surprised Primble actually thought it over, but finally he put up the gun, then tossed it onto the bed. He showed Sangster his empty hands.

"So," Primble said. "Have you come to kill me?"

"I told you, Ed," Sangster said. "I don't do that any more."

"What about O'Malley?"

"He's not dead. He's in the hospital, but he's not dead."

"And Silk?"

"I suspect he's in the emergency room, about now," Sangster said, "but not dead. He'll probably need some dental work, though. I expect you'll stand good for all their medical bills?"

"You did all this without killing them, and without a gun?" Primble asked.

"That's right."

Primble smiled.

"And you said you were retired."

"I am."

"Retired, but not rusty."

"Very rusty," Sangster said. "Luckily, the men you sent against me weren't very good."

"I didn't send them," Primble said. "They volunteered."

"You pay them, and you told them where I was."

"They're not being paid," Primble said.

"Oh, that's right," Sangster said, "there was a bet."

"The winner gets your old job."

"Which you've held open for three years, hoping I'd come back?" Sangster asked.

"Of course."

"I'm flattered, Ed."

"Don't be," Primble said. "You're one of a kind, Sangster. A natural. I never saw anyone take to it the way you did. No conscience, and no soul. The perfect killing machine."

"Not any more."

"Why?" Primble asked. "Just tell me why."

"I woke up one morning, and there they were," Sangster said. "My soul, my conscience."

"Just like that?"

"Just like that."

Primble frowned.

"I've lost it, Ed. It's gone. I can't do it any more."

"Maybe if you . . . tried?"

"What about today?" Sangster asked. "Your O'Malley and Silk. If it was in me—anywhere in me, any more—don't you think I would have killed them? And you?"

"Well, them, maybe," Primble said, "but not me. We go back a long ways, Sangster."

"Were we friends, Ed?" Sangster asked. "Were we ever friends?"

"Sure we were. We were—"

"When's my birthday?"

Primble didn't answer.

"Where am I from originally?"

No answer.

"What's my first name?"

"Okay," Primble said, "so I sluff off the personal details. They never mattered, Sangster. What mattered was you did the job. Every time. No hitches."

"Read my lips, Ed," Sangster said. "Not any more."

He got up from the chair and Primble tensed, his eyes going to the gun on the bed, then the bullets on the floor. Sangster started for the door, stopped next to Primble, who was several inches shorter than he was. He leaned down to speak into the smaller man's ear.

"Don't send those two after me again, Ed. Don't send anyone else after me. Or we might have to really test out your theory that it's still in me."

"Sangster—"

"Shhh," Sangster said. "Don't say anything else. There's nothing else to say. The next time I see you, Ed, I'll kill you."

"But . . . you just said you can't—"

"Assassinate," Sangster said, "I don't—can't—assassinate any more. Maybe, though—just maybe—I can still kill in self-defense."

He patted Primble on the shoulder—felt the man start—and then went out the door.

8

"Why do you have to leave?" Burke asked.

They were sitting on Sangster's porch, having one last chess match. Next to Sangster was his packed suitcase. Just one. When he traveled now, he traveled light.

"They'll leave you alone, won't they?" Burke asked. "They haven't come back yet."

"It's only been three days," Sangster said. "They might get their courage back up. I don't want to be here if they do. I don't want to think about what might happen."

"Oh, well," Burke said, moving a piece. "Checkmate."

Sangster smiled, stood up and put out his hand. Burke stood and shook it.

"It's been fun, Burke."

"Stay," Burke said. "If they come, I can help you."

"No, I can't."

"Where will you go?"

"I can't tell you that," he said. "What you don't know, you can't tell."

"I'd never tell."

"They wouldn't ask politely, Burke."

"At least take a gun—"

"No," Sangster said. "Good-bye, Burke."

"'Bye, Sangster."

He picked up his suitcase and went down the steps. He hadn't reached the end of the walk when Burke shouted, "Hey."

"What?" he asked, turning.

"Is Sangster your real name?"

He shrugged and said, "It's the only one I've used since I was fifteen. I guess it's as real as any name can be."

He was sitting down at the ferry depot when it hit him. Just leaving was not going to be the answer. They would come, and they would ask Burke where he was. And once they believed that he did not know, they'd kill him. Could he, in all good conscience, leave Burke in that position?

It was four days later—a full week since Primble had found Sangster waiting for him in his suite at the Lafitte House. Primble entered his Brentwood home, tossed his keys into a vase he kept by the front door for that purpose, then went into the den to pour himself a drink. It was a routine he always went through when he got home. He stopped short, though. Sangster was there, seated in a chair. His position was exactly the same as it had been in the wicker chair in New Orleans.

"I knew it," Primble said. "I knew you'd be back. I just didn't think it would take you this long."

"I was just wondering how long it would have taken you to send someone else after me, or looking for me, in Algiers. When they didn't find me there, they'd question my friend Burke, torture him, then kill him. I couldn't let that happen. I didn't want that on my conscience."

"So you came back."

"Just to remove any possibility of that happening."

"Welcome home, then, Sangster. In fact, I just today got an assignment that would be right up your alley."

Sangster stood up, approached Primble. He removed his gloved hand from his pocket, holding a small throwaway piece, a Saturday Night Special. When Primble saw it he said, "Hey, wait—" but Sangster pressed the barrel to the man's belly and fired. There was only a low pop. Primble's body jerked. As he started to fall, Sangster caught him and eased him to the floor. Primble's eyes were glazed, confused, as he stared up at Sangster.

"B-but . . . your soul—"

"Is probably damned anyway," Sangster said. He stood up. "But this way, at least my conscience will be clear."

He aimed the gun at Primble's head and fired.

Karma Hits Dogma

BY JEFF ABBOTT

Jeff Abbott is the author of three novels of suspense set on the Texas Gulf Coast. One of them, *Black Jack Point* (Onyx, 2002), was nominated for an Edgar. His short story "Bet on Red" was also nominated last year from the Randisi anthology *High Stakes* (Onyx, 2003). This story features one of the more unusual motives for someone to hire a hit man.

"HE KILLED MY DOG," Massini said, "so I want you to kill him."

Ames sipped at his coffee. It tasted of hazelnut, which surprised him. Massini didn't look like a man who would drink sweet coffee. He was in his seventies, with the look of a gnarled old piece of wood, a face only dogs could love. Ames smelled the barest reek of stale deodorant over the tang of old skin and cigarette smoke when Massini leaned close.

"Killing a man over a dog. It's a big step," Ames said. Thinking, *Jesus, this won't be worth the money or the pat on the head from my boss, wondering if he could talk this old coot out of misguided revenge.*

"What goes around comes around," Massini said, solemn as a mourner. "You a dog lover?"

Ames fought down the urge to answer, "No, I've never made love with a dog," but he saw the pain in the old man's face, a grief hiding behind the scowl. So instead he drank some more of the nutty-sugary coffee and said, "Yeah, Mr. Massini, I like dogs a lot."

"Good," Massini said. "It shows character to be fond of dogs. Because anybody can be mean to an animal, but being nice to an animal takes thought. Consideration." He put his hand on his chest. "It takes a heart. Now. This man I want you to kill. His name is Johnny Walker. Like the whiskey except Johnny spelled with a y."

"How'd he kill your dog?"

"Ran over her. A great little bitch named Mona. Pomeranian." He stared down at his coffee cup.

"Mr. Massini. With all due respect, that sounds like it was an accident."

"Doesn't matter. My dog's still dead and he's still driving. He's a public menace." Massini stared at him. "I want vengeance, my money's good. You want a client or not?"

"Murdering a man is serious business, sir. I don't have to take the job. I need to know exactly what I'm getting into before I go and, um, avenge Mona."

Massini lit a cigarette with a hack, blew out smoke, frowned. "You think I'm an old fool. A dead dog, not worth all this trouble. But I loved that dog. My ingrate kids don't bother to call me. I outlived three wives. All I had was Mona."

"I could get you a new dog, sir," Ames said. "It's less trouble than homicide."

"New dog. And here'll come Johnny Walker with his old Jaguar and turn my new dog into pudding. No. I want him dead." He pointed the lit cigarette at Ames. "You work for Tessarella, and he owes me a lot of favors. A lot. He said you'd help me, not debate me."

"A new dog might bring you closure." Ames's ex-wife loved to talk about closure.

Massini stubbed out the cigarette in anger, half of it unsmoked. "Closure's overrated. Revenge is what lets you sleep at night.

Knowing you've made the bastard who hurt you pay a price, and the bastard knowing that you did it to him. It's Rule Number One in life, and I have never wavered from it."

Ames kept back a long sigh. These old men lacked perspective as much as a small child. What about wisdom coming with age? It had passed by this old man. "Fine, I'll help you, Mr. Massini."

"Good. It's not too early to drink, is it? It's five o'clock somewhere." Massini got up, fetched a bottle from the kitchen cabinet, and set it down in front of Ames with two glasses. Johnnie Walker Red.

"Never say I don't have a sense of humor," Massini said with a wicked-sick grin.

Johnny Walker lived a block down from Mr. Massini, in another small tidy condominium that faced the Atlantic. The Florida sky was faultless blue, and Ames, happy to be out of the blear and cold of Chicago, wanted to lie on the welcoming sands and hang out in the bars in South Beach and drink mojitos or Jamaican beer, which, he imagined, was how a tourist in Miami spent his time. He had never been to Florida before. Instead he sat in his car, as obvious and noticeable to a neighborhood of old people as he could be, waiting for Mr. Walker to show up. Massini provided a detailed schedule for Walker, who was as reliable in his movements as the sun. Walker was due home in thirty minutes. So Ames got out of the car, dressed in a nice suit that no burglar would wear, walked to the front door with the firm spine of a person with an appointment, and he jimmied the knob with a lockpick and was inside in a matter of seconds.

The air was cool, the room lit only by the faint glow of a lamp. There was no alarm system in the condo, or at the least it had not been activated. He moved quickly through the room. He was not going to sit and wait for Walker; Massini had stressed this could not be seen as murder. Massini and Walker screamed and argued over poor dead Mona in the cul-de-sac, each blaming the other for the tragedy, Walker trying to shrink back into his skin under Massini's verbal onslaught. The neighbors knew of their feud.

Massini had publicly forgiven Walker last month at the home-owners' association meeting, to warm applause. Walker wasn't there; he kept a low profile, didn't mix, didn't mingle, according to Massini, who found such privacy highly suspect. But Massini couldn't be suspected when Walker turned up dead.

So poison or a staged accident were the best bets.

He went straight to Walker's medicine cabinet to find a fast over-dose he could pour down Walker's throat. Nothing. No blood med-ications, no pain relievers beyond aspirin, no bottles of syrup to ward off wintertime coughs. Nothing except a sample package of Viagra and an unopened box of condoms, and he thought Massini would prefer that Walker expire without a smile on his face. He shut the medicine cabinet. No electronics in the bathroom that could, oops, slide into the tub and make Walker dance the last second of his life away. He went back into the den and inspected the stairs—they turned twice while leading up to the second floor, making for too short of a fall to break a neck.

Fate was funny, he thought, when it prodded a dog to dart into a not-busy street and change three lives—not counting the unfortunate dog. Massini's, Walker's. Even his, Ames knew, if he got caught. He won-dered what he had been doing at the exact moment Mona made her fatal dash. Probably watching TV back home in Chicago, blissfully unaware he'd soon be flying down to avenge a hyperactive dog.

If there were no medications to tamper with or accidents to stage, it was back to basics. Strangle or knife the old guy, make it look like a robbery interrupted. The old folks would freak but the suspicion would certainly not be on the humorous Mr. Massini. He could take the old man's wallet and watch. There didn't seem to be much else in the condo that could tempt a burglar. A small TV, no VCR or DVD player, no computer, no women's jewelry. He could tear the mattress open, leave a ten wedged in the tatters to suggest Walker kept a stash of cash. But that implied that the killer knew Walker—burglars didn't hunt in mattresses any more—and therefore wouldn't work. He needed to create a sense of the random. So trash the place, make it look like the burglar had expected to find a bounty and killed the old man in a rage. Not much of a story, but he didn't have much to work with. Murder had been done for pennies. It would have to do.

Ames sat to wait for Walker. Let his eyes wander the walls.

Odd. No pictures. There were no photos of Walker or his loved ones in the house, nothing to indicate the man had a life. The condo had all the personality of a hotel room. A couch, a TV, a few magazines on a cheap coffee table, a bare desk in the corner.

The minimalism bothered Ames. Such sterility was not how old people lived; they clung to the clutter of their lives, especially photos of kids and grandkids. Ames pulled a handkerchief from his pocket and used it to open a desk drawer. Empty, except for a slick black Glock in the desk drawer. Cleaned and primed and loaded. He unloaded and replaced the gun, a wary tickle feathering his gut. He checked the bedside table. No gun, but a peek under the pillow showed a Beretta. He unloaded the second gun.

"You old fart," Ames said to the absent Walker. He kept searching—under the bed, behind the drawers, in the toilet's tank. Nothing. He went to the refrigerator. The top section held the freezer—and, hidden behind rock-hard chicken breasts and a dented box of waffles, he found the third gun.

Well. The refrigerator sealed it for Ames. He might have thought Walker to be a collector, or a citizen keeping guns on hand for protection, but stashing a gun in the fridge implied you needed to get to it when company was around. It was a preparation for betrayal. Now either Massini had mouthed off to the point old Walker thought he was in mortal danger, or Walker wasn't some harmless old man with substandard driving skills and a simmering hatred of small yippy dogs.

Ames left the third gun loaded. One reason for the firepower might be money; Mr. Walker might not be a believer in banks. He went back to the bedroom, started pulling out the bureau drawers. On the back of the first one he found an envelope taped; he started prying open the envelope, saw a wad of bills.

Then he heard a key sliding into the front door's lock.

Calmly, he eased the drawer home, ducked backward into the old man's closet. He would ask old Walker a few questions: why the armory, why the cash; then he would stage a suicide with Walker's remaining loaded gun, get the rest of his money from Massini, and hit the beach.

He heard the old man come into the bedroom, pick up the phone, punch numbers. Ames waited; not a good idea to kill someone while they chatted on the line.

"Hi. Yeah. Listen, I got to pull up stakes." A pause. "No, no problem with the papers you did. I got a serious hassle with a neighbor who might know some rough types. So I need new papers. License, birth cert, credit cards, the works." A pause. "I need it yesterday, Roger. How soon?" Another pause. "Yeah, okay, I'll meet you there. Okay. How much?" A third pause. "You price-hiking bastard. All right. All right. Yeah, cash. Make the license for Alabama, please. I'm gonna go to Mobile. I got spoiled by the warm weather down here." Then Walker said his goodbyes and hung up.

Well, Ames thought. This is interesting.

Through the crack of the door, Walker came into view, heading back into the kitchen, an old guy but one who walked with a tall bearing. Seventy, at least, but well-built. Ames counted to ten and followed him. He had his back to Ames, washing his hands at the sink.

Ames moved forward, silently, but Walker sensed him and started to turn and Ames pressed the gun into the man's temple. Walker didn't scream in terror or start babbling questions or begging for mercy. It was what most people did. Guns made people forget basic breathing or piss themselves or freeze in absolute terror. But Walker just stopped washing his hands and he left his palms open, dripping bubbles of soap.

"There's a towel over there if you want to hand it to me," Walker said. "Or are you just going to shoot me?"

"Who are you?"

"Johnny Walker."

"I know your name. I'm just wondering what you are. *What* you are."

"I'm retired."

"Most harmless old men don't have three guns in the house and a need for fake identities."

Walker gave off a long sigh. "Who you with?"

"That doesn't matter."

Walker laughed, to Ames's surprise. "I knew it. Is this about that dog?"

"Yes." Ames decided he owed the man the truth about why he would die.

Walker tilted his head slightly so that it rested against the gun's barrel. "I figured Massini might hire a gun. He's ex-mob, isn't he?"

This, Ames wasn't willing to admit, even to a dead man walking, and he said, "No, I don't think so."

"Please. He got drunk on cheap beer at the Super Bowl party up at the clubhouse last year, he bragged about his connections up in Chicago when he was trying to impress a new lady. Mentioned a number of Italian names. He was a dentist to important men, he says."

Ames knew that part was true: Massini had filled cavities and done root canals on some of the most dangerous and powerful crime families in the Midwest. He had also removed teeth from mob-killed corpses so they could not be identified from dental records after gasoline burning. DNA testing made Massini less useful. But favors done were favors done. Regardless, Massini didn't need to be tossing around names. "I have no comment."

"I can't believe you're going to kill me over a dog."

"He loved his dog," Ames said.

"Sure he did. But accidents happen. You going to kill me over an accident, son?"

Maybe not when you might be a very interesting opportunity, Ames thought. "Who are you really? Why are you hiding?"

Walker stayed quiet.

"Don't make our dealings more difficult," Ames said.

"More difficult? Jesus, you're going to kill me," Walker said.

"Listen, son, whatever's Massini's paying you, I can double it if you let me go."

"Sorry. That's against the rules. My boss would disapprove of me cutting a separate deal with you."

"You don't say that with great conviction," Walker said. "Think about what's best for you—"

Ames did. He clubbed Walker with the butt of the gun and the old man collapsed. He was careful not to hit Walker too hard because he didn't want him dead. Ames found an extension cord in the closet and he tied Walker with it, wrapped masking tape over the man's mouth, leaving the nostrils clear, checking for and finding a steady tide of breath.

Ames thought: sometimes you get a bit of good fortune, out of the blue, and you have to recognize it for what it is. A bit of providence floating down from God, maybe, or just life tossing you a real sweet break because you've been a good boy.

He went back to the bedroom. After another thirty minutes of searching, he found over fifty thousand hidden in the bedroom, in the dead spaces behind drawers and under furniture. No more guns, no other evidence pointing to why Walker lived a hidden life.

He hit redial on the phone, waited for an answer.

It came on the fifth ring. "Yeah?" Presumably this was Roger. His voice sounded like he swallowed gravel on a regular basis.

"Roger, hello. I have Mr. Walker here in my own private custody. I understand you were to create new papers for him."

Roger hung up.

Sighing, Ames hit redial again. Pickup on the fifth ring again.

"Roger. Hi. Now don't be difficult. It makes me irritable. Here's the deal. I'm guessing you supply Mr. Walker with his papers, you know who he really is. I just need a name. Or I can give him to the cops and let them sort it out. But if I give him to the cops, I'm going to give them you along with him. It's double-coupon day. Now. Save me and you a world of grief. Who is he?"

Silence.

"Roger, I'm going to write your name and phone number on Mr. Walker's forehead when I leave him tied up and call the cops to report him as a fugitive from justice. If you want to save your business, I suggest you help me."

"Who the hell is this?" Roger's voice lost the gravelly growl, had risen an octave in panic.

"I'm either your new best friend or your worst enemy. There's not a thing you can do to help Mr. Walker. All you can do is help yourself. Now. What's his real name?"

"I don't have any proof you have him."

"Hold, please." He filled a pot full of cold water and dumped it on Walker. The man jerked awake, moaned, looked around in confusion and fear.

"Say hi to Roger," Ames said, yanking the tape loose from Walker's mouth and holding the phone where Walker could speak into it.

"Roger?" Walker said. "Jesus, help me. . . ."

"You got that, Roger?" Ames took the phone away from Walker's mouth, smoothed the tape back over the lips. "Here's what he said to you when he called." And he repeated Walker's side of the conversation, nearly verbatim. "He's an old man. You sound young. Years to live. Tell me his real name."

Silence again. "Jerry Patrick. That's all I know, okay? Leave me out of this."

"Thank you. Do you know why he was running?"

"Jesus, man, they don't fill out questionnaires. I told you what I know. We never talked." He hung up.

Ames hung up the phone. "Roger," he said to the wide-eyed Walker, "has abandoned you to my tender mercies."

Ames's cell phone rang. He answered it.

Massini. "Is the job done?"

Hell. He didn't want to kill Walker until he found out if there was more money to be made from this stroke of luck, if someone somewhere was willing to pay for Mr. Patrick. But he also didn't want

Massini to know about any side deals. "You're not supposed to call me. Ever. You know the rules. I'll call you. Later." He hung up, switched off his phone.

"Mr. Patrick," Ames said to the man, and at the name Walker closed his eyes. "Do you have a computer around here I could please borrow, sir?"

Walker/Patrick didn't, so Ames tied him more completely, gave him another love tap on the back of the head so he'd sleep, locked him in a closet, and drove to a nearby library that offered free computer access. He fired up a search engine and started hunting for Jerry Patrick, adding words like missing and crime to the mix.

He found him fast. Jerry Patrick had vanished a year ago. He was a CPA in Brooklyn, no wife, no kids, no criminal record except for a couple of tickets for reckless driving. The article mentioned rumblings and rumors that Patrick laundered money for the Quintana crime family, but nothing had been proven. The Quintanas were still alive and kicking, so Mr. Patrick had presumably not gone to the Feds. The picture in the newspaper did not do Walker justice; he looked healthier and happier now: Florida had agreed with him but had not improved his driving.

Back at Walker's, Ames made a couple of calls to friends, got a direct number to reach Lucio Quintana.

He took a deep breath and dialed.

"Yeah?"

"Mr. Quintana?"

"Who's this?"

"My name doesn't matter. I'm the guy who's going to make your day. I got Jerry Patrick tied up in a Florida apartment. He's yours for a price."

A long pause, long enough that Ames knew he'd hit a jackpot. "I don't know no Jerry Patrick."

"Sure you do, sir. I think he took off, and he took off with a great deal of your money. I can either keep what's left of your money and off Mr. Patrick, or I can give you back Mr. Patrick so you can find where he's hidden the rest of your green. And you can pay me a nice reward." His heart pounded. This was pushing the limits, this was the big score he had dreamed of.

Silence, just like Roger at first. It was the sound of bad luck for Walker, good luck for Ames.

"Let's talk," Quintana said.

That night Ames kept Walker tied up in the closet, fed him dry cereal and water, gave him a bathroom break if he remembered. Ames glanced out of the windows every few hours and saw lights burning, all night long, at the Massini condo.

The next morning, Quintana sent a man to collect Walker and the cash. Quintana's man took a long hard look at Walker, spat in the old man's face, and then opened a briefcase. Fifty thousand. Sweet. Massini paid him ten to off Walker, so this was more money than he ever made in a day. A tidal wave of good luck, all because an old man ran over a dog. Life was crazy.

"One question," Quintana's man said. "How'd you get interested in him?"

"Not your worry," Ames said.

"Yes my worry," the man said. "It will put Mr. Quintana's mind at ease to know who you are."

"Just a concerned citizen," Ames said. He nodded to Walker, who had been stoic during the night but now had tears welling in his eyes. "Good luck to you, sir." He gave a little laugh, shook the hand of Quintana's man, left the house with his cash. Quintana's man let him go.

Massini, five doors down, misted water over his flowerbeds.

Hell, Ames thought. Massini'd pitch a fit, over nothing, Walker was as good as dead. Quintana's people would work him over, wring the last of the money from him, kill him and dump him in the ocean. That was as sure a deal as the setting sun.

So he slowed as he passed Massini's yard, he gave the slightest of nods, he held up his fingers in an O of okay, jerked a thumb toward his trunk.

Massini nodded and frowned, and glanced down the street. Quintana's man's car wasn't parked in front of Walker's house, but maybe Massini had seen him head into the condo, maybe he wondered if Ames spent the night in the condo, and Ames could see the questions forming in Massini's mind.

Ames kept driving, not looking back.

Three days later, Ames had vroomed through a nice chunk of the Quintana money, spending green on a South Beach hotel room, a high-priced Swedish whore, and several excellent meals. At night he watched the jewel-like stars wink over Florida, his lucky stars. Over breakfast he read about a disappearance in a Miami neighborhood. Johnny Walker, a retiree from Kansas City, had vanished from his house during the past week. His car was missing, but he had not indicated to any neighbors that he was planning a trip. One neighbor, Dominic Massini, described him as pleasant but a man who kept very much to himself. The authorities asked for anyone who had contact with Mr. Walker to call.

His cell phone rang. "Yeah?"

"Mr. Ames. This is Dominic Massini. How are you enjoying your vacation?"

"I thought we agreed not to be in touch right now."

"Well, I assume the job is done."

"Yes." He had already thought of his lie. "It's done. It's best you don't know details, but it's done."

"Please allow me to show you my gratitude."

"That's not necessary, sir. Your happiness is all the thanks I need."

"Don't BS me, son," Massini said. "Come over for dinner. I'll cook you up a steak."

"Thanks, but we should really keep our distance."

"Hey, I talked with your boss, he said it was fine. If it's fine with him, I'll bet it's fine with you."

Old men, Ames thought with amused contempt. They always had to try and pay you back with kindness. Whatever. He'd do it to keep peace with his boss, Massini's friend. He'd have to cancel dinner with the Swedish call girl, just have dessert with her. Or on her. The thought made him nearly laugh.

"See you at seven," Massini said.

"If it's not too forward," Ames said, "I thought you'd like a new dog." He handed Massini the mutt that he'd found at the pound. He was unsure of what had possessed him to come bearing a puppy; guilt, perhaps, although guilt was not an emotion with which he had deep acquaintance. The dog reminded him of Massini: tough, small, determined. He loathed the reek of the pound, worried about the dog smell worming its way into his new Armani suit, picked the puppy that seemed to want to leave its cage the most and hurried out.

The dog wriggled in Massini's arms, gave the old man's ugly face a quick inspection, then licked his chin.

"Ah, hell," Massini said. "Hello, baby. Hello—hello—hello," he cooed.

"I'm glad you like him," Ames said.

"My weakness." Massini went inside, still cradling the dog. "Damn, I wasn't ready for another dog but now that you forced the issue. . . ." He settled the dog onto the floor, picked up a yellow plastic bowl marked MONA with careful black block letters, gushed water into it from the faucet. "Mona wouldn't mind, no she wouldn't."

He scratched the dog's head and glanced up at Ames. "Thank you, son," he said.

"You're welcome."

Dinner was steak, grilled to bloody perfection, salad, pasta laced with Parmesan and butter, a steady flow of good Barbera wine, and Ames felt himself mellowing. Massini seemed a new man, bright and cheery, the weight of his revenge eased from his shoulders. The new dog sat close to Massini, overwhelmed with the affection the old man showed, and drunk on tossed chunks of rare steak.

"I got to name this dog," Massini said.

"Mona Junior," Ames said. He'd drunk most of the wine and he felt giddy in his bones.

"No. No one could replace Mona, I got to love this puppy-pup in a whole new way. And he's a he. I think I'll call him Niccolo. He looks like a Niccolo."

"Yes, actually he does," Ames said.

Massini scratched the dog's ears. "I want to see the body, please."

Ames swallowed a gulp of Barbera. "Excuse me?"

"Walker's body. I'd like to see it, please."

"It's in the Everglades, Mr. Massini, I don't think I could find it again."

"We'll try," Mr. Massini said.

"I have another appointment this evening," Ames said, thinking of the Swedish girl. "I'm sorry."

"I want to see the body, right now, and I want you to take me there." He reached for his phone. "I got your boss on my speed-dial, Mr. Ames. I think you've had a hair too much to drink, so I'll drive."

"It's not good to revisit the site of a body dumping. What if the police have found it and we show up there?"

"Then you didn't do a very good job, did you?" Mr. Massini said. "Let's go."

Niccolo rode between them, hind legs on the seat, front legs on the dashboard. Ames's throat burned like he had a fever. Massini drove. They took Alligator Alley, the thin line of toll road that shot west from Miami across the green and damp of the 'Glades. It was late, little traffic, and the stars glistened above like wet eyes watching.

"Here," Ames said, afraid they would run out of Everglades soon. There were very few exits on the road, and as they went past the Big Cypress National Preserve they hit a small highway that cut across the Alley.

"Go south," Ames said. Massini took the exit onto Highway 29, drove toward the small hamlet of Copeland.

"I think it was near here," Ames lied. He rubbed his bottom lip. It felt raw. "There was an abandoned road. It headed east. . . ."

He knows I didn't kill Walker. But how could he? He couldn't know. He couldn't. That was the deal with Quintana, not a word spoken. No. This was just an old man, wanting to be sure, making sure he got his money's worth. It was an insult, where had trust gone? He'd told Massini Walker would be dead; Walker was dead.

He could bluster his way through this. Massini was a soft old fool, he would tire of being out in this netherworld of gators and mosquitoes and muck after about an hour or so. An hour of tromping around and they would be done. And if not . . . he had his gun. He saw the solution clearly. He could manufacture a sweet lie for his bosses if Massini vanished. Ames had killed Walker; Walker, let's say, was under the shield of the Feds; the Feds made Massini vanish into WitSec. Or killed him. Yeah. It would work. No one the wiser.

You get an hour, old man, he thought. He felt a sick twist of regret that he might have to kill the dog. It would be cruel to leave a dog out here for the gators to eat, and he couldn't take Niccolo back to the pound. He liked the dog. Maybe he could take it back to Miami, leave it in Massini's neighborhood. Another old person would find it and love it. Oh, well, he thought, let the show begin.

"It was off this road," Ames said, grasping at an opportunity, pointing at an unpaved track that threaded back into the deep of the Glades. Massini turned. They drove for another ten minutes and then Ames said, "Here."

They both got out of the car. The ground was a patchwork: dry humps, wet mud, fingers of swamp burrowing through, the grass high and lazy and silvered in the moonlight. Massini brought a heavy flashlight and he pressed it into Ames's hands.

"Show me the way," he said.

"You got to remember," Ames said, "It was night and I sure wasn't planning on finding it again. It's not like I parked the old guy near markers."

"Night. When I saw you driving away during the day."

"He was in the trunk then, sir. I had other business in Miami. By the time I got out here it was night." The explanation sounded lame to his own ears, but he had learned long ago to stick to a story.

"You got a sharp memory, you can find it again," Massini said. "Let's go." He picked up a shovel from the trunk of the car, holding it in one hand, holding Niccolo in the other.

They trudged into the damp, following the circle of light Ames played along the ground. Ames started to lead Massini in a careful dance.

"Here," he would say. Then: "No, it was further," he would announce after ten stiff digs with the shovel. "The dirt looks wrong."

Massini didn't complain, he would simply hand the flashlight back to Ames and take the shovel.

"I don't think you know where it is," Massini said.

"No, I don't think I do," Ames said. "I'm sorry, sir. The ground all looks the same, I was in a hurry, it was dark, it was raining a little. Maybe the gators pulled him loose. Or the pumas, or whatever the hell those cats out here are called." He turned to suggest that they give up, go back to his hotel for a nice drink, offer to buy a gift for Niccolo and as he turned he heard Niccolo hit the ground on all four paws.

"Don't set him down, there might be snakes—" Ames said and the shovel hit Ames full in the face, then again, and he fell back into the water.

"You cheated me!" Massini screamed. "You didn't kill him, you had someone else do it! Rule Number One! I wanted him to know I'd done it to him, he was dying because of me."

Ames's nose was broken, he couldn't see past the blood in his eyes. He said: "What does it matter?"

"Because I paid you to do it. Not to turn him back over to his bosses, not to make a profit for yourself."

Quintana had talked. Probably bragged about catching Walker, to let folks know no one could escape his reach. Oh, God.

He thought fast. Massini was retired. Fixed income. Bribe him. "I didn't cheat you. You want some of the take? There's plenty for both of us, we're both happy."

The shovel hit him hard again in the head and then Massini scooped up Niccolo and ran.

Ames staggered to his feet. Old dentist running with a dog. Not a problem. Ahead a dancing light showed Massini's threading path through the grass. Ames pulled his gun, fired. Once, nothing. Twice, and the light vanished.

Massini'd fallen on the flashlight, he hoped. Ames staggered forward, barely conscious, teeth loose in his mouth, his nose aching like it had been flattened against his face. No sound of old man breathing through a bullet wound, no yip from the dog.

"I got you a damned dog and you try to kill me!" Ames hollered. He plunged back and forth through the grasses. No old man. No dog.

He heard a car start. His good luck wasn't over yet. He ran in the direction of the engine. He barreled out of the grasses to see Massini behind the wheel of the car, the headlights go bright in his eyes and then dim, and the engine rev hard. The tires squealed against the damp earth and Ames steadied himself to fire, blinking against the afterimage of the lights and blood coursing into his eyes.

He aimed, wavered, fired a shot. The car kept coming and then the car hit him and he flew out of his shoes, the gun parted from his hand, and he landed thirty feet away, into cold mud and water. Cold. Shouldn't be cold, Florida was warm. Cold in Florida should be against the rules.

Above him he saw Massini standing, raising the shovel, blocking the lucky stars.

The Greatest Trick of All

Lee Child is the author of the best-selling "Jack Reacher" series, including last year's *Persuader* and this year's *The Enemy*, both from the Dell Publishing Group. We're pleased to have this neat little tale from him, as he doesn't often contribute to anthologies. I think you'll find yourself drawn in from the first paragraph by the voice.

I COULD HAVE SHOT you in one ear and out the other from a thousand yards. I could have brushed past you in a crowd and you wouldn't have known your throat was cut until you went to nod your head and it rolled away down the street without you. I was the guy you were worrying about when you locked your doors and posted your guards and walked upstairs to bed, only to find me already up there before you, leaning on the dresser, just waiting in the dark.

I was the guy who always found a way.

I was the guy that couldn't be stopped.

But that's over now, I guess.

None of my stuff was original. I studied the best of the best, long ago. I learned from all of them. A move here, a move there, all stitched together. All the tricks. Including the greatest trick of all, which I learned from a man called Ryland. Back in the day Ryland worked all over, but mainly where there was oil, or white powder, or money, or girls, or high-stakes card games. Then he got old, and he slowly withdrew. Eventually he found the matrimonial market. Maybe he invented it, although I doubt that. But certainly he refined it. He turned it into a business. He was in the right place at the right time. Getting old and slowing down, just when all those California lawyers made divorce into a lottery win. Just when guys all over the hemisphere started to get nervous about it.

The theory was simple: a live wife goes to a lawyer, but a dead wife goes nowhere. Except the cemetery. Problem solved. A dead wife attracts a certain level of attention from the police, of course, but Ryland moved in a world where a guy would be a thousand times happier to get a call from a cop than a divorce lawyer. Cops would have to pussyfoot around the grief issue, and there was a general assumption that when it came to IQ, cops were not the sharpest chisels in the box. Whereas lawyers were like razors. And, of course, part of the appeal of a guy like Ryland was that evidence was going to be very thin on the ground. No question, a wife dead at Ryland's hands was generally considered to be a lottery win in reverse.

He worked hard. Hit the microfilm and check it out. Check newspapers all over the States and Central and South America. Look at Europe, Germany, Italy, anyplace where there were substantial fortunes at stake. Look at how many women went missing. Look at how old they were, and how long they had been married. Then check the follow-up stories, the inside pages, the later paragraphs, and see how many hints there were about incipient marital strife. Check it out, and you'll see a pattern.

The cops saw it too, of course. But Ryland was a ghost. He had survived oil and dope and money-lending and hookers and gambling. No way was he going to get brought down by greedy husbands and bored wives. He flourished, and I bet his name was never written down in any cop's file. Not anywhere, not once. He was that good.

He was working back in the days when billionaires were rare. Back then, a hundred million was considered a threshold level. Below a hundred mil, you were poor. Above, you were respectable. People called a hundred mil a unit, and most of Ryland's clients were worth three or four units. And Ryland noticed something: rich husband, rich wife. The wives weren't rich in the sense their husbands were, of course. They didn't have units of their own. But they had spending cash. It stands to reason, Ryland said to me. Guys set them up with bank accounts and credit cards. Guys worth three or four units don't like to trouble themselves with trivia down at the six-figure level.

But the six-figure level was where Ryland worked.

And he noticed that the blood he was spilling was dripping all over minks and diamond chokers and Paris gowns and perforated leather seats in Mercedes Benzes. He started searching purses after a while. There were big checking balances in most of them, and platinum cards. He didn't steal anything, of course. That would have been fatal, and stupid, and Ryland wasn't stupid. Not stupid at all. But he was imaginative.

Or so he claimed.

Actually, I like to believe one of the women handed the idea to him. Maybe one a little feistier than normal. Maybe when it became clear what was about to transpire, she put in a counter-offer. That's how I like to think it all started. Maybe she said: "That rat bastard. I should pay you to off him instead." I know Ryland's ears would have pricked up at that. Anything involving payment would have gotten him interested. He would have run the calculation at the same hyper speed he used for any calculation, from a bullet's trajectory to a risk assessment. He would have figured: this chick can afford a six-figure coat, so she can afford a six-figure hit.

Thus, the greatest trick of all.

Getting paid twice.

He told me about it after he got sick with cancer, and I took it as a kind of anointment. The nomination of an heir. The passing of the baton. He wanted me to be the new Ryland. That was okay with me.

I also took it as a mute appeal not to let him linger and suffer. That was okay with me too. He was frail by then. He resisted the pillow like crazy, but the lights went out soon enough. And there it was. The old Ryland gone, and the new Ryland starting out with new energy.

First up was a stout forty-something from Essen in Germany. Married to a steel baron who had recently found her to be boring. A hundred grand in my pocket would save him a hundred million in hers. Classically, of course, you would hunt and strike before she ever knew you were on the planet. Previously, that would have been the hallmark of a job well done.

But not any more.

I went with her to Gstaad. I didn't travel with her. I just showed up there the next day. Got to know her a little. She was a cow. I would have gladly killed her for free. But I didn't. I talked to her. I worked her around to the point where she said, "My husband thinks I'm too old." Then she looked up at me from under her lashes. It was the usual reassurance-seeking crap. She wanted me to say. "You? Too old? How could he think that about such a beautiful woman?"

But I didn't say that.

Instead, I said, "He wants to get rid of you."

She took it as a question. She answered, "Yes, I think he does."

I said, "No, I know he does. He offered me money to kill you."

Think about it. How was she going to react? No screaming. No running to the Swiss cops. Just utter stunned silence, under the weight of the biggest single surprise she could have heard. First, of course, the conceptual question: "You're an assassin?" She knew people like me existed. She had moved in her husband's world for a long time. Too long, according to him. Then eventually, of course, the inevitable inquiry: "How much did he offer you?"

Ryland had told me to exaggerate a little. In his opinion it gave the victims a little perverse pleasure to hear a big number. It gave them a last shot at feeling needed, in a backhanded way. They weren't wanted any more, but at least it was costing a lot to get rid of them. Status, of a sort.

"Two hundred thousand U.S. dollars," I said.

The fat Essen bitch took that in and then started down the wrong road.

She said, "I could give you that not to."

"Wouldn't work for me," I said. "I can't leave a job undone. He would tell people, and my reputation would be shot. A guy like me, his reputation is all he's got."

Gstaad was a good place to be having the conversation. It was isolated and other-worldly. It was like there was just her and me on the planet. I sat beside her and tried to radiate sympathy. Like a dentist, maybe. When he has to drill a tooth. I'm sorry . . . but it's got to be done. Her anger built, a little slow, but it came. Eventually she got on the right road.

"You work for money," she said.

I nodded.

"You work for anyone who can pay the freight," she said.

"Like a taxicab," I said.

She said, "I'll pay you to kill him."

There was anger there, of course, but there were also financial considerations. They were forming slowly in her mind, a little vaguely, but basically they were the exact obverse of the considerations I had seen in the husband's mind a week previously. People like that, it comes down to just four words: all the money, mine.

She asked, "How much?"

"The same," I said. "Two hundred grand."

We were in Switzerland, which made the banking part easy. I stuck with her, supportive, and watched her get her fat pink paws on two hundred thousand U.S. dollars, crisp new bills from some European country's central reserve. She gave them to me and started to explain where her husband would be, and when.

"I know where he is," I said. "I have a rendezvous set up. For me to get paid."

She giggled at the irony. Guaranteed access to the victim. She wasn't dumb. That was the single greatest strength of Ryland's idea.

We went for a walk, alone, on a snow-covered track rarely frequented by skiers. I killed her there by breaking her fat neck and leaving her in a position that suggested a slip and a fall. Then I took the train back to Essen and kept my rendezvous with the husband. Obviously he had gone to great lengths to keep our meetings secret. He was in a place he wouldn't normally go, alone and unobserved. I collected my fee and killed him too. A silenced .22, in the head. It was an article of faith for people like Ryland and me. If you get paid, you have to deliver.

So, two fees, and all those steel units cascading down to fractious heirs that would be calling me themselves, soon enough. All the money, mine.

It went on like that for two years. Check the microfilm. Check the papers. North America, Central, South, all over Europe. Cops in a lather about anarchists targeting rich couples. That was another strength of Ryland's idea. It rendered the motive inexplicable.

Then I got an offer from Brazil. I was kind of surprised. For some reason I imagined their divorce laws to be old-fashioned and traditional. I didn't think any Brazilian guy would need my kind of help. But someone reached out to me and I ended up face to face with a man who had big units from mineral deposits and an actress wife who was sleeping around. The guy was wounded about it. Maybe that's why he called me. He didn't strictly need to. But he wanted to.

He was rich and he was angry, so I doubled my usual fee. That was no problem. I explained how it would work. Payment after the event at a discreet location, satisfaction guaranteed. Then he told me his wife was going to be on a train, some kind of a long private club-car journey through the mountains. That was a problem. There are no banks on trains. So I decided to pass on Ryland's trick, just this one time. I would go the traditional single-ended route. The old way. I checked a map and saw that I could get on the train late and get off early. The wife would be dead in her sleeper when it rolled into Rio. I would be long gone by then.

It was comforting to think about working the old way, just for once.

I spotted her on the train and kept well back. But even from a distance I saw the ring on her finger. It was a gigantic rock. A diamond so big they probably ran out of carat numbers to measure it with.

That was a bank right there, on her finger.

Traceable, theoretically, but not through certain parts of Amsterdam or Johannesburg or Freetown, Sierra Leone. Potentially a problem at customs posts, but I could swallow it.

I moved up the train.

She was a very beautiful woman. Skin like lavender honey, long black hair that shone, eyes like pools. Long legs, a tiny waist, a rack that was popping out of her shirt. I took the armchair opposite her and said, "Hello." I figured a woman who sleeps around would at least give me a look. I have certain rough qualities. A few scars, the kind of unkempt appearance that suggests adventure. She didn't need money. She was married to it. Maybe all she needed was diversion.

It went well at first and I found a reason to move around the table and slide into the chair next to her. Then within an hour we were well into that train-journey thing where she was leaning left and I was leaning right and we were sharing intimacies over the rush of the wind and the clatter of the wheels. She talked about her marriage briefly and then changed the subject. I brought it back. I pointed to her ring and asked her about it. She spread her hand like a starfish and let me take a look.

"My husband gave it to me," she said.

"So he should," I said. "He's a lucky man."

"He's an angry man," she said. "I don't behave myself very well, I'm afraid."

I said nothing.

She said, "I think he wants to have me killed."

So there it was, the opening that was often so hard to work around to. I should have said, "He does," and opened negotiations. But I didn't.

She said, "I look at the men I meet and I wonder, is this the one?"

So then I got my mouth working and said, "This is the one."

"Really?" she said.

I nodded. "I'm afraid so."

"But I have insurance," she said.

She raised her hand again and all I saw was the diamond. Hard to blame myself, because the diamond was so big and the stiletto's blade was so slender. I really didn't see it at all. Wasn't aware of its existence until its tip went through my shirt and pierced my skin. Then she leaned on it with surprising strength and weight. It was cold. And long. A custom piece. It went right through me and pinned me to the chair. She used the heel of her hand and butted it firmly into place. Then she used my tie to wipe the handle clean of prints.

"Goodbye," she said.

She got up and left me there. I was unable to move. An inch left or right would tear my insides out. I just sat and felt the spreading stain of blood reach my lap. I'm still sitting there, ten minutes later. Once I could have shot you in one ear and out the other from a thousand yards. Or I could have brushed past you in a crowd and you wouldn't have known your throat was cut until you went to nod your head and it rolled away down the street without you. I was the guy you were worrying about when you locked your doors and posted your guards and walked upstairs to bed, only to find me already up there before you, leaning on the dresser, just waiting in the dark.

I was the guy who always found a way.

I was the guy that couldn't be stopped.

But then I met Ryland.

And all that's over now.

Dr. Sullivan's Library

BY CHRISTINE MATTHEWS

Christine Matthews is the co-author of the "Gil & Claire" series, the third of which, *Same Time, Same Murder* (SMP), appeared in 2005. Her crime story "Dirty Girl" was optioned for a film. She is also the editor of the anthology *Deadly Housewives* (Avon, 2006).

IT WAS ALWAYS THERE in the eyes. Close to the surface. And after sixteen years of looking into so many of them, ever respectful of each life spread out in front of him, he started cataloguing his patients.

Romances took slow, lazy blinks. Soulful eyes fringed with long lashes, usually. Smoky colored eyes hiding secret passion. *Biographies* were self-involved, so very insecure. Always looking for a mirror on the wall or rummaging through a purse for a compact. Wondering how they measure up, comparing everything they do to what the next guy's done. *Westerns*: Like an old Gene Autry movie, everything for them is in black and white. In their world, only two groups of people exist: good guys and bad guys. When they make a decision, they stick to it. No in-betweens—no going back. Intolerant eyes, opinionated, arched eyebrows. Now *Science Fictions* were the complete opposites of Westerns. Gullible, lonely. They joined support groups, tried every fad diet, sent hard-earned money or savings to televangelists. Contradicting what he'd originally thought to be the case, this group had the least imagination or creativity. It took a few years, but Dr. Maxwell Sullivan finally learned that those who lived, worked, and vacationed outside the box were *Mysteries*. Colored lenses covered their naturalness. They thought before speaking, took nothing at face value; whenever he ran into a wall, he was usually dealing with a Mystery.

As he flipped on the light, he perused his calendar, looking for his favorite type of Mystery. Not just a nice, uncomplicated *Who-dun-it*, no, today he desperately needed a *Thriller*.

"Mr. Hargrove, please, have a seat."

Sid Hargrove sat. The brown pin-striped suit jacket stretched across his broad shoulders. The white shirt looked as though he had just unwrapped it, fresh from the cleaners. His tie—art deco, a twenties kind of look. It all worked.

Dr. Max Sullivan sat behind his desk, facing the man. "So," he leaned back, studied the man a moment, then said, "tell me about yourself."

"No."

"You are aware, Mr. Hargrove, that I've been appointed by the court?"

"Yes."

"So you're going to have to talk to me sooner or later. . . ."

"Look, I don't have a problem. This is all nuts. That ex-wife of mine, talk about your nut jobs, she was one of the biggest. But that was over twelve years ago."

"Then how did this domestic incident occur? Why were you at her home?" It was all there in the file, but it was better coming from the patient. Each word carried emotion. Each emotion carried clues.

"It wasn't anything like she told the cops. I have friends in the neighborhood. That's all. That's the only reason I was there at all."

"What about Jessica?"

"I get her on the weekends."

"And this 911 call was made on a Wednesday."

"I stick to the rules. I don't need no more judges telling me how much and for how long I gotta kiss that bitch's ass just to get to spend time with my kid."

"Your daughter's ten years old."

"Yeah. She's beautiful. And smart. Always on the honor roll. Amazing, isn't it, how something so beautiful can come out of a slut like her mother."

"So, if you were just in the neighborhood, how did you end up in your wife's—"

"Ex-wife."

Max leafed through the papers. "Judy. How did you end up inside her house, beating her up?"

"It ain't like she said."

He never flinched. Steady. He was lying, and damn good at it. According to the latest statistics, one in every twenty-five people have no conscience. The number was staggering, even to him. It was unbelievable that of the seventy-six patients he had seen in the last two years, three of them were cold. Unfeeling, uncaring, and detached. Experience showed him those three could not be reached. They'd play with him and he'd play right back, cashing their checks or the state's or the insurance company's, and try not to think about them once the hour was up. Three.

Two more to go.

Madeline Whitney. History of manic depression, migraines, lapses in memory that she attributed to alien abductions. After their second session, he'd catalogued her as a *Gothic*. Easy to tears, drooping lids that half-covered gray eyes. Colorless, odorless, she instigated her own sadness and wore it like a coat of armor. Rusty armor. Even if someone pried her out of that suit, she'd crawl right back in. It was the only safe place she knew. Comfortable in the discomfort.

"Why did you cancel our last session?"

"I couldn't get out of bed. Look at my arm."

"What happened?"

"It wasn't there when I went to bed last night."

"Maybe you did it in your sleep. Sometimes my fingernail snags—"

"No. We both know it wasn't that."

She did it all for attention. We do everything for the attention, don't we?

"Madeline, does it sound logical to you that while you were sleeping someone—"

"Or something—"

"—came into your house, walked into your bedroom, and, without waking you, cut your arm and then just left?"

"Yes . . . it does."

He adjusted his glasses. "Do you remember when we talked about how normal actions result in logical reactions?"

Her neck seemed to suddenly be made of rubber, enabling her to lift her head even further from her rigid body.

"How many times must I tell you not to say my first name? To you I'm Mrs. Whitney. If we are to ever figure out how all these terrible things are happening, why I out of millions of people in this world have been singled out, if we are ever able to go to the authorities, you must remain objective. Professional. Please, I'm recording this session like all the rest, and if you keep crossing that line, that spiderweb line separating hired help from friend, we'll never be able to present an accurate, scientific thesis."

Six months he had been seeing her, and still she ranted. The more she spoke, the more anxiety filled each word. Breathing exercises hadn't worked, visualization, medication, nothing seemed to cut through her paranoia. He studied her eyes. The belief was still dominant. She took cover behind every strange word she uttered. And that total belief released her from any responsibility for her own actions. No fault ever landed on her doorstep. No fault equaled no guilt. The purity of her delusion made her almost perfect.

Almost.

Before making his decision, however, he had to see Owen Sawyer.

Sunday dinner with the family.

"Max, sweetheart." She hugged him so tightly, her gardenia perfume fouled his collar. "I made your favorite. Are you alone?"

Every week she asked.

Every week he was alone.

No need answering.

She took the bottle of wine he offered. "Daddy's in the basement. Fooling with those damned trains of his. Go have a visit while I finish up the salad."

As Max clomped down the wooden stairs, the sound of miniature wheels racing along metal tracks made him smile. The first train set had been one of those cheap things that circled the Christmas tree. No landscaping, no toy commuters, only one cardboard drugstore cut out from a box top and folded into shape. But it had hooked them. The next year, Max had bought a plaster house with money he'd saved from his allowance, with white glitter glued to the roof. To his eight-year-old eyes, it had looked like real snow and when the Christmas tree bulbs flashed on and off . . . wow. By the third year a real scale-model train looped and raced through station after station in the basement.

"Hey! Get in here, mister fancy doctor." Big Max held his arms open.

Max smiled and carefully gathered the frail man into a hug. "You look good, Pop."

"Liar."

"Do I look like I'm lying?" He stepped back to give his father direct access to his eyes.

"All's I can tell you is, never play poker. They'd cut you to pieces and then play with them pieces until there weren't nuthin' left."

"Nice image, Pop. You always did have a way with words."

He shrugged. "It's a gift."

Max dragged a metal stool over to a spot next to his father. Big Max lifted an engineer's cap off the desk behind him and pulled it down onto his son's head. Forty-five years old, and Max still got a kick out of it.

It was nice. The two of them sitting together, the aroma of meatloaf spicing the air around them. As Max gazed across the large table covered with green felt and miles of track, some peace started to filter down through his tension. But then Big Max had to go and spoil it.

"How's it comin'? You know. How much longer 'til you decide somethin'?"

Owen Sawyer twitched. When he was in the office, Max made sure this patient stretched out on the couch; otherwise, once that foot of his started shaking, furniture rattled, lamps flickered—it all made Max slightly nauseous. A *Travelogue*. Just as a joke to himself, Max had likened this particular patient to a travel book only because of his constant movement. When they'd met for the first time, Sawyer had rocked back and forth in his chair for the full hour. The even, incessant, maddening motion had started an end table vibrating, causing a vase to finally crash to the floor. Traveling. Unsettled.

But after six months of reading the man, Max had learned he was a total contradiction to what he'd originally thought. He'd never seen such a calm person. Dead calm inside. Thoughtful, even, emotionless. Secrets lived deep down inside that psyche. So deep that Max hadn't been able to shine the tiniest bit of light on any of it in all the time he'd been working with Sawyer. And he'd worked especially hard with the man. But something else bothered him . . . something he'd never mentioned to a colleague or noted in his file. Owen Sawyer frightened him. Max struggled with himself, re-examined his compassion, fought this irrational fear. But then he had his own breakthrough and reclassified Sawyer as a *True Crime*.

By the time Sawyer was fourteen, both of his parents were also in therapy. For his fifteenth birthday, he decided to treat himself and stole both his brother's car and his nineteen-year-old girl-friend and headed for the liquor store. When the clerk refused to sell either of the teens alcohol, they'd beaten the man and grabbed all the beer they could carry in addition to one hundred seventeen dollars from the register. It only took the police an hour to track down the car and haul the two off to jail.

In and out of juvenile court, Sawyer had developed a cocaine habit that never went away. Today, at forty-two, he worked as a dish-washer at a café one town over. Married twice, divorced twice, no children. Apparently no one could stand the man.

"What would you like to talk about today, Mr. Sawyer?"

"You know what, Doc?"

"No, what?"

"I don't know a damn thing about *you*."

Max scrutinized Sawyer's wet grin. "You're not paying me to tell you—"

"You're supposed to make me feel better, right? Talking to you is therapy?"

"Yes."

"So, spill your guts. Ahh, come on, Doc. I could use a good laugh. It'll make me feel better. Promise."

Those eyes. Calculating. Trying to undo him. Make him doubt himself. Max felt his face flush with hatred for Owen Sawyer.

Time was running out. As Max watched the timer count down one last minute on the treadmill, he wondered what the hell he was going to tell his father. Or even worse, how would he handle his mother?

Heading for the locker room, his only thought was of a hot shower. Clear his head and his body. Almost there, he spotted the vending machine and was struck with the urgent need for a soda. Unzipping the pocket of his sweatpants, hoping to come up with exact change, he caught parts of a conversation between two women coming from somewhere around the corner.

"That slimy sonofabitch. I'd like to hang him up by his balls. And while he's squirming up there on that meat hook, screaming for me to let him down, I'll ask him, calmly, if he's sorry for all the shit he's put me through."

"That's so mean."

"Whose side are ya on, here? You know all the crap he's pulled on me."

Max thought he recognized one of the voices.

"Imagine it, the bastard's hangin' there, beggin', and I tell him to bite me. No mercy for that fuckin' creep."

"Yeah, he deserves whatever he gets. More, even."

"But he begs. An' keeps on cryin'. And I say, 'No. Never. You lose.' An' I start cuttin'."

Laughter and then she saw him. "Oh, Dr. Sullivan, I didn't know you were—"

"Jeanine, hi."

"Kelly, this is Dr. Sullivan. Dr. Sullivan, this is my friend Kelly."

"Hi." He gave her a quick smile.

"The boss," Kelly said. "I've heard a lot about you."

He didn't ask what she'd heard because he was looking at Jeanine, wondering how she could be smiling so sweetly at him now, when just a second ago she'd been so brutal, so crude.

"I've never seen you here before," his receptionist said demurely.

"I joined last week."

"Well, I'm sure it's just to stay in the shape you're in; you certainly don't need to lose one pound."

"Thanks." Was she flirting, he wondered.

"And your hair," she tucked a damp curl behind his ear, "it looks sexy all messed up like that."

Yep, she was flirting.

• • •

"Jeanine, where's my three-o'clock?"

"She just called; she'll be fifteen minutes late."

Max snapped off the intercom. Passive-aggressive. He of all people should know what his patient was doing. But waste aggravated him the most. And the older he got, the less forgiving he became of those who wasted his time. He'd have to work on that, especially in his profession.

He got up to tell Jeanine to charge Mrs. Hornberger for the full hour plus an extra hundred to teach her a lesson. As he opened the door a crack, he stopped.

"You know the rules, Mr. Hargrove. Your appointments are always on Tuesday. Today is Thursday—"

"Get out of my way, you dumb bitch. I need to see the doctor and I'm going in there."

Max pulled the door open enough so he could watch what was happening.

Jeanine threw her stapler at the back of the man's head and then raced around her desk. "What did you call me, asshole? Who the hell do you think you are?"

Like a whip snapping, Hargrove turned and slapped Jeanine across the face. "I'll have your job for what you did. I'm bleedin' here."

Max stood fascinated, hoping Jeanine didn't need rescuing—not just yet.

"You like to beat up women, don't you? I type up all the Doctor's reports and I know all about you. I've dated bums just like you. You're weak. Just an overweight, stupid, fucked-up bully!"

Hargrove's face reddened. It was glorious to watch. This bout with Jeanine would do him more good than months of therapy. Max almost rushed in when he saw the man make a move toward Jeanine, but then realized she was all over him. She pulled her arm back and whacked the man across his pock-marked cheek. The sound was thrilling.

"That's it, lady, you're dead."

Jeanine grabbed her letter opener. "A threat? You assaulted and then threatened me! Now you can either get the hell out of here or wait while I call the police. What'll it be?"

"Sullivan!" Hargrove shouted. "Doctor Sullivan!"

Max hesitated long enough to give the impression he'd been clear on the other side of his office, seated behind his desk when the commotion started.

"What?" He even managed a look of surprise at seeing Jeanine holding a long, silver letter opener up near Hargrove's neck. "What on earth—"

"Either you fire this whore, or I'll have your license. She should never work in a doctor's office. With sick people. Fragile people. . . ."

No apologies. Jeanine stood defiant. "Fragile, my ass!"

And that's when Maxwell Sullivan knew he was in love.

Sunday dinner with the family.

"Max, sweetheart." She hugged him close. No gardenia perfume this week, his mother's cheek felt slick and smelled of suntan lotion. A sure sign she had been working in the garden before starting dinner.

"I'm making lasagna. Hope you're hungry. Are you alone?" Expecting no answer, she turned back to the stove.

"No, Mom, I'm not." Max waved for Jeanine to come into the kitchen from the living room, where he'd left her.

Gracie Sullivan turned around to see her son standing next to an attractive redhead.

"And who have we here? Come on, don't be shy." She held out her arms.

Jeanine obliged with a polite hug. "Hi. I'm Jeanine. Max's secretary. It's nice to meet you, Mrs. Sullivan."

"Let's have a good look at you."

Max watched as the women sized each other up and was surprised

that his mother's premature familiarity wasn't putting Jeanine off in the slightest. In fact, she seemed amused. Good. Today had to go well.

"So? Where have you been keeping her, Max?"

"Be gentler, Mom, this is only our sixth date and if you keep this up, it'll be our last."

"Oh, no, I don't think so. She seems pretty sturdy to me."

Jeanine smiled.

"No, honey, go down and say hi to your father. Dinner will be ready in twenty minutes. Jeanine, come help with the salad. We can talk."

"Yeah, honey," Jeanine said, sarcastically, "run along."

"Okay by me."

The first thing Max noticed as he walked down the basement steps was the silence. No trains, no whistles.

"Hey, Pop, ya down here?"

"And where else would I be?"

As he came around the corner, Max saw his father stretched out on the brown-and-orange tweed recliner his mother had bargained for, twenty years ago in a garage sale. The large chair practically swallowed his old man up. Big Max was wearing a maroon cardigan instead of his favorite B&O sweatshirt. Max realized for the first time how few strands of hair were actually still attached to his father's shiny head. He looked so old. Max hated this.

"Come on, Pop, let's try out that new engine I got you last week."

"Not now. I'm tired, Max. Sit, talk to me."

Max sat.

"I thought I heard another voice upstairs."

"Yeah, I brought a date—Jeanine—for dinner. You'll like her."

"Is she anything like that Sarah girl? So much blond hair and pale skin. Ahh," he waved his hand, as if trying to dismiss the memory, "too weak, too pale, no character. You need a woman like your mother. . . ."

"I know, Pop, I know."

"Do you?" Big Max's eyes brightened. "Do you really understand how important a strong woman is? For sure one of the biggest assets you'll ever have in our business."

"Jeanine has been working in my office for almost a year now, but I never really noticed her until a few months ago. She's great."

"So, ya screwed her yet?"

He never changed. Sick, healthy, old or young, his father was crude. It didn't matter if they were in front of hundreds of people or sitting together with the trains, the old fart was always blurting out something that made Max hate being related to such an asshole. But every wave of anger was immediately followed by one of guilt. And here he was again, trying to ride it out, back to shore, where he could regain his balance until it happened again. And it always did.

"No, Pop, I haven't screwed her."

"Why the hell not? You have to establish who's in control from the beginning. Power, Max, how many times do I hafta tell you? It's all about power. Running a business, keeping a broad . . . ya gotta stay strong. In control."

Max nodded.

"Are you listening to me, son?"

"Yes." How could he not be listening? Big Max was shouting. Always loud. Max took after his mother, if he had to liken himself to either parent.

"Dinner!"

Big Max stood up. "Let's go and have a look at this girl. See if she's got what it takes."

"I really love your mom, you know? And your dad's a sweetheart."

Ten more dates and he still wasn't sure. Being in love was great, but he did have a business to run.

"Isn't it fun that my birthday falls on a Sunday this year? That way we can have dinner with your folks . . . oh, did I tell you she called?"

"My mother called here?"

"Yeah, she and your dad have a big surprise. Do you know what it is?"

He knew exactly what was going to happen, but he said, "Haven't got a clue."

"Really?" She cocked her head in that little-girl way that he found so endearing.

Forcing himself back to work, he asked, "Is my one-thirty here yet?"

"I'll go check."

"If he is, could you stall for a few minutes? I have to make a call."

"Sure." She threw him a kiss before closing the door behind her.

Quickly he dialed the phone. "Mother, pick up. Mom? Are you sure it's time? I really like this one; I hope you're right. I don't want to scare—"

Gracie picked up on her end. "Stop worrying. Trust me."

"Trust you? That's what you said last time. With Brenda. Remember?"

"Let it go, Max. So I made a mistake—one time. Believe me, Jeanine is going to love her present. This will be her best birthday ever. One to remember. One that will change all our lives."

"If you say so."

"Why are you doing this to me?"

Jack Beckley fought against the duct tape fastening him to a splintered chair.

"Shut up!"

Big Max snapped the hedge clipper. Jack screamed as his right index finger dropped onto the concrete floor.

"Hold on!" Gracie ordered. "You're going to spoil everything."

Max parked next to his mother's black Mercedes.

"Why are we out in the middle of nowhere? Wait a minute." Jeanine grinned. "Is this part of my birthday surprise?"

Max leaned over and gave her a serious kiss. "I hope you like it."

Jeanine looked through the windshield. "But everything's closed up out here."

"You'll see."

Max got out of the car and walked around to open her door.

"Listen . . . I think I hear a car door." Gracie said.

Jack prayed somehow the cops had gotten wind of his situation. "Over here! Help me!"

Max led Jeanine to a side door of the old depot.

"Watch your step."

"Are you really sure this is the right place?" Jeanine asked, more confused than ever after hearing some commotion from inside.

"I'm sure." Why hadn't they gagged him? Amazing. Thirty years in the business, and still so sloppy.

Once inside, the couple headed for the single light in the back.

"Surprise!" Gracie and Big Max yelled.

Jack's eyes bugged out when he saw her. "Jeanie? Baby? Oh, thank God it's you."

It took Jeanine a moment for her eyes to adjust to the light from the lantern on the floor. It took another moment for her to recognize her ex-boyfriend.

"Jack? Why are you . . . ? Mrs. Sullivan?"

"Come here, birthday girl," Big Max said. "I got somethin' real special for you. Asshole, imported from Newark. Special delivery."

"We picked it out ourselves." Gracie laughed at her own joke.

"See? I remember," Max said, "from that first day we bumped into each other at the gym. You were so upset. Because of him." Max kicked Jack in the shin. "I'm never going to let anyone hurt you again. Ever."

"You know these people? For Chrissake, Jeanie, look what they're doin' here."

Big Max held out a power drill. "Too serious. Is this a friggin' party or ain't it?"

"Noooooo!" Jack blacked out before the drill went completely through his thigh and into the chair.

Max watched Jeanine closely, waiting for her to crack. To scream. To run. But she didn't. Overwhelmed by her strength, Max knew the time was right and lowered his weight, balancing on one knee. "I have a surprise for you, too, honey."

The birthday girl turned toward the diamond ring.

"I want you to marry me, be my wife. My partner."

"Isn't it all too perfect?" Gracie asked. "Just like Big Max and me. Living together, working together. Now we'll all be one big, happy family. . . ."

"Max? I don't understand. Your parents are psychiatrists, too?"

"They're talking about the family business—not my practice. That's just something to do until I found the right person. I thought it would be a partner to work with. To train so when Mom and Dad retire . . ."

"Boca Raton. It's gorgeous there," Big Max said.

". . . but I never dreamed I'd find someone like you."

Gracie smiled proudly. "I took the business over from my mother. She started it right after Daddy was killed. It was just for revenge that first time, but she found she was good at it. And she really loved the work."

"What exactly is 'the work'?" Jeanine asked.

"Ma was a . . . cleaning lady. That's how she thought of it."

"But instead of using a mop, she used a .45, some wire . . . whatever it took," Big Max said with admiration. "She was somethin' else. You remind me a lot of her."

"And your dad?" she asked Max.

"Oh, he takes a contract now and then, but mostly he keeps books, makes contacts, sets up appointments."

Gracie walked over to Jeanine, putting an arm around her, said, "Look, we both know women are stronger, more . . . thorough. Aren't you sick and tired of kissin' ass?"

Jeanine nodded, still fairly stunned by the turn of events.

"Do you love my son?"

"With all my heart."

"And isn't it great how easily you can resolve your anger right now? This very minute." Gracie nodded toward Jack. "No such thing as therapy in my world. Give back as bad as you get, that's what Ma used to say. Plus there's lots of money in our line of work, travel, fancy clothes. You get to meet more than a few very interesting people. So you have to clean up a few messes, get your hands dirty every now and then, but the benefits are far greater than the actual work."

Jack moaned and the foursome looked over in his direction.

Max joined the women. "In case I have to remind you, Jeanine, I love you very much."

Big Max shouted across the room from his position next to Jack, "So, what do you say, kid? Wanna join the family?"

"Would I be replacing you, Big Max? Staying put in the office while Max gets to have all the fun?"

"No, I've got just the right person to fill in for dad," Max told her. "Mr. Sawyer."

"Owen Sawyer? Wednesday? Four o'clock Mr. Sawyer?"

"Yes."

Jeanine frowned, thinking a moment. "But he's so . . . so . . . oh yeah, he'd be perfect."

"Good, that's all settled," Big Max said, "so can we please finish up here and go get some dinner?" He handed the drill to Jeanine. "There ya go, hon. Enjoy. But remember, this is a gift. After this you only do it for money. After all, it's a business."

She stood there looking from the drill to Jack, then from Jack back to the drill. "I still can't believe you did all this for me. It's the best present I ever got." Taking care, she pressed the tool into Jack's right shoulder, waiting for his reaction before she squeezed the trigger.

"Don't do it! Come on, Jeanine, you can't really be this angry just because of a few smacks now and then. We had some good times. Remember?"

"I remember the black eyes, two loose teeth, five stitches, and most of all the—"

Her coldness suddenly made him angry. "You deserved all of it—"

"—abortion. I remember how you said I didn't have to go to a real doctor, Jack." She pressed the trigger and the drill bit dug into his shoulder, chewing up his flannel shirt as shreds twisted and reddened with blood.

Now his face. She came at his eye, oblivious to the screams. Long, raw strings of agony.

"You know, Jack, I do think this will make us even."

Max watched, overcome with love. Everything was going to change now. His life in that office, that suffocating, ugly office was over. What a fool he'd been looking for his partner among the dark patients, the damaged. He'd wasted so much time searching all the wrong shelves. Jeanine was a *New Age* book, enlightened. Willing to try new and exciting lifestyles, an unconventional outlook on life. And those eyes. Clear, wide, and that complexion—except for the blood spatters—so smooth and clean . . . she was inspiring.

Retrospective

BY KEVIN WIGNALL

Kevin Wignall is the author of *People Die* (Kensington, 2002), which features a hit man as its main character. His second novel, *For The Dogs*, was published by Simon & Schuster in July 2004.

THERE WAS MORE DEATH and misery in this room than was fit for any civilized place. Mutilated bodies, the diseased and the starving, the fearful and the grief-stricken; and all those empty eyes, the haunted and expressionless faces—it was all here, and it was all his.

Tomorrow night, the Dorchester Street Gallery would open its doors and the celebrities and art world players would get their vicarious thrill as they socialized and flirted and exchanged business cards over wine and morsels amid the horror of his life's work.

Most of his life's work, at any rate; the landscape photographs of recent years had been shunted off into one small side gallery. He didn't mind that, either, conscious of the fact that the landscapes hadn't earned him this retrospective.

When people thought of Jonathan Hoyle, they thought of the images that had been used to fill both the two large gallery spaces and the big fat accompanying catalogue. For nearly twenty years,

he'd produced these iconic photographs of the world's war zones
and he suspected he was alone in seeing what he'd done. Far from
exposing the truth, he'd reduced human tragedy to the level of
pornography, or worse, for pornographers were at least honest.

He heard a noise behind him and turned to see the young gallery
assistant approaching. Her name was Sophie, he thought, and she
looked pretty and mousy in the moneyed way of gallery assistants.
If he were a different type of photographer, he'd be trying to seduce
her into sitting for him.

"Having a final look around, Mr. Hoyle?"

He wasn't sure how to respond, so he said, "Please, call me Jon."

"Thank you." She blushed, and again, he thought maybe he
should move from his current obsession to the landscape of the
female body. "It's a bit cheeky of me, I know, but do you think you
could sign my copy of the catalogue?"

He looked at the catalogue in her hand, and his thoughts crumbled into dust. There was the dead Palestinian boy whose picture
had once appeared on newspaper front pages the world over. The
gallery had offered him a choice of two photographs for the cover
and he'd opted for this one without a second thought, but it still
depressed him to see it.

"Of course." He took the catalogue and the pen she proffered. "It's
Sophie, isn't it?" She nodded and he wrote a simple inscription,
thanking her for all her help.

She studied it, apparently happy with the personal touch, then
looked at the cover and said, "It's such a beautiful picture, incredibly
moving." She looked up at him again and said, "Why did you stop . . .
I mean, why didn't you take any more war photography after this one?"

He sighed. These questions would always haunt him. The life he'd
lived, the person he'd been, out there on the ragged edges of the
world, it would always get in the way of the simpler things. You're a
pretty girl, he wanted to say, I'd like to go for a drink with you and
talk about art, and I'd like to see you naked. But she was right, the
Palestinian boy had been the last.

"I stopped because I'd finally captured the truth; there was nothing left to say after that."

She smiled, uncertain, as if she feared he might be teasing her. "But your photographs are *all* about the truth."

"Are they?" She didn't know how to respond. "Good night, Sophie, I'll see you tomorrow evening." He drifted toward the door, enigma intact, almost self-satisfied.

It was already dark and there was a cold wind picking up, but he decided to walk back to the hotel, wanting to clear his head out there on the streets. As he stepped outside, though, he was faced with a black Range Rover, tinted windows, a young guy in a suit waiting by one of the rear doors.

"Evening, Mr. Hoyle. Your car." He was Australian, like most of the people keeping London's service economy afloat. The guy opened the door in readiness for him.

Jon was about to tell him that he felt like walking, but stopped himself and said, "My car? No one ordered a car for me."

If he'd had a moment longer, he might have figured that the guy's suit was a little too expensive to suggest a chauffeur. He didn't have time, though. Before he'd even finished speaking, the guy had produced a gun from somewhere, a silencer already attached. He was pointing it at Jon, but holding it in a casual, almost non-threatening way.

"Get in the car, mate. I don't wanna have to kill you here, but I will."

The thought of running had died even before it was fully formed. He remembered seeing that French journalist getting shot in Somalia, remembered how sudden and arbitrary it had been—one minute talking to the soldiers, the next crumpled in the dust, oozing blood. There was no running, and he felt bad because, right at this moment, he couldn't remember that French journalist's name, even though he'd drunk with him a couple of times.

Jon got in the back of the Range Rover and the young guy got in after him, closing the door.

"Okay, let's go." Another guy was in the driving seat, but it was soon clear the car belonged to the gunman. They lurched forward, nearly clipping another parked car, and the Australian said, "Mate, if you scratch my bloody paintwork!" He turned to Jon then and said, "Gotta blindfold you." He put the blindfold on, tying it behind Jon's head, surprisingly gentle. "How's that feel?"

"Okay, I suppose, under the circumstances."

"Yeah, sorry about that. The name's Dan, Dan Borowski." Bizarrely, Jon felt him take his hand and shake it like he was introducing himself to a blind man. And it was bizarre mainly because he knew this was it; whoever they were, they were going to kill him.

I don't wanna have to kill you here, that's what the guy had said, and he'd given his full name, which meant he saw no danger because he was talking to a dead man. He couldn't help but be amused by the irony of it, that he'd traveled unscathed through every impression of hell the world had to offer, only to die in London.

"You're gonna kill me."

He waited for the voice, and when it came it was a little regretful. "Yeah. Client wants to meet you first, but your number's up. I'm sorry."

"Why? I mean, why does he want me dead?"

"Didn't say." His tone was casual again. "Gotta be something to do with your work, though, don't you think?"

Jon nodded. He was surprised how calm he felt. He wondered if experienced pilots felt like this when their planes finally took a nosedive, if they serenely embraced the void, knowing they'd defied it too long already.

Jon didn't want pain, but he could imagine this guy, Dan, making it easy for him anyway; he was clearly a professional killer, not like some of the monstrous amateurs he'd seen parading around in their makeshift uniforms. He didn't want to die either, but he'd tap-danced around death for so long, he could hardly complain now as it reached out to rest its hand upon his shoulder.

He was curious, though, trying to think which aspect of his work had angered someone so much that, even now, a few years after he'd stopped being a war photographer, they were still determined to kill him for it. It couldn't be for offending some cause or other.

He could only imagine this being a personal bitterness, the result of a photograph that had so intruded on someone else's grief or suffering that this seemed a justifiable retribution. That ruled out the landscapes, but not much else.

He supposed a lot of the people who knew and loved the subjects of his photographs would have killed him if they'd had the means. The fact that this person clearly had been able to hire a contract killer perhaps narrowed it down a little further. It made the Balkans, the Middle East, and Central America more likely as the source. It hardly mattered, though; whoever it was, whichever photograph, they were striking a blow for all the unknown families.

"You *are* a contract killer, I take it."

"Among other things," said Dan.

Jon was already getting attuned to having no visuals to fall back on, and although Dan had fallen silent again, he could sense that he had more to say. Sure enough, after a couple more beats, a stop at traffic lights, a left turn, Dan spoke again.

"You know, in a way, you and I are a lot alike. Our jobs, anyway."

Jon laughed and said, "I'm cynical about the work I do, but that's a bit rich. I photograph death. In a strange way, I think I sanitize it, but at least I can hold my hands up and say I've never caused it."

There was a slight pause, during which Jon realized he'd talked in the present tense, even though it was a while now since he'd photographed the overspill of war. Dan seemed fixed on something else, the distraction audible in his voice as he said, "I'm picking up some negative vibes here, like you're dismissing the work you've produced. I've gotta tell you, Jon, you're wrong about that. You're a great photographer, and it's a document of our times, good or bad."

"Well, we'll have to agree to differ on that."

"No way!" He laughed as if they were old friends disagreeing over favorite teams or dream dates. "Seriously, I'm such a fan of your work. I've even got the book of landscapes. It was one of the reasons I agreed to this job."

It was Jon's turn to laugh. "You agreed to kill me for money because you're such a fan of my work! Well, thanks; I'm touched."

Another pause, and Dan's response was subdued, even a little hurt. "The contract would have gone to someone else, anyway. I took the job because I wanted to meet you, and I wanted to make sure it was done right."

He couldn't ignore the final point, because it was what he'd hoped for, that he wouldn't let him suffer. And maybe another man, certainly one in another profession, wouldn't have looked at his own killer's intentions in quite the same way, but Jon *was* touched by the sentiment now that he thought about it.

"Thanks, Dan. I do appreciate that, and I know if it hadn't been you, it would have been someone else."

"Yeah, it's too bad."

"You didn't say how we were similar."

He was relaxed again, almost cheery as he said, "I just meant the way we go into areas, not just geographical areas, you know, areas of the human condition that most people don't ever experience. We drop in, I do what I've been paid to do, you get your picture, and we're back out again, onto the next little screw-up."

"I still don't see it. From my point of view, you're part of the problem. I may not be part of the solution, but at least I'm letting the world know what's really happening."

Dan laughed and said, "See, we're already getting somewhere; you're looking at your own work in a more positive light." The car stopped and the engine was turned off. For the first time, Jon felt a nervous twitching in his stomach. "We're here."

Dan helped him out of the car, a brief reminder of the cold night air, a coldness he wanted to savor, to fill his lungs with it like he was about to swim underwater for a long time. They walked through a door and it was still cold but no longer fresh, then up several flights of stone steps.

At the top, they walked through another door and then Dan took off the blindfold. They were in a large loft which looked as if it had only recently stopped being used as a factory or workspace. No doubt its next reincarnation would be as a couple of fabulous apartments, and neither of the new owners would ever imagine that it had been the scene of an execution.

There were two chairs in the middle of the floor, facing each other, a few yards apart. He noticed too, over to one side, what looked like a picture under a sheet, resting against a pillar. Jon wondered if that was it, the evidence of his crime, the photograph that had cost him his life.

He'd seen that happen to other photographers, their determination to get the ultimate shot drawing them too far into the open. It felt now like a stray bullet had hit him sometime in the last twenty years, the day he'd taken that picture, whatever it was, and ever since, he'd simply been waiting to fall.

"Take a seat. We shouldn't have to wait long."

"Will you do it here?" Dan looked around the room as if weighing up its suitability. He nodded. Jon pointed at the picture under the sheet. "Is that the photograph under there? Is that why he wants me dead?"

"I don't know, but you'll find out soon enough. Best you just sit down."

Dan sat on one of the chairs, so Jon took the other. He took a good look at Dan now. He looked young but he was probably thirty, maybe older, good-looking in that healthy Australian way, and his face was familiar somehow; but then Jon had seen so many faces in his life, they all ended up looking a little familiar.

Suddenly, he thought of the blindfold. He had no idea which part of London they were in, though they hadn't driven far. But if he was definitely to be killed, he couldn't understand why he'd had to be blindfolded.

"Does this guy definitely want me dead? There's no way out of it?"

Dan shook his head regretfully and said, "Why do you ask?"

"The blindfold. If he definitely wants me dead, I can't understand why I had to be blindfolded."

"He's just really cautious. And he doesn't know that when I bring someone in, they stay in."

"How much is he paying you?"

Dan smiled and offered the briefest shake of his head. He stared at Jon for a while then, still smiling, intrigued, and finally said, "I don't suppose you recognize me?"

"Your face is vaguely familiar, but I don't know where from."

"You took my picture once." He could see the look of surprise on Jon's face and waited for it to sink in before adding, "Not only that—it's in the exhibition."

"I . . . I don't remember."

"Yes, you do. Near the Congo–Rwandan border. You were taking pictures of the refugees escaping the fighting. Remember, there were thousands of them, just this silent broken river of people pouring over the border. I walked past you, didn't think anything of it. Then I see the picture, all those refugees walking toward the camera, me walking away from it."

Jon shook his head, astonished, because he did remember now. He'd been taking shots for an hour or more, never quite feeling he'd captured what he was after. Then a Western soldier had walked past him in black combats, heavily armed but still looking suicidally ill-equipped for where he was heading, a war zone of mind-altering barbarity. That was his picture, another one which had been dubbed iconic.

And the amazing thing was, he'd seen him again, five days later, back in the hotel. He'd recognized him just from the easy confident gait of his walk, from his build, the cut of his hair. Jon had asked someone who he was and he'd been told he was a mercenary, that he'd gone in for the German government and brought out some aid workers who'd been taken by the guerrillas. It had always intrigued him, that a man could walk so casually into hell and still come back.

"You saved those German aid workers."

Dan shrugged and said, "I saved three of them. One had already been killed by the time I got there. Another died on the way out."

"I've always wondered about that. Weren't you scared at all, going in there, knowing what was happening?"

"No," he said, smiling dismissively.

"I've been to some pretty freaky places, but I would have been scared going in there."

"That's because you only had a camera. I was armed; I knew I could handle it. I didn't know I could get them out alive, I was nervous about that, but I knew I could handle a few drug-crazed guerrillas."

"So you're not just a contract killer."

"No, like I said, I do all kinds of stuff. But don't paint me like Mother Theresa—I got paid more for bringing those people out of the jungle than you probably got paid in five years."

"At least you brought them out. You saved someone; it's more than I ever did."

"It wasn't your job to save people."

"It wasn't my job, but it was my duty as a human being. I used to look at some of these people and think they were savages, and yet I'd watch people dying and worry about things like light and exposure." Dan was shaking his head, the blanket disagreement of a true fan. Hoyle continued, "Tell me something: if you'd been in the jungle and stumbled across those hostages, would you have left them there to die? It wouldn't have been your job to save them, no payment, but would you?"

"Yeah, I probably would have had a go."

"That's the difference, Dan. You may be a cold-blooded killer, but you're still human. I never saved anyone."

Dan seemed to turn it over for a few seconds and then said, "You know, certain times of year, if a croc finds a baby turtle on the riverbank, it'll scoop it up in its mouth, take it down to the water, and let it go. See, they're programmed to help newly hatched crocs, so they just help anything small that's moving toward the water. Six months later, that croc, he'll kill that turtle."

Jon wondered if that was true, but was struck then by something else. "I don't follow. What's your point?"

Dan laughed and said, "I have absolutely no bloody idea!"

Jon laughed too, and then they were both silenced as the street door down below opened and closed and heavy steps worked laboriously toward them. Jon expected to feel nervous again, but if anything, their conversation had left him even more prepared. Maybe the nerves would come again later, but with any luck, he wouldn't have too long to think about it.

Dan stood up now, but gestured for Jon to stay where he was, and as if the approaching man were already in earshot, he said quietly, "You know, if there'd been any other way. . . ."

"Don't. And I'm glad I met you, too. I was always curious about the guy in that photograph."

Dan nodded and walked over to the door as it opened and a heavy-set guy in his fifties walked in. He was balding, wearing an expensive gray suit, an open collar. At first, Jon had him down as an Eastern European, but then he quickly realized the guy was an Arab.

The guy looked across, a mixture of disdain and satisfaction, but spoke to Dan for a minute or two in hushed tones. Their conversation seemed relaxed, as if they were filling each other in on what had happened recently, and when it was over, Dan nodded and left.

The client walked across the room without looking at him, picked up the picture, still under its sheet, and placed it on the chair facing Jon. He walked around the chair and stood behind it, finally allowing himself to make eye contact.

"You are Jonathan Hoyle." His voice was deep, the accent giving it an added gravitas. "May I call you Jonathan?"

"People call me Jon."

He gave a little nod and said, "So, Jon, do you know anyone called Nabil?" Jon shook his head. "It's my name. I am Nabil. It was also my son's name. I know you don't have children, so I also know that you don't understand what it is to lose a child. And I know you don't understand what it is for your dead child's photograph to be made into a piece of art, bought and sold, put on the covers of books. I know you don't understand any of this." There was no anger in his words; they were no more than statements of fact. And Jon couldn't question them, so he remained silent. "That is what I know about you. And this is what I know about me. I know that killing you tonight will not bring my son back and will not ease my pain. Indeed, the pain may become worse because your death will bring even more interest to your work; but, still, I must insist on your death. First, I want you to look again at my son's photograph, knowing his name, knowing. . . ."

He stopped, suddenly overcome, and took a deep breath. Jon lowered his gaze slightly, not wanting to stare at this man who was still so visibly torn by grief. He heard the sheet being pulled away, saw it drop to the floor, and a part of him didn't want to look up, because he had a feeling he knew which picture it would be, and the memory of it was already making him feel sick.

"Look at my son, Mr. Hoyle. Jon, look at my son."

He looked up. There was the print of the Palestinian boy, blown up life-size. His name had been Nabil and he'd been fourteen years old, and now Jon could think of no good reason why he shouldn't die tonight.

The boy's father wasn't crying but he had the look of a man who had no more tears left, a man who'd been beaten by life and was spent. Jon thought of all the times over the last four years that this man had chanced upon that picture and had the wound torn afresh.

Jon knew something of that, because he'd experienced it too. He'd seen the picture pulled from image libraries and used to illustrate newspaper and magazine stories—no context, no explanation, just a cynical, exploitative pathos.

He'd been fêted for that photograph; and yet, as ambivalent as he'd been about it, as much as its appearance had made jagged shards of his memory, he'd never once given thought to the boy's family. He could see it now, of course, how they'd probably come to hate him even more than the unknown Israeli soldier whose bullet had killed Nabil that day in Gaza.

"Do you have anything to say?"

"That was the last photograph I ever took in a war zone."

Nabil laughed a little, incredulous, as he said, "That's not much of a defense."

"I don't have any defense. It isn't right for you to kill me, but I can make no sound argument for sparing me. If it means anything, if it offers any comfort, I'm sorry."

Nabil nodded once, almost like a bow of his head. Jon wanted it over with now, he wanted Dan to come back into the room and end it, but Nabil looked contemplative, as if he was still dwelling upon something and wanted to ask another question. He suddenly became grim and determined, though, and started toward the door.

Jon felt his stomach tighten into a spasm, his blood spinning out of control with adrenaline, a mixture of fear and of self-loathing, knowing that it was wrong to leave it like this, without at least telling him the truth. "Nabil." Nabil stopped and turned to look at him. Jon felt ashamed because he knew it looked like he was stalling, and he wasn't; his nerves were for something else, for the things he wanted to say for the first time. He wanted to offer this man something more than a trite apology, and he wanted to get something off his own conscience before he died. "Before you call Dan back in, I want to tell you something about the day your son died. It won't change anything, but I want to tell you anyway."

Nabil's expression was unyielding, but he walked back toward the chair and stood a few paces behind it. "Go on."

Jon took a couple of deep breaths, looked at the photograph again, then at Nabil. "I took a lot of good photographs that day, and in the days before. You remember how volatile it was at that time, almost like there was something unstable in the air."

"I remember."

"So I was there, and there were Palestinian boys, young men, throwing stones at an Israeli patrol. I saw your son."

Nabil prickled defensively and said, "Yet you have no pictures of him throwing stones."

"Because he wasn't throwing stones. Like a lot of people those days, he was just trying to get from one place to another without getting caught up in it. He didn't look scared, he just looked like a kid who was used to it, confident, almost carefree." He looked at the photograph in front of him and wished, as he had many times, that he'd captured that carefree face as a counterpoint. "I wasn't even wasting film at that point. Stone throwing, that was just becoming routine. Then someone started firing on the soldiers and one of them got hit. They fired back and one of the stone throwers took a bullet in the shoulder. I got some good pictures of his friends helping him, this hive of activity and this dazed, strangely calm kid in the middle of it all. There were a couple of other photographers with me. And within another ten minutes it was all over. I was walking away on my own when I saw blood on the ground. I walked around the corner, into the yard of a house that had been bombed the week before, and I saw the body lying there. I recognized him right away, the kid I'd seen earlier. I guessed he'd been hit by a stray bullet, had managed to drag himself into the yard. He looked so young, and all the clichés were there—he looked peaceful, his face angelic, and the only thing that went through my mind at that moment was that I knew this photograph would make front pages all around the world. I took it, just one shot, and I knew I'd got it, the bloody hole in the side of his chest, the angelic face. I felt satisfied. I'm ashamed to say that, but I did, I felt like I'd found that day's star prize. And then the strangest thing happened. I kept looking through the lens, looking at his face, and I just knew something wasn't right, somehow. It took a moment, but I saw it in the end." He got up out of his chair and walked toward the picture. Nabil glanced at the door, as if ready to shout, but Jon kept his course. He picked up the picture and turned it for Nabil to see. "This is the truest photograph I ever took, and it's a fake. It shows a dead Palestinian boy, your son, but when this photograph was taken, the boy wasn't dead."

Nabil looked at him, surprised and yet wary, as if suspecting an attempt to earn his forgiveness. Jon didn't want that, though, and wasn't even sure that it was in this Nabil's power to grant it. He wanted only to tell the truth of how this photograph had been taken.

"Remember, I told you this won't change anything. The circumstances matter to me, but it doesn't change a thing."

"Please, continue."

Jon nodded and said, "I knelt down beside him and checked for a pulse, but I didn't need to. As soon as my hand touched his neck, his eyes opened, and he started to mutter something, very quietly, like he was afraid we'd be overheard. I knew he was really bad." Jon shook his head, the memory of his own helplessness briefly overpowering him again. "I just didn't know what to do, and in the distance I could hear the Israeli armored cars and I thought, if I could just get out to them, they'd have a medic with them, or there might be an ambulance. I put my camera down and I went to leave, but he grabbed my arm and I couldn't understand what he was saying but I could see it in his face, that he didn't want me to go, and I knew he was dying and there was nothing I could do. The injury was bad. He'd lost a lot of blood. And he looked so alone—I'd never noticed that before. So I just held his hand and I looked at him. I was muttering back to him, telling him I was still there." Jon could feel tears in his eyes, but they weren't stacked up enough to run down onto his cheeks, and he didn't want them to, because he didn't want any sympathy. "I couldn't save him. All the horrors I've witnessed, all the death and mutilation, but I didn't know how to save that boy."

Nabil was staring at him blankly, overcome with the onslaught of new information about his son's death.

"You stayed with him? Till he died?"

"It wasn't long after that. It was almost like he'd been waiting for someone to find him, so that he didn't die alone. And he didn't die alone, I gave him that much, but another person could have saved him, I'm sure of it. That's why I stopped being a war photographer."

"Because you watched my son die?"

"I've seen plenty of kids die. No, it was because I had the illusion of detachment snatched away from me, and once you've lost that, you never get it back." Jon put the picture back on the chair and took one last look at it. He was glad it was over. "You can call Dan in now. I'm ready."

Without looking at him, Nabil walked across to the door and opened it. Jon could see Dan sitting on the top step outside. He jumped up and by the time he came into the room, his gun was already in his hand. It would be quick, Jon told himself, and it would be done.

Dan looked at Nabil, surprised that he was still there, and said, "Wouldn't you prefer to leave first?"

"No, but there's no need for the gun. You can take him back."

Dan shrugged, expressing no emotional response, no disappointment, no relief, and said simply, "You do realize this doesn't change anything?"

He was talking about the fee and Nabil nodded and said, "Of course, and I'm sorry if I've wasted your time."

"Time's never wasted," said Dan, smiling.

Nabil finally looked at Jon again. "It's some comfort that you were with my son in his final moments, but that isn't why I'm sparing you. I was determined to kill the man who took that picture because I knew he had absolutely no understanding of what he'd done by taking it. I was wrong. I see now, you did understand."

"That once, I understood. But there are thousands of mothers and fathers out there to whom I could offer no answers, none at all."

The grieving father in front of him said no more. He offered Jon his hand, and when he shook it, he was surprised to find his own palm clammy and Nabil's dry as parchment. Nabil must have given some slight signal then, because Dan touched Jon on the elbow and the two of them left.

He looked back before descending the stairs. Nabil was sitting in the chair he'd occupied himself, and he was staring at the picture of his son, broken, the universe refusing to reform itself around him.

Jon wished he could go back in there and say something else to comfort him, but he'd already given him everything he had.

The driver had gone, and Dan drove back with Jon in the passenger seat. He still didn't recognize this part of London. At first neither of them spoke, but after a few minutes, Dan said, "What the bloody hell happened back there?"

"I don't know." Jon tried to think back, but all he could think of was Dan coming in with his gun already drawn, then his insistence on getting his fee. "You would have killed me, wouldn't you? I mean, you wouldn't have given it a second thought."

"Of course. But I thought I explained all of that. I wouldn't have been killing *you*, Jonathan Hoyle, I just would have been hitting a target."

Jon smiled. He could imagine this guy being completely untroubled by what he did, sleeping well, walking lightly through the world. He'd been like that himself once, and maybe Dan's moment would also come, but he doubted it somehow.

He'd killed people, he'd saved people, he'd inhabited the same world as Jon, and on at least one occasion, they'd even crossed paths. But Dan Borowski was a natural in that world, someone who wore death easily and saw it for what it was.

No doubt if Dan had found the young Nabil dying in the ruins, he'd have known what to do. If the boy could have been saved, Dan would have left him and gone for help. If he couldn't, Dan would have stayed with him, just as Jon had, but when it was all done, he'd have left it behind.

"When you were talking earlier, about our jobs being similar, you missed something."

Dan glanced over, casually curious, and said, "What's that?"

"The need to detach what you're doing from the individual on the end of it—your target, my subject."

Dan nodded, and at first it didn't look like he'd respond further, but then he said, "I wonder how many people around the world have died since I picked you up earlier. Hundreds? Thousands? It doesn't matter. None of those lives matters to us. If I'd killed you tonight, the vast majority of the world's population wouldn't have even known about it. If I die tomorrow, it won't matter to anyone. So you see, it's just not worth thinking about. I live well, and that's enough for me. Should be enough for you too."

Jon nodded, even though he felt like he needed a few minutes to work out what Dan had just said—on first pass, it wasn't much clearer than the crocodile story. Then he realized that they'd turned into Dorchester Street and a moment later Dan had pulled up outside the gallery.

"Oh, God, sorry mate, I've brought you back to the gallery. I'll take you to the hotel."

"No, this is fine, really. After everything that's happened, I could use the fresh air."

Dan laughed and said, "I bet!" He looked serious then as he added, "It's been a pleasure, Jon, and for what it's worth, I think you handled yourself really bloody well. Not many people would've stayed calm like that."

"I had nothing to lose." He smiled and said, "So long, Dan."

"You take care now."

Jon got out of the car and watched as Dan pulled away. He heard his name then and turned to see Sophie coming out of the gallery, her coat on, bag over her shoulder, catalogue under one arm. She managed to lock the door without putting anything on the ground, then walked over to him.

"Hi, what are you still doing here?"

"Long story. I was somewhere else, and then I got dropped off here by mistake." She smiled, showing interest, the slightly awkward way people did when they felt they had to be interested but weren't really. "Sorry, don't let me keep you. I'm sure you wanna get home."

"No, it's fine. I don't have anything to rush back for." Maybe he needed to go back to photographing people in some form or other because it seemed he'd read her completely wrong.

"Well, I'm only heading back to the hotel—would you like to come back for dinner?"

She looked staggered, maybe even suspecting he wasn't serious, as she said, "I'd love to, but do you mind? The general word is that you don't care for company."

"I never used to."

They started to walk and he couldn't help but smile. A contract killer named Dan Borowski had shot him in the head this evening, a death he'd accepted, even embraced—from now on, everything else was a gift.

The Right Tool for the Job

BY MARCUS PELEGRIMAS

Marcus Pelegrimas's stories have appeared in the anthologies *Mystery Street* (Signet, 2001), *Guns of the West* (Berkley, 2003), and *Lone Star Law* (Pocket, 2005). His first novel, *The Man from Boot Hill* (Harper Torch), appeared in July 2004. It was the first of a series. He has written in the horror, western, and mystery genres. This story is a perfect example of what I said in my introduction about how you'd find characters in here who, although killers, are likeable. Meet Cecil and Eddie.

EDDIE BALLARD HAD ALWAYS ENJOYED hurting people.

When he was a kid, he wanted to be a cop. He'd just liked the idea of pinning a badge to his shirt, strapping a gun around his waist, and kicking ass in the name of justice. By the time he was old enough to get a start on his career, he realized there was a whole lot of work involved with fighting the good fight. It also required that he keep his own nose relatively clean in the process.

That last part had always been Eddie's biggest problem.

He joined the Army after high school because it seemed like a good deal. Free food, clothes, and all the guns a growing boy could want. But even with those things under consideration, it wasn't worth putting up with superior officers who never wanted to give Eddie a fair shake. He left when his time was up and started looking around for a line of work that suited him better.

It turned out that he didn't care about the law or enemies, foreign and domestic. He just liked to hurt people. He came to that realization over drinks with an old friend from the neighborhood. When that friend offered to put in a good word with some business associates of his own, Eddie knew he'd stumbled upon something that fit him like the black gloves that would be wrapped around his fists almost a year later.

From the streets to boot camp, Roy had always looked out for him. It had been Roy's idea for Eddie to do what he loved and start demanding real money for his skills rather than settle for a civil servant's salary.

Those years in the Army were barely a memory. The dreams before that of wearing a badge seemed to have come from someone else's head altogether. All that concerned Eddie nowadays was getting paid for doing things that had been at the heart of every other aspiration he'd ever had.

Eddie's leather-clad fist slammed into the bigger man's face like a hammer tenderizing a side of beef. The impact wiped away every trace of the grin that the man had worn only moments ago, replacing it with a wet crimson mask.

"You want to tell me where to find Dennison?" Eddie asked, being careful to keep his voice just above a whisper.

The man with the bloody face was built like a linebacker. His hands were thick as generously sliced steaks and his fingers opened and closed like animated sausages. When he tried to reach up and take hold of Eddie's wrist, the guy just got another punch in the mouth for his trouble.

"All right," Eddie grunted as he pulled the nine-millimeter pistol from its shoulder holster. "Start talking, or you're dead meat."

Doing his best to maintain his tough facade, the linebacker

actually started to tremble when the pistol in Eddie's hand was jammed against his forehead. "Upstairs," he blubbered. "Room 312."

Eddie nodded and took in the sight of the bigger man who'd been reduced to a scared little kid in a matter of seconds. "Thanks. You did the right thing." With that, he reared back his gun arm and dropped it against the linebacker's temple. The pistol's grip, wrapped within his hand, made a satisfying crunch as it knocked against flesh and bone. The linebacker dropped into an unconscious heap.

After holstering the pistol, Eddie reached back and found the doorknob, which had been pressing against the bottom of his spine. Twisting it, he stepped backwards into a tastefully decorated hallway. After closing the door, he wiped his hands on his shirt and walked away.

The room he left behind was a maintenance closet about twenty feet from a bank of elevators. As he walked past those elevators, Eddie glanced up at a row of narrow signs marked with directions to the stairway as well as various blocks of room numbers. Every door he passed from then on was identical: white painted metal, electronic card reader, number on a black plate. Only the occasional DO NOT DISTURB sign hanging from a brass-plated knob broke up the monotony.

Eddie buttoned up his jacket to cover the bloodied shirt as well as the holster strapped under his arm. Glancing around casually, he made sure that nobody was around before opening the door at the end of the hall and stepping into a harshly lit stairwell. Through the large windows, he could see a parking lot, a highway, and a large block of office buildings on the other side of it.

After jogging up a few sets of stairs, he pulled open the door to the third floor and stepped through. Compared to the lower floors, this one was bustling with activity. There were men in suits posted at three of the doors further down the hall. Similarly dressed men were near the elevator at the opposite end. There were even a few muscle-bound specimens standing on either side of the door to the stairs that Eddie was currently using.

"Excuse me," Eddie said as he walked into the hallway. "I'm looking for the ice machine."

Neither of the men said a word. Instead, they glared at Eddie as if he'd just insulted their mothers.

"The machine on this floor's broke," the first of the guards said. "Try someplace else."

Pretending not to hear anything the man said, Eddie shrugged and started walking past him and his twin. He waited until he felt one of them grab his shoulder before balling his fist and making his move.

First, he took hold of the hand grasping his shoulder. Keeping that hand in place, Eddie used his free arm to take a swing at the second guard who was just starting to reach under his jacket when Eddie's fist caught him in the stomach.

As the second guard crumpled over, the first one was still trapped with one hand on Eddie's shoulder. He wasn't content to keep still as his partner was dropped, so he slammed one fist into Eddie's ribs.

Feeling a dull explosion of pain in his side, Eddie gritted his teeth and viciously slammed his forehead into the first guard's face. The impact sent a loud crunch through both men's ears, but it was the guard who started to wobble. Eddie let go of the man's hand so he could get a grip on the guy by his chin and twist his head to one side. Another wet crunch could be heard as the guard's neck snapped.

Eddie turned to walk down the hall as his hand went for the nine-millimeter under his jacket. The first two guards had fallen in a matter of seconds, but the rest of the men had taken up their positions and most of them already had their weapons drawn. Now that Eddie was the only one standing at the door, thunder filled the hall as all those guns started going off in the enclosed space.

Eddie wasn't the first to fire, but he was the first to actually hit anything. Bullets punched into the walls around him as he took quick aim and pulled his trigger. His face twitched reflexively as the nine-millimeter jumped in his hand. That twitch became a victorious smirk when he saw one of the men in the hall jerk back and fall over amid a spray of blood.

Walking down the hall toward the door marked 312, Eddie felt a certain calmness fall over him like a blanket which shielded his ears from the roar of gunfire. He fired every step of the way, knowing that he would never have gotten a moment like this wearing any sort of uniform. By the time he made it to his destination, Eddie had put three men out of their misery and sent the others running for the closest exit.

Eddie sent his last shot into the twitching body of a guard slumped against the door. He then brought one knee up to his chest and sent his heel straight into a spot next to the door's handle. Although the door rattled against the frame, his foot bounced off of it without much progress. One more kick, though, was enough to fracture the bolt, and a third impact got the door swinging inward.

"Come on out, Dennison," Eddie snarled. His eyes darted about the room as his hand reached into a jacket pocket to retrieve a clip for the nine-millimeter. By the time his gun was reloaded, his eyes had settled upon a figure huddled in the next room.

Will Dennison's face had been burned into Eddie's mind during the flight from Kansas City as well as during the drive to the hotel. All that time, he'd been picturing the way Dennison would look when Eddie finally met him in person. The defiant sneer was just what Eddie had expected. Wiping that sneer off was going to be a pleasure.

Dennison was a squat man in his forties with a full head of greasy brown hair. His round face was drenched in sweat and he was breathing as though he'd just completed a few laps around the parking lot. "You stupid son of a bitch," he said between gasps.

Just then, Eddie heard heavy footsteps coming from every direction. The door to the bathroom was kicked open and a man carrying a shotgun rushed out. Two others popped their heads up to level their gaze as well as a pair of automatics at Eddie.

Eddie blinked once and then started firing.

The nine-millimeter was emptied in a matter of seconds, filling the room with blood and the stench of death. A wisp of smoke curled from the barrel as he slipped the pistol back into its holster. While stepping over one of the bodies, Eddie reached down and picked up the man's automatic, which had yet to be fired.

It was a small, box-shaped pistol with an extended clip. The barrel had been extended as well, to accommodate the silencer which protruded from the end of the gun. Once the automatic settled into his grasp, Eddie stood over Dennison, who'd curled himself up in a ball between the bed and the air conditioner/heater which took up most of the wall beneath the window.

"You pissed off the wrong people, Dennison," Eddie said.

Dennison did his best to regain some dignity, but was having a hard time of it with his legs tucked up against his chest like a baby. Rather than struggle some more on the floor, he propped his arms on his knees and shook his head. "You want to make some real money? I'll double whatever you're getting paid for this."

"All right," Eddie said. "Where's the money?"

Dennison's eyes narrowed and he cocked his head a bit to one side. "In the suitcase," he said, nodding toward a metal stand at the other side of the room. "In the lining on the side, right against my socks."

Keeping his gun trained on Dennison, Eddie walked over to the suitcase and rummaged through it. Sure enough, he found a wad of money right where Dennison said it would be.

"There's over ten grand in there," Dennison said. "Keep it. There's plenty more once I make it out of here."

Eddie pocketed the money and walked back over to Dennison. "Actually, this is more than enough."

Before Dennison could say another word, the automatic came to life in Eddie's hand and tore his body to shreds.

Four days later, Eddie was walking down another hallway wearing the same self-satisfied grin that he'd worn in the blood-spattered hotel room that was Will Dennison's final resting place. This hallway was a little wider and didn't have as many doors as the previous one.

There were fewer guards posted, but plenty of cameras mounted on the walls to take up that slack.

The building wasn't that much different than any of the other office buildings in downtown St. Louis. There were secretaries doing their business and men in suits doing theirs. All in all, Eddie felt like he could have been applying for a loan rather than attending a meeting with a man who handed out death warrants and million-dollar deals every day of the week.

The door where Eddie stopped didn't look different from the others, but was definitely the toughest one to pass. Apart from being thicker than a vault door, it was guarded by three men wearing enough ordnance to stage a revolt in a small country. "Assuming the position," Eddie smiled as he approached one of the guards and raised his arms.

The man who searched him was of average build and displayed as much emotion on his face as the door he was guarding. He removed Eddie's weapons before stepping back and nodding to another man who sat on a chair three feet away. That one said something into a small microphone connected to an earpiece before opening the door.

Eddie stepped inside and walked straight up to the clean, mahogany desk which took up most of the room. "You hear about the job?"

Pyotr was the name of the man behind the desk. He appeared to be in his mid to late fifties and had the build of an old soldier. Smooth, olive skin covered an iron physique. His face had been filling out over the last few years, but that did nothing to take away from dark eyes which burned like coals in his skull. Nobody in the building knew his last name, so his closer acquaintances called him The Greek. Everyone else called him Sir.

"You call that a job?" Pyotr asked.

Eddie winced a bit, but recovered instantly. "Dennison was supposed to wind up dead. He's dead."

"Did you get him to talk?"

"He wouldn't say a word. Tough guy, right up to the end." W

that, Eddie made a gun with his fingers and pulled the imaginary trigger. That brought an amused smile to his face.

Pyotr wasn't as easily amused. "As far as hits go, it was a grade-A fuckup. I want that kind of job done, I'll hire some dumb-shit punks off the street for a quarter of the price."

"Look, Greek, I—"

Pyotr stopped him right there with an upraised finger which cut a whole lot deeper than Eddie's imaginary gun. "I brought you in here as a favor to Roy. You're still on trial with me. You understand?"

"Yeah. I understand."

"It took some major pull to get you out of there clean after that shit you pulled. You know that was a hotel full of regular people, right?"

Eddie let out an aggravated breath. He nodded, but saw that wasn't enough. "I know. I watched the place for—"

"For what? Five minutes?"

"I might've gotten a little carried away. . . ." Eddie stopped himself when he saw that Pyotr was about to explode. Before the older man could say another word, Eddie quickly added, "Maybe even a lot carried away. I just want to do a good job for you and you said that it didn't matter if there were some other bodies when the smoke cleared. Nobody knew who I was or who I worked for."

"I provide a service," Pyotr said in a tone that was like a blade sinking quietly into the back of Eddie's neck. "You don't even know half of what I do, but I can tell you that you're a speck on a fly's ass compared to the rest of this operation. You want to wave your gun around? Then go show it to some dumb bitch who'll be impressed by it."

Like a kid who just realized he wasn't about to be expelled for smoking after class, Eddie nodded and relaxed a bit. "I'll do better next time. When is the next time, by the way?"

Pyotr moved his other hand for the first time since Eddie had walked into the room. Until now, that hand had been lying flat upon a folder on top of his desk. Stretching his arm forward, he slid

the folder toward Eddie. "It starts right now. There's someone I need you to take care of. I wanted to talk to him myself, but he decided to run."

When Eddie tried to take the folder, Pyotr kept his hand pressed down firmly upon it. He brought up his other hand to stab a beefy finger at Eddie's face. "This won't end up like the last job. You understand?"

Eddie nodded.

"A professional needs a soft touch," Pyotr continued. "You either get yourself a softer touch or you'll be out of a job. It don't matter how much I like you or Roy or anyone else. I can't afford to have that kind of heat turned my way again. I want this job done quiet and professionally. You screw this up, and there won't be no other jobs for you. Not ever."

"I'll do what I do," Eddie said, feeling himself getting backed into a corner. "But I can't do it all." Opening the folder, he flipped through the few sheets of paper which included some addresses, some brief descriptions of security systems, but not one photograph. "I might not even be able to shut these alarms off quick enough to do any good."

For the first time since Eddie had known him, Pyotr smiled. It wasn't exactly a pleasant sight. "I'm glad you brought that up, because that shows you can think if you need to. There's someone coming along with you on this one."

"W-what?" Eddie stammered. "Who? Why?"

"Just someone to handle the technical part of it. You know, get through security, maybe even show you a thing or two."

Eddie puffed out his chest and snatched the folder from the top of the desk. "I've seen plenty."

"You know how to pick a lock? What about hacking a computer? This jerk-off you're after has got himself wrapped up in more technology than a Sharper Image store. You know how to get through that, or did you just plan on calling in an air strike? That'd be quieter than the bullshit that went on in that hotel."

As much as he wanted to answer the challenge written all over Pyotr's face, Eddie didn't have anything to say. Nothing, that is, that wouldn't cause the older man to lunge over the top of his desk.

"Take it easy, boy," Pyotr said. "And meet your partner."

Eddie looked around as the room's only door was opened and a small man was allowed inside. The guy, a good bit older than Eddie, looked like someone Eddie would have beaten the shit out of in high school, if they'd been in high school together.

"This is Cecil," Pyotr announced. "He'll be along for the ride."

The sports car rumbled around its two passengers like a cat wrapping around its master's leg. Sitting in the driver's seat, Eddie worked the wheel and pedals like every turn was a command and every stop had to be announced with a stomp. As always, he allowed the other man a few minutes to soak up the grandeur of the automobile before asking the guy to speak. After all, the little fellow was only human.

"So," Eddie said after giving the guy in the seat next to him enough time to adjust to the impressive machinery around him, "your name is Cecil?"

For a moment, it seemed as though the guy hadn't heard Eddie's question. His eyes rarely moved from the newspaper he was holding and the only time he moved was in response to the motion of the car. Then, after a few more pressing looks from the driver, Cecil nodded. "Yes. It is."

"I'm Eddie."

His eyes were already back to the newspaper and his hands were busy shaking it to straighten it out. "I know."

Nodding, Eddie slowly shifted his eyes back to the road. "Nice car, huh?"

Cecil looked around as though he was only now noticing the vehicle that was carrying him from one point to another. "Sure."

"What do you do for The Greek?"

That question brought Cecil's eyes over to Eddie and held them there. Shaking his head, he glanced out the window at the highway. "Didn't he tell you?"

"He said you know about security systems and computers and shit."

"That sounds about right."

"Sounds boring."

Cecil shrugged and looked back to the paper.

After allowing a few seconds to pass, Eddie put on a friendly grin and looked over to the passenger. "I kill people."

The statement had been intended to allow Eddie to get a feel for the other man. He watched Cecil's reaction the way he might stare someone down across a poker table. Although there was a little flicker that could have been fear or nervousness, it wasn't enough to crease the smaller man's brow.

"I heard about that," Cecil replied with a vague glimmer of a smirk.

"You did? From The Greek?"

Nodding, Cecil said, "Sounds like it was a sloppy job."

Eddie looked over to Cecil, back to the road, back to Cecil and then slammed his foot on the brake while wrenching the wheel to the right. He got a bit of satisfaction from the way Cecil grabbed at the dashboard to keep himself from going through the window, but Eddie was more concerned with keeping his car in one piece as he skidded to a halt along the side of I-70.

"Look here, you little shit," Eddie growled as soon as he'd slammed the car into park. "I do my job damn well and if things get a little messy, then that's the way it is. What the hell do you know about anything?" The longer he looked at the skinny man with the sunken face taking up his passenger seat, the angrier Eddie got. "How the fuck did you find out about my last job anyway? That shit is between me and The Greek."

Although he'd looked rattled by the sudden stop, Cecil hadn't lost his composure. In fact, now that the car wasn't about to careen into oncoming traffic, his face had reverted back to its normal emotion-less, if somewhat pasty, expression. In response to Eddie's question,

Cecil snapped the newspaper straight, folded it in half, and turned it toward the other man.

FOUR DEAD AND SEVERAL WOUNDED IN GANG-RELATED SHOOTOUT

"It's not the front page," Cecil said. "But I'm guessing that's only because there's a war going on somewhere else in the world."

Looking at those big, black words plastered across Cecil's newspaper, Eddie could almost hear Pyotr's voice bellowing through his ears.

"I . . . uhh . . . didn't see that one," Eddie mumbled.

"It's a good idea to read the local papers for a while after you finish a job," Cecil told him. "That gives you an idea of how big a splash you made and what's being done about it."

Suddenly, Eddie wasn't so angered by the sight of the skinny guy in his passenger seat. He didn't even feel the overwhelming need to punch the man just to see if his face was as fragile as it looked. Nodding, Eddie put the car in drive and stomped on the gas pedal. "I'll have to remember that," he said as the car's engine roared and they were thrown into the stream of commuters.

St. Louis's Lambert International Airport was only a few more minutes away.

The plane ride had taken just under an hour, but Eddie felt like an entire day had been mercilessly stripped from his life. Not only was his seat cramped and stuck somewhere between upright and reclined, but it was close enough to Cecil's for him to see every move the smaller man made.

Eddie couldn't decide which drove him crazier: the fact that The Greek had sent along a babysitter, or that this particular babysitter had less personality than a limp noodle.

The check-in process had been excruciating. As soon as they'd walked into the airport, Cecil had acted as though Eddie didn't even exist. He'd dumped his newspaper in a trash can, only to replace it with the first *St. Louis Post-Dispatch* that he could find. Ever since then, the little prick had been strutting ahead of Eddie as if he was in charge of the whole job.

Eddie knew well enough that it was best to keep up appearances, but there was also a matter of respect between the two men that wasn't being observed. The Greek said that Cecil was supposed to show him a thing or two. So far, all Eddie had been shown was a newspaper.

"Care for something to drink before we land?" asked the pretty blonde stewardess as she pushed the cart down the aisle.

She'd been flirting with him like that since he'd gotten onto the plane. Even though he didn't have his guns on him, Eddie still carried himself like a dangerous man. Women could sense that about him and, no matter what they said to their friends or therapists, they loved it.

"I'll save my drink for after we land," Eddie said in a voice that was smooth enough to be a purr to her ears. "Care to join me?"

She looked away for a moment and then gave him a smile. "We'll have to see about that."

Knowing that she couldn't say too much more without getting in trouble, Eddie nodded and winked at her. "Oh yeah. We sure will."

She giggled and turned away to look at one of the other stewardesses further up the aisle. From what Eddie could see, she couldn't wait to tell her friend about what she wanted to do to him once the flight was over. Too bad none of that would happen. Eddie had some dangerous business to handle. Of course, there was always the flight home.

When he looked over to Cecil, Eddie held his eyes there until the skinny guy finally looked back. The speaker over Eddie's head crackled and the pilot's voice sounded throughout the cabin. He didn't listen to a damn word that was said. Instead, Eddie put on his own shit-eating grin and sent a friendly little wave in Cecil's direction.

"I hate that little bastard," Eddie grumbled under his breath.

Even though the plane ride had been short and uneventful, Cecil was glad it was over. The change in altitude hurt his ears more than it did for most people, making the first part of any flight feel as though he was getting an ice pick driven through his head. Not too long after his ears had popped, the plane started descending for its landing and the process started all over again.

It would have been good to get some work done, but that wasn't going to happen. Cecil felt like his head was going to crack and his partner was too busy making an ass out of himself with the flight attendant to worry about a thing like earning his pay.

Once the plane came to a stop at the gate, Cecil started getting his things together. All it took was a little shuffling of papers to get Eddie frustrated enough to shove his way into the aisle so he could come to a stop about two feet from where he'd started.

Most lines were for prisoners and people too stupid to know that just about anything they were after would still be there once the rest of the lemmings had cleared the path. Shaking his head, Cecil waited until enough of the passengers had cleared out for him to step into the aisle and exit the plane without being rushed.

"Thanks for flying with us," the blonde flight attendant said in the same tone that had brought a victorious grin to Eddie's face when he'd walked past that same spot.

Cecil nodded and moved on. He took his time leaving the plane and kept a leisurely pace once inside the airport itself. Eddie was waiting for him as though he'd been standing in the terminal for the better part of the day.

"Jesus," Eddie grunted as he fell into step next to Cecil. "You walk like an old man."

"You know we still need to wait for our luggage, right?"

"Yeah, and if we don't hurry, we won't get a spot right by where it dumps out onto that turntable thing."

Shaking his head, Cecil passed up the chance to tell Eddie that, contrary to popular belief, all of the luggage made its way around the entire track no matter what airport it was in. Instead of getting too upset by the hyperactive younger man, Cecil let him scamper ahead and shove into a spot near the front of the baggage claim.

They waited there for a good twenty minutes before it started moving.

Eddie's brain rattled in his head. Watching Cecil's plodding steps and deliberate movements only made it worse. He doubted the skinny little jerk could take a shit without making an appointment for it and then scribbling it into his planner. That image brought a smirk to Eddie's face as he dropped himself into the driver's seat of his rented car and turned the key.

"You ever been here before?" Eddie asked.

So far, Cecil hadn't even glanced out a window. Upon retrieving his bag, he'd dug out a small shaving kit, which he was now opening. From the leather bag, he removed a smaller leather pouch as well as a plastic container that resembled the one Eddie used to hold the removable faceplate of his car's CD player. The shaving kit went into an inner jacket pocket, and the bag went onto the floor behind his seat.

"Never been here," Cecil replied as he opened the plastic container and removed a narrow electronic device. "But that doesn't matter."

Eddie recognized the device before too long. "That one of them GSP things?"

"GPS."

"Yeah, yeah. An electric map thing. Soccer moms love having those in their vans. You know, for family trips and shit."

"Or," Cecil added while tapping his fingers over a touch-sensitive pad, "for finding an address without having to worry about maps or written directions." After his fingers had been still for a few moments, Cecil pointed toward the front widow. "Pull out here and take a left. Get on the highway heading east."

"Yes, sir," Eddie muttered. The sarcasm in his voice was lost upon the skinny man sitting next to him.

Driving from highway to side street and then back to highway again, Eddie was nearly lulled to sleep. The only thing to keep him alert was the occasional instruction delivered by Cecil's sharp, demanding voice.

"This place in the city or out of it?" Eddie asked.

Cecil looked up from the electronic box in his hand and glanced at the drab scenery sliding past his window. "Looks out of the city to me."

"I barely even remember what city we're in."

"Does it matter?"

Eddie thought about that for a moment and shrugged. "I guess it doesn't."

"But you still want to know, don't you?"

"Yeah. Maybe I do. Is that wrong?"

Now it was Cecil's turn to shrug. "Not wrong, per se, but unnecessary. When some guy in a suit sits in his chair and fills out his reports, do you think he knows exactly where his reports go or every last detail they refer to?"

"What kind of office?"

"Does it matter?"

"No," Eddie said with a short laugh. "I guess it doesn't."

"There's an exit coming up here in just over a mile." After getting the acknowledging nod from Eddie, Cecil fidgeted with something inside his jacket pocket. "You know what your problem is?"

Twitching as if he'd just been asked to drop his pants, Eddie looked over at the skinny guy next to him. "My problem?" Knowing he wasn't going to get much more than the dry look in return, he asked, "Why don't you tell me?"

"You're not a very good hit man."

"I'm what?"

"Isn't that what you like to call yourself? A hit man?"

"Sure." Although his voice was reserved, the way he straightened up in his seat and puffed out his chest was hard to miss. Suddenly, he remembered the words that had come just before his glamorous title. "How the fuck would you know if I'm any good?"

"Being sent on a shit job like this is a good indication. From what I could tell, Pyotr wasn't too happy with you."

"Yeah? Maybe he's not too happy with you, either."

Cecil shook his head and glanced at the road stretching out in front of the rental car. "You're probably not that good at poker, either. The exit's coming up right here."

Gnashing his teeth, Eddie let out a measured breath as he steered for the exit marked by a rectangular green sign. The sky had turned gray and was spitting a mist down onto them. It was a greasy kind of mist that smudged the windshield but avoided getting caught by the wiper blades.

Cecil's eyes were on Eddie and stayed there until the car was well onto its new course. The road quickly became rougher and the scenery thinned out even more until there was nothing more than trees and open space on any side.

Pushed well past his limit by the maddening silence that hung around Cecil like a fog, Eddie smacked the top of the steering wheel and sent a few venomous looks in the skinny man's direction. "Look, you're working for me on this job. I don't have to take any lip from some fucking geek who's just along to hack a computer."

"I don't work for you."

"Yeah, well, if you keep talking out of line, maybe I should . . ." Eddie's threat was cut short by nothing more than the look in Cecil's eyes. It wasn't a murderous look, or even a threatening look. Instead, it was a look so completely devoid of emotion that Eddie saw his own death flash in front of him. "Who the hell are you?"

"I'm someone who's been in this business for a long time," Cecil replied calmly. "I've seen plenty of potential talent come and go. You might even say that's my specialty."

"How long have you worked for The Greek?"

"I don't work for anyone in particular. My services get hired out when they're needed, and I only work for people who can do me some good."

"Are you higher up than The Greek?"

"Look, you've got some potential. If you didn't, you'd be dead already."

"I'm damn good at my job," Eddie said defensively.

"Then maybe your problem is that you don't know what your job truly is. An assassin is supposed to be professional."

"I am a professional."

"No. You're a killer. There's a difference."

"Is there?"

Cecil's eyes narrowed and he leaned forward so he could look Eddie in the face. "The difference is that assassins are in and out like a diamond-edged drill bit. They don't wind up on the front page of a newspaper because of a bloodbath that they were too fucking stupid to avoid."

Eddie's hand moved instinctively toward the holster under his arm. He'd missed having the gun with him during his time on the plane and in the airports, but now it was a familiar weight in his grasp. As he pulled the gun out, he was already planning what he would say and how the skinny little bastard in the passenger seat would piss himself with fear.

Those thoughts were cut short by the touch of warm steel against his throat.

Eddie hadn't actually seen Cecil reach for the leather pouch in his pocket, but his brain put the pieces together after the fact. Unfortunately, the blade that had been inside that pouch was already out and pressing against the flesh just beneath his chin.

Cecil's eyes hadn't wavered. His shoulders were in the same position and the GPS was still clutched in his other hand. It seemed as though his left arm had come to life and taken action on its own, with the rest of Cecil's mind and body a mildly interested spectator.

Squirming in his seat, Eddie barely realized that his foot had slipped off the gas pedal. Since the road was as straight as it was empty, there was plenty of room for the car to veer as it rolled to a gradual stop.

"You see that?" Cecil asked as he shifted the knife against Eddie's throat. "You're like a big kid strutting down a high-school hallway. That makes you predictable and sloppy because you're too anxious to prove how tough you are."

"You want to kill me?" Eddie grunted as best he could without pushing himself against the blade in Cecil's hand. He couldn't see the weapon, but he could feel that the blade was only a few inches long and curved as if it had been custom made for this very moment. "Then what are you waiting for? Do it. I bet you don't even have the stones to kill a man."

The shift in Cecil's face was all but imperceptible. "There's no way you could possibly believe that."

The words hung in the air like cigar smoke until Eddie thought he was going to choke on them. Finally, he no longer felt the blade against his neck. When he dared to move above the waist, there was nothing stopping him.

"What about the job?" Eddie asked, still confused by the fact that he was still alive. "Who's going to finish the job?"

Glancing around the car as though he was looking for someone, Cecil said, "*We* do the job, of course. Who do you think?"

"I mean . . . after what you said . . . are we still working together?"

"You've got talent," Cecil announced. "I've seen plenty who've started a shootout like the one in that hotel, but not many who would've been able to walk out in one piece. All you need to do is know where your strength lies and behave accordingly." More to himself, he added, "The rest is just a matter of putting you on the right job."

Enough time had passed for Eddie to pull himself together and get his mind back on track. He even felt a pinch of anger biting into his stomach as he gunned the rental car's engine and skidded onto the road.

The next few seconds dragged by with Eddie at the wheel and Cecil calmly studying the GPS. If someone had looked away for the last few minutes, they might have thought nothing had happened between the time just before the rental car had turned off the main highway and now.

But Eddie knew better.

Plenty had changed.

Eddie's life had been flipped like a quarter off of somebody's thumb. Whether he'd flipped toward a fat promotion within The Greek's organization or toward the end of his road, he couldn't quite say. Not just yet, anyway.

"The turn's ahead about two and a half miles," Cecil said with less enthusiasm in his voice than the fat redhead from whom they'd rented the car. "There's a grocery store at the turn. Pull in there so we can get some supplies."

"Supplies? What supplies?"

Although Eddie knew Cecil was much more than just some passenger, he also figured out that Pyotr hadn't been lying about the skinny man's talent with security systems. The dot on Cecil's GPS was a small house in the middle of nowhere at the end of a long stretch of rough road. Cecil made him pull over more than half a mile away and cut the engine.

It was dark. In fact, it was the kind of dark that made a city boy feel like he was on the moon. Without the glare of streetlights or even the distant glow of civilization, Eddie started to feel like he was in a bad horror movie. The occasional sounds of nature made him twitch in several directions as his hand lingered over his holstered pistol.

"Stay here," Cecil said impatiently. "These grounds are wired."

"How do you know?"

Cecil's only response was a quick, downward stab of his finger. When Eddie looked in that direction, he saw a single thread stretching between what appeared to be two blades of grass.

"Because there's the wire," Cecil announced to drive his point home.

Eddie nodded and kept the rest of what he had wanted to say in the back of his mind, where it belonged.

Stepping over the nearly invisible tripwire, Cecil made his way across a field which was only about twenty yards long. He moved like a cartoon hunter trying to keep very, very quiet. Both of Cecil's hands were open and at waist level. Every one of his steps was taken on deliberate tip-toes. Every now and then, he would stop and turn another way or hop over some other unseen obstacle in his path. He would then crouch down, examine something that could barely even be seen in the darkness, and then fish something from one of the pockets in his jacket. After putting the tool back in its place, Cecil moved on.

Finally, he made it to a black blob of shadow at a cluster of trees at the edge of the clearing. Cecil reached out to what appeared to be one of the trees and started brushing off the trunk. Eddie's eyes were becoming used to the darkness and he eventually saw that Cecil wasn't dusting off a tree. Instead, he was pulling away branches and some sort of blanket to reveal a rectangular metal box.

The box came to Cecil's chest level. It opened at the front with a squeak that seemed more like a scream in the quiet night. Once the box was opened, Cecil squatted slightly so he could look straight into its contents. He reached into his jacket pocket and removed something from what had appeared to be the grooming kit from his bag in the car.

Eddie blinked and felt his muscles tense. He hadn't seen Cecil take that from the bag and knew damn well that it hadn't been on him when he'd gone through the metal detector at the airport. All this time, he'd been keeping a close eye on the skinny little prick and something still got past Eddie's eyes.

The more he thought about it, the more certain Eddie became that Cecil was probably armed to the teeth.

A brief spark and an electrical crackle snapped Eddie out of his worried thoughts. Cecil's face was briefly illuminated by the discharge from the box. Although he didn't seem to react to the sparks, Cecil did look over to Eddie and nod once.

"All right," Cecil whispered. "It should be safe for you to come here."

Keeping his body low and his eyes jumping from one dark shape to another, Eddie stretched out with his senses and tried to identify every noise he heard and every hint of movement he spotted. By the time he got to where Cecil was waiting, he found the skinny man smirking and shaking his head.

"What's so fucking funny?" Eddie asked with a snarl.

"You've seen way too many movies. For a moment there, I thought you were going drop and roll."

Eddie's hand clenched around his gun.

"Stay here and let me deactivate the next set of perimeter alarms," Cecil said.

"This place is like some kind of fortress, huh?"

Cecil responded to that with something close to a laugh. It was more like watching his face squirm. "Fortresses have more than motion sensors and tripwires. We're not through yet, but I shouldn't have much trouble."

That was enough to get Eddie to relax a bit. As far as he knew, things like silent alarm systems and security perimeters were like magic and voodoo rituals.

In Cecil's experience, the security precautions here were fucking pathetic.

Cecil crept ahead and went through a similar set of motions until he got to another carefully hidden circuit box. After the sparks flew, he motioned for Eddie to follow. They leapfrogged like that two more times, before coming within spitting distance of a weathered, ranch-style home.

Holding up a hand, Cecil got Eddie to freeze before going any closer. "There's the alarm system for the house," he said while pointing to a flat metal box on the side of the building. "I'll shut it off but keep the power on, so we don't tip off our friend inside." After taking half a step toward the box, Cecil stopped and looked over his shoulder. "Once I'm done here, it's your show. Feel free to make all the noise you want."

Eddie let out a sigh while grinding his teeth together.

"Too many movies," Cecil said as he turned his attention toward the junction box.

Just as Eddie was about to spit out the first insult that had come to mind, he spotted something that he'd been looking for ever since he'd left the car. From the corner of his eye, he saw a trace of movement, which was followed by the sound of heavy steps coming his way.

Before he had a chance to think, Eddie was rushing toward the source of the movement. One of his hands was wrapped around his nine-millimeter. As soon as he got a look at the man stepping out of the house, Eddie was grabbing hold of him and pulling him out.

The look of surprise on the other man's face bordered on comical.

All Eddie needed to see was that the other man wasn't the target and he wasn't a friendly face. Knowing that, he pumped two nine-millimeter rounds into the man's chest at point-blank range. The shots were muffled by the guy's body, but the impact of the bullets was enough to lift him off his feet.

Picking out one wire from the tangle inside the junction box, Cecil snipped it and pulled its neighbors from their plugs. He then closed the box and said, "Alarm's off. I guess we can sneak inside without being seen."

The sarcasm in Cecil's voice almost made Eddie turn his still-smoking gun toward the skinny man.

"Go on and finish what you started," Cecil said with a wave toward the front door. "There's no reporters around, so you can make all the noise you want."

Eddie took a look through the newly opened door and found a small room filled with coat hooks on the wall and dirty shoes lined up on the floor. When he turned back around to look at Cecil, he couldn't see a trace of the skinny security expert.

Another door on the opposite end of the coat room was opening. Eddie stepped inside and waited until it was fully open so he could get a look at who was on the other side. After spotting the approaching guards, he allowed his instincts to take over.

Once he got moving, Eddie felt like he was sliding down a muddy hill. While he could control himself a bit, it was limited to changes in direction as he shifted his aim from one armed man to another. After sending a few of them to the ground with a few well-placed head shots, Eddie started firing the nine-millimeter at anything that moved.

His ears rang with the sounds of gunfire. His vision started to blur and his heart pounded against the inside of his ribs. Some of the guards got a shot or two off, but not before they'd felt some of the fury Eddie was dealing out. When he ran out of ammo, Eddie used the butt of his gun to smash one guard's face into a bloody pulp. He then snapped the last guard's neck with his bare hands.

A few seconds later and Eddie could hear movement coming from the next room. He reloaded with a clip from his pocket and stormed in there with his gun held in front of him. Even before the door had a chance to smack against the wall, Eddie had chambered the first round and lifted the gun to aim at a man who matched the rough description he'd been given of his target. Shock jolted through his system like a splash of cold water.

"Roy?" Eddie asked the man standing in front of him. "Is that you?"

"Y-yeah," the man said to erase any doubt from Eddie's mind. "It's me. What the hell are you doing here? Why the fuck did you shoot my guys?" Suddenly, Roy focused on the gun in Eddie's hand. His eyes widened and he stumbled backward. In fact, he looked as though he probably hadn't slept for at least a week. His clothes were rumpled, and thick, uneven stubble marred his face. "Holy shit. Are you here to kill me?"

Eddie glanced at the nine-millimeter he was holding as if it was the first time he'd ever seen it. Lowering the gun, he started shaking his head. "No, Roy! Jesus Christ, I'm not here to kill you."

A door at the other end of the room swung open, allowing yet another familiar figure to walk in. Unlike Roy, there wasn't a single hair out of place on this man's head. In fact, Pyotr looked just as he had the last time Eddie had seen him. "Don't lie to the man, Eddie."

As Eddie looked around, the blood had begun to slow in his veins. The rush he'd felt earlier was fading, allowing him to finally see more than potential targets in his environment.

The room was some sort of den, complete with a large fireplace on one wall. Flames crackled in the stone space, tossing awkward shadows across the entire room. The opposite wall had a window with curtains drawn tightly over it. A tattered rug covered most of the floor and a cold breeze shifted through the air, chilling the half of Eddie's body that was farthest from the fire.

And just when Eddie was getting his mind around the fact that Pyotr was there, yet another familiar person stepped into the room behind The Greek.

"What do you say, Marker?" Pyotr asked. "How did our little Eddie do?"

Cecil looked over to Eddie as though he was studying a fast-food menu. "So far, so good."

Pyotr nodded and smirked, knowing exactly what kind of an impact he was having on Eddie and Roy.

"What's going on here?" Eddie asked, not sure whether he was talking to Cecil or Pyotr. "And who's Marker?"

"Cecil's a good man to have around," Pyotr explained. "He's damn good at his job and he knows how to pay back a favor. That's all he deals in. His marker is good as gold. He owes you a favor and it gets done. You want something from him and he gets a marker to call in on you. I don't know who started calling him the Marker Man, but it got cut down to Marker before too long."

Cecil rolled his eyes at the story, obviously uncomfortable with the joy that Pyotr was getting from watching Eddie squirm.

"Where's the rest of the guards?" Eddie asked.

"You got 'em all," Pyotr replied. "Nice job. Of course, they were just a bunch of punks who thought they were tough, but it's probably all Roy here could afford. Now it's time to wrap this up so we can go home."

Pyotr's eyes were fixed upon Roy the way a tiger eyed a limping antelope. Eddie had no trouble interpreting that predator's glance, but shook his head at it.

"No fucking way, Greek," Eddie said. "Roy's my homie."

"Cut the street talk, boy, you sound like some jerk-off kid at the mall. I say kill that stupid shit, so that's what you do."

The anger in Eddie's eyes was fading a bit, soon to be replaced by a vague sadness. "Why? What did he do?"

"What did he do? He vouched for you! That's what he did." Pyotr kept both his hands stuck in his pockets as he stepped forward and leaned in, as if that was enough to keep Eddie from moving a muscle. He was right. "Roy came to me and told me what a great guy you were. He said you knew how to handle yourself like a real pro, no matter how rough the job got. What did I say to that, Roy? Go on. Tell him what I said."

Roy was unable to look up into Pyotr's face. His body was trembling enough to rattle the tips of every strand of hair which hung down over his eyes. The outdated mop looked slick in the orange light of the fire.

Pyotr smiled at him. "You're sweating like a whore in church. Go on and tell your homie what I told you."

Roy clenched his eyes shut at the mocking tone in Pyotr's voice. Scrounging up the last shred of strength he had, he lifted his chin and met the other man's glare. "You said it would be my ass if Eddie didn't work out."

"You read the papers lately?"

Roy's nod was so weak that it almost went unnoticed.

"What about the news? I've seen that fucking hotel hallway on CNN more times than fucking Iraq. Does that seem like Eddie's worked out to you?"

Reflexively, Roy glanced over to Eddie. He couldn't hold it long and immediately dropped his focus to the floor. Soon, a beefy hand came into his line of sight and a few sausage-sized fingers came under his chin. Once his face was forced upward, Roy was looking directly at Pyotr.

"Does it?" The Greek asked.

". . . no."

"Then here I am to make good on my word." Stepping back, Pyotr paid no mind whatsoever to the gun still clutched in Eddie's hand. "You're a fuckup, Eddie. There's no two ways about it. You pull this cowboy gunfighter bullshit one too many times and now one of my jobs winds up all over the news. And," he added with a quick glance back in Cecil's direction, "you don't play too well with others."

Eddie looked over to Cecil and found the skinny man was no longer standing in the same spot. He'd positioned himself a few paces closer to Roy by the time Eddie spotted him.

"But we'll deal with that later," Pyotr continued. "For now, I've got too many problems to deal with. You can work through being a fuckup and you sure as hell know your way around a gun. But I'll only keep you if you earn your merit badge for loyalty.

"Someone needs to pay for what happened at that hotel, Eddie, and it's either going to be you or the dumb shit who brought you into my organization. I know Roy's your friend, so if you kill him for me you'll prove your loyalty. If you don't, then you're not only stupid and reckless, but you can't even take orders."

Nobody in the room spoke for a solid minute.

Eddie and Pyotr were staring each other down, trying to figure the other one out. Cecil looked on as if he already knew what was going to happen, and Roy was already resigned to his fate.

Strangely enough, it was Cecil who broke the silence. "I'll take care of him."

"That's not your job, Marker," Pyotr said without taking his eyes from Eddie.

"This is going nowhere. I'll take care of them both."

Eddie pulled in a sharp breath and raised his gun. "The hell you will, you skinny son of a bitch. You take one more step and I'll blow your head off."

The threat didn't land. Not only that, but Cecil didn't even break his stride.

In a move that seemed impossibly fast coming from a man of his size, Pyotr reached out and snatched the gun from Eddie's hand. Without a single word, he pressed the nine-millimeter to Roy's head and pulled the trigger.

The gun coughed once and sprayed the contents of Roy's head over the mantel behind him. Some of the heavier chunks smacked wetly against the brick fireplace as the sound of the shot rolled around inside the room.

Pyotr's face was beaming. The smile he wore stretched from one ear to the other and only grew more when he saw the mortified expression on Eddie's face. "You see that, you stupid bastard? That's what happens to people who put my fucking business on the goddamn news! Take a good look, Eddie."

There was a slight rustling sound behind Eddie, but he was too distracted to notice. He barely even noticed the slender arms that wrapped around the top of his chest and neck like a pair of steel bands.

"You talk too much," Cecil muttered as he took hold of Eddie and wrestled with the younger man. Twisting the wrist of the arm wrapped around Eddie's chest, Cecil showed the small curved knife in his fist.

Eddie struggled with every ounce of his strength. He grabbed hold of the arm wrapped around his neck while trying to pull away from the skinny man holding him, but Cecil was latched on as if he'd been welded there. The muscles under Cecil's sleeves were like iron snakes wrapped around the bones of his arms.

If he'd had another couple of seconds, Eddie might have been able to break free.

But Eddie didn't have another couple of seconds.

His time was up.

Using Eddie's momentum against him, Cecil twisted himself around until his back was to Pyotr. Eddie came along for the ride and when his feet hit the ground again, he was facing the door that he'd used to enter the room an eternity ago.

In one, viciously efficient move, Cecil raised Eddie's chin with one arm while reaching up and slicing the curved blade across his throat with the other.

Even Pyotr was taken aback by the detached efficiency of Cecil's actions. From his angle, he could only see the back of Eddie's head and his struggling limbs. He'd wanted to get a look into Eddie's eyes when he died, but The Greek nodded approvingly when he saw the spray of blood fill the air and Eddie's body go limp in Cecil's grasp.

After lowering Eddie to the floor, Cecil stood over him and wiped the dripping blade onto his sleeve. When he turned around, he saw Pyotr stepping over Eddie's silent body with the nine-millimeter still in his hand. Cecil reached out and plucked the gun from him with a fluid extension of his arm. "I'll dispose of this, as well as the bodies."

Pyotr was still eyeing Eddie's corpse. After a few seconds, he looked up and said, "I want to make sure."

"You want to make sure? How about you stand around for a while longer to make sure someone sees you with all this blood on your hands. I told you coming here yourself was a bad idea, but what do I know, right?"

Pyotr stopped him with an upraised hand. "Point taken. I just didn't come all this way to miss out on how this ends."

"You want to see how this ends? Then wait outside for a few minutes and you can roast some marshmallows after I set a match to this place. Before then, just let me do my work."

There was an unmistakably hungry look in Pyotr's eyes. It was the look of someone who'd gotten to sop up steak juices with a roll rather than sink his teeth into the meat. Those eyes drifted toward the knife in Cecil's hand, but finally found their way to the blood-drenched sleeve of Cecil's arm. That seemed to give him the taste he was after. Soon, the bigger man was nodding.

"You're right, Marker. You did your part."

"So this clears up my account with you." There wasn't a trace of a question in Cecil's voice. It was a statement of cold, hard fact.

"Yeah," Pyotr said as he looked around at the two bodies littering the room. "Now you just need to forget about those other things I owe you and we can be square."

Cecil grinned. It was a particularly chilling sight considering the bloody, little curved blade in his hand. "Nice try. My account with you is settled. Your account with me is wide open."

"How about I buy you dinner? Maybe let you sit in on one of my poker games?"

"That might do the trick."

Reaching out with the hand that had so recently been wrapped around a dead man's gun, Pyotr slapped Cecil on the shoulder and walked out. He made sure to clear his throat and spit a juicy wad onto the back of Eddie's head.

"I don't know how I kept from whacking that son of a bitch," Eddie grunted as he reached back and wiped the spit from his scalp.

Cecil gunned the engine and drove down the lonely road, putting the burning cabin behind him. Flames lapped at the sky in his rearview mirror, reminding him of the fireplace which was now a smoking ruin. "Actually, I'm pretty surprised myself."

Reaching across with his right arm, he kept his left elbow on the steering wheel while tugging his sleeve down. It took some work, but the fact that his right sleeve was already sliced along the bottom made it easier to remove it. Underneath the sticky, torn fabric, was a mess of red liquid, ripped cellophane and duct tape.

Eddie watched what Cecil was doing and instinctively touched the dried liquid on his neck. The supplies they'd bought earlier at the grocery store had all been put to good use. The tape and cellophane had secured to Cecil's arm a bag of fake blood that had been made from a mixture of food coloring and corn syrup. With Eddie facing away from Pyotr, one quick swipe from the curved blade had put on a sufficiently gruesome show.

As Cecil pulled off the tape and plastic, he revealed a wicked gash running down the length of his forearm. Wincing, he grabbed some paper towels from the floor of the car and started cleaning himself up. "Looks like I cut a little too deep when I sliced through that tape."

"You all right?"

Another few swipes from the towel and more of Cecil's arm could be seen. Apart from the fresh cut, there were plenty of older scars of roughly the same size. "I'm fine. Sorry about your friend. There wasn't anything I could do for him."

Eddie's face expression became somber as he nodded. "I know." He shot a few nervous glances over to Cecil. For a while, it seemed everything was catching up to him. Finally, he managed to pull in a breath and give a voice to the question hanging over his head. "Why'd you go through all of that?"

"Because you're good at what you do."

"No. You and The Greek were right. I fucked up."

"I agree. I didn't say you were a good assassin, but you're a hell of a killer. Someone like you could come in real handy someday."

"The Greek talked like you're his boss."

"I'm not. We've already gone through that."

"I know. But it still sounds like you're high up on the chain."

"I set things up, build them nice and high, and see to it that they don't fall down. On either side of the law, big jobs need someone like that. I'm the carpenter on those jobs."

"What does that make me?"

"You're a hammer. The problem so far has been that everyone's been trying to use you for precision jobs. A hammer should never be expected to do the job of a set of tweezers. You understand?"

Eddie grinned and nodded. "I think I can understand that. A hammer. I get it."

"Thing is, every carpenter needs a hammer. I've got a few, but you'd make a fine addition."

"That's why you did this? To recruit me?"

Cecil nodded. "You proved your loyalty back there by not killing your friend and by trusting me to follow through on this little production we put on for Pyotr. After all of that, I can throw some jobs your way and you can start doing the work you're actually good at."

"Like what? Pounding in a nail?"

"I'm sure I can put you to good use. First off, you might be able to help me take care of your friend The Greek. I don't think he's willing to abide by our previous arrangement any longer. He sounded a little too anxious to be free and clear of the debt he owes me."

"What debt?"

"That's between me and him. All you need to worry about is doing what I tell you and wrecking what needs to be wrecked."

That caused Eddie to perk up like a kid who just remembered it was his birthday. "You mean I get to wipe the grin off that asshole's face?"

"He's a stubborn nail surrounded by a whole lot of dead wood. Sounds like every hammer's dream. I'll set it up and you can walk in to do your worst. Just be sure to tell him hello from Roy."

"Oh, I'll do that after spitting in his fucking face. You sure you can arrange this?"

"It'll take some time and effort, but I can do it. Since I am doing all this for you, don't forget one thing."

"What's that?"

"You owe me."

For Sale By Owner

BY JENNY SILER

Jenny Siler is the author of several thrillers, including *Easy Money*, *Iced*, *Shot*, and *Flashback*. The common theme in all the books is that of strong women faced with deadly situations. While the main character here is a man, I think you'll find she's carried the theme over to her short fiction.

"A KID!" ERNESTO ROJAS BELLOWED. "Can you believe it? My brother's doing twenty-five years in Coleman, and that bitch's got a fucking kid." Rojas smacked his palm against the formica tabletop and leaned forward, causing the table to list slightly, as if the café was a boat and they'd just sailed into a storm. The other patrons glanced cautiously in their direction, then turned back to their coffees.

Normally, Martin made it a point never to meet his employers in public. In fact, most of them he never met at all. But Ernesto Rojas was not someone it was wise to say no to. The café belonged to Rojas, as did most of its customers, in one way or another; but still, the whole thing made Martin nervous. Exactly as Rojas wanted it, he thought, glancing at his watch.

"You got a picture?" Martin asked, hoping to move the process along. It was nearly ten, and if he was going to make it to Bonita Springs by lunchtime, he would have to leave soon.

Rojas picked up an arepa with his meaty hand and shoved the entire pastry into his mouth, then licked the grease off his fingers. "Jesus, man. Lighten the fuck up, will you? You in some kind of hurry?" He nodded to his bodyguard, and the man stepped forward from his place by the wall and handed a photograph to Martin.

The picture was at least fifteen years old, a drunken snapshot taken at one of Rojas's brother Gabriel's notorious pool parties. The crowd was mostly Colombian, dressed in the Miami Vice style that had been popular at the time. Bright suits and thin ties. All the women looking like whores.

"That's her," Rojas said, leaning forward, pointing to a blonde woman off to the side of the picture. She was wearing high heels and a skin-tight purple mini-dress, her bare right arm marked by a thumb-sized bruise, her hand clutching a drink, her face half-masked by a sheaf of pale hair.

"This is it?" Martin asked.

"What are you," Rojas snapped, "the fucking DMV? I'm telling you, it was her."

Martin nodded. What did he care? If Rojas thought he'd seen the woman, then Rojas was right.

"Man, that bitch had a set of tits on her," Rojas remarked. He put his hands to his own chest and mimed two grapefruit-sized shapes. "Still does, too. And fresh as a milkmaid. Must be that Montana air."

Martin turned the picture over. There was an address on the back side, and two names. Vicky Bolin and Victoria Yates. "Yates is the name the Feds gave her?" he asked.

Rojas nodded absently. "Perfect, man," he sighed. "Even with the kid. You know how some women let themselves go."

Yes, Martin thought, I know. Rojas's wife, Lupe, included. Fat and dumpy after four kids, like an overstuffed sausage in Versace casings.

"Not this one," Rojas continued. "Walking out of that gas station just like she used to walk out onto the stage at Sensations. All the cowboys stopping to watch her go. Sexy but without seeing it, you know? That's what made her so goddamn hot."

Martin tried to imagine the scene as Rojas described it. Rojas and his boys on their big fly-fishing vacation out west, the whole crew in stiff Levis and brand-new fishing vests, Eddie Bauer shirts still marked with the store creases. Rojas himself like a giant manatee in his green chest waders. Not the woman those cowboys were staring at, Martin thought.

He glanced down at the picture in his hand again, Vicky Bolin in her tight purple dress and strappy silver shoes. Vicky Bolin, sucking down Gabriel Rojas's good Colombian cocaine. Sucking him off in one of the private rooms at Sensations. Velvet drapes and black leather banquettes, fake zebra skins on the floor, lights dim enough to hide the stains. And Gabriel's hand on her arm, his thumb gripping her to him.

"Well?" Ernesto wanted to know. "You gonna do this thing, or what?"

Martin slipped the picture into his pocket and looked across the table. "You got my money?" he asked.

Outside, the heat was oppressive. Not yet mid-morning and already pushing ninety degrees. Late summer heat, the worst kind, sticky and stale. Martin got into his Malibu and turned the air conditioner way up, sending a burst of tepid air across his face. Out on the sidewalk, a group of young girls walked by, a jumble of brown skin and neon halter tops, gold hoop earrings shining in the tropical sunlight.

A good day to drive, windows up, air blasting a refrigerator chill, tires coasting along Alligator Alley with nothing but the long flat sea of the Everglades on either side. And yet Martin was dreading the trip, as he always did, this monthly pilgrimage to Bonita Springs.

He took the picture of the woman from his pocket and laid it on the dash, face-up, like a portrait of a saint, then shifted into DRIVE and pulled out onto the street. Montana, he thought, tall mountains and big sky, John Wayne and Clint Eastwood riding down through the sagebrush. A better life than this one, though it seemed to Martin that most were.

Martin's mother looked the same as she always did. No better and no worse. Matchstick ankles sticking out from her pajamas, skin puckered and pale, veins gnarled like banyan roots, eyes wild with confusion, with the shock of constant forgetting. And what would it be like, Martin always wondered, to have to confront yourself anew each day, the reality of old age a fresh terror each time?

She didn't remember him, of course, thought he was her kid brother, just back from the war. She kept asking him about someone named Charles, insinuating things Martin didn't want to know, that they had slept together, she and this boy. Martin didn't know quite what to say, except to remind her again that he was her son, but she didn't believe him. And then, on the way down to lunch, she remembered, finally, unmercifully, about the boy. How he'd been shot in the head at Normandy and died there, fresh off the boat.

Martin wanted to take her back to her room, but the nurses insisted that she stay in the dining hall and eat.

"Better for them to come down if they can," one of the nurses said with saccharine cheer, shouting to be heard over his mother's sobs. "Keeps their spirits up."

So Martin sat dutifully in his chair while his mother hurled her peas and jello salad and swore at him and the staff. Until lunch was over and he could take her back to her room. And then it was time to go.

"I'm going to Montana tomorrow," Martin told his mother before he left.

She was lying in her bed, propped up on pillows, her feet in a pair of hand-knitted booties Martin had never seen before. A gift, no doubt, from the church ladies, the ones who left religious literature on his mother's bedside table. Pictures of weeping Jesuses and happy little children, flocks of the saved swarming toward the pearly gates.

"You bastard," she hissed, narrowing her eyes, turning away from Martin to face the wall. And then she was crying again.

"Sometimes I think it's a blessing when they finally go," one of the nurses, not the one from lunch, told Martin on his way out, and Martin thought, sometimes?

But on the drive back to Miami, Martin couldn't stop thinking about what she'd said, about how easy it would be. After all, this was what people paid him to do. And in his mother's case, it would just be a matter of a few extra pills, or a few minutes alone with her and a pillow. And yet Martin knew he could never go through with it.

The plane out of Salt Lake City the next day was a tiny commuter jet. Two narrow rows of seats and a set of rickety metal stairs like in the old movies. Though, instead of Bogart in a trench coat, Martin's fellow passengers were mostly tourists or salesmen, or both. Fat guys in patterned polo shirts carrying Orvis fly rods and sample cases.

Martin had never been much of a fisherman. One of his mother's boyfriends had taken him out in his boat a few times, down by Marco Island. And there'd been a lake, back before they'd left New York, where his grandfather kept a small outboard, a rusty little dingy that always seemed to have two inches of water in its hull. But it just never seemed like much fun to Martin. All that male posturing, and the boredom.

The pilot brought them in low over the mountains, banking wildly toward the runway, wings dipping over ranchland and new subdivisions, giant houses adrift on the plains, some still half-finished, bulldozers asleep in their scarred front yards. Like the distant Florida of Martin's childhood, the land slowly giving way to retirement communities and golf courses. And Martin, who never liked to fly, found himself wishing he had said yes to the beer the flight attendant had offered him on the way up, though he'd given up drinking years earlier.

The airport was overly ambitious. Four gates and a cavernous terminal, two dozen security guards sitting around telling bad jokes.

Someone's idea of vision. Build it and they will come. And yet they obviously hadn't.

The clerk at the rental-car counter was excited to see him. Twenty years old, if that, smiling awkwardly out from behind her computer, answering "yessir" and "nosir" to all of his questions, not even seeming to notice just how out of place he was in his leather jacket and creased pants, his Havana shirt with the pleats down the front.

"Yessir, the road out front goes right into town. Just hang a left out of the parking lot."

"Nosir, we're all out of midsized cars, but I can give you the next size up for the same price."

At the end of their transaction, she handed him a map with his keys, and a brochure for a local motel. "Nicest place in town," she told him sincerely. "Right on the river, close to the school, heated swimming pool. And cable, of course. You can't miss the signs once you get into town."

"No, thanks," Martin said, offering the brochure back to her. The color photo of the motel, the river in the foreground, riffles winking the late afternoon sun. Not for him.

But the girl was insistent. "At least think about it."

And in the car on the way into town, driving past the farmers' supply and the John Deere outlet and the thirty-nine-dollar-a-night strip motels, Martin had thought about it. And then thought, what the hell? After all, this wasn't like most of the trips he made. Driving straight through to Trenton or Syracuse, sleeping in some fleabag dive off the interstate, eating at the truckers' buffet.

You've got to spend your money on something, his mother had said once, back when she'd been well enough to think like that.

The girl was right: the motel was easy to find, just off the main drag, with plenty of signs pointing the way. Not the Fontainebleau, not by any stretch. The lobby was done up in a sort of seventies woodsman chic, with large chain-sawed friezes of bears and antelopes, and dirty red-and-gold carpet. But there were complimentary chocolate-chip cookies at check-in, and Martin's room, if not completely clean, had a balcony that hung right out over the river, and from which he could see the wide bowl of mountains that encircled the town, like a jawful of jagged and rotting teeth, still spotted with snow even though it was August. And across the river, "the school," as the girl at the airport had called it, the playing fields and architectural jumble of the state university.

Down on the rocky beach, a fisherman was casting relentlessly to the same stretch of river, his arm moving in tin-soldier fashion, the line snapping out before him, smacking the surface in a way even Martin knew would do more to scare the fish off than anything. It was late, past eight o'clock, but it was full-on daylight still, the sun hours away from setting. Two hours later for Martin, but watching the man fish made him restless.

Martin dug the photograph of the woman from his wallet, along with the address Rojas had given him. He set the picture on his bedside table and pulled the phone book from the nightstand drawer, then flipped to the map index in the back. He had no intention of doing the job that night, but he figured he could at least give the woman's house a drive-by, see what he was up against.

FOR SALE BY OWNER, the sign in the front yard said. The house itself was neat as a pin, a white cottage with green shutters, set back from a maple-lined street just a few blocks from the campus, in what was obviously the respectable part of town. She'd become a gardener, this Vicky. The beds were planted with a profusion of flowers, the windowboxes overflowing.

Martin drove by once, then circled the block and came around slowly again. He'd thought about bringing a gun with him from Miami but had decided against it in the end, hadn't wanted to draw the extra attention checking one required these days. Besides, the way gun laws worked out west, Martin knew it would be easy enough to pick up a cheap pistol at a pawn shop, something he could toss before he left town. Now, taking in the property and the neighboring homes, Martin made a mental note that he'd need something small and quiet if he was going to do the job at the house.

The woman's front door was open and as Martin cruised slowly down the street he could see movement inside, a shadow at the screen, peering out. No husband, for now, though Rojas had said there was one, a teacher at the college, of all things. And the baby? Sleeping, perhaps. And then, before Martin realized what was happening, the screen door swung open and the woman was out on the porch, waving to him.

Martin fumbled with the unfamiliar window controls, but it was too late. She'd caught him looking, and now she was coming down the walk.

"Hi!" she called. She was barefoot, in shorts and a loose t-shirt, her legs long and athletic, the arches of her feet crossed with neat white tan lines, the ghosts of whatever sandals she'd worn through the summer.

"Sorry to chase you down." She smiled apologetically and stepped into the street while Martin rolled to a stop and set the car into PARK. "It's just that I saw you looking at the house. I thought you might like one of these." She lifted her hand to the open window and offered Martin a piece of paper, a homemade fact sheet with a black and white picture of the house, taken in another season. "If you have any questions. . . ."

Martin nodded his thanks and took the paper, feigned interest. What else could he do?

"So you're from out of town, then?" The woman asked, leaning down toward the open window, her gaze wandering toward the passenger seat, the motel brochure where Martin had left it.

"Yes," Martin said, offering no further explanation.

The woman blinked nervously, anxious for his approval. Her hair was pulled back and her face was naked, her nose spattered with faint freckles, her eyes dark and slightly tired. "There are three bedrooms and two baths," she explained. "We redid everything just a couple of years ago. New kitchen, new bathrooms. All the wood floors have been refinished."

"It's a little out of my price range," Martin mumbled. He handed the paper back through the open window, but the woman drew her hand away.

"Keep it," she told him, shrugging. "You never know. Our number's there, if you change your mind."

Martin smiled as best he could, then slipped the car back into DRIVE, hoping to make an escape.

"Well, I won't keep you," the woman said. Then she turned and, waving slightly, made her way across the jewel-green lawn and up the walk.

The fisherman was gone when Martin got back to his room, the riverbank empty save for a gangly blue heron picking his way along the rocky bed, angling for his supper. Martin had stopped at a Mexican fast-food restaurant on the way back to the motel, and he set his own dinner on the table by the window. Salsa packets and plastic silverware. Food wrapped like a mummy bound for the tomb.

In the next room over, the TV was on. Martin could hear it through the wall, two distorted voices, one male and one female. And beneath the TV voices, the sounds of the real couple staying in the room. A man and a woman, talking themselves to sleep.

Martin took the paper the woman had given him from his pocket, then sat down at the table and unfolded it. *Beautifully remodeled, charming bungalow on large corner lot with a view of the mountains,* the description of the house read. *Fenced yard, perennial garden, patio. Walk to campus.*

A nice life, he thought, remembering the way the woman had looked coming down the walk, the spikes of purple blossoms along the fence, flowers, the names of which he didn't know. For a moment, Martin felt just the slightest pang of regret, and then it was gone. She should have known better, he told himself, should have been smarter than to rat out Gabriel Rojas to the Feds. She should have known they would find her in the end.

Martin ate his dinner in the last of the failing light, then took a shower and climbed into the king-size bed. He'd left the windows open and he could hear the river outside and the hush of traffic on the nearby bridge, the occasional whoop of an exuberant teenager driving by, the faraway rattling of a car stereo. The sounds of summer and of this small town.

He should have been tired, but he wasn't. For a long time, he lay awake thinking about the woman, about her face outside his car window, the nakedness of it. And then she was there, as she'd been in the photograph, kneeling before him in the purple dress, her breasts pushed up against the fabric, her blond hair like a shield across her face. And then her lips were on him, the pearls of her teeth sliding across his skin.

Martin drove the few short blocks into downtown the next morning and had breakfast at a mock nineteen-fifties diner on the main street. Bad coffee and greasy hashbrowns, and a waitress who looked like she'd seen one too many late shifts, who kept glancing hopefully at Martin from behind the counter, smiling and making small talk with him when she came to refill his coffee.

An ex-stripper, Martin thought, or a cocktail waitress, put out to pasture here among the milkshake machines and old forty-fives, the bubblegum walls and the jukebox crooning "Strawberry Hill." And for a moment, Martin allowed himself to think about going home with her, back to whatever trailer or sagging house near the train tracks he knew was hers. He could see the two of them on her flow-ered bedspread, her deflating body tucked strategically into a black bra and panties, and from where he was, none of it looked too bad.

When she came with his check and he asked her where the pawn shops were she seemed both disappointed and relieved at the same time.

"You'll find most of them down by the old train station, at the far end of this main drag," she said, her hand still leaning on the table where she'd put the check. Her fingernails were painted a bright beachy orange, chipped in places. "There's one called City Pawn where I like to do business. Run by a guy named Hap, real fair." She smiled at him again, but this time there was pity in it, a look of having been there, of knowing how easy the return trip came. And Martin could see that whatever might have been between them, though not exactly ruined, had been tainted.

Martin found the train station easily, though it obviously had not served in such a capacity for some time. The old brick building's windows were dark and boarded, the latest attempts at its renewal—a defunct bridal shop with a few dusty mannequins in the window, and an empty travel agency—had decidedly failed. But the pawn shops had persisted, clustered limpet-like along the street to the west of the old station.

There wasn't much to distinguish City Pawn from the rest of its counterparts, but Martin took the waitress's advice and went inside. He wasn't looking for much, something small and cheap, discreet enough to slip into his pocket. There was a nice Beretta under the case, and a Colt Pony thirty-eight, but in the end it was a Lorcin twenty-two with a sixty-five-dollar price tag that Martin asked to see. It was a woman's gun, short barrel, pink plastic handle, but Martin didn't care.

For my girlfriend, Martin told the man behind the counter after he'd talked him down to a flat fifty bucks. Hap, the waitress had called him. Then the two of them sat there bullshitting while the National Instant Background Check ran Martin's fake ID.

"I knew you'd change your mind," the woman said. "How about noon?"

Martin looked out his window at the river. The same fisherman from the night before was back again, fishing poorly and in the same poor spot. Martin had the urge to go down and talk to him, set him straight.

"Or some other time," the woman offered. "Whenever it's convenient for you."

Martin looked at his watch, though why, he didn't know. It was just after ten. "No," he told her, "noon will be just fine." He could hear the baby in the background, babbling incoherently, and the sound of a faucet running. A handful, he thought, and still no sign, or sound, of the husband.

When she'd caught him cruising the house the night before, Martin had been concerned. She was in witness protection, after all, no doubt used to looking over her shoulder, waiting for someone like him, and the last thing he wanted was to scare her. But eventually he'd come to realize there was nothing to worry about, to see the meeting as the piece of luck that it had been, an opportunity for him to get inside the house.

It was partly the woman herself who'd convinced him, the ease with which she'd sauntered out to Martin's car and stood there talking. And there was the town as well, the rows of shady bungalows, each with its door wide open, and the way everyone smiled at him, the guilelessness of it all. Nothing to be afraid of, ever.

"See you then," she said, and Martin nodded into the phone.

"See you at noon."

The day was perfect, warm and clear, the sky an alien blue, the land pushed up so that it seemed to touch the liquid bowl of heaven. Martin found the sporting-goods store the man at the pawn shop had recommended and bought a box of bullets, then drove out to the target range on the edge of town.

He wasn't much interested in the way the gun shot, knew whatever work he did would be close enough that accuracy wouldn't matter. But it felt good to pull the trigger, felt good to be out there in the woods, plinking shots off the various targets the local kids had left behind. Battered tin cans and stolen stop signs, a smashed parking meter that had been ripped from its pole. He wasted an hour easily, and before he knew it, it was almost noon, time to go.

The woman was waiting for him in the front yard when Martin got to the house. The kid was with her and the two of them were playing with a ball, the baby careering after it through the grass in what looked to Martin like one long, barely controlled fall.

"She's still getting the hang of this walking thing," the woman said as Martin came up the walk. Then she ran after the baby and scooped it up in her arms. "Let's go inside."

Martin nodded, following the woman's bare calves up the front steps and in through the screen door.

The house was remarkably cool, cold even, and Martin shivered slightly beneath his jacket, but the woman seemed not to notice even though she was wearing much less. Shorts again, and a tank top. She set the baby down and the girl darted across the room, squealing as she went.

"I'm Vicky, by the way." She smiled, waiting for Martin's response, and when it didn't come gestured nervously to the house around her. "I guess we can start upstairs," she said, picking the reluctant toddler up again, leading Martin up a narrow staircase.

Yes, Martin thought, there was definitely a husband. A man's clothes in the bedroom closet, sports magazines in a neat pile in the bathroom. And yet there was only one toothbrush in the holder, one set of towels on the towel rack.

"Why are you selling the house?" Martin asked, as they started back down the stairs.

"My husband has a new job," the woman answered. "In Florida, of all places."

"You sound disappointed," Martin said.

The woman shrugged. "I lived there years ago, when I was younger." Martin felt his gut tighten, fought back the color from his face.

"It's not my favorite place," she continued. "But that was Miami. We'll be going to Gainesville." She reached the landing and shifted the baby on her hip, then turned and looked back at Martin. "How about you? Where are you from?"

"New York," Martin said, and it was true in a way, though not for decades now. Not since he and his mother had moved to Florida when he was six.

"Well, you'll like it here," the woman told him, somewhat wistfully. "It's a beautiful place."

Martin smiled awkwardly. He could feel the gun in his pocket, the stock still warm from the hour at the shooting range. So easy, he thought, and then the phone rang.

"Excuse me," the woman said, turning and padding into the kitchen.

"Hello?" Martin heard her through the doorway. A pause and then laughter, low and conspiratorial. And then her voice again. "Can you hold on a minute? There's someone here looking at the house."

She reappeared with the cordless phone in her hand. "I'm sorry." She smiled at Martin again, always that smile. "Would you mind showing yourself around the basement while I take this? The door's right back here, through the kitchen."

Martin nodded, let himself be led through the kitchen to the basement steps.

"This'll only take a minute," the woman reassured him, then she turned back to her conversation.

Martin started down the stairs and the woman's voice faded. Something about the baby and the flight home tomorrow, how the conference had gone. The husband, he thought, away with his toothbrush.

Martin reached the basement and stopped, letting his eyes adjust to the semi-darkness, counting out the minutes to himself. How long should he stay? He wondered. Long enough for the make-believe of checking the furnace and the pipes. And what else? How did a person act when buying a house? He could hear the woman above him, the floor creaking beneath her bare feet, and the low reverberations of her voice, the sounds muffled by the earth and the house around them.

She was laughing, and then there was a moment of silence and her voice at the top of the stairs, calling to him. "Everything okay down there?"

Martin glanced around the basement at the sleeping hulk of the furnace, the washer and dryer sitting side by side. The stacks of boxes pushed up against one wall, labeled, *Christmas, maternity,* and *baby clothes.* Here, he told himself. This was where he would do it. Not now, but tonight.

"Sir?" she called again, and this time Martin answered.

"Fine," he called back. "Everything's just fine."

It was her, Martin told himself, no doubt about it. He picked the picture up off his bedside table and stared down at the woman, as if searching for something. Fifteen years on, and almost everything about her was different, her face, or what he could see of it, fuller, her body more defined. Yet Rojas was right. And she'd confirmed it herself at the house. Though when she'd introduced herself to him, Martin had wanted her to say anything but what she did. Vicky.

Not a choice, Martin reminded himself, not his decision to make. He slipped the picture into his pocket and slid the screen door open, stepped out onto the balcony. The temperature had dropped a good thirty degrees since the sun had set and there was a steady wind blowing in from the canyon on the eastern edge of town. Across the river, the cottonwood trees rattled and tossed, the lights of the campus winking beyond them.

Nothing fair about the way we went. Either it was your time or it wasn't. Eighteen and scared, puking up seawater on a beach halfway across the world. Or rotting slowly away in the morgue-like chill of a sterile room in Bonita Springs. Clean sheets and someone to wipe your ass. Someone to tell you your name each morning.

Martin ducked back into the room and pulled the balcony doors closed behind him. He wanted a cigarette or a drink, or both, something to take the edge off. Vices he hadn't used in years. Shivering, he reached for his leather jacket, slipped the Lorcin from the pocket, and checked the clip, running his thumb along the nine fresh bullets. Eight more than he'd be needing.

Three A.M. and the town was empty, the streets quiet except for the steady murmur of the trees, the maples, thick and erotic above him, leaves glossed with sap, limbs snapping and creaking in the wind. Martin parked the rental car one street over and made his way down the alley toward the house.

It was a good night to be working, overturned garbage cans and clanging gates, the wind loud enough to cover any missteps. Up ahead in the darkness a dog was barking itself raw. Martin paused for a second by the woman's back fence, then lifted the latch and slipped in through the gate.

They'd made a quick tour of the back yard that afternoon before Martin had left, but everything was different in the dark, and it took Martin a moment to orient himself. The yard was long and deep, surrounded by trees and shrubs. Apricots, the woman had said, gesturing to the thicket along the back fence. And in the side yard, lilacs. Though she could have said anything and Martin wouldn't have known the difference. A maze of flower beds stretched from the patio, and farther back, toward the alley, there was a square vegetable garden, neat rows of bush beans and tomatoes.

Martin moved carefully forward, scanning the back of the house as he went, the dark dormers of the woman's bedroom, and the baby's room below, a night light glowing softly behind the open curtains. And the back door off the kitchen, through which he would enter. No deadbolt, he'd noted that afternoon, and the lock an easy pick.

The wind gusted and the chimes on the back porch clattered and rang. Bamboo and brass, a circle of metal birds that clanged heavily against each other, the hollow sound of wood or bone. Martin crossed the patio and started up the steps, put his hand on the first riser and stopped. In the upstairs bedroom, the light flared on.

Martin took a step back and peered up at the windows, the diorama inside. Wooden headboard and taupe walls, a print of a deer's skull and mountains behind. The woman appeared, her silhouette skating across the window, her back to Martin, naked from the waist up. And then she was gone into the dark house.

Out on the street a car rolled by and came to a stop. Martin caught his breath and held it. There was a slamming of doors, goodnights shouted into the wind. And then, in the ensuing quiet, Martin could hear the baby crying. Through the kitchen window and the inside doorway beyond he saw a flicker of movement. Shoulders and neck, hair tousled by sleep, the woman's shadow silvered by the street-light's gritty reflection. She crossed the living room and disappeared again. Then the light in the baby's room winked on and she was there at the window. She'd put a bathrobe on, a red kimono with a pattern of birds in flight, and she looked like a bird herself, a jewel-feathered geisha on a bright stage.

Almost close enough to touch, Martin thought, moving instinctively back. And yet there would be nothing, he knew, for her to see. Nothing but her own reflection in the black panes, her face still sleep-creased, her eyes caught mid-dream. Emboldened, Martin inched forward across the patio till he was standing just a few feet from the window, till he could see the whole of the room, bright yellow walls and little blue dresser, wooden rocking chair.

The woman bent and picked the baby up from its crib, and held it to her, rocked it gently back and forth. But the girl was inconsolable, locked in the lonely terror of sleep, her eyes black and panicked, screaming.

Cradling the baby in one arm, the woman sat down in the rocking chair and pulled the sash of her kimono loose, then pushed the fabric aside, revealing her left shoulder and breast. *Perfect*, Martin could hear Rojas say, his hands on his chest, the gesture now even more obscene than it had seemed at the café. The woman's breast was pale and engorged, etched with faint blue veins, the nipple round and thick. She cupped her hand beneath it and bent forward slightly, and suddenly the baby was quiet, her fist gripping the woman's arm, her eyes closing, her whole being given to the singular pleasure. Then the woman closed her eyes as well and leaned back into the chair.

They stayed like this for some time. The three of them, the woman and the baby and Martin, each fastened to the other. And then, without warning, the woman's eyes snapped open and she looked out the window, out into the garden, toward the spot where Martin stood. Hidden, Martin reminded himself. Nothing but her own reflection looking back. And yet her gaze lit there and stayed for some time, her face unblinking, her jaw set hard.

Tomorrow, Martin told himself as he climbed into the rental car and pulled the door shut behind him. He slipped the key into the ignition and started the engine, illuminating the green dash lights, the soft glow of the instrument panel. Tomorrow he would go back and finish the job, even if it meant killing the husband, too. Not his choice to make, and yet he had, knew even as he told himself otherwise that this job wasn't for him.

Martin pulled slowly away from the curb and circled the block, cruising the woman's street as he'd done that first evening. The baby had evidently gone back to sleep, for the house, or at least what Martin could see of it from the street, was dark again, and for a moment Martin thought about stopping. He could finish it now, he told himself, and yet this wasn't what he wanted at all. His real desire was for her to know, to understand that it was he who had spared her. But of course this was impossible.

He tapped the brake with his foot, then accelerated again, turning north at the end of the block, heading back toward the river and his motel. Past the craftsman cottages and professors' homes. Fake tudors and colonials with unnaturally lush lawns. Garden flags whipping in the wind, bright tulips or birds, WELCOME stitched in banner letters. Though their doors, which that first evening had seemed so welcoming, now were anything but.

He cruised past the campus and started into the hook turn that led to the bridge, then lowered the passenger side window, reached into his pocket, and pulled the Lorcin out. The night air poured into the car, the earthy smell of the river, fish and cottonwoods, last spring's runoff on the dry rocks. The distant smell of Martin's child-hood, a lake somewhere in the Adirondacks, the water like a piece of polished onyx set into the trees. And on the shore, her towel spread on the rocky beach, her legs sleek and muscular as the arching tail of a bass, Martin's mother.

Martin coaxed the car up onto the bridge, then stopped at the midway point, slid across the seat toward the open window, and tossed the Lorcin over the guardrail.

It was raining the next morning, the mountains shrouded in clouds, the gray river reflecting the gray sky. Autumn already, nearly cold enough to snow, though Martin had trouble believing such a thing possible in August. Martin called the airline and booked a seat on the afternoon flight home, then drove downtown to the diner where he'd eaten breakfast the day before.

Nothing had changed since his last visit. The Happy Days jukebox was still there, the booths still upholstered in the same plastic leather, but the restaurant seemed different somehow. Martin's wait-ress was gone, and the young woman who served him his coffee and eggs made no attempt to hide her disdain.

Back at the motel, Martin made a beeline for the bar. He hadn't given much thought the night before to what he was going to tell Rojas, but he was thinking about it now, knowing whatever he did tell the Colombian wouldn't be good enough. He took a seat at the counter and ordered an Irish coffee. One for the flight, he told himself.

Outside, there was a sudden gust of wind, and the rain picked up momentarily, fat drops hammering the bar's wide bank of windows. Martin ordered a second drink and looked out at the river. The fish-erman was back again, his line fighting the wind as he cast toward the water's frothy spine, his jacket stained dark by the rain. Martin shook his head, caught the bartender's eye, the two of them thinking, stupid bastard.

Wrong girl, Martin said to himself, testing the lie and Rojas' response. Not good, in this case, though nothing looked good. If he lied and Rojas found out, he'd be a dead man. Worse. And if he told the truth, Rojas would kill him and send someone else to finish the job. No, he'd screwed up and he would have to pay for his mistake.

He downed the second drink and called for a third, straight up whiskey this time, then paid his tab and headed back to his room. Maybe he could stay, he thought, feeling good now, the whiskey sitting warm in his stomach. Buy the woman's house and disappear, as she had. Maybe even take up gardening.

Stopping in front of the door to his room, Martin slid the key card from his wallet, then slipped it into the narrow slot above the handle, watched the security light flash green, and let himself inside.

It was freezing in the room, the patio doors wide open. The maid, Martin told himself, though he should have known better. He'd told the front desk himself that morning that he would be checking out late. From the room's narrow foyer he could see the very end of the bed, the spread dishevelled, as he'd left it. And in the bathroom, the previous night's towels strewn across the floor.

"Hello?" he called, getting no answer. He stepped forward, feeling in his pocket for the ghost of the Lorcin. It wasn't until he reached the room itself that he saw the woman, Vicky. She was sitting at the table by the window with the detritus of Martin's Mexican dinner spread out in front of her.

"Hello," she said. She was breathing hard, as if she'd run the whole way from the house. Her hair was dripping wet, her shirt clinging to her shoulders and chest, showing the exact shape of her body underneath, and what Martin thought wasn't tits, but muscle, the power visible in her arms and chest. There was a gun in her hand, not some pocket pistol, but a Sig Sauer, the barrel elongated by the cylindrical shape of a silencer. "You should have killed me last night," she told him.

"Yes," Martin agreed, though a part of him was happy she knew what he had done. That she understood that he had saved her. He started to say something about how he could be useful to her alive, about throwing Rojas off her trail, then thought better of it.

Not his choice, he reminded himself as he'd done so many times before. It was either your time or it wasn't. And then, suddenly, it was.

The Closers

BY PAUL GUYOT

Paul Guyot is an award-winning television writer whose credits include *Snoops*—the David E. Kelley show starring Gina Gershon and Paula Marshall as private eyes who tended to lick whipped cream off each other during sweeps; *Level 9*—created by former MWA president Michael Connelly; and *Judging Amy*—the CBS courtroom drama currently in its sixth season. Paul has sold pilots to Twentieth Century Fox and the Fox Network and just completed filming *The Dark*, a pilot co-created with Stephen J. Cannell.

But here he crafts a clever, unusual story that is made all the more so by the fact that it is his first.

DO YOU THINK ABOUT DEATH *a lot?*

Dennis Collins was standing on line with Cindy Bradshaw, but he was thinking back to last night when he was listening to *Night Lies*—the late night talk radio show hosted by "Stella." A girl had called in and asked what happens to a person after they die and is it any different than when they're killed.

Dennis had the same thoughts now and then.

"Go," said Cindy.

Dennis looked up and saw the pharmacist waiting. The people behind them were hemming and hawing, making the point that their lives were on hold while Dennis stood there daydreaming.

I could kill all of you with that box of condoms, thought Dennis.

Cindy and Dennis stepped up and Cindy handed in the prescription. The pharmacist asked for a name.

"Bradshaw," said Cindy.

The pharmacist typed away and Dennis lost himself in his earliest memory of death: going deer-hunting with his father.

He smiled, thinking back to those halcyon nights, sitting in his car seat in the back of his father's battered Plymouth Fury as they drove the winding roads up through the Coconino National Forest, hour after hour, until little Dennis felt the torque of the Fury's 360 as Daddy mashed the gas pedal, followed by the percussive energy of impact as the Fury slammed directly into a headlights-hypnotized deer at seventy-five m.p.h.

"Says here you're allergic to penicillin," said the pharmacist.

"No, I'm not," said Dennis, popping back to the present.

"He's talking to me, sweetie," said Cindy. Then to the pharmacist: "It's not for me, it's for my mother, Ellen Bradshaw."

"Do you want to wait for this?" the pharmacist asked. "It'll take about twenty minutes."

Cindy looked at her Daniel Roth, then turned to Dennis. "Axelrod's retirement thingy is this morning. We should get going." To the pharmacist she said, "I'll come back at lunch."

Dennis and Cindy left the pharmacy and walked two blocks east, then two blocks north. On the way Dennis glanced a few times at his girlfriend's ass—one of those perfect heart-shaped asses—and listened to her.

"I just don't know if they'll ever give me a chance," she said.

"Why wouldn't they?" Dennis said. "You're a good worker, you know the biz. You just have to put your time in like everyone else. Shit, I spent three years in the mailroom before making junior VP, and four years doing that before becoming a VP."

"I think the company is biased against women," said Cindy.

"Stop thinking so much," Dennis said. "Look at Lyla or Carol, they're VP's. You just have to put your time in." He watched Cindy's mouth start to open and said, "Don't say Hanrahan, that guy was an anomaly. He's the only one the company ever promoted straight to executive and that was only because he came up with the whole NC idea."

As they waited for a light to change, Dennis said, "I've got an idea. Why don't you enter the contest?"

"That idea thing?" asked Cindy. "Come on."

"Seriously, why not you?" he said, as they crossed the street. "It's just thinking up something to help the company. Hell, Wally won it one month because he figured out a better place for the fucking water cooler. And we know you have no trouble thinking about things."

"Stop," she said, smacking his arm. "What's the point? It's not like the winner becomes a VP or anything."

"The point," Dennis explained, "is to impress the execs. Show them you're VP material. Besides, you get a nice blender, too."

Cindy smiled. "I would love a new blender."

They reached the forty-seven-story glass-and-steel edifice that was home to OmniDat.

"Okay, I'll give it a shot," Cindy said. "I can come up with an idea or two." She put her arms around Dennis and said, "Thanks, sweetie, for talking to me. I feel much better. But did we solve your problems?"

"I don't have any problems, babe. Life is good." And they entered the building.

"Morning, Jasper," they both said to the hulking security guard manning the reception desk and the bank of monitors behind it.

"Morning, ladies," replied Jasper.

Dennis always wondered if that was Jasper's way—kidding out of affection—or if he really questioned Dennis's manhood. He caught Jasper checking out Cindy's ass as they stepped onto the elevator.

Dennis puffed out his ordinary chest and draped an arm over Cindy. *I know sixty-eight different ways to kill you*, Dennis thought as the doors closed.

OmniDat occupied the top three floors of the building. The forty-seventh floor—the penthouse—was the domain of Edgar Maddox, founder and CEO of OmniDat. The stocky, venerable eighty-year-old made appearances from time to time on the lower floors, but for the most part Edgar Maddox remained on the forty-seventh floor.

The only time anyone was invited to join him up there was when a VP had been exalted to the revered position of "Executive." It was the ultimate, the brass ring, the end of the rainbow for an OmniDat employee.

Rumors abounded about what went on during the ceremony—drinking unblended scotch and smoking cigars with the man; doing hookers and cocaine; learning all the company secrets—but no one really knew. The few lucky enough to experience it never had time to discuss what went down, as they almost immediately began traveling the world—one of the perks, along with a fat seven-figure income—overseeing OmniDat's global operations. There were nine executives in the company of three hundred and eighty-one employees.

Dennis Collins desperately wanted to be number ten.

The elevator doors opened to the forty-fifth floor. Dennis kissed Cindy and stepped off. He said hello to Margery—the office manager—who nodded from behind the large kidney-shaped reception desk under a metallic sign that read:

OMNIDAT

TOMORROW'S TECHNOLOGY SERVING TODAY'S NEEDS

The forty-fifth floor was one giant area, stuffed to the gills with row after row of fabricated cubicles, where VP's and junior VP's all worked together in a manmade prairie-dog town.

Dennis walked down the main aisle, tossing nondescript greet-
ings to co-workers who did the same, finally coming to his cube,
which looked exactly the same as everyone else's.

Dennis sat down in front of his computer. He stared at his reflection in the dark monitor for a brief moment, as he did every
morning before firing up the PC. Forty seconds later, he entered his
password, then his second password, and saw his next bond was
already waiting for him. He briefly thought he might make the chart
this year. He typed in another password and looked at the photo
and dossier on his screen.

Robert "Bob" Carmichael lived on Palm Lane in Scottsdale, Arizona, had a wife, three kids, and two dogs. Bob worked at a chem-
ical plant. Dennis scanned the photo just like his training had
taught him; first give a quick glance, then go back and study every
inch. Start at the top of the head—commit to memory the shape of
the skull—then slowly move down the forehead—picking out any
scars, bumps, fissures, etc.—before focusing on the eyes—color, size,
shape, how far apart, how far from the nose, how far from the tem-
ples. Then do the same with the rest of the face, and finally, when
you have all the finite details locked into your brain, you look at the
triangle—the distance from the corners of the eyes to the center of
the mouth. It was something the government used in identifying
potential terrorists from security camera photos. Regardless of how
much plastic surgery one has, it is virtually impossible to alter the
God-given triangle of the eyes and mouth.

Dennis knew this was all overkill. Bob had no idea he had
become a client of OmniDat. He would have no reason to have surgery done. Bob was living as if he had all the time in the world.

Poor Bob, thought Dennis. Then he thought, *Why did I think
poor Bob?*

He looked over everything again, noting the word "client"
above Bob's name. *Client*, thought Dennis. *The emptor should be the
client. Why do we call clients emptors and subjects clients? And why do
we call contracts bonds?* Dennis thought OmniDat hid behind

fancy euphemisms. Regardless of the language, it all meant the same thing.

People hired OmniDat to murder other people.

"Hey, Denny. How goes it?"

Dennis rose up and peered over his cubicle to see the cherubic face of Wally Waxman, a doughy VP, looking back at him.

We are prairie dogs.

"What's up, Wally?"

"Same old, same old. Can you believe Axelrod is calling it quits? Thirty-four freaking years. That's as long as I've been alive."

"Then I guess it's time," offered Dennis.

Wally's thick eyebrows made one as he struggled with that. "Hey, did you hear about Ackerman? He finally closed that Jersey bond."

"Really?"

Dennis was surprised. Ackerman had drawn one of those bonds that just seem to be fraught with one problem after another. "Melons," they called them. Seemed like Ackerman had been on that same bond for sixteen months or more.

"Yeah," said Wally. "Came in this morning, early, like seven-thirty. He looked like shit. At least that's what Lyla said. She was here then, I came in later. God, Lyla's hot, isn't she?"

Dennis ignored him and looked across the expanse of cubicles. There were a few others "prairie-dogging," like he and Wally were. He looked toward the southeast corner where Gil Ackerman's cubicle was, wondering just how shitty he looked.

"Maybe I'll go congratulate him," Dennis said.

"Yeah, do. I did already. Gave him the Waxman high-five-down-low-crosstown move," said Wally, waving his hand in a way that looked to Dennis like he was directing a plane to its gate.

Dennis walked to Ackerman's cubicle and peered around the fabricated corner. He saw the tall, athletic Ackerman sitting in his ergonomic chair with his head on his desk. Dennis thought he might be crying.

"Uh, Gil?"

The man's head slowly came up and Dennis saw the two black eyes and swollen jaw.

"Holy shit. What happened? Who was the fucking client?"

Gil Ackerman stared at Dennis. "Rita Moreno."

"You killed Rita Moreno?"

It was out of Dennis's mouth before he knew it. You *never* used the K word.

In any context.

Ever.

It meant immediate termination.

Dennis shot a quick glance over the cubes to see if anyone had heard. Apparently most of them were on their way to the retirement party.

"Sorry, Gil," Dennis said. "I didn't mean, you know . . . I just . . . but Jesus Christ, Rita fucking Moreno? She did that to your face? I mean, I know she can dance, but Jesus Christ."

Gil shakily stood up. "Stop talking, Dennis, and help me to the party."

Dennis noticed that the veteran VP was limping as well. He led the man toward the elevators as Gil told the story.

"It wasn't *the* Rita Moreno, you moron, it was someone using the name as an alias. And no, the client didn't do this to me, it was her fucking sons. Five of them. The dossier said there were two. That's just one of the things that went wrong on this fucking bond."

They stepped onto the elevator and Dennis hit forty-six. "Well, at least you completed it. That's gotta make you feel good."

Gil turned his raccoon face toward Dennis. "You think this job is about feeling good? It's about survival. It's about making your quotas and not letting some young, upstart asshole junior veep pass you. It's about doing the job, making enough money so that when it's your time to walk, you have so much fucking cash that you can go anywhere and do anything and they can never find you."

"They? They who?"

The doors opened, they stepped off and then Gil took hold of Dennis's arm. "How long have you been a VP?"

"Uh, I don't know, like almost two years."

"And you were a junior how long?"

"Four. Years."

Gil's voice dropped to a near whisper as he said, "You worked some bonds as a junior, right?" Dennis nodded. "And you've done what, maybe twelve or fifteen since being a VP?"

"Eighteen," said Dennis.

"Nice," said Gil, impressed. "But all those bonds, and you still don't know who 'they' are?"

"No. Tell me who they are."

Just then the elevator doors opened and Edgar Maddox stepped off.

"Gentlemen," said the CEO. "Shall we?"

Dennis and Gil followed behind the towering five-foot-seven presence of Edgar Maddox.

Bernie Axelrod was crying. The retirees always cried—nobody wanted to leave OmniDat. Axelrod was sixty, maybe? Sixty-five? His shape, once described as barrel-chested, had succumbed to the gravity of age and now more resembled a beer belly.

Axelrod had been with OmniDat thirty-four years, starting in the mailroom and working up to his current position as executive. His reputation was both ruthless and wonderful. Like a crusty old professor who'd forgotten more than you'd ever learn, he was as hard as nails on you, but in the end cared deeply.

Debbie Klein, the only female executive in OmniDat, gave a nice speech about how much Axelrod had meant to the company, talked about the unprecedented run he had in the late eighties when he was "VP of the year" four out of five years, and the mentor program that Axelrod had helped create—something Dennis participated in—and then gave him the twenty-four-carat gold Breguet pocket watch each retiree was handed.

Axelrod cried harder.

Edgar Maddox, up to this point quietly standing off to the side, stepped up and shook Bernie Axelrod's hand, then turned to the crowd and, in that subdued, nasally voice with just a hint still lingering of his South African upbringing, said, "I remember the day Bernie came up to the forty-seventh floor. I knew he was special." Edgar then turned and put an arm around Axelrod's waist, looked up into the bigger man's eyes and said, "I am going to miss you."

Everyone clapped and cheered.

Axelrod sobbed.

Later, back inside his cubicle, Dennis printed out his plane ticket to Arizona as Cindy rubbed his shoulders.

"That was sad, huh?" she mused.

"Yeah," said Dennis. "Axelrod was the first one to sort of take me under his wing. But why was he taking it so hard? I'd be jumping up and down if I were retiring with the kind of cash Axelrod must have."

Cindy shrugged.

"I was talking to Ackerman earlier," Dennis said.

"What a wild bond, huh? Did you see his face?"

"Yeah. Have you ever heard anyone talk about 'they'?

"They who?"

"Just they."

Debbie Klein appeared at the cubicle. She looked over her rhinestone-covered glasses at Cindy. "I didn't realize you and Mr. Pearson had transferred to this floor, Ms. Bradshaw," said Klein. Mr. Pearson was Cindy's boss. Klein's voice sounded as if she were chewing gravel, the result of years spent smoking those horrid More cigarettes.

"I was just passing by, Ma'am," Cindy said, and she moved off.

Klein turned to Dennis. "Interoffice relationships are discouraged, Mr. Collins."

"I know that."

"Keep it on the street," gargled Klein. "Now . . . you have everything you need for your current bond?"

"Yep. All ready to go."

"Good. Get gone. Close this one and you might make the chart."

Dennis glanced across to the west wall with the giant production

chart on it. Written in beautiful calligraphy were the top ten VP's—
those who closed the most bonds—for both the current month and
for the year.

Dennis's name was nowhere.

"Right now I think you're hanging around number eleven or
twelve this month. You just passed that asshat Waxman," Klein said
and then sauntered away.

Wally Waxman peered over his cubicle with a hangdog look.

Prairie hangdog, thought Dennis. He gave Wally a shrug, gathered
his things and walked out.

On the street outside OmniDat's building, Dennis saw Gil Ackerman sitting near a fountain, dragging on a cigarette.

"Hey," Dennis said walking up to him. "You want to tell me who
'they' are?"

Ackerman stood, sucked his Camel down to the filter, then flicked
the butt into the water. "Look, Dennis, just keep your head down
and do the job. Don't think about things. Thinking only gets you in
trouble."

"I don't know what that means."

Ackerman gave an exasperated sigh and sat back down. "There's
this radio show," he began, massaging his swollen jaw. "It's called
Night Lies. It's an all-night talk show, live across the country."

"Stella by the shore, I know it," said Dennis, excited he wasn't the
only one with insomnia.

"Huh," said Ackerman, giving Dennis a look. "You're the first
person I've met who listens. Did you hear it last night? There was
this caller . . . talking about death and dying. Talking about what
happens after. . . ."

Dennis started to say he'd heard it, too, but something stopped
him.

"If you listened to this chick," Gil continued, "from Seattle, I
think, you could tell that what she was really talking to Stella about
was wetwork."

"You think?" Dennis asked.

"Sure. Maybe not bond type of stuff, but you could tell the girl had eliminated someone, or was thinking about doing it."

"So, what's your point? What does this have to do with 'them'?

Ackerman narrowed his eyes. "My point is, this chick was thinking. Thinking way too much about things. She's going to have her ass handed to her because she thinks too much. Wonders, like a fucking toddler."

Something popped inside Dennis's mind, like a light bulb burning out.

Ackerman continued. "My fucking point, Dennis, is that we're all playing with the house's money. You asked me about feeling good. You feel good when the game's over and you can walk away from the table with a pile of chips and your ass still intact."

Ackerman hobbled back inside the building, but Dennis never saw him. He was lost. Staring into the fountain water.

Thinking too much. Have her ass handed to her.

Ass.

Thinking.

Cindy.

Scottsdale was hot. Even on a late afternoon in March, it was in the nineties. Dennis quickly realized that all that "dry heat" bullshit was bullshit. Hot was hot. Wet, dry, or whatever. He silently thanked God he didn't have to wear any prosthetics for this bond—Dennis had been blessed with one of those completely average, completely ordinary, completely forgetful faces—and usually a wig was enough. Like now.

Dennis finished his bucket of balls and started cleaning his clubs, keeping an eye on Bob Carmichael, six stalls down the driving range. Bob was three balls from finishing his bucket—Dennis had timed it perfectly. He would be just ahead of Bob leaving the range.

On the way to the parking lot, Bob stopped to talk to another golfer. Dennis slowed the process of changing from golf shoes to sandals just enough to keep the interval the same, but not so much anyone would notice. Bob said goodbye to the golfer and made his way to his Buick Le Sabre. Dennis watched him take out a cell phone and make a quick call. Dennis knew who he was calling. After nine days of surveillance, Dennis knew everything about Robert "Bob" Carmichael.

Including that he would die today.

Bob's Buick turned right out of the driving range and traveled north on Miller. Dennis had turned right just before Bob and had his Toyota Corolla two cars ahead. Dennis always used a Corolla. Not only were they a hundred percent reliable, but there were more of them on the roads than just about any other vehicle and there were dozens of cars that had the same basic shape and size.

Color was important, too, and Dennis followed the OmniDat training guidelines by choosing one of those in-between colors the automakers are so fond of these days. This Corolla was "Aspen Green," which looked green in certain light, gray in other light, and occasionally even blue.

The training also taught that one never rents a vehicle for wet-work. If your bond is to be closed in Scottsdale for instance, you fly into a city a couple hundred miles from there—Dennis had chosen San Diego—buy a used car with cash, drive to Scottsdale, close the bond, then ditch the car and fly out of the local airport. The cherry on the sundae of this endeavor was calling the police—in this case the San Diego police—and reporting the car stolen. All this done using your false identity, of course.

Dennis made a left on Camelback, as he knew Bob would do, then turned north on Hayden. He stayed two cars ahead of his client for a couple of miles until Bob did something unexpected.

He turned around.

Dennis hit the brakes, watching the Buick head back south on Hayden. The traffic was too much for Dennis to make his own U-turn and he sat there helpless, waiting for it to clear like a schoolboy waits for the bell to ring. By the time he could make the turn without causing a noticeable commotion, he knew Bob could be anywhere.

So Dennis went to the GPS.

He had planted a chip on Bob's Buick the first day of surveillance—an optional expense—and now was glad he had. He watched the screen and saw that Bob had stopped only a half mile down the road.

At a Taco Bell.

Dennis exhaled, turned the Corolla around again, and drove to where he knew Bob was originally headed—the apartment of his mistress, Stephanie Ritts. Dennis parked the Corolla in a nearby Walgreen's parking lot, grabbed a backpack and towel from the trunk, removed the wig, and then walked the two hundred yards to the apartment building.

He entered the pool area—three days ago he'd been able to pick the lock on the gate in nine seconds—nodded to the two gorgeous coeds that had been sunning themselves the past two days just like Dennis, and chose a deck chair—or was it a lounge chair?—that afforded a full view of the gate as well as being just steps away from the hot tub. He removed his golf shirt and stuffed it into the backpack. He took out sunglasses, suntan lotion, and a *People* magazine, then stretched out on the long chair and waited.

Three hours later the sun had mercifully begun to set, dropping the temperature to a frosty eighty-six. The coeds were gone. The fat woman and her three brats who'd splashed Dennis had come and gone, and the place was now empty.

Dennis removed a can of sea salt from the backpack, and quickly dumped it into the hot tub, then turned the dial. The tub's jets churned to life.

He moved back to his chair, stuck the can into the pack, and looked at his watch. He knew that Bob and the mistress were due any second, but when he looked at the dial his first thought was that the *Night Lies* show started in five hours. Dennis blinked. He couldn't remember ever being on a bond and having something break his focus like that. One of the first things you learn as a junior VP is—when you're on a bond, clear *everything* out of your mind except closing the bond.

The gate swung open and Bob and his mistress appeared. Dennis took note of Bob's flabby middle, thinking that he didn't need to be stopping at Taco Bell, then thought, *What the hell, it's his last day on earth*. The pair went straight to the hot tub as they always did. Dennis pretended to be engrossed in his *People*. He watched Bob check the tub timer—still had twenty minutes left. Bob and the woman stepped into the swirling bubbles.

It didn't take long for Bob and the woman to forget Dennis was there and start nuzzling each other. Dennis waited another two minutes, then stuck the *People* back in his pack and pulled out a Stun Master 775,000-volt stun gun. He stood up, concealing the weapon behind his back.

"Mind if I join ya for a quick bit?" Dennis said in an unidentifiable accent.

"Uh, yeah. Sure," said Bob, clearly not happy about the company.

Dennis's world suddenly morphed into slow motion, as it always did when he was closing a bond. It was like a dream state almost, all movement slowed like the world was inside a Jell-O mold.

Dennis moved to the edge of the hot tub. "Let me just test the water."

Dennis lowered the hot end of the stun gun to the water's surface and fired.

Bob and the woman began the taser dance. After ten seconds, Dennis returned the device to his pack and slipped on rubber gloves. He moved to the other side of the tub—everything still in slow motion—making sure to stay on top of his rubber-soled sandals. Bob was splashing mildly and drooling heavily. Dennis gripped Bob's thick sandy mane and pushed him under the bubbling water.

The woman sounded like she was having an orgasm. Dennis reached over, grabbed a fistful of her hair, and pushed her head under the surface. Suddenly there was no sound but the bubbles.

With the help of the electricity interrupting the communication between brain and muscles, and the salt water making a much better conduit than fresh water, Dennis didn't have to wait long for his client and his client's mistress to die. He held them under for a good two minutes after they stopped moving—just to be safe. Someone walked past the pool area to their apartment, but from where they were it just looked like a guy testing the hot-tub water.

Everything returned to normal speed.

Once Dennis was sure all life was gone, he casually walked out of the pool area and out of the apartment complex.

He slipped his shirt back on as he walked to the Corolla. He returned the backpack to the trunk, got in, and drove toward Sky Harbor International airport.

On the drive there, he replayed everything. The deaths would appear to be from drowning—the autopsies would reveal no marks on the body, taser or otherwise. Maybe saltwater in the lungs, but who gives a shit? And if Scottsdale happened to have a really good ME, then maybe there would be some evidence of seizure prior to death, but the likelihood was nil.

Just what the emptor had requested. The bond was for Robert "Bob" Carmichael to be killed by any means necessary. There was no specific request for anything to appear accidental, or the really expensive option—natural causes. But OmniDat had its own natural causes department, and the NC people specialized in that and that only. The bond had also contained a bonus clause for the mistress's demise. Dennis had done well. Maybe he'd even win VP of the month. He could use a new set of steak knives.

He pulled out his cell and dialed OmniDat.

"Hi, Margery. Dennis Collins. Bond nine-four-six-five-six-nine-six is closed." Margery said thank you and hung up. Not one for small talk, Margery.

Dennis felt a smile climb out of his mouth and felt good for the first time since arriving in Arizona. He turned off the AC and rolled down the windows, letting the dry warm air blow over him. He quickly went back to the AC.

A few miles from the apartment complex, Dennis pulled behind a Home Depot and dumped the wig, stun gun, and sea salt into a large dumpster. He was still smiling as he climbed back into the Corolla.

Dennis was nearing where he had planned to ditch the car when he passed another Taco Bell. He looked at the colorful sign as he rolled by and suddenly the smile and good feelings vanished. Dennis got that knot in his gut that he'd gotten after the Telluride bond. He felt like crying again and didn't know why. He thought of Ackerman. He thought of Axelrod. He thought of Robert "Bob" Carmichael and Stephanie Ritts. He had thought about the woman only as *the mistress* the entire time he was in Arizona. Why was he now thinking of her by name?

What the hell was happening?

"Hello again, Sandy from Seattle."

Dennis sat in his dark Arizona hotel room and listened intently. Stella's voice sounded like smoke, if smoke could talk.

It was just after eleven in Arizona—after two on the east coast, presumably where *Night Lies* broadcast from. Instead of boarding his scheduled flight to Houston Hobby—from where he'd take a cab to Houston Intercontinental, catch a flight to Denver, and then to Kansas City, where he would pick up the OmniDat company car he'd left in the long-term parking lot and drive back to St. Louis— Dennis had remained in Scottsdale so as not to miss the show.

"Hi, Stella," the female voice said.

Dennis was sure that it was his Cindy.

"Are you still in a conundrum over this thing called life?" she asked.

"I don't know."

"Well, tell us what you do know. Drop some science on your fellow night liars out there, Sandy from Seattle."

"I think . . . it's wrong to play God."

"Unless you're Morgan Freeman," said Stella. "He can play anything."

Dennis dialed Cindy's cell phone. Voice mail. He dialed her home phone. No answer.

She was on the other line.

"Have you been playing God, Sandy?"

"Sort of," the voice said. "Well, not me. But a friend. Someone I'm close with."

Dennis felt his stomach crunch again.

"But he's just doing his job."

"And your friend's job is to play God?"

"Sort of."

"What is he, one of those parking enforcement cops?"

"No."

Dennis was suddenly aware that despite the cranked AC, he was sweating like Michael Jackson in a Toys-R-Us.

"Is your friend a drug dealer, Sandy from Seattle?"

Dennis's cell phone chirped. He grabbed it, thinking, hoping it was Cindy.

It was Gil Ackerman.

"Collins. That chick's back on *Night Lies*! The one from Seattle, she's on right now!"

"Uh, hey, Gil. I don't have a radio in my hotel room."

"You're not home? I heard you closed your bond. Where are you?"

"I, uh, missed my flight," Dennis said, trying to listen to Gil and the radio simultaneously.

"This chick has a friend who's whacking folks," Gil said. "I'd bet my left nut on it."

"Listen, Gil, I'm beat. I'll see you at the office." Dennis ended the call and cranked the volume on the radio.

But the caller was gone.

Dennis sat in his cubicle staring at fish swimming slowly across his computer screen. He imagined one fish killing all the other fish, and then swimming alone for the rest of its life.

He had gotten in to town early this morning but hadn't contacted Cindy. He wasn't sure what to say.

Are you telling a nationwide radio show that I'm murdering people?

Bob Carmichael and Taco Bell suddenly flashed in Dennis's mind. He felt a tear forming in one eye and literally shook it out of there.

"Nice job in Scottsdale. You made the chart."

It was Wally prairie-dogging over his cubicle.

"Thanks."

"I would have made the chart," said Wally. "If that Omaha bond hadn't gotten so screwed up."

"Yeah, well, it's always good to make sure there are bullets in the gun."

Wally shrugged and asked, "You going to the company picnic this weekend?"

"I don't think so."

"I'm going. I was supposed to be out on a bond, but Cindy came down—said Pearson was taking it on account of the emptor had decided he wanted NC instead of accidental. Guess it's for the best. Who wants to go to Birmingham, anyway?"

"Birmingham's nice. I killed a guy there once," said Dennis.

Wally Waxman nearly fell over. His eyes bulged out, his mouth opened and closed, trying to form words, and his knuckles tightened around the cubicle wall. Finally he was able to say, "Holy cats, Collins, what's wrong with you?"

Wally's head then spun around like Linda Blair's, looking for anyone who might have heard. "I, I . . . Jesus, Collins. Don't say stuff like that! Not around me!"

Wally disappeared down into his cubicle.

Dennis didn't care. He was sick and tired of the euphemisms, of the pretending. Everyone knew what was going on at OmniDat. Everyone knew they were killers. Cindy was right—who are they to be playing God? Live or die, it's all up to the highest bidder.

Your life is worth exactly what someone will pay to have it ended.

"Dennis Collins."

Dennis literally jumped in his chair. He spun around to see Heidi Moss, the girl from accounting. "Oh. Heidi. Scared me."

"I have your check for the Scottsdale bond. In addition to your expenses they deducted two percent for not returning on time." She handed him an envelope and walked away.

Dennis opened the envelope and stared at the check. Pay to the order of Dennis Collins . . . thirteen thousand dollars and eighteen cents. *After* the deductions, he thought. That mistress bonus was nice.

Cindy would be proud. Or would she think he's a monster? He thought about her wanting so desperately to be a VP. That didn't jive with her calling Stella and saying Dennis was a murderous God-playing monster. *Which is it, babe?* he thought. *Can't have it both ways. You're either in or you're out. If you're not part of the solution, you're part of the problem.*

Or was *he* part of the problem?

Dennis suddenly crumpled the check, stuffed it into his pocket, and bolted from his cubicle. He took the stairs to forty-six, not waiting for the elevator, then made a beeline for Pearson's office—where Cindy worked. She looked up and smiled when she saw him.

"Come with me."

"What?"

"We have to talk. Right now."

"Dennis, I'm working—"

"Take an early lunch."

"It's almost four, I already had lunch."

"Then leave early. Please, Cindy. We have to talk."

Cindy looked at him for a long moment. Finally, she put some files into a drawer and picked up the phone.

"Hey, Mr. Pearson, mind if I take off early today? I've got some family stuff to do . . . thanks."

She stood up and let Dennis lead her out.

"You think I'm calling a radio show?"

"Come on," Dennis said. "I know it's you."

They were sitting on the sofa in Dennis's apartment.

"I'm not the only one who knows," he said.

"What are you talking about?"

"Ackerman heard you, too. God knows who else."

"And what is it you think I'm saying to this Stella person?"

"You know, that we're all playing God. Saying who lives and who dies, like we have that right."

"Dennis—"

"But you're right, babe. That's what I want to tell you. I get it. You're right!"

"I'm right?"

"Yes. I've been feeling it too, just didn't know it until I heard you. Remember how sick I got after that Atlanta bond?"

"You said it was food poisoning."

"I thought it was. But then I felt sick after Telluride, and Arizona, damn, I don't know if I can ever eat Taco Bell again."

"What does food have to do with all this?"

"Nothing. It's about what you've been talking to Stella about. Playing God and all that. We have no right. All that OmniDat propaganda about every client has done something bad, otherwise they wouldn't have a bond on them—it's bullshit. We don't know who the emptors are. We don't know why they want these people killed."

"Yeah. . . ." Cindy said. Dennis felt like she was finally letting her guard down.

"We're just mindless fucking robots," he continued, "going along, killing whoever they tell us to kill. For what? Thirteen thousand dollars and eighteen cents."

Cindy's eyes widened. "You made thirteen thousand on Scottsdale? Dennis, that's awesome!"

"There was a bonus clause. But no, it's not awesome! It's disgusting."

Cindy put her arms around him. "Do you love me?" she asked.

"Absolutely," he said.

"Well . . . do you think you could live without doing this? Without working for OmniDat?"

"I know I could. If you were with me."

"You'd be walking away from a lot of money. Health, dental, paid vacations."

"You can get that without killing people."

Dennis watched Cindy think. She got up and paced. He watched her ass.

"If this is really making you sick," she told him, "I don't want you to do it. But . . . what about me? What do I do about a career?"

"Do you really want to become a VP?" Dennis asked. "As conflicted as you already are. If you think it's hard working with people who kill, what do you think it's going to be like when *you* have to do it?"

Dennis saw he had stung her with that. He moved to her. Wrapped his arms around her from behind. He felt her begin to cry.

"I know it's wrong," Cindy said quietly. "Always have. But . . . it's not like we can quit. Nobody quits OmniDat. You have to retire."

She suddenly spun around. Wiped her eyes. "It is wrong, but we're already too deep. We have to stop talking like this. We could get into trouble."

"If Ackerman recognizes your voice, we're already in trouble." He kissed her gently. Hugged her. "I just want us to be happy. If being at OmniDat is tearing you up, tearing both of us up, we should leave."

"But you're a VP," she said. "You're on the chart now. You could be an executive one day."

Executive. God, that sounded good. But Dennis shook the thought from his mind.

"No. If I keep going like I am, I'm going to have an ulcer before I'm forty."

Cindy wiped more tears and said, "I had a dream last week. Just before that first call to *Night Lies.* I dreamed I made VP. And my first bond was . . . on my mother."

"Oh, babe," Dennis said, and held her as she began to sob.

"There's no way out," Cindy said through tears.

"Yes, there is," Dennis assured her. "We'll find it. I promise."

• • •

The next several days were better. Dennis wasn't given a new bond and busied himself with paperwork, mentally trying to work out an escape plan from OmniDat. At night, he and Cindy would usually have dinner at his place. They loved to cook together. They'd cook, eat, watch some TV, make love, and then fall asleep listening to *Night Lies.* "Sandy from Seattle" never called in again.

One morning on the way to work Cindy said, "I might have found something in Pearson's files that could help us."

Dennis asked what, but she said she wasn't ready to tell him. Not until she knew for sure.

"Then why mention it?" he asked.

Cindy smiled and kissed him. "I guess I wanted to give you hope. I'm a drugless hope addict."

Dennis knew right then that he would marry this woman.

They entered OmniDat's building and gave their perfunctory hellos to Jasper, but instead of his expected "Morning, ladies" he said, "Mr. Collins, package for you."

Cindy said, "I've got to run up and get there before Pearson. Come see me when you can."

Dennis nodded and Cindy stepped onto the elevator as Dennis made his way over to Jasper's desk. The large man set down a shoebox-sized package swaddled in brown parcel paper.

"Sign here," said Jasper.

As Dennis did, he said, "I like your sense of humor, Jasper. The 'Morning, ladies' thing always gets me."

Jasper just stared and Dennis stepped onto the elevator.

Inside his cubicle, Dennis opened the package. The return address was from an Internet site he sometimes bought from, but he didn't remember purchasing anything recently. Inside was a twill ball cap with a smiling stick figure seated in a yoga position. On the bill were the words: LIFE IS GOOD.

His phone rang. "Dennis Collins," he answered.

"Do you like it?" asked Cindy.

"You sent this?"

"Yeah. That's why I ran up the elevator. I didn't want to be with you when you opened it."

Dennis looked at the hat and smiled. "I love it."

"I thought it was perfect right now, you know?"

"It is."

"Listen," said Cindy. "I gotta run. Pearson's leaving for a bond today. But come to my place tonight. You make your famous chicken cacciatore and I'll throw together a salad. And I'll show you the stuff I found."

"Sounds great."

"Oh, my mother had her prescription refilled. Can you pick it up for me?"

"Of course."

"Thanks. Kisses."

And she hung up.

Dennis put his new hat on and looked into the black reflection of his monitor. He smiled. He'd been smiling more lately. Maybe life was good.

He turned his PC on and immediately heard the chime—a new bond had arrived.

Dennis typed in his passwords and watched the dossier appear.

His smile vanished along with the color in his face.

On screen was a photo of Cindy along with all her vitals. In large red letters were the words: HIGHEST PRIORITY, ALPHA CLEARANCE—FAILURE TO ACHIEVE WILL RESULT IN IMMEDIATE TERMINATION.

Dennis had heard of these bonds—red balls, they were called—a bond ordered on an OmniDat employee. From time to time, for a variety of reasons, OmniDat had to *clean house*, is how Axelrod had put it. But why Cindy? She wasn't even a junior VP.

They know about Night Lies, Dennis thought. He also thought maybe Pearson realized she'd been digging in his files, and now they wanted her terminated.

Killed. They wanted her fucking killed.

He brought up his address book and found Bernie Axelrod's number. He dialed.

"Hello?"

"Uh, Mrs. Axelrod? This is Dennis Collins from OmniDat . . . is Bernie around?"

Mrs. Axelrod screamed, "You bastards! Thirty-four years he gave you, and you can't let him live? You have to kill him!"

"What?"

"He had a bad liver, did you know that? Why couldn't you let him have those last few years?"

She slammed the phone down.

Dennis dialed Ackerman's extension. His voice mail said he was out on a bond.

Dennis hung up. He looked at the dossier again.

Failure to achieve will result in immediate termination.

Fuck them. He wouldn't do it. He'd run before he'd do it. *Go get Cindy and walk out of the building and straight to the airport. Go to Brazil or Madagascar, the company doesn't have an office in Madagascar.*

"Mr. Collins?"

Dennis jumped at the sound of Debbie Klein's voice.

"I assume you have your current bond?"

Dennis stared at the woman. Those fucking rhinestone glasses and that stupid brown cigarette. *I oughta buy a bond on you, you grisly old bat.*

"Yes."

"Is there a problem?" she asked, taking a long drag on the cigarette.

Dennis thought about putting the lighted end in her eye. "Actually, there is, Ms. Klein. . . ."

"Red balls have a way of changing people's lives, Mr. Collins."

"Huh?"

"With the departure of Mr. Axelrod, OmniDat is in need of a new executive," she rasped.

Dennis blinked. "Executive?"

Debbie Klein took another drag, and as she exhaled the blue smoke she said, "Red balls have a way of changing people's lives."

Dennis watched her walk away. He turned back to his computer, looked at his girlfriend smiling back at him.

He took off his new hat and dropped it into the trash can.

Dennis used his foot to knock on Cindy's door. His hands were full of utensils and ingredients for chicken cacciatore . . . and Mrs. Bradshaw's penicillin. Cindy opened the door, gave him a big kiss, and took the bag of utensils from him.

"I got stuff to make a Waldorf, that sound good?" she asked.

"My favorite, babe," Dennis said. He watched her walk to the kitchen.

I'm going to miss that ass.

Later, as they prepared the meal, Dennis had suggested Cindy make the salad in the dining room, giving the kitchen over to the cacciatore, which was the bigger project. He eyed the vial of penicillin.

"Are you sure Pearson doesn't know you've been snooping?" Dennis asked as he removed five caplets.

"No, he's dense," Cindy answered.

"So, what did you find in his files that could help us?" Dennis asked, grinding up the pills, then dusting the chicken with it.

"There's all this info on NC bonds," Cindy explained. "But not just about the bonds and how they were closed, but all this stuff about NC ways to kill."

"How does that help us?"

"Because what's also in there is what Pearson calls 'flags.' Basically notes on how to fake a death. We can fake a Romeo and Juliet suicide thing. You know, because we're so despondent over OmniDat."

"Sounds great, babe," said Dennis. He thought it was a ridiculous plan.

Dennis placed the cacciatore on the table between them. He didn't quite know how loud someone might be when poisoned with penicillin—he hadn't had time to research—so he asked Cindy to put some music on.

Bruce Springsteen was singing about being lost in the flood as Cindy and Dennis started in on the salad.

"Mmm, best Waldorf you've ever made, babe," Dennis said, eating as if everything was normal.

Dennis watched Cindy load her plate with cacciatore. Then everything went into slow motion.

First the fork dropped, crashing onto the plate. Then the gagging due to the lack of oxygen, the grabbing of the chest, the sweat pouring out of the pores as the body's defense system kicked in, trying to quash whatever was invading. Hands at the throat, face turning deep blue, and then the eyes . . . as they found their lover and stared across the table silently screaming *Why?*

Then finally, the convulsing, the spasms, the body fighting instinctively for life. The sound of plates crashing to the floor, followed by the thud of dead weight.

Bruce sang about the angel wielding love as a lethal weapon.

"I'm sorry, sweetie," Cindy said as she stood over Dennis's dead body.

"That was disgusting," said Wally Waxman, appearing from her bedroom. "Did you see the color his face turned?"

"I told you not to watch, you putz." Cindy walked over and put her arms around Wally. "But you're my putz."

They kissed. Wally's hands went to her butt and he thought, *Not much of an ass, but nice jubblies.*

"Thanks for the help," Cindy said. "I don't know shit about poisoning . . . was it cyanide?"

"Sodium azide," said a grinning Wally. "Coroner won't find it unless he's looking for it." His grin widened. "When I got the red ball for Denny, I knew I was gonna get back on the chart!"

The elevator doors opened to the forty-seventh floor and Cindy stepped off. The place was exquisite. Decorated in an Asian theme, Ming Dynasty, Cindy thought, and she figured all the vases and sculptures were probably authentic.

"Welcome," said Edgar Maddox. "Please sit." He motioned to a beautiful silk-covered chair and Cindy sat.

"Obviously, I am very impressed with you," the old man said.

"Thank you, sir."

"Please, I'm just Edgar. A simple man. All I did was see a need in the world and provide a service accordingly. Consumer demand—know it and you'll always be successful."

"Yes, sir."

"I imagine this was difficult for you, dear," Edgar said.

"Not as much as I expected, sir."

"Edgar, my dear," he said. "I'm glad it was not a problem. When the reports came in about Mr. Collins and his use of prohibited language around the office, well, something needed to be done.

"I must say, Miss Bradshaw, when I saw your contest entry, well, I haven't seen that kind of fortitude since the late Mr. Hanrahan . . . to use interpersonal relationships as a means of achieving red balls. Simply brilliant, my dear."

"Thank you."

"And isn't serendipity a wonderful bedfellow? You and Mr. Waxman having different goals, but attaining both by working together for the same end. That type of joint effort is what OmniDat is all about."

"Yes, sir."

"Now," said Maddox. "As you know, no one is asked up here unless they are being made an executive. And no one since Hanrahan has been made executive without climbing the appropriate ladders . . . no one until you. Welcome to the executive life, Miss Bradshaw."

"Thank you, Edgar."

They sipped their tea, and the old man asked, "Do you have any questions at all, my dear?"

"Just one, sir," Cindy said. "Do I still get the blender?"

Chapter and Verse

BY JEFFERY DEAVER

Jeffery Deaver is the *New York Times* best-selling author of the "Lincoln Rhymes" books, including *The Bone Collector*, filmed with Denzel Washington, and the recent *The Vanished Man* (Simon & Schuster, 2003). However, a recent book is the stand-alone thriller *Garden of Beasts* (S&S, 2004), which, coincidentally, featured a hit man as its main character. This story appeared on his Web site, but this is the first time it has been in print.

"REVEREND . . . CAN I CALL YOU 'Reverend'?"

The round, middle-aged man in the clerical collar smiled. "That works for me."

"I'm Detective Mike Silverman with the County Sheriff's Department."

Reverend Stanley Lansing nodded and examined the ID and badge that the nervously slim, salt-and-pepper-haired detective offered.

"Is something wrong?"

"Nothing involving you, sir. Not directly, I mean. Just hoping you might be able to help us with a situation we have."

"Situation. Hmmm. Well, come on inside, please, Officer. . . ."

The men walked into the office connected to the First Presbyterian Church of Bedford, a quaint, white house of worship that Silverman had passed a thousand times on his route between office and home and never really thought about.

That is, not until the murder this morning.

Rev. Lansing's office was musty and a gauze of dust covered most of the furniture. He seemed embarrassed. "Have to apologize. My wife and I've been away on vacation for the past week. She's still up at the lake. I came back to write my sermon—and to deliver it to my flock this Sunday, of course." He gave a wry laugh. "*If* there's anybody in the pews. Funny how religious commitment seems to go up around Christmas and then dip around vacation time." Then the man of the cloth looked around the office with a frown. "And I'm afraid I don't have anything to offer you. The church secretary's off too. Although between you and me, you're better off not sampling her coffee."

"No, I'm fine," Silverman said.

"So, what can I do for you, Officer?"

"I won't keep you long. I need some religious expertise on a case we're running. I would've gone to my father's rabbi, but my question's got to do with the New Testament. That's your bailiwick, right? More than ours."

"Well," the friendly, gray-haired reverend said, wiping his glasses on his jacket lapel and replacing them, "I'm just a small-town pastor, hardly an expert. But I probably know *Matthew, Mark, Luke,* and *John* better than your average rabbi, I suspect. Now, tell me how I can help."

"You're heard about the witness protection program, right?"

"Like *Goodfellas,* that sort of thing? The *Sopranos.*"

"More or less, yep. The U.S. Marshals run the federal program but we have our own state witness protection system."

"Really? I didn't know that. But I guess it makes sense."

"I'm in charge of the program in the county here and one of the people we're protecting is about to appear as a witness in a trial in Hamilton. It's our job to keep him safe through the trial and after we get a conviction—we hope—then we'll get him a new identity and move him out of the state."

"A Mafia trial?"

"Something like that."

Silverman couldn't go into the exact details of the case—how the witness, Randall Pease, a minder for drug dealer Tommy Doyle, had seen his boss put a bullet into the brain of a rival. Despite Doyle's reputation for ruthlessly murdering anyone who was a threat to him, Pease agreed to testify for a reduced sentence on assault, drug, and gun charges. The state prosecutor shipped Pease off to Silverman's jurisdiction, a hundred miles from Hamilton, to keep him safe; rumor was that Doyle would do anything, pay any money, to kill his former underling—since Pease's testimony could get him the death penalty or put him away for life. Silverman had stashed the witness in a safehouse near the Sheriff's Department and put a round-the-clock guard on him. The detective gave the reverend a generic description of what had happened, not mentioning names, and then said, "But there's been a setback. We had a CI—a confidential informant—"

"That's a snitch, right?"

Silverman laughed.

"I learned that from *Law and Order*. I watch it every chance I get. *CSI* too. I love cop shows." He frowned. "You mind if I say 'cop'?"

"Works for me. . . . Anyway, the informant got solid information that a professional killer's been hired to murder our witness before the trial next week."

"A hit man?"

"Yep."

"Oh, my." The reverend frowned as he touched his neck and rubbed it near the stiff white clerical collar, where it seemed to chafe.

"But the bad guys made the snitch—found out about him, I mean—and had him killed before he could give us the details about who the hit man is and how he planned to kill my witness."

"Oh, I'm so sorry," the reverend said sympathetically. "I'll say a prayer for the man."

Silverman grunted anemic thanks but his true thoughts were that the scurvy little snitch deserved an express-lane ride to hell—not only for being a loser punk addict, but for dying before he could give the detective the particulars about the potential hit on Pease. Detective Mike Silverman didn't share with the minister that he himself had been in trouble lately in the Sheriff's Department and had been shipped off to Siberia—witness protection—because he hadn't closed any major cases in a while. He needed to make sure this assignment went smoothly, and he absolutely could not let Pease get killed.

The detective continued, "Here's where you come in—I hope. When the informant was stabbed, he didn't die right away. He managed to write a note—about a bible passage. We think it was a clue as to how the hit man was going to kill our witness. But it's like a puzzle. We can't figure it out."

The reverend seemed intrigued. "Something from the New Testament, you said?"

"Yep," Silverman said. He opened his notebook. "The note said, 'He's on his way. Look out.' Then he wrote a chapter and verse from the bible. We think he was going to write something else but he didn't get a chance. He was Catholic, so we figure he knew the bible pretty well—and knew something in particular in that passage that'd tell us how the hit man's going to come after our witness."

The reverend turned around and looked for a bible on his shelf. Finally he located one and flipped it open. "What verse?"

"*Luke* twelve, fifteen."

The minister found the passage and read. "'Then to the people he said, "Beware! Be on your guard against greed of every kind, for even when someone has more than enough, his possessions do not give him life."'"

"My partner brought a bible from home. He's Christian, but he's not real religious, not a bible-thumper. . . . Oh, hey, no offense."

"None taken. We're Presbyterians. We don't thump."

Silverman smiled. "He didn't have any idea of what that might mean. I got to thinking about your church—it's the closest one to the station house—so I thought I'd stop by and see if you can help us out. Is there anything in there you can see that'd suggest how the defendant might try to kill our witness?"

The reverend read some more from the tissue-thin pages. "This section is in one of the Gospels—where different disciples tell the story of Jesus. In Chapter Twelve of *Luke*, Jesus is warning the people about the Pharisees, urging them not to live a sinful life."

"Who were they exactly, the Pharisees?"

"They were a religious sect. In essence, they believed that God existed to serve them, not the other way around. They felt they were better than everyone else and put people down. Well, that was the story back then—you never know, of course, if it's accurate. People did just as much poiltical spinning then as they do now." Rev. Lansing tried to turn on the desk lamp but it didn't work. He fiddled with the curtains, finally opening them and letting more light into the murky office. He read the passage several times more, squinting in concentration, nodding. Silverman looked around the dim place. Books, mostly. It seemed more like a professor's study than a church office. No pictures or anything else personal. You'd think even a minister would have pictures of family on his desk or walls.

Finally the man looked up. "So far, nothing really jumps out me." He seemed frustrated.

Silverman felt the same way. Ever since the CI had been found stabbed to death that morning, the detective had been wrestling with the words from *The Gospel According to Luke*, trying to decipher the meaning.

Beware! . . .

Rev. Lansing continued, "But I have to say, I'm fascinated with the idea. It's just like *The Da Vinci Code*. You read it?"

"No."

"It was great fun. All about secret codes and hidden messages. Say, if it's okay with you, Detective, I'd like to spend some time researching, doing some thinking about this. I love puzzles."

"I'd appreciate it, Reverend."

"I'll do what I can. You have that man under pretty good guard, I assume?"

"Oh, you bet, but it'll be risky getting him to court. We've got to figure out how the hit man's going to come at him."

"And the sooner the better, I assume."

"Yessir."

"I'll get right to it."

Grateful for the man's willingness to help, but discouraged he had no quick answers, Silverman walked out through the silent, deserted church. He climbed into his car and drove to the safehouse, checked on Randy Pease. The witness was his typical obnoxious self, complaining constantly, but the officer babysitting him reported that there'd been no sign of any threats around the safehouse. The detective then returned to the department.

In his office Silverman made a few calls to see if any of his other CIs had heard about the hired killer; they hadn't. His eyes kept returning to the passage, taped up on the wall in front of his desk.

"Beware! Be on your guard against greed of every kind, for even when someone has more than enough, his possessions do not give him life."

A voice startled him. "Wanta get some lunch?"

He looked up to find his partner, Steve Noveski, standing in the doorway. The junior detective, with a pleasant, round baby face, was staring obviously at his watch.

Silverman, still lost in the mysterious bible passage, just stared at him.

"Lunch, dude," Noveski repeated. "I'm starving."

"Naw, I've gotta get this figured out." He tapped the bible. "I'm kind of obsessed with it."

"Like, you think?" the other detective said, packing as much sarcasm into his voice as would fit.

• • •

That night Silverman returned home and sat distractedly through dinner with his family. His widower father had joined them, and the old man wasn't pleased that his son was so preoccupied.

"And what's that you're reading that's so important? The New Testament?" The man nodded toward the bible he'd seen his son poring over before dinner. He shook his head and turned to his daughter-in-law. "The boy hasn't been to temple in years and he couldn't find the Torah his mother and I gave him if his life depended on it. Now look, he's reading about Jesus Christ. What a son."

"It's for a case, dad," Silverman said. "Listen, I've got some work to do. I'll see you guys later. Sorry."

"See you later sorry?" the man muttered. "And you say 'you guys' to your wife? Don't you have any respect—"

Silverman closed the door to his den, sat down at his desk, and checked messages. The forensic scientist testing the murdered CI's note about the bible passage had called to report there was no significant evidence to be found on the sheet and neither the paper nor the ink were traceable. A handwriting comparison suggested that it had been written by the victim but he couldn't be one hundred percent certain.

And, as the hours passed, there was still no word from Rev. Lansing. Sighing, Silverman stretched and stared at the words once again.

"Beware! Be on your guard against greed of every kind, for even when someone has more than enough, his possessions do not give him life."

He grew angry. A man died leaving these words to warn them. What was he trying to say?

Silverman had a vague memory of his father saying goodbye that night and later still an even more vague memory of his wife saying goodnight, the den door closing abruptly. She was mad. But Michael Silverman didn't care. All that mattered at the moment was finding the meaning to the message.

Something the reverend had said that afternoon came back to him. *The Da Vinci Code.* A code . . . Silverman thought about the snitch: the man hadn't been a college grad, but he was smart in his own way. Maybe he had more in mind than the literal meaning of the passage; could it be that the specifics of his warning were somehow encoded in the letters themselves?

It was close to four A.M., but Silverman ignored his exhaustion and went online. He found a Web site about word games and puzzles. In one game you made as many words as you could out of the first letters from a saying or quotation. Okay, this could be it, Silverman thought excitedly. He wrote down the first letters of each of the words from *Luke* 12:15 and began rearranging them.

He got several names: *Bob, Tom, Don* . . . and dozens of words: *gone, pen, gap* . . .

Well, *Tom* could refer to Tommy Doyle. But he could find no other clear meaning in the words or any combination of them.

What other codes were there he might try?

He tried an obvious one: assigning the numbers to the letters, A equaled 1, B 2, and so on. But when he applied the formula, all he ended up with were sheets of hundreds of random digits. Hopeless, he thought. Like trying to guess a computer password.

Then he thought of anagrams—where the letters of a word or phrase are rearranged to make other words. After a brief search on the Web, he found a site with an anagram generator, a software program that let you type in a word and a few seconds later spit out all the anagrams that could be made from it.

For hours he typed in every word and combination of words in the passage and studied the results. At six A.M., utterly exhausted, Silverman was about to give up and fall into bed. But as he was arranging the printouts of the anagrams he'd downloaded, he happened to glance at one—the anagrams that the word "possessions" had yielded: *open, spies, session, nose, sepsis.* . . .

Something rang a bell.

"Sepsis?" he wondered out loud. It sounded familiar. He looked the word up. It meant infection. Like blood poisoning.

He was confident that he was on to something and, excited,

he riffled through the other sheets. He saw that "greed" incorporated "Dr."

Yes!

And the word "guard" produced "drug."

Okay, he thought in triumph. Got it!

Detective Mike Silverman celebrated his success by falling asleep in his chair.

He awoke an hour later, angry at the loud engine rattling nearby—until he realized the noise was his own snoring.

The detective closed his dry mouth, winced at the pain in his back, and sat up. Massaging his stiff neck, he staggered upstairs to the bedroom, blinded by the sunlight pouring through the French doors.

"Are you up already?" his wife asked blearily from bed, looking at his slacks and shirt. "It's early."

"Go back to sleep," he said.

After a fast shower, he dressed and sped to the office. At eight A.M., he was in his captain's office, with his partner, Steve Noveski, beside him.

"I've figured it out."

"What?" his balding, joweled superior officer asked.

Noveski glanced at his partner with a lifted eyebrow; he'd just arrived and hadn't heard Silverman's theory yet.

"The message we got from the dead CI—how Doyle's going to kill Pease."

The captain had heard about the biblical passage but hadn't put much stock in it. "So how?" he asked skeptically.

"Doctors," Silverman announced.

"Huh?"

"I think he's going to use a doctor to try to get to Pease."

"Keep going."

Silverman told him about the anagrams.

"Like crossword puzzles?"

"Sort of."

Noveski said nothing but he too seemed skeptical of the idea.

The captain screwed up his long face. "Hold on here. You're saying that here's our CI and he's got a severed jugular and he's playing *word* games?"

"Funny how the mind works, what it sees, what it can figure out."

"Funny," the senior cop muttered. "Sounds a little, whatsa word, contrived, you know what I mean?"

"He had to get us the message and he had to make sure that Doyle didn't tip to the fact he'd alerted us. He had to make it, you know, subtle enough so Doyle's boys wouldn't figure out what he knew, but not so subtle that we couldn't guess it."

"I don't know."

Silverman shook his head. "I think it works." He explained that Tommy Doyle had often paid huge fees to brilliant, ruthless hit men who'd masquerade as somebody else to get close to their unsuspecting victims. Silverman speculated that the killer would buy or steal a doctor's white jacket and get a fake ID card and a stethoscope or whatever doctors carried around with them nowadays. Then a couple of Doyle's cronies would make a half-hearted attempt on Pease's life—they couldn't get close enough to kill him in the safehouse, but causing injury was a possibility. "Maybe food poisoning." Silverman explained about the sepsis anagram. "Or maybe they'd arrange for a fire or gas leak or something. The hit man, disguised as a med tech, would be allowed inside and kill Pease there. Or maybe the witness would be rushed to the hospital and the man'd cap him in the emergency room."

The captain shrugged. "Well, you can check it out—provided you don't ignore the grunt work. We can't afford to screw this one up. We lose Pease and it's our ass."

The pronouns in those sentences may have been first person plural, but all Silverman heard was a very singular "you" and "your."

"Fair enough."

In the hallway on their way back to his office, Silverman asked his partner, "Who do we have on call for medical attention at the safehouse?"

"I don't know, a team from Forest Hills Hospital, I'd guess."

"We don't know who?" Silverman snapped.

"I don't, no."

"Well, find out! Then get on the horn to the safehouse and tell the babysitter if Pease gets sick for any reason, needs any medicine, needs a goddamn bandage, to call me right away. Do *not* let any medical people see him unless we have a positive ID and I give my personal okay."

"Right."

"Then call the supervisor at Forest Hills and tell him to let me know stat if any doctors or ambulance attendants or nurses— *anybody*—don't show up for work or call in sick or if there're some doctors around that he doesn't recognize."

The young man peeled off into his office to do what Silverman had ordered and the senior detective returned to his own desk. He called a counterpart at the county sheriff's office in Hamilton and told him what he suspected and added that they had to be on the lookout for any medical people who were close to Pease.

The detective then sat back in his chair, rubbing his eyes and massaging his neck. He was more and more convinced he was right, that the secret message left by the dying informant was pointing toward a killer masquerading as a health-care worker. He picked up the phone again. For several hours, he nagged hospitals and ambulance services around the county to find out if all of their people and vehicles were accounted for.

As the hour neared lunchtime, his phone rang.

"Hello?"

"Silverman." The captain's abrupt voice instantly killed the detective's sleep-deprivation haze; he was instantly alert. "We just had an attempt on Pease."

Silverman's heart thudded. He sat forward. "He okay?"

"Yeah. Somebody in an SUV fired thirty, forty shots through the front windows of the safehouse. Steel-jacketed rounds, so they got through the armored glass. Pease and his guard got hit with some splinters, but nothing serious. Normally we'd send 'em to the hospital, but I was thinking about what you said, about the killer pretending to be a tech or doctor, so I thought it was better to bring Pease straight here, to Detention. I'll have our sawbones look 'em both over."

"Good.

"We'll keep him here for a day or two and then send him up to the federal WP facility in Ronanka Falls."

"And have somebody head over to the Forest Hills emergency room and check out the doctors. Doyle's hired gun might be thinking we'd send him there and be waiting."

"Already ordered," the captain said.

"When'll Pease get here?"

"Any time now."

"I'll have the lockup cleared." He hung up, rubbed his eyes again. How the hell had Doyle found out the location of the safehouse? It was the best-kept secret in the department. Still, since no one had been seriously injured in the attack, he allowed himself another figurative pat of self-congratulation. His theory was being borne out. The shooter hadn't tried to kill Pease at all, just shake him up and cause enough carnage to have him dive to the floor and scrape an elbow or get cut by flying glass. Then off to the ER—and straight into the arms of Doyle's hit man.

He called the Detention supervisor at the jail and arranged to have the existing prisoners in the holding cell moved temporarily to the town police station, then told the man to brief the guards and warn them to make absolutely certain they recognized the doctor who was going to look over Pease and his bodyguard.

"I already did. 'Causa what the captain said, you know."

Silverman was about to hang up when he glanced at the clock. It was noon, the start of the second guard shift. "Did you tell the afternoon-shift personnel about the situation?"

"Oh. Forgot. I'll do it now."

Silverman hung up angrily. Did he have to think of everything himself?

He was walking to his door, headed for the Detention Center intake area to meet Pease and his guard, when his phone buzzed. The desk sergeant told him he had a visitor. "It's a Rev. Lansing. He said it's urgent that he sees you. He said to tell you that he's figured out the message. You'd know what he means."

"I'll be right there."

Silverman winced. As soon as he'd figured out what the passage meant that morning, the detective had planned to call the minister and tell him they didn't need his help any longer. But he'd forgotten all about it. Shit. . . . Well, he'd do something nice for the guy— maybe donate some money to the church or take the reverend out to lunch to thank him. Yeah, lunch would be good. They could talk about TV cop shows.

The detective met Rev. Lansing at the front desk. Silverman greeted him with another wince, noticing how exhausted he looked. "You get any sleep last night?"

The minister laughed. "Nope. Just like you, looks like."

"Come on with me, Reverend. Tell me what you came up with." He led the man down the corridor toward Intake. He decided he'd hear what the man had to say. Couldn't hurt.

"I think I've got the answer to the message."

"Go on."

"Well, I was thinking that we shouldn't limit ourselves just to verse fifteen itself. That one's just a sort of introduction to the parable that follows. I think that's the answer."

Silverman nodded, recalling what he'd read in Noveski's bible. "The parable about the farmer?"

"Exactly. Jesus tells about a rich farmer who has a good harvest. He doesn't know what to do with the excess grain. He thinks he'll build bigger barns and figures he'll spend the rest of his life enjoying what he's done. But what happens is that God strikes him down because he's greedy. He's materially rich but spiritually impoverished."

"Okay," Silverman said. He didn't see any obvious message yet.

The reverend sensed the cop's confusion. "The point of the passage is greed. And I think that might be the key to what that poor man was trying to tell you."

They got to the intake dock and joined an armed guard who was awaiting the arrival of the armored van carrying Pease. The existing prisoners in the lockup, Silverman learned, weren't all in the transport bus yet for the transfer to the city jail.

"Tell 'em to step on it," Silverman ordered and turned back to the minister, who continued his explanation.

"So I asked myself, what's greed nowadays? And I figured it was Enron, Tyco, CEOs, Internet moguls. . . . And Cahill Industries."

Silverman nodded slowly. Robert Cahill was the former head of a huge agri-business complex. After selling that company, he'd turned to real estate and had put up dozens of buildings in the county. The man had just been indicted for tax evasion and insider trading.

"Successful farmer," Silverman mused. "Has a big windfall and gets in trouble. Sure. Just like the parable."

"It gets better," the minister said excitedly. "There was an editorial in the paper a few weeks ago—I tried to find it but couldn't—about Cahill. I think the editor cited a couple of bible passages about greed. I can't remember which but I'll bet one of them was *Luke* twelve, fifteen."

Standing on the intake loading dock, Silverman watched the van carrying Randy Pease arrive. The detective and the guard looked around them carefully for any signs of threats as the armored vehicle backed in. Everything seemed clear. The detective knocked on the back door, and the witness and his bodyguard hurried out onto the intake loading dock. The van pulled away.

Pease started complaining immediately. He had a small cut on his forehead and a bruise on his cheek from the attack at the safehouse, but he moaned as if he'd fallen down a two-story flight of stairs. "I want a doctor. Look at this cut. It's already infected, I can tell. And my shoulder is killing me. What's a man gotta do to get treated right around here?"

Cops grow very talented at ignoring difficult suspects and witnesses, and Silverman hardly heard a word of the man's whiny voice.

"Cahill," Silverman said, turning back to the minister. "And what do you think that means for us?"

"Cahill owns high-rises all over town. I was wondering if the way you're going to drive your witness to the courthouse would go past any of them."

"Could be."

"So a sniper could be on top of one of them." The reverend smiled. "I didn't actually think that up on my own. I saw it in a TV show once."

A chill went through Silverman's spine.

Sniper?

He lifted his eyes from the alley. A hundred yards away was a high-rise from whose roof a sniper would have perfect shot into the intake loading dock where Silverman, the minister, Pease, and the two guards now stood. It could very well be a Cahill building.

"Inside!" he shouted. "Now."

They all hurried into the corridor that led to the lockup, and Pease's babysitter slammed the door behind them. Heart pounding from the possible near miss, Silverman picked up a phone at the desk and called the captain. He told the man the reverend's theory. The captain said, "Sure, I get it. They shoot up the safehouse to flush Pease, figuring they'd bring him here and then put a shooter on the high-rise. I'll send a tactical team to scour it. Hey, bring that minister by when you've got Pease locked down. Whether he's right or not, I want to thank him."

"Will do." The detective was miffed that the brass seemed to like this idea better than the anagrams, but Silverman'd accept any theory as long as it meant keeping Pease alive.

As they waited in the dim corridor for the lockup to empty out, skinny, stringy-haired Pease began complaining again, droning on and on. You mean there was a shooter out there and you didn't fucking know about it, for Christ's sake, oh, sorry about the language, Father. Listen, you assholes, I'm not a suspect, I'm the *star* of this show, without me—

"Shut the hell up," Silverman snarled.

"You can't talk to me—"

Silverman's cell phone rang, and he stepped away from the others to take the call. "'Lo?"

"Thank God you picked up." Steve Noveski's voice was breathless. "Where's Pease?"

"He's right in front of me," Silverman told his partner. "He's okay. There's a tac team looking for shooters in the building up the street. What's up?"

"Where's that reverend?" Noveski said. "The desk log doesn't show him signing out."

"Here, with me."

"Listen, Mike, I was thinking—what if the CI didn't leave that message from the bible."

"Then who did?"

"What if it was the hit man himself? The one Doyle hired."

"The killer? Why would he leave a clue?"

"It's not a clue. Think about it. He wrote the biblical stuff himself and left it near the body, as *if* the CI had left it. The killer'd figure we'd try to find a minister to help us figure it out—but not just any minister, the one at the church that's closest to the police station."

Silverman's thoughts raced to a logical conclusion. Doyle's hit man kills the minister and his wife at their summer place on the lake and masquerades as the reverend. The detective recalled that the church office had nothing in it that might identify the minister. In fact, he seemed to remember that the man had trouble even finding a bible and didn't seem to know his desk-lamp bulb was burned out. In fact, the whole church was deserted and dusty.

He continued the logical progression of events: Doyle's boys shoot up the safehouse and we bring Pease here for safekeeping at the same time the reverend shows up with some story about greed and a real estate developer and a sniper—just to get close to Silverman . . . and to Pease!

He understood suddenly: there *was* no secret message. *He's on his way. Look out—Luke 12:15.* It was meaningless. The killer could've written *any* biblical passage on the note. The whole point was to have the police contact the phony reverend and give the man access to the lockup at the same time that Pease was there.

And *I* led him right to his victim!

Dropping the phone and pulling his gun from its holster, Silverman raced up the hall and tackled the reverend. The man cried out in pain and gasped as the fall knocked the wind from his lungs. The detective pushed his gun into the hit man's neck. "Don't move a muscle."

"What're you doing?"

"What's wrong?" Pease's guard asked.

"He's the killer! He's one of Doyle's men!"

"No, I'm not. This is crazy!"

Silverman cuffed the fake minister roughly and holstered his gun. He frisked him and didn't find any weapons but figured he'd probably intended to grab one of the cops' own guns to kill Pease—and the rest of them.

The detective yanked the minister to his feet and handed him off to the intake guard. He ordered, "Take him to an interrogation room. I'll be there in ten minutes. Make sure he's shackled."

"Yessir."

"You can't do this!" the reverend shouted as he was led away roughly. "You're making a big mistake."

"Get him out of here," Silverman snapped.

Pease eyed the detective contemptuously. "He coulda killed me, you asshole."

Another guard ran up the corridor from intake. "Problem, Detective?"

"We've got everything under control. But see if the lockup's empty yet. I want that man inside ASAP!" Nodding toward Pease.

"Yessir," the guard said, and hurried to the intercom beside the security door leading to the cells.

Silverman looked back down the corridor, watching the minister and his escort disappear through a doorway. The detective's hands were shaking. Man, that was a close one. But at least the witness is safe.

And so is my job.

Still have to answer a hell of a lot of questions, sure, but—

"No!" a voice cried behind him.

A sharp sound, like an axe in a tree trunk, resounded in the corridor, then a second, accompanied by the acrid smell of burnt gunpowder.

The detective spun around, gasping. He found himself staring in shock at the intake guard who'd just joined them. The young man held an automatic pistol mounted with a silencer, and he was standing over the bodies of the men he'd just killed: Randy Pease and the cop who'd been beside him.

Silverman reached for his own gun.

But Doyle's hit man, wearing a perfect replica of a Detention Center guard's uniform, turned his pistol on the detective and shook his head. In despair, Silverman realized that had been partly right. Doyle's people had shot up the safehouse to flush out Pease—but not to send him to the hospital; they knew the cops would bring him to the jail for safekeeping.

The hit man looked up the corridor. None of the other guards had heard or otherwise noticed the killings. The man pulled a radio from his pocket with his left hand, pushed a button and said, "It's done. Ready for the pickup."

"Good," came the tinny reply. "Right on schedule. We'll meet you in front of the station."

"Got it." He put the radio away.

Silverman opened his mouth to plead with the killer to spare his life.

But he fell silent, then gave a faint, despairing laugh as glanced at the killer's name badge and he realized the truth—that the dead snitch's message hadn't been so mysterious after all. The CI was simply telling them to look out for a hit man masquerading as a guard whose first name was what Silverman now gaped at on the man's plastic name plate: "Luke."

And, as for the chapter and verse, well, that was pretty simple too. The CI's note meant that the killer was planning the hit shortly after the start of the second shift, to give himself fifteen minutes to clock in and find where the prisoner was being held.

Right on schedule . . .

The time on the wall clock was exactly 12:15.

Permissions